CW01430701

Armchair

Hero

A Planet Glob

Legend

As related and embellished

by

WGWL

AnotherPlanet

AnotherPlanet

PO Box 72, Caldicot, Monmouthshire NP26 3ZG

www.anotherplanet.eu
www.planetglob.com
www.armchairhero.co.uk

Contents © WgWl 2010

British Library Cataloguing in Publication Data available.

ISBN 978-0-9565858-0-6

Set in Times
Printed by Lulu.com

Book cover design: WgWl

PREAMBLE

In the beginning...there was nothing. To be more exact, before the beginning there was nothing: a big void of anything that was colourless, dimensionless and endless. A perfect void. Well not quite.

Nothing is perfect, and from what was the most infinitesimal imperfection, over aeons developed into a sizeable blemish, until it quite suddenly discovered that it was something. As something to do it spread into the empty space, and declared itself The Great Being because there was a nice ring to the name. Having done this, The Great Being wondered what to do next. It experimented for several centuries until it settled on a comfortable form of crinkled folds of skin and long flowing locks of white hair, and designed for itself a desirable environment.

Unintentionally, The Great Being started to develop feelings and emotions, and the first complex one was boredom. So spreading itself over vast swathes of the remaining nothingness, it started a hobby - CREATION. First a vegetable garden, and then a shed to be able to potter about in and do the other things it didn't do in the veggie plot.

After scratching what it presumed was its head for an age or two, The Great Being started some serious creation. A bit rough and ready at first, but as it put together a collection of prototypes of things it later called planets along its workshelf, The Great Being stood back and allowed itself a smile of satisfaction.

It then decided to build a bigger shed, as it had just stepped out through the wall, and as a secondary thought wondered where to put the things it had made.

I

A violent stench escaped screaming from the kitchens of Castle Gloom. Making a break for freedom it smashed into walls and curled fixtures and fittings as it ran riot along the maze of dark corridors.

Formed from the pungent odours of decomposing carcasses and a variety of putrefying vegetables boiled in rusty cauldrons, it brawled with everything in whiffing distance. Two dark cloaked figures stopped and sniffed with tingling nostrils as the putrid stench howled passed them, bouncing off the dripping walls.

"Stop salivating like that. He doesn't like it, you know. Disturbs Him to the marrow, you dribbling like that."

"Sorry. It's just that dinner smells so good."

"Bad!"

"Sorry. Yes – bad. Bad. Bad! Bad!"

"And stop saying sorry."

"Sorry?"

The Balck Warlock of Murk sighed. It would not be long before the body of this new apprentice was fed to the Gloops that terrorised the castle moat. The warlock shivered and the slime on his tail felt almost tepid at the thought.

"You may be new here, but as Balck Warlock, I can't have an apprentice who is ignorant of Murkspeak. Globspeak is a serious offence, and it is not good for my image. Got that?"

The apprentice's knobbly head shook so hard its three eyes jangled against each other on their antennae.

"Yes, yes, yes…or should that be no, no, no?"

"It's yes. Haven't you read the Balck Book yet?"

There was an embarrassed silence only tempered by the squelching sounds of their feet as they progressed towards the dark double doors at the end of the passage.

"Can't read," snivelled the apprentice sorcerer apologetically.

The Balck Warlock's hooded reptilian eyes blinked under the pungent light of the burning rush braziers. His tongue darted in and out of his lipless mouth as he pondered on the sorcerer's career path.

"How do you read the future then?"

"It's a gift. Mum said it was from the great Trachi…"

"Shush!" the warlock interrupted quickly. "Don't mention His name out loud! If a troll hears you, it's instant shredding."

"Sorry."

"And don't say sorry…"

"Sorry."

The Balck Warlock sighed again. His apprentice was destined not to last another two changes of the skin. It was a shame. Somewhere behind the stupid expression and the jangling eyes was a real talent for reading the giblets of all kinds of sacrificial animals.

They stopped in front of doors to the Great Hall, decorated in over-excited high gothic carved embellishments. As the warlock pulled the bell rope next to a grille in the gargantuan doors, he admired the sorcerer's slime trail. At least that was a good sign, he thought.

"Bog off!" bellowed the purple-mouthed giant troll through the rusty grille.

"The Balck Warlock and the Scrofulous the Sorcerer to see his Disgusting Darkness, Lord of Murk."

"Right'o," said the troll. "You'd better come in then."

Locks jangled and bolts snapped. After an excruciating squeal of hinges, a small section of the massive door opened as a cat-flap hidden amongst an extravagantly demonic carved panel.

"Mind your hat, wizard," the troll remarked casually, as the most powerful magician in Murk and his assistant crawled through the opening.

"It's Warlock! And one more bit of lip like that and yours will be sprouting a bunch of pansies," snapped the Balck Warlock.

"Can't you take a joke? Hur-hur-hur," the troll mumbled into his scraggy beard.

"The Dark Lord is just dispensing a bit of injustice. It won't take long – never does, hur-hur! Might as well go up and see the action," the troll said.

The sound of creaking leather and clinking chains of the troll's uniform accompanied the slithering of the masters of the balck arts as they marched up between the slime stained bombastic arches. The colonnade of pillars halted abruptly and opened out into a vast expanse of dripping blue stone. Through the dank spectral mist that dribbled through the slit windows high in the walls (controlled to keep the hall at the correct level of mouldering dampness) the warlock and sorcerer apprentice adjusted their eyes to the dim blue light.

Hidden in the shadows they waited as a kitchen devil, presumed guilty of cleaning a pot, tried to mitigate its crime in a flood of squeaky whines.

A stony silence bore down on the prostrate figure weighed down in manacles and heavy chain links, its pointy ears and bony membrane wings laid flat in submission.

A dark figure sat shimmering in a darker outline against the high-backed throne of pure refined jet. His shadowy velvet robes of deep extra royal blue and trimmed with pure black sable somehow glimmered in the poor light. What was difficult for the eye to distinguish, the other senses made up for, as they trembled in the presence of unadulterated ultimate evil. Trachidambabble, otherwise known as The Great Evil, the Dark Lord of Murk, and any other title that took his fancy, glimmered with a dark potency.

When he spoke it was with a rasping whisper that echoed loudly around the Great Hall.

"It is my opinion, that your excuse that the pan accidentally slipped from your talons into a sink which just happened to be full of water infected with detergent, and you were merely retrieving it, is nothing more than the truth."

Trachidambabble, terrible Lord of Murk and All Black Rain Clouds, paused.

He smiled in a manner that indicates that whatever followed was not going to be very funny at all.

"…And as such, can only be punished in the nicest way possible. You shall be sentenced to 10 years re-education at the Cleaning and Laundry Camp at the Neverend of Murk."

The kitchen devil, which had been gibbering annoyingly, let out a piercing wail of horror as the sentence was pronounced.

"Oh no, please your Imperial Filthiness. Not clean socks, pressed trousers, and white shirts smelling of pine freshness. Not hygiene…three showers a day – with soap. Mercy, have merceeee…"

The devil's pleading trailed off as it was dragged away between two smirking guards.

"Next!" hissed Trachidambabble.

The troll snapped to attention and announced: "The Balck Warlock and Scrofulous the Sorcerer to advise on what augers for the Secret Plan."

With a loud 'SPLATT!' Scrofulous was ceremonially chucked to the floor.

In recognition of his position as chief executive of the Future Planning Department of Castle Gloom Glob Enterprises, the troll expertly executed a more respectful throwing to the ground for the warlock, whose face hit the slime coated flagstones with a more dignified SQUELCH!.

"Well?"

The sinister decibels floated down to the spread-eagled figures on the floor. "Don't just lie there. Get on with it – I haven't got all night."

The Balck Warlock prised himself from the slippery stone, and placing several mystical signs in a special order to create a magic poly-pentagon. Theatrically rolling up his sleeves, the warlock mumbled incantations and revolved his head. A click of his finger joints produced a puff of smoke. It cleared to reveal a coughing alligator-headed spirit in a snappy suit and sharp shoes, standing nonchalantly in the centre of the magic poly-pentagon.

"Hi there folks. Tastie Gobbledigook here. The spirit with the know-how to tell you how. There ain't no greater gator with his claw on the pulse of what's going down, and what's being thrown up, in this and other dimensions. Surveys, reports, and public relations exercises undertaken, utilising the biggest data base for *the* most professional results."

"Skip the self-promotion, and get on with it," the voice from the throne reverberated with a menace that rattled the spirit bones of Tastie Gobbledigook. It gulped, its ethereal outline quivering cravenly.

After a pause to regain its cocky composure the spirit puffed out its chest and grinned all its teeth.

"You called on the services of Tastie Gobbledigook to discover the likeliness of whether the Secret Plan would achieve its aim of turning Murk into the prime mover of Glob. Due to the difficulty of not knowing what the plan is – because it is secret – it was decided to pester…haha…er conduct a survey of The Far-Seeing spirits."

Tastie gestured, and paused for a screen to materialise by his side.

"As you will see from the charts, we asked 1,000 grumpy spirits renowned for their knowledge of the future and general know-all nature: "what augurs for the Secret Plan?" and these were the results…"

A series of taps by Tastie's tail and an instantly assembled screen displayed a succession of highly coloured charts and graphs. He talked his way through the squiggly lines, pie charts, and representative diagrams, and saying a lot and nothing all at the the same time.

"…And so you will see that due to the pessimistic disposition of most spirits of the NeverEther World, the consensus of opinion is that the Secret Plan will be an unmitigated disaster."

"Terrible, oh terrible. Not just a disaster, an unmitigated disaster!" grinned Trachidambabble from his throne.

The screen disappeared, replaced by a pile of glossy report brochures which floated separately into the hands of Trachidambabble, the warlock and his apprentice.

"So glad you appreciate the professionalism of the primary agency of the ether – Tastie Gobbledigook for all your communication needs. Unfortunately, due to collating difficulties, there are certain incremental costs - which had not been foreseen in the original estimate - but nevertheless need to be added to the invoice. Payment loans come at very competitive rates. "

The spirit was cut short as it was vaporised by a by a zap of blue light originating from Trachidambabble's black gloved hand.

"Account closed. Somehow I don't think we will be using that spirit agency again," the black god of Murk muttered almost contentedly, blowing at the smoke curling from his finger.

"Nevertheless, may I venture that the Secret Plan will achieve its aim," the Warlock whined in his most servile voice.

"And it's a very GOOD report. Lots of photographs, and all, on quality paper. I do like three-ply velour paper," Scrofulous chipped in equally crawling tones, and immediately wished he hadn't.

"A *GOOD* report, did you say?" said a voice that resonated of biting arctic winds sweeping across plains of permafrost.

The sorcerer trembled at the timbre of the words echoing around the Great Hall.

"Er…No, a very *BAD* report. Yes, a very, bad, bad, bad report," the sorcerer quavered.

He did not quaver long. A twist of a dark wrist and what had been a promising illiterate sorcerer was a steaming pile of dung.

The warlock sighed to himself, picked up his mystic signs and put the remains of his apprentice in his pocket to keep as soup stock.

It could be very trying working for the Dark Lord, even if it did mean having an impressive number of titles. The loss of his best spirit world source and a most promising sorcerer was a heavy price to pay for one night's work.

It was difficult enough getting sorcerers of any potential at all, without those few that did come forward being biodegraded on their first audience with the Dark Lord.

"Well, it looks like the signs bode disastrously for target goal achievement in the Secret Plan," he said and prostrated himself on the floor to leave.

"I would have settled for disaster, but unmitigated disaster – I feel like celebrating," grated the voice of iron filings responsible for the dispensation of misery throughout glob.

"Oh, yes," the warlock thought despondently.

The floor suddenly disappeared beneath him and the Balck Warlock shot, hat first, towards the Gloop-infested radioactive sludge of the castle's moat, chased by sinister howls of laughter tickling at his curling shoes.

The trolls of the Imperial BlackGuards clinked uneasily at attention. It was not lucky to be in such close proximity to the Lord of Murk when he was in such a zap-happy mood.

The spectral outline of the face of the keeper of Castle Gloom creased in a mirthless grin, and thought of how different it would be once he had changed the face of Glob, and turned it topsy-turvy with the implementation of the Secret Plan.

"The time has come," the cloaked figure on the jet throne bellowed, and his BalckGuard trolls trembled in expectation of imminent biodegradation as their lord's laughter peeled amongst the damp arches of the Great Hall.

ANOTHER AMBLE

The Great Being didn't know how long it had been working on new intricate geopolitical stratas. It did this on principle, and stuffed the imitation cotton wool ear plugs deeper into the ears to drown the incessant ticking of TIME. Although as The Great Being it was the omnipotent source of every living and invented thing – and all its own work – there were some things The Great Being could not control.

TIME was a very uncontrollable manifestation if you wanted it to stop. It had appeared suddenly without warning, and insisted on annoying The Great Being by loudly declaring its progress. The Great Being presumed that it was a by-product of creation, and put up with the loud phenomenon with very little grace. Creation filled up the wide open spaces of The Great Being's existence. Designing and putting a planet together was an intricate task that was enjoyable because of the effort involved in getting the balance right, from the size of grains of sand, through to the food chains and the layered design of the grand physical features. The Great Being spun on the real fake-leather executive chair and looked out of the shed window at the universe for all the planetary creations that sat like a rubbery bladder depository in the middle of the vegetable plot. It now covered most of the rhubarb patch and wobbled worryingly as its contents bumped and crashed into each other.

Feeling satisfied with the work it had already completed, The Great Being sat back in its chair, put its feet up on an instantly materialising stool, and took a look at animated route-planner to the universe pinned on the shed wall.

"I wonder what happened to that funny little prototype that somehow slipped into Galaxy Mk.XXXVI," Tthe Great Being thought out loud in a nostalgic sort of way.

Instantly the macro atlas micro-ed in on Galaxy Mk.XXXVI and chased around the night sky, until a strange little world appeared, lolloping along as it sprayed a golden tail behind it, chasing two pink suns while orbiting its own green moon.

The Great Being beamed with affection. It was one of the earliest efforts at making a properly working planet that orbited correctly in the confines of a universe. Well before the idea of worlds with molten cores designed to zip about in space, the Great Being had experimented with gravitational force drives, powered by the forces of good and evil strapped onto opposite poles. The theory was for a delicate balance of forces counteracting each other, with the jealous black boot of Murk constantly chasing the golden anvil of Heaven. Meanwhile heaven was busy producing a heavy liquid of golden particles, which gave the planet its impressive tail in the night sky, and pushed the planet at the correct speed for its constant revolutions to prevent it falling out of the sky.

It still worked. Eccentrically, but it worked .

II

Ceremonial duties was not something Fyrsil was good at. Unfortunately it was a large part of his job as Spearholder and Cupbearer to Hap-i-Glob, Great God of the Golden Palace of Heaven, Protector of the Orbs, Spindoctor Supreme, and Professor of the Eternal Ness – usually referred to as Hap, the top god in Heaven.

"Come on, look lively. Left..right..left..right. Slope spear.. and don't wave it around like a broomstick at a witches' sabbat," yelled the Bobo, the last survivor of Glob's colourful breed of birds of war, as it tried to drill its raw recruit. This recruit had been raw for a very long time, but the Bobo's military temperament insisted that it would succeed in licking even this poor specimen into shape.

Fyrsil tripped clumsily in his usual way and reminded himself that there was only one week to go before his contract was up. He thought wistfully of his alpine home town of Alpoi, which nestled in the mountains at the foot of the Stairway To Heaven, and of his interrupted career path of becoming a Nutgatherer Mystic like his father, and his father before him, and even his mother. He wasn't too sure about his grandmother, but he was sure she liked eating nuts.

Fyrsil gazed numbly at the Golden Palace as he stumbled around in a half-military fashion to the yells of the Bobo. It was nothing to write home about, he told himself for the twentieth time that morning. It was becoming a very repetitive and tedious thought. To try and make that particular thought more interesting he decided to imagine he was writing a tourist guide to Heaven, and had to think of a snappy *mot juste* to sum it up. 'Neo-classic-drive-thru-wedding-cake-post-modern-supermarket' was the snappiest it got. Hap being the top god in Heaven and unhampered by planning regulations had indulged in his own whimsical taste and then plastered everything with gold. The end result had met with universal disapproval from the rest of the pantheon who had to live in it, but to Hap there seemed little point in being top god unless you could impose your tastes on everyone else.

"It might help your bleedin' eyesight if you removed those damned sunglasses from your pecker," shrieked the exasperated Bobo from its perch on Fyrsil's helmet.

Fyrsil's thoughts collected quickly as he swerved to avoid marching into a sunken ornamental pond.

"It's the glare. All this gold just makes me giddy," answered Fyrsil. "And can't we go somewhere else for a change? I've nearly finished my tour of duty and all we do is march up and down in front of the Golden Palace. Couldn't we try round the back for once?"

"Halt! Halt you bleedin' num-dum!" the Bobo screeched.

The badly fitting ceremonial armour clanked to a stop shortly after Fyrsil cut short his forward momentum. Outrageously coloured plumage spluttered nosily from the top of the helmet. Suddenly, where there had been golden vistas of tasteless architecture, Fyrsil's immediate horizon was filled with two manic bloodshot eyes and an ugly upside-down beak.

"Listen carefully to me, you useless baggage of bones," the inverted head of the Bobo menaced. "Your job is to guard and protect Hap-i-Glob, Great God of the Golden Palace of Heaven, Protector of the Orbs, Spindoctor Supreme, and Professor of the Eternal Ness. The traditional way of doing that is to march up and down in a suitably military manner to indicate to any potential horrible horde from Murk that any attack would be futile. Believe it or not, you are supposed to be versed in all arts of modern warfare and so would be able to fight off a dirty legion of would be assassins. So, as your sorely put upon instructor and muse in all things military pertaining to the defence of Heaven, pick up those great useless platters of yours, and putting them one in front of the other, let's see if we can't do a march and about-turn or two in something of a semblance of a military demeanour? Or should I ask you please?"

In a movement that would have defied an acrobat, the Bobo righted itself from its inverted position in front of Fyrsil's quivering nose.

"Spearholder! Huh! The Administration in Alpoi has rigid guidelines for what is required, and what do we get? Heaven is sent a lanky weed who doesn't fit the uniform, can't march, and can't even hold a spear properly. How did you end up here?" the gaudy bird muttered as it smoothed its ruffled feathers.

Fyrsil sighed heavily.

It wasn't his fault; it was a computer error.

"ADAM sent me," he muttered to his feathered tormentor.

＊　　　　　＊　　　　　＊

Fyrsil had been quite happily preparing for a life as a Nutgatherer Mystic, one of the many semi-religious cults that thrived in the high altitudes of Alpoi. As the gateway community to the Stairway to Heaven, it had been decreed a very long time ago that the security guard for the Golden Palace in Heaven was the strongest and fittest youth with the best dental records that Alpoi could supply.

Once there had been armies. Now there was a solitary security guard.

Over the centuries Hap had got sick of the armies of guards cluttering up Heaven. There might be the ever-present threat of attack from the nasty things that dwelled on Murk, but that did not stop Hap getting thoroughly sick of the constant bugle calls, the tramping of massed hob-nailed boots, and the thoroughly annoying attack alert practices.

Hap had waited for several millennia for the forces of Murk to attack Heaven and carry off the Golden Orbs of Heaven. These were rather important as in them was stored the Golden Ness, which made the world go round when it was tipped off the end of Heaven. No invasions had happened. So being top god, he did the only sensible thing, and called in the accountants for a cost cutting exercise. Hap had hoped this would reduce the noise of the toughest hunks from all over Glob prancing around and preening themselves for the daily routine of parades and route marches. He would have been happy with the recommendation that the brass marching band and groaning massed choir should both be disbanded. The result of the eight volumes of the cost effectiveness and functionality report was even better.

Hap was extremely pleased with the findings: a token force of one would suffice to fend off an attack.

After all, Murk had made no hint of an attack in all the centuries that Hap had been making Ness.

There were a lot of things Hap didn't understand about his role on Heaven, but that was mainly because he had lost the instruction manual.

That was a shame as the introduction of the manual explained what kept Glob in constant motion. This boiled down to the combined energies of the forces of Heaven at the top end of the planet and Murk on the bottom end constantly chasing each other. A major factor in this process was Hap manufacturing Ness, and tipping it off the edge of Heaven. The dispersal of the elemental Ness produced a gravitational roll in Glob's rotation as it circled in its haphazard way between its two pink suns that shone above the planet. But it was Murk's hateful envy of Heaven's role as Glob's prime mover that gave the planet up-thrust to keep it on course, and prevented it from careering through space and crashing into the elasticated wall of the universe.

Hap did not realise any of this. He was a happier not tripping over various members of the Golden Guard playing war games and sounding off trumpets all over Heaven, disturbing his afternoon naps, and generally molesting the peace.

Being a practical god, Hap then decided to leave the choice of the single token security force to Alpoi, the closest human settlement to Heaven. To be more precise he sent a messenger down to the city state's ruling body which called itself the Goatherd Senate, and told it to get on with the job, and send the first guard up as soon as possible.

Traditionally a nation of poor crofters scraping an impossible living off the beautiful but harsh environment of the Golden Mountains, the one thing that most of its citizens were good at doing was arguing. They were so good at it, that no decisions were ever made between elections. Suddenly they had the problem of actually making at least one decision every year, and secondly cope with the problem of a massive influx of fit and aggressive young men from all corners of Glob vying for the honour of being Heaven's sole security guard.

Patrolling shepherds reported a worrying 582% increase in the number of reported cattle-worrying incidents as joggers in full armour rushed up and down the most inaccessible slopes making for the moral high ground. The arrival of these unwanted ethically motivated muscle bound meatheads publicly wanting to display their suitability for service in Heaven also severely interrupted the normal day to day practices of bribery and intimidation that passed for administration in the absence of any decisions from the Goatherd Senate. Disturbed by the alarming reports of citizen's arrests and good deeds committed by well-meaning foreigners the Goatherd Senate was forced to make a decision. It bought a computer which make would decisions for it.

The computer system was called ADAM (short for Administrative And Municipal), as a niche market configuration of heavy hardware and complex applications that had been developed to solve all problems for inner city states and urban sprawls. But it had one design fault – it took up the space of several blocks of expensive real estate, and so had failed to be attractive for its original target market of the rich metropolises. As Alpoi had several worthless bare mountain tops, and a desperate salesman cobbled together a ridiculously cheap deal, ADAM was installed to make the annual security guard selection from Alpoi's citizenry. Against the laws of probability, and definitely only in an idle moment, a dull functionary in the Goatherd Forum (uncivil) Civil Service discovered that ADAM could do a whole lot more. In fact it could virtually do their job for them.

So that is what happened in Alpoi. ADAM decided on virtually every matter in Alpoi, from the 'in' fashion colours for the year, to the complete career path for all of its citizens.

Remarkably, ADAM was such a spectacular piece of computer engineering that there no teething problems at all. So for centuries a succession of strong, fit and healthy young men were sent up to Heaven for a one year tour of duty. There were no bribes, no lawsuits against officials, and no problems. Every citizen was allocated a job according to their natural ability – or lack of it - and the Goatherd Forum was able to get back to arguing about making laws on intrusive urban development of areas of Outstanding Heavenly Beauty, and the provision of cattle grids on remote mountain outcrops.

Then the guarantee ran out. Within a week after a lot of un-normal whirring and beeping ADAM crashed. When the computer was rebooted it was not its old self, and was suffering severely from concussed circuits.

Fyrsil, who at 15-years-old, along with every other citizen, had registered his qualifications and had sat the aptitude test at the Forum Administrative Centre, and was awaiting the automatic allocation to trainee Nutgatherer Mystic. He knew that was what he was going to be, because he answered the aptitude test with the same answers that had been given by his father, and his father before him. All that was needed was the formality of the computer read –out confirming that a man of his dental records, non-membership of gyms or any active clubs, and general gawky appearance could only have one destiny. When the slip arrived three weeks late, Fyrsil couldn't believe his eyes: ADAM had judged him the most suitable candidate in Alpoi for Heaven's security guard, including the titles of Spearholder and Cup Bearer to Hap-I-Glob, Heaven's top god.

When Fyrsil attempted to report the obvious mistake to the Forum Administrative official, he found that he had been processed, dressed and dispatched to the foot of the Golden Stairway to Heaven, before he could voice any sort of protest.

"I know you look like a mistake, but it is the rules. ADAM's decision is final. And it's time for my snack break," the unsympathetic official told Fyrsil as she pushed him onto the moving stairway.

"But I don't want to go to Heaven!" Fyrsil shouted, attempting to run back down the escalator as he was whisked up at breakneck speed.

He fell over backwards in a clank of ill-fitting armour.

"You're late!" a shrill squawk in his ear told him.

"So this is Heaven," Fyrsil thought, as he peered through his favourite shades at a psychedelic bundle of lurid colours in boots and feathers, as the Bobo gave him the traditional abusive pep talk outlining his duties for the next 365 days of his life.

∗ ∗ ∗

That was then.

Now, the Bobo stiffened to attention on top of Fyrsil's helmet and fanned its tail feathers into a plume. The effect was an ugly pattern of clashing day-glo colour combinations that would have shocked even the most gauche of interior designers.

"Hsst. Look lively and get stood to attention. We've got Aquavita, goddess of Gushing Water and Muddy Places, coming up 'ere. And I want to see a smart salute," the bird whispered frighteningly loudly in the manner of sergeant-majors everywhere.

"I'll make a Spearholder of you yet, my lad!" it added hopefully.

Across the giant yellow mock-marble slabs, which made up the grand patio in front of the Golden Palace, sloshed something that looked like a moss-infested weeping willow wearing green galoshes. Despite appearances, it was the frumpy goddess Aquavita, much worshipped in the bogs and wetlands of Glob.

Fyrsil tried a snappy salute. The shaft of his spear clanged against an overhanging edge of his outsized breastplate. The Bobo hopped round on its perch on Fyrsil's helmet to hide its embarrassment, and drooped its tail feathers into Fyrsil's face. The helmet swayed under the exasperated sobs of a distressed Bobo bird of war, and the day-glo feathers tickled Fyrsil's wrinkling nose. Before the Spearholder knew what he was doing, another parade ground gaff had been committed as he sneezed loudly.

"Oh hello Spearholder," said Aquavita. "Nasty cold you've got there. Ought to take something for it. Don't know why they have not been banished. After all, this is Heaven."

With that medicinal advice, the goddess of Gushing Water and Muddy Places wandered off towards the ornamental pond on the Golden Palace's grand patio, where she intended to sit amongst the plastic lily pads and golden statues of gnomes with fishing rods, thinking wet thoughts.

"Gawd. I don't believe it. I just don't believe it,' sobbed the Bobo. "To think it has come to this. Me, the only surviving Bobo, the most feared and terrifying warbird on Glob. Me, trained in all martial arts since pecking me way through the egg shell; disciplined on the parade ground; and survivor of more fights and battles than the Gastrognomes of Hotchili have had hog-roast feasts. Me, having to witness the most dismal display of parade ground drill since a soldier was first ordered to 'Jump to it!' and knowing it has been ME who was given the task of licking YOU into shape! You...you useless great gangling nam-dam."

Being used to this sort of litany of abuse since his first bewildered days as Spearholder to Hap, Fyrsil ignored the flood of insults. Mentioned in dispatches of the Bobo's torrent of abuse was the cursing of his family right through to his maternal second cousin; questioning his parentage – anything from a one-cell amoeba to a humpback bum-beetle; and finally Fyrsil's own appearance, including the unusually large ears, the button nose, and oversized feet which were the only part of his anatomy which fit his uniform.

"You're about as much use as a security guard to the Golden Palace as a chocolate fireguard, you great stringy num-dum," the Bobo finished excitedly in a flurry of day-glo feathers.

During this excited tirade Fyrsil studiously tried his best to adjust his breastplate, and stop his sword belt from making its habitual dive to his ankles.

He put the abusive nature of the Bobo down to the psychological problems of being the last of the species of the fiercest form of birdlife on Glob. Although ugly, smelly and too intelligent for its own good, the very rarity of the Bobo made them a rare culinary delicacy – purely because of that fact. Especially to the tribe of food-orientated Gastrognomes of Hotchili whose cultural make-up was to scour the planet for strange and interesting things to add to the menu. And the stranger the better, because the higher the price which was paid for them by restaurants fighting to keep their place at the forefront of *haute cuisine*.

Cunning hunters devised special gasmasks and clothing to protect them from the Bobo's noxious intestinal pellets fired from its bum, to be able to reap the reward of the high prices paid in Hotchili. The record price was paid for the last known Bobo on Glob, which was eaten by the Gastrognome ruler, the Machomuncher, in front of a live televised audience of salivating food critics.

In fact it was almost the last Bobo.

Sorefoot, god of Travellers, had picked up a Bobo when on a fact finding tour of his shrines on the Upsiedown continent near the bottom of Glob. He gave it to Hap as a colourful souvenir. And from that moment it became the bane of the life of all security guards of the Golden Palace.

It was this souvenir that was now getting up Fyrsil's nose.

However, as he still harboured hopes of becoming an apprentice Nutgatherer Mystic in his uncle's cave when he returned from Heaven, Fyrsil thought he ought to be philosophical about the Bobo's behaviour.

He was trying to understand the Bobo's problems, and had often tried to be sympathetic – simply because the Bobo was the last of the Bobos. He actively encouraged the bird to talk openly, and get its anger off its luridly coloured chest.

Stoically, Fyrsil applied the therapy of letting the Bobo talk its frustrations out, and so inserted a pair of earplugs, which he found useful for these sessions. So, he didn't hear the whispering automatic doors of the Golden Palace open as Hap stepped out into the sunlight and laughed heartily.

He practised this regularly, as he felt it was required of the top god in Heaven.

He was a big god. They didn't get much bigger. Paving slabs were heard to creak as he indented their surface with a footprint. Being a big god, he had a big voice to match, and when the cry of "Cup Bearer!" filled the golden air, the gilded particles of heaven tinkled with the resonance.

Fyrsil longed for that eardrum-threatening call. It meant that Fyrsil had to transform from Spearholder to Cup Bearer via a lightning change of clothes – part of the cost-cutting and efficiency at work programme for Heaven's security guard – but more importantly it took him out of the company of the Bobo.

He rushed to the sentry box and shed the complicatedly buckled breast plate, shook out of the leg armour and grieves, and kicked off the 22 lace-holed war boots. Then as Cup Bearer he donned a holy yellow toga, secured about the waist by an imperial purple sash, high-tied thong sandals, and dashed with symbolic golden goblet to be at Hap's beck and call.

The other reason "Cup Bearer!" or even "Cup Bearer! Cup Bearer!" was Fyrsil's favourite sound in Heaven was it meant he could slip away to the Golden Palace library, where he could pull down from the dusty shelves a neglected encyclopaedia or two and watch in fascination as the books constantly up-dated the information on cities, towns, villages, rivers, mountains and plains of Glob. On pushing back the doors of the library it was like entering the engine room of an enormous super liner. As he walked down the aisles of fading dun coloured spines titled with every subject that existed on Glob, the air was thick with a hum of busy activity, as the words in the encyclopaedia automatically erased and rewrote paragraphs, pages and maps. Political upheavals, wars, floods, disasters - natural and un-natural – all constantly adding and changing the entries in volumes of the ultimate encyclopaedias.

To Fyrsil the library was what Heaven was all about. But what it was about at that moment was delivering a fresh round of sandwiches to Hap in his laboratory.

III

A soft, baggy, imperial yellow leisure suit tried to disguise the great bulk of Hap as he moved heavily around the mass of apparatus and scientific bric-a-brac. Even the official uniform of the toga he wore on official occasions seemed to constrict the bulging slabs of fat that hung off his body. Bloated on the vapours of Ness that hung in every particle of air in the Golden Palace laboratories, Hap filled his leisure suit like a lumpy blancmange fills a carrier bag.

He sighed happily, and pulled a well-used lever to release a secret recipe of chemicals into a vat to start another batch of Ness.

Hap had happily waved goodbye to countless millennia since as a slim young god he had filled the first gleaming vat to produce the fresh, heavy Ness to fill the pristine Golden Orbs. He grabbed a large handful of his drooping midriff and wobbled to his comfy chair.

"Sandwich, your Venerable Golden Holiness?" Fyrsil said as he proffered a large platter of nut and honey crust-less triangles.

"Thank-you Cup Bearer," said Hap. He pressed a button on a 203-function remote, and from the side of the chair a tray on a mechanical arm instantly appeared to take the neat pile of sandwiches Fyrsil had carefully prepared.

"Oh, and stop all that "your Venerable Golden Holiness" stuff. Hap will do for the laboratory. Leave the formal nonsense for official occasions."

The god heaved his legs into mid-air, and pressed another button. The floral patterned comfy chair instantly produced a footstool for Hap's puffy feet. He looked out of the large plate glass at the golden clouds floating around Heaven as honey dribbled down his beard.

"Yo Hap!" said Fyrsil, entering into the spirit of the god's request.

"Noth that inthormal," Hap said sharply through his stuffed mouth.

A pensive silence filled the space between the next sandwich, so Hap said: "Talk to me Cup Bearer."

"What about?"

"Anything."

After a short pause while he tried to decide what was considered a good subject of conversation between mortal and god, Fyrsil looked out the window and said: "Looks like rain."

"Don't be so stupid. It never rains in Heaven. It's a rain-free zone. And that's official."

The word of the top god might be final, but Fyrsil, who knew a thing about rain, was convinced he was looking at a very black rain cloud. Not only a rain cloud, but one which had VERY WET spelt in large letters. Thinking it strange, he picked up his ceremonial golden goblet and went to get a pair of binoculars from the storeroom to investigate the matter.

With his attention drawn to the black cloud that was scooting across the sky towards the palace, Hap scratched his head. It definitely did look like a stormy black rain cloud. But all storm clouds were manufactured in Murk, where they launched into the skies of Glob to compete with the showers of Golden Ness. Everybody knew that, except the cloud that was now hovering above the Golden Palace's laboratory.

After guzzling another sandwich, Hap was still puzzling about this strange phenomenon when something that looked like rain to someone who had never seen it before started dropping from the cloud.

At least from a distance it looked like rain. As the raindrops got nearer, they came into focus as hundreds of red imps in black raincoats and black gumboots, and black demons in red raincoats and red wellingtons, all parachuting with umbrellas down onto the Golden Palace. Hap found out that it was exactly what they were when one of the imps smashed through the plate window and landed on his lap.

"Hoi! Careful. Mind my sandwich," he shouted. Only then did he realise what was happening: The long-dreaded attack on Heaven had begun.

"Smash, smash, smash. Hit, hit, hit," gibbered the imp from underneath its oversized sou'wester hat, and so Hap obligingly swatted the imp off his lap and into the honey and nut mess on the floor.

"Spearholder! Spearholder! And don't bother changing," Hap roared, wishing that he had not been persuaded by the management consultants into being defended by a stringy looking boy who was rather good at making nut cutlets. Frantically he pushed buttons on his remote to transform his chair into a whirling sea of mechanical fly swats, which hit out at the swirling horde of umbrella-wielding imps and demons pouring like a multicoloured ocean through the smashed window.

The tranquil rhythms of Heaven were shattered – replaced by wild blood-curdling yells, and sounds of gilded concrete statues being whacked by furled umbrellas. Windows crashed, glass tinkled and everywhere fixtures and fittings shrieked as they were pulled to their destruction. And a distressed Bobo squawked desperate spelling corrections to the crude illiterate graffiti sprayed on the walls of the Golden Palace, as it was chased by a posse of imps with aerosol cans.

Fyrsil did not hear the loud call of "Spearholder" in the storeroom. One reason was that he was concentrating on trying to work out the organised confusion that passed for a filing system. Another reason was that the palace intercom was not switched on, and so he could not hear the rumpus in the laboratory. His concern was why 'binoculars' was not listed under 'B', or even 'O' for Optical Aids.

At that moment, the storeroom filing system was not something that was bothering Hap at all. Pinned down by a net of pure slime, that effectively stopped him swatting at the imps and demons which were poking at him with their umbrellas, he was thinking of who was going to rescue him. The security guard was nowhere to be seen, and he thought he had heard the squawk of the Bobo running down the corridor. What was needed was a charge of fearsome war-like deities like Crusher, the god of war, and Knucklehead, the god of military strategy and the rest of the heavenly host. Unfortunately, along with most of the rest of the pantheon, they had gone off for the annual tennis club picnic in one of the more distant unspoilt beauty spots on the edge of Heaven.

Even the comfy chair had given up trying to swipe at the uniformed invaders through the layers of slime netting.

But for Hap the worst part about the experience was the sound of crashes, clangs and tinkles that told him that every instrument and appliance in his beloved laboratory was being trashed with maximum depraved prejudice.

As the clamour of destruction rose, so did the colour of Hap's face. His complexion darkened from the normally golden bronze, into a seething and boiling beetroot red.

"GRRRSTOPPIT...STOPPITT...STOP...IT!"

Suddenly, the comfy chair bucked under the restraining slime net, and Hap roared like an enormous novelty lemon jelly on steroids, as the pent up force of his temper exploded in a small vocal gale of sound. The restraining imps who had been piled on Hap shook their heads and blankly wondered where their hearing had gone. The rest of the demons and imps were scattered on the floor or frozen in mid bash as the roar of Hap's bellow reverberated around the laboratory in a solid wall of sound.

"Who's in charge of this despicable rabble," roared the incapacitated top god of Heaven.

The nearest imps and demons continued merely to blink in an empty-headed fashion, still wondering why they couldn't hear anything. But from the back of the crowd a big black umbrella wielded by a burly demon thwacked and shoved a corridor to the comfy chair.

"I am," said the demon, pointing with a gnarled talon to a badge on the breast of his red raincoat. The badge read: 'Most Horrible of the Horribles (1st Class)'.

"You are now a prisoner of the Suicide Demon Legion – the big stormtroopers of Murk."

"No, I am," shouted a vicious imp, as he cut a swathe with a viscously spiked parasol through the dazed umbrella parachutists to the other arm of the comfy chair. Pointing to a badge on his black shiny mackintosh with the legend 'The Biggest Big Trouble' the diminutive red imp whisked its tail angrily and said: "And don't listen to anything he says. It's me what commands the Totally Disloyal Impi of Imps – the real stormtroopers of Murk."

"No, I do," said the Most Horrible of Horribles, leering threateningly at his rival.

"You don't. I do," shouted back The Big Trouble.

"But, I was promised. Lord Murk appointed me with this badge," whined The Most Horrible of Horribles, and petulantly stamped his foot to get his point across.

"My badge is bigger," said The Big Trouble, tapping it importantly, "and He pinned it on me mac – personal like. I was number one, He said." To emphasise his point he hit the demon over the sou'wester with his brolly.

Not slow to pick up a line of argument, the demon responded with a resounding whack on the imp's sou'wester, to which the imp replied with gusto in a remarkably similar fashion. Feeling that he could continue this dispute using the 'eye for an eye' dialogue, the imp bashed the demon, and was answered with the same sort of retort, and was answered in kind like a demented clockwork tin toy.

After watching this display above his head in the nodding manner known to crowds at tennis matches, Hap decided that the game should end.

"Right, that's enough," Hap shouted at them. "You are both in charge, so you can both get on with whatever you were going to get on with before you started getting on with this display."

The umbrellas wavered in mid-air, more because the combatants were trying to work out what had been said than because they wanted to stop hitting each other. They were beginning to enjoy the argument. But after a suitable pause, and a straightening of mackintoshes, they both pulled out a poster from an inside pocket, and thrust close in front of Hap's face, declaring in unison: "We is after this here god what calls himself Hap."

The top god in Heaven gave a start. Not because in every temple of Glob he was normally referred to as nothing less than: Hap-i-Glob the Golden, Tippity-Top of Heaven's Golden Palace. (More usually several other appendages such as Protector of the Orbs, Great Cook of the Golden Gleam, and Professor of the Eternal Ness, were added to fill up the priests' services, and sound pompous.) Nor was it because scrawled across the poster was:

WANTED!
Criminal!!
The enemy of Murk: Hap –
sometimes known as Hap-i-Glob.
Many other aliases used included
Protector, Great Cook and Professor.

What left him speechless was the slightly out of focus picture showing a lean, young Hap beaming proudly as he stood in front of the newly constructed Golden Palace. According to myth, because his memory wasn't that good, it would have been shortly after Glob first tumbled from the workbench of the Great Being and fell into the universe - which fortunately was lying open at the time.

"By the Golden Orbs," he exclaimed, "that's me. Where did you get that picture?"

"Can't be you. Him in that picture is thin, trim, and good looking," said The Most Horrible of Horribles.

"And you is fat and blobby. And also, we is the ones with the questions. That's because you is our prisoner. Right!" The Big Trouble told Hap.

"But it is me. That is how I used to look ...centuries –probably eons – ago. Of course I couldn't possibly fit into that toga now. Pity, it always was one of my favourites."

"What's your name then?" demanded The Big Trouble, narrowing his already heavily hooded eyes.

"Hap-i-Glob the Golden, Protector of the Orbs, Professor of Eternal Ness and a whole lot more I keep on forgetting which order they come in..."

"Alright, that's enough. Fairly conclusive I would say," said the Most Horrible of Horribles, licking his black lips and baring his fangs with satisfaction.

"Incriminating, even," said The Big Trouble, winking and wrinkling his red nose in a delightedly threatening manner.

As one they discarded the posters, pulled out identical parchment rolls from their mackintoshes, and in unison cleared their throats noisily, and announced importantly:

"His Unbelievably Mightiness, The Unmentionable, Lord of Murk and Keeper of the Castle Gloom, Stormdoctor, and Dispenser of Misery to Planet Glob, has sent his distrusted servants..."

"The Impi of imps," said The Biggest Big Trouble, as he inflated his chest.

"The Demon Legion," said The Most Horrible of Horribles, smugly picking his nose in pride.

"...to bring back the secret formula of Ness and Golden Orbs, what was stolen at the beginning of Time by the arch criminal Hap of Heaven..."

"What's all this rubbish!" Hap interrupted angrily." It wasn't stolen. It has always been mine..."

"Interjections during the reading of proclamations of the Lord of Murk will be dealt with in the traditional manner..." The Most Horrible of Horribles hissed in Hap's face gleefully.

"Of Putting a Sock In It," finished The Big Trouble. The demon fished from a pocket a large soiled sock that smelled of a unimaginable pot-pourri of foot-rot, verrucas, and festering swamps.

This he stuffed forcefully into Hap's protesting mouth and sealed his lips with industrial packing tape.

"Now, where were we?" said the Big Big Trouble rhetorically above the muffled noises of Hap's taste and smelling senses reacting to the murky sock.

"Ah, yes. Stolen at the beginning of Time…"said The Most Horrible of Horribles. Together they cleared their throats and continued: "Stolen at the beginning of time by the arch criminal Hap of Heaven, and so the true order of the world of Glob can be restored – with Murk making the world go round."

Pausing, they both grinned gargoyle smirks.

"Any reticence in handing over the Golden Orbs or the secret recipe for Ness will be punished by the tried and tested methods of interrogation perfected in the lower recesses of the malcontents resting rooms of Castle Gloom. Signed: The Unmentionable (Trachidambabble to those who don't know) Lord of Murk. P.S. Pillage and destruction of everything in Heaven is considered essential to the success of this mission."

"Right, that's the boring bit over with," said The Big Trouble, as they threw the parchments over their shoulders. "Let's get down to a smidgen of friendly interrogation. Where are your balls, and where is the formula – fatty?" demanded The Big Trouble.

"Yeah! Spill the beans wobblebottom!" demanded the Most Horrible of Horribles "then we can work you over for pudding! Or is that dessert? Menus always confuse me."

Being the top god in Heaven, Hap was not used to being tied up in a slimy net, nor have the most vile sock in creation stuffed unceremoniously into his mouth.

He was definitely not used to anyone calling him "fatty" or "wobblebottom".

Discrimination, especially weightism, was not big in Heaven, which was understandable when the god who ran the show was of such generous proportions. Hap had come to think of himself as 'big-boned'. It was just the bones kept on getting bigger.

Hap did try to express his dismay at his sudden loss of dignity for a very important god, but all he could achieve was an almost inaudible grunting through the sock.

"I didn't understand any of that, did you 'Orrible?" smirked The Big Trouble.

"Not a word," snickered The Most Horrible of Horribles.

"Well, we'd better ask again then. But this time with a little persuasion," said Trouble, grinning menacingly through his fangs. He pressed a button on the handle of his umbrella, and with a vicious hiss the spike at the end of the brolly opened up into a nasty looking barbed bit of metalware that had no attractive features and plenty of unpleasant ones. The stunted imp commander prodded various more globular parts of Hap's anatomy, which produced muffled howls of pain through the sock.

"Not very co-operative, is he? A little more encouragement is needed, I think," commented The Most Horrible of Horribles. With a twist of the handle, the end of the demon's umbrella transformed into a multi-spiked club, bristling with rusty nails.

"We want your secret formula and your BALLS, Mr Flabby," the demon menaced, and to emphasise his point, brought the club down on the appropriately sensitive part of Hap's anatomy.

The force of the reaction surprised even the interrogators. An enormous howl of pain projected the murky sock out of Hap's mouth like the shell from a howitzer, breaking through the slime net, and ricocheting off walls, ceiling and a large number of imps and demons. What followed in the wake of the sock was an aural tidal wave of sound that was so powerfully awful and piercing, it splintered every smashed article in the laboratory. The crowd of warriors from Murk who were not crushed under the wave of sound were frozen to the spot.

It was at this moment that Fyrsil chose to enter the laboratory.

Not being able to find the binoculars Fyrsil had gone to look for, he had decided to make some more sandwiches. The feeling that something was wrong in Heaven strengthened as he walked along the corridors that had been recently daubed with sprayed messages reading: MURK ROOLZ OK! and SCUM WOZ EAR!

It was emphasised as he was flung flat against the wall as the Bobo rushed by, firing a stream of noxious pellets from its red bum at a clattering posse of demons shouting: "Luverly pong. Yum-yum. More, more."

Still clutching his ceremonial goblet, Fyrsil ran headlong through the swing doors into the laboratory. Instantly he was frozen to the spot by the howl of anguish of the god he should have been protecting.

As a result, this daringly uncharacteristic rush into the fray went completely unnoticed. When those stormtroopers of Murk who could pick themselves up, did so, they didn't notice that the only unbroken thing in the laboratory was a statue with a goblet in its hand. The one demon who did notice Fyrsil was so dazed that instead of tearing Fyrsil apart limb by limb – which is the usual demon reaction to something they haven't seen before. Pulling out a paint gun, it wrote 'MURK ROOLZ' up and down Fyrsil's toga, and as a final touch bashed the golden goblet of the Cup Bearer of Hap onto Fyrsil's head.

The Cup Bearer, and erstwhile Spearholder of Heaven wasn't to discover this until he recovered consciousness.

It also meant Fyrsil didn't see a demon poke his head through what once was a laboratory window and say: "Got the balls boss. They're in the warehouse out the back."

Nor did he see the imp take the formula for Ness from the memory board where it was pinned among brochures, prayer ribbons, and various souvenirs from temples on Glob.

III

Some people always dream of being a hero and saving the world. Others have observed that most heroes die young as a result of their heroics, and so do their best to avoid getting into situations where they might be pushed into brave and very rash acts.

For someone who thought he was destined for the quiet life of a Nutgatherer Mystic, heroics was not something that Fyrsil had planned for in his career development profile.

As far as he could see, even through his coal-black dark glasses, there was not much to be said for the work of a hero. For a start it is very seasonal – times of trouble only – and secondly it's positively dangerous.

Naturally seeing that most people end up doing things they do not want to do - and Fyrsil's luck had been hiding from him recently - he got lumbered with the ultimate heroic task by being the wrong man at the wrong time.

The wrong time was when he was moping around the grounds of Golden Palace after the meeting of the Council of Heaven.

The council meeting, like most of its ilk, had been an eye-opener on the great and the good in the pantheon of gods living in Heaven. After an appeal by Hap for volunteers to go to Murk and rescue the Golden Orbs and the recipe for Ness, there had been an uncomfortable silence and a lot of shuffling of papers. From Crusher the god of War, to Verity the cynical god of Truth, they all made their excuses. Hap stormed out of the council chamber amid a chorus of excuses after Knucklehead, the god of military strategy, declared it would take at least a year to plan a proper campaign to effect this sort of operation.

The last words of Hap, chairman of the council, as reported in the minutes circulated days later, were: "This is the end. If Trachidambabble doesn't start making Ness soon, Glob will spin out and be flattened on the walls of the universe. And even if Murk does start doing my job, it's still curtains for the planet. You can't put the back legs of a donkey at the front and expect it to work properly."

Fyrsil knew all this because he had been there. But after that Hap had taken to his inner sanctum, and could not be tempted out even for a honey and nut sandwich. So the Bobo had set Fyrsil the task of gluing the various limbs, noses and other appendages back on the ornamental statues that had once graced the patio outside the Golden Palace, but were now piles of puzzling bits of gilded stone and marble.

He was standing back and wondering whether the nose he had just glued on a damaged statue was really the right one, when a familiar voice barked behind him: "Hoi, dopey!"

"The name's Fyrsil," he told the Bobo with a resigned sigh.

"Well, whatever it is, pick up your spear and make you way in an orderly fashion into the presence of Hap-i-Glob – until recently Protector of the Orbs, as well as top god of Heaven. There you will listen and obey like the Spearholder you have been trained to be – or meet a gory fate. And I will see to the latter personally. Got that?" the warbird squawked in its best parade ground manner.

"Well...What's this all about?" asked Fyrsil, who had been rather hoping that now the end of the world was nigh, he would be able to go back to Alpoi, and at least be a Nutgatherer Mystic for the time before Glob fell out of its orbit and dived towards the universe wall.

"Dunno," replied the Bobo brightly, "probably instructions for tidying up the Palace and giving it a new lick of paint before Doomsday."

"That's on my list anyway. So why all this bit about a gory death? We're all going to die anyway."

"Oh, that's just traditional before a private audience with the top god, just in case it's a Death or Glory mission. We haven't had one of those for eons, but it does give a sense of occasion."

Still not 100 per cent sure that the threat was hollow, Fyrsil tentatively picked up his spear and clanked to the palace as the Bobo squawked in his ear: "Right, let's being having you...left-right-left-right-left...and slope that spear properly.

The Bobo guided Fyrsil down corridors in the palace he had never seen before, until they halted beside an ornate door with an embossed golden plaque declaring the room behind to be Hap's Inner Sanctum. The Bobo pulled a bell rope, and a merry electronic tune played annoyingly before a pre-recorded message asked them to enter Hap's personal apartment, and make sure to wipe their feet at the door.

Once inside, Fyrsil glanced at what had been once a sort of sumptuous décor, before rampaging stormtroopers of Murk had wielded their umbrellas in a destructive frenzy. The once grand canary yellow waterbed still dominated the room, but the damp patch that surrounded its half-deflated state and the scattered parts of several puncture repair kits on the floor told the story of the holy bed.

Hap was frowning as he tried to re-arrange a few broken favourite mementoes on a now three-legged occasional table, which wobbled ominously every time he touched a cluttered ornament. At the sound of Fyrsil clattering into the Inner Sanctum, he thankfully gave up the task, and sank into the comfort of his loyal floral covered chair.

As he saluted in front of the top god, Fyrsil could see worry lines below a turban of bandages on a once wrinkle-free forehead. His features drooped, and every overflowing dollop of his body sagged in every direction.

"Ah, Spearholder, at ease, at ease. Fuzzy, isn't it?"

Fyrsil looked perplexed, before answering: "Sorry?"

"Your name! Fuzzy isn't it."

"No, actually it…Ow!"

The Bobo, sensing that an essential part of protocol was about to be breached, pecked Fyrsil hard on the ear. "If he calls you Fuzzy, then you is Fuzzy – right!" it whispered hoarsely.

Getting the message, Fyrsil executed a smart salute with his spear, and managed to hit himself on the nose and stamp the shaft down onto his foot. Even the Bobo was impressed by this almost impossible display of lack of co-ordination.

"Absolutely, Your Golden Hap-I-Ness," he said through gritted teeth, as he tried to suppress a howl of pain.

"Oh good. Well, Absolutely Fuzzy, I've summoned you here to ask you to do something for me."

"Your wish is my command, Your Golden-Ness," the security guard said, remembering the Bobo's lines about gory death.

"Quite so, quite so. I was just coming to that. What I want you to do is…save the world."

There was an incredulous silence from Fyrsil as Hap twiddled his thumbs and beamed with beatific confidence at his security guard.

"You can't be serious," a pop-eyed Fyrsil blurted out, knowing that the god in the lemon yellow joggers was exactly that. Momentarily he wondered whether it was in his contract that the Bobo had made him sign after he first tripped off the escalator on the Stairway to Heaven.

"Oh absolutely, Absolutely Fuzzy," Hap replied as Fyrsil received another sharp peck from the Bobo. "You saw what happened in the council chamber. Every one of those useless gods cried off! For centuries they have been hanging around Heaven, not really doing much, apart from ignoring the prayers and sacrifices of their congregations. Then, on the only occasion that they are asked to do anything that would be a useful contribution to the future of the planet, they all vanish. They should have jumped at the chance of saving Glob from eternal Murk and destruction."

Hap paused to adjust his bandage, which his quivering indignation had caused to slip over his left eye.

"And so, in the circumstances, that only leaves you."

There was a small silence that Hap intended for Fyrsil to say something enthusiastic. Not a speech, but something that summed up the historic proportions of this event with a good turn of phrase. He didn't. He was speechless.

"The thing is," Hap continued, slightly miffed by the silence, "after the rest of the gods and goddesses, you - according to your contract - are my personal representative, and so the only other official representative of Heaven."

"It is not just for the preservation and the greater glory of Heaven. I have this nasty feeling that we might have underestimated the importance of the Golden Orbs and the manufacture of Ness in the basic scheme of things for making this planet run properly."

Fyrsil could hear a knocking sound, and wondered what it was before realising it was his knees shaking uncontrollably.

"As it happens, I understand from messages from my priests that there have already been quite a few disasters on the face of Glob: mountains springing up where they shouldn't be; seas disappearing; that sort of thing. And that is just from the theft of the Golden Orbs. Who knows what will happen if Murk starts making Ness. It's probably in my manual to Heaven, but I can't find it in the storeroom anywhere. The filing system is terrible."

"I see," said Fyrsil, who didn't at all, but felt he had to say something anyway.

"What I suspect will happen is that Glob will drop out of the sky and after a lot really appalling catastrophes - the odd plague or environmental disaster will seem like a jolly jaunt after these – Heaven and Murk will fall off, and Glob will crash into the perimeter wall of the universe."

Fyrsil gulped appreciatively at the awesome prediction.

"So all you have to do, is go to Murk and bring back the Golden Orbs and recipe for Ness, and I will be able to get back to making Glob work properly again. Not much to ask really, in the circumstances," Hap said confidently, and nonchalantly looked at his fingernails with the air of someone who has just asked someone to change a light bulb.

"Well, I'm not too experienced at saving worlds," Fyrsil said shakily, consciously defying a peck from the Bobo.

"Good point, Absolutely Fuzzy, good point. Don't think I would send you out to save the world without the proper equipment. That would be silly."

Hap fumbled around underneath a floral cushion on the comfy chair, and pulled out a brightly coloured bumbag with the legend emblazoned across it in gothic script: God on Tour!

All across Glob a tourist is instantly identified by this handy luggage belt, in which invariably there is stuffed essentials such as passports, money, incomprehensible train timetables, and information on how to operate inflatable lifejackets in 10 obscure languages.

Fyrsil took the bumbag in his hands, looked at it, felt it, weighed it up, shook it, and looked at Hap questionably. It was a bit beyond him as to how he was meant to save the world with an article of convenience luggage.

"Amazing little thing, Fuzzy," Hap told him, who was looking at the bumbag as if it had already saved the world.

Nodding politely in agreement, Fyrsil hooked the belt around the waist and adjusted it for size and comfort.

"All my favourite colours, and that logo just hits the spot."

Fyrsil looked at the yellow bag and nodded somewhat less enthusiastically.

"And even more amazingly everything fits into it. Rather lucky, otherwise you would be loaded down with all sorts of clobber. A clever little cherub managed to muck around with molecules and dimensions and the like, and has come up with this ingenious little space-saver. What we've done is make it a sort of Hero's starter pack – most things for most situations. Even managed to fit in a *Shield of the Righteous*. I never thought it would get through the zipper."

Like a child with a new box of toys, Hap had become very animated. He took the bumbag off Fyrsil, and only just remembering in time to de-activate the Snapper anti-pick-pocket device (guaranteed to rip the hand off anyone foolish enough to tamper with a bumbag of the gods), stuck his arm in and pulled out a small pile of various weapons, implements and assorted chattels.

Along with the *Shield of Righteousness* (including dust cover), Crusher (God of War – Warriors, Weapons and Devices) had contributed a 4 metre *Sword of the Mighty MkIV*, complete with manual and solar-charge batteries; lie-detector ear-phones from Veritas (God of Truth & Small Places; Fair Corker (Goddess of Lust & Fashion Accessories) had contributed an expensively presented phial of scent labelled RAW LOVE (a single sniff and any living creature – and some dead ones – are driven crazy with desire).

A pile of useful, inappropriate, and useless articles grew around Hap's feet as he dug deeper into the bumbag.

" ...And what do we have here? Ah yes, Anti-Mate for dragons, a guide to 11 of the best restaurants in Hotchilli, and lots, lots more. Essentially everything you will need to help you save Glob, generously donated by the pantheon of gods in Heaven."

Hap rambled on as he balanced travel freshen-up kits precariously on variously coloured thermal underwear, looking for more obscure articles that had been packed into the space-saving bumbag."How do I find Murk?" Fyrsil ventured.

"Don't know. Try the library, there must be a map somewhere," Hap scowled, waving his hand airily in the manner that indicated that the top god in Heaven does not concern himself with trivialities like directions.

Fyrsil watched uneasily, not at all sure about the confidence placed in him to return the Golden Orbs and the necessary recipe for Ness. Apart from coming to Heaven, he had never ventured off the craggy outcrops of Alpoi, and he had no desire to find out what was on the rest of Glob.

"Now," said Hap, interrupting Fyrsil's thoughts, "if you're wondering how long you have to complete this mission..." And so saying pulled out a pouch from a pocket of the bulging lycra leisure suit. He emptied the contents, and held up a small and perfectly formed golden spherical nugget in front of Fyrsil's eyes.

As it turned slowly in Hap's plump fingers, the globe drew Fyrsil's attention to it with a fascination which went beyond the beauty of its translucent golden yellow colouring.

"This is the *Being Stone*. At the beginning of Time it was wrapped in the recipe for Ness. When all is well with Glob it shines with a light that can never be matched, and with a golden-ness that is more gold than pure gold. There was a time when no mortal could look at it without being blinded by its brilliance."

Hap's eyebrows arched high on the plump peach of his face.

"But the light is fading. The fortune of Glob is mirrored in the heart of the stone, and as you can see, there are already veins of blue clouding its surface. If you do not return the Golden Orbs, and new production of Ness is not started before the *Being Stone* turns completely blue, then the planet is doomed."

Hap made a face that mirrored his predictions.

"Glob will have a fate worse than the worst fate imaginable – whatever that is."

Solemnly Hap place the stone in Fyrsil's hand, and closing the security guard's fingers around it declared: "Glob depends on you Fuzzy, my boy. Bring back the Orbs and set the world to rights."

Standing dumbstruck, Fyrsil examined the stone of gold, before putting it carefully back in its pouch, which he hung around his neck. At least he wouldn't lose it, if it was there, he thought.

"Oh, and another thing: clear up this mess from the bumbag before you go," Hap told his security guard and soon to be hero of the planet, as he sank back into the comfy chair.

"Erm…just one question," Fyrsil said with his finger on chin.

"Yes, yes, well get on with it Fuzzy."

"How do I get there? I mean, it doesn't look as if I have much time, if I am going to save the planet, and Murk will be a very long walk."

Hap looked at the gangling guard with a troubled expression.

"Good point, good point. I hear what you are saying," said the lemon lycra wrapped god. After a moment's pause he reluctantly shifted his weight out of the chair.

"I suppose it's a time of sacrifice for everyone," he said wearily. Indicating to the chair, he announced it as not merely a comfort for the posterior, but as the 11th wonder of the world, called the Comfy Chair. Designed by a team of worshippers from Egg, renowned for their needless over-intelligence and inventiveness, they had put into it every feature that could be of possible use and quite a few that wouldn't. These operated on manual or semi-remote, as well as fully automatic, and all simultaneously.

"Let's try and find the manual. It will explain everything far better than me," Hap said, after pushing a few illustrative buttons on the remote control.

After digging down the sides of the chair, the large god pulled out a fully indexed manual still in its golden presentation plastic, and gave it to Fyrsil to browse through while he had one last play with the remote.

In quick succession the Comfy Chair sprouted an umbrella, produced a pot of tea and four place settings, and then, after a lot of whirring and buzzing, apertures opened in the sides of the chair as it grew a pair of gigantic wings that matched the floral pattern of its covers.

"There you are," Hap shouted triumphantly. "Simple really. All you need to do now is read the manual – it took me years to learn which buttons to press for those wings – and you will find that the Comfy Chair is one of the most wonderful creations on Glob. Constant contentment to your backside, a friend, a useful thing to know, and a constant companion."

Patting the Comfy Chair in the way people do when they come across an impressive piece of technological machinery that they have no understanding of, Hap tried to explain a few basic features.

"Oh, and I almost forgot."

He patted his pockets, and after a couple of minutes searching pulled out an old handkerchief. Unwrapping, it he revealed a battered gold badge with *HERO* inscribed on it.

"I found this in the storeroom," he said pinning it with difficulty onto Fyrsil's toga. "I think that completes the formalities. Oh, you better take the Bobo with you, and that's an order. It is very good on military things and fighting. Bound to come in useful, and I am sure it will be a perfect companion for your journey."

The Bobo squawked unhappily in answer to the command by the only superior it recognised.

The god in his sagging yellow leisure suit beamed contentedly. He was pleased with the interview, and now he let it known that it was over as he turned his attention back to the wobbly occasional table with his mementoes.

Fyrsil tried a last salute, and failed miserably again. He headed down the corridor from the Inner Sanctum to his future with a brightly coloured bird on his helmet, a bumbag around his waist, and following at his heels a comfy chair wearing covers of decorous floral patterns.

V

The howling wind made fists against Fyrsil's freckled cheeks and grabbed at this tousled hair as the Comfy Chair sped at a dizzying height above the mountain peaks at the top end of Glob. Fyrsil tried not to look down, because every time he did so, he felt sick. Despite all his misgivings, he felt he had to accept that he was now an official hero – after all he had a badge to prove it pinned to his toga. And he was sure that heroes were never air sick.

The reference book about flying he had taken from the Golden Palace library had indicated that the first experience of flight to any creature not born to using it as their primary mode of transport, would be likely to feel a heightened sense of relaxed exhilaration and freedom. It did not mention the mounting nausea, sweaty palms on the joystick, and the conviction that the stomach had migrated from its normal position below the ribcage to take up position just below the tonsils.

The usually brilliant golden skies dotted with lemon souffle puffs of clouds appeared to be different from normal. Maybe it was his coal black shades refracting the light differently at this height, or the fact that his eyes were watering heavily behind them, but it seemed that a tint of menacing purple was beginning to lurk at the edges of the horizon.

If he had not been still trying to master the delicate controls of a flying floral comfy chair, Fyrsil would have tried to look at the Being Stone to examine its golden depths for any more blue veins. For an unwilling security guard and fledgling hero the task of saving the world was an almost impossible task. Returning the Golden Orbs to Heaven before the Being Stone turned blue made an impossible task even more impossible.

First things first, thought Fyrsil, trying to establish in his mind a logical process of going about saving Glob. The immediate problem was to get the navigational instruments working.

Like a lot of things recently, flying was a new experience for the boy whose sole ambition before being unwillingly dragooned up to Heaven was to have become in the fullness of time a quite adequate Nutgatherer Mystic amongst the caves of Alpoi.

The Bobo had assured him that flying must be easy.

"Got to be simple. That's the reason Bobos stopped doing it. Too easy, and not as impressive on a parade ground – naturally," the flightless bird told him, as it donned a leather flying cap, goggles, and wound a white scarf around its neck.

A glance through the copy of *DIY Flying In 30 Minutes* from the library was not very reassuring. The book had been posthumously published after the author had imprinted himself permanently on the side of a mountain.

Fyrsil had mentioned this to Hap as he pushed reference books and guides down the sides of the Comfy Chair. The top god of Heaven merely snorted, and told the new hero that saving the world was unlikely not to involve a bit of personal danger, but it would be all worthwhile in the end.

"Just think of me! I will be constantly worrying about how your are getting on. It is bound to affect my digestion. It is a lonely position when the ultimate responsibility for the continued existence of a planet weighs upon your shoulders, and the only person you can send out is a weedy security guard. I am looking forward to sleepless siestas and excruciating headaches from post-Hap-i-Ness trauma until you return," he told Fyrsil, and stalked off to rustle up a send-off party to launch Fyrsil on his mission.

Finishing the strapping down of the last of the essential provisions, Fyrsil turned to find Crusher sidling up to him.

The god of War was leaning heavily on a medically approved walking stick as he limped along with a heavily bandaged toe.

"Ahem," the god said apologetically to announce his presence.

"Yes," said Fyrsil irritably. He blamed Crusher in particular for being landed with the role of trying to save the world. Fyrsil regarded it as the responsibility of all bellicose gods, and not one for the security guard whose contract was nearly up.

"Ever saved a world before?" asked Crusher, polishing the tip of his shiny boot on the back of his cavalry twills to avoid having to look Fyrsil in the eye.

"No," Fyrsil replied shortly.

"Me neither. Ever been in a battle?" the god asked, as he inspected very closely a piece of fluff on his tunic.

"Nooo..."

"Ah. Oh. Ever been in a fight?"

"No. It's not something that happens amongst Nutgatherer Mystics," a puzzled Fyrsil told the warrior god.

"No, I suppose not. An odd lot those mystics – pacifists or some such rot. Most of them anyway," Crusher said, and looked as if he wished he hadn't. This small talk was obviously taxing his thinking processes.

"Take a bit of advice from an old – recently invalided – warrior," the god said at last, his face happy with the achievement of a constructive thought. "Go to the island city of Loot in the Blood Sea and recruit some the pirates there to help you go and biff Murk. Nasty lot those pirates. Scourge of the whole planet, and equal to any demon in the amount of mischief they can cause. To say they are an evil, fearless bunch of misfits would be an understatement – they even stopped sacrificing to me a couple of years ago. The chance of a scrap like this will be like a red rag to a bull. They'll jump at it, especially if there's a chance of some gold and booty, and plenty of that Knockout punch they all drink to oil the wheels of the whole operation."

Despite his reluctance to even talk to Crusher, this was the first bit of help any god had given Fyrsil for his mission. In the absence of any other, as a plan it was quite an acceptable one – Fyrsil had racked his brain several times thinking of how to achieve his mission. His plan so far was to head down to Murk and hope he thought of something on the way. He was sure he would recognise Murk, because it was at the bottom end of Glob, and it chucked out rain clouds and thunder storms into the atmosphere. The map Fyrsil found in library even had Castle Gloom marked clearly, but was a bit hazy about the rest of Trachidambabble's domain.

"So where is Loot," he asked, fishing out the atlas from behind a cushion.

"Don't know," the god replied, and produced a hard thinking expression to dominate his features. "One of my high priests once took me there for a binge. I think he said it was some sort of missionary work, but it involved a lot of downing large quantities of that Knockout punch.. It was quite a party – at least I think. Couldn't remember a thing afterwards. Lucky to get back to Heaven in one piece."

The big god in his military attire smiled at the memory, then with a comradely pat on the back for Fyrsil, Crusher walked off, almost forgetting to limp.

Another trip to the library for Fyrsil, and another tome was added to the luggage stuffed down the sides of the Comfy Chair. The volume marked 'L' of the official Heaven Encyclopaedia of Glob buzzed loudly as Fyrsil pushed it behind the cushions. With Hap impatiently asking at every opportunity whether Fyrsil was packed yet, there was going to be no time to discover more about Loot until they were well on their way. It would have to do as in-flight entertainment.

But a sneak peak at the pages of the encyclopaedia was worrying. The writing and re-writing of events and the features of Glob used to be carried out at a relaxed ambling pace as the world slowly evolved. But flicking through a couple of pages had left Fyrsil with an uneasy feeling that things were going awry. Letters were sprinting down the page in phrases and sentences, chased by completely new formations of black paragraphed type, in waves of wild-formed fonts. Pie charts were spinning like multi-coloured tops, and graphs moved like a helter-skelter heliograph. Even to Fyrsil it was clear that there had been a seismic change on the face of Glob. Quick glances at occasional pages indicated violent changes in weather patterns, volcanoes sprouting in prairies, and lost tides wandering around desserts looking for new seas. Minor species were written out history as food chains packed up and left the territory, and new seasons set up shop wherever they felt like it.

It was obviously too much for some of the print in Heaven's official encyclopaedia. Margins were littered with burnt out calligraphic squiggles, too exhausted to be able to define the sudden changes that had gone on.

A quick look at the appropriate page assured him Loot had not sunk into the Blood Sea. The relevant pages were just as confused as the rest of the volume, but at least the history of the island did not make his eyeballs jump up and down with the movement of the indecipherable letters rushing around like headless chickens.

Loot was one of those places which most people had heard of, but no one knew its exact location. Which was lucky, as no one in their right mind wanted to find out where Loot was. 'Civil' was a rusty and neglected word among the pirate brotherhood, and the only use for civilisation as far as Loot's citizenry were concerned was for plundering,.

What Fyrsil did learn was that the pirate citadel was one of a many identical marshy insect infested islands that wallowed in impenetrable and uncharted parts of the Blood Sea. There was no tourist office, official holidays were frequent but had no fixed dates, (as all it depended on when was someone willing to pay for a big party) and the official currency depended on which country had been recently laid waste.

The encyclopaedia was the last of the items to be stuffed under cushions or strapped to the Comfy Chair before Fyrsil straddled the joystick, and with the Bobo squawking instructions from the chair's manual, taxied down to the top of the Stairway to Heaven. There Hap and an assembly of gods had gathered to see Fyrsil off on his trip to save the world. The turn-out was acceptable for the occasion, but they were getting restless by the time Fyrsil had got to grips with steering the chair and its enormous outstretched wings into the take-off position marked out in white paint on a cloud at the edge of Heaven.

Hap wobbled forward, his girth drooping alarmingly out of the folds of the ceremonial toga.

"Gods, goddesses and anyone else who has bothered to turn up."

A couple of cherubs giggled as they played with each other.

"I feel a few words are appropriate at the outset of this heroic mission. Absolutely Fuzzy has been totally selfless in volunteering for this task. We all depend on him succeeding. The future of Heaven, the future of Glob, rests in his –ahem – capable hands, and I'm sure we would all want to wish him well. He's an example to us all in this act of selfless devotion to duty, and getting your hands dirty by doing something that is unpleasant - but necessary."

A weak cheer mumbled its way out of the crowd of deities.

"Right, that's enough speeches. Bring back my Golden Orbs and my Ness recipe, and you'll have Glob at your feet. Fail and you have condemned the world to oblivion," shouted Hap enthusiastically. "Oh, and good luck!"

Borrowing a phrase he had read in the DIY flight manual he shouted: "chocks away Bobo" in what he hoped were heroic tenor.

The Bobo chose to ignore this flippancy and barked out directions read sternly from the Comfy Chair manual (chapter XXXV Auxiliary Applications.)

"Flying: take off. Select options mode from functions panel by pressing button marked 'O'. The monitor in left arm console will display options. Select booster by pressing buttons 'R' and 'B' simultaneously on the remote. A green light will indicate when booster is primed. De-activate safety cover on booster button (red) on joystick. Brace and push button for ignition."

Having followed the instructions to the letter, Fyrsil braced his thumb and pushed. Nothing happened. He cursed under his breath, looking nervously at the crowd of gods shifting their feet impatiently to cheer him off. He pushed again using both thumbs, and forgetting to brace. Someone started humming a tune, as Fyrsil hit the button with his fist.

With a sudden jolt the Comfy Chair was suddenly propelled off Heaven and into the nothing that is solid air as Hurr! (god of Unnecessary Strength) let out a blood curdling yell and pushed the chair on its castors over the edge. The mammoth deity had better things to do than save the world – there was a record pile of weights waiting in the gym to be lifted to win yet another title he had thought of.

Momentarily, the chair, its occupants and overloaded contents, seemed to hang in suspended animation as the pantheon waved their handkerchiefs and managed a brief cheer. Then it plummeted out of sight, and the gods and goddesses dragged themselves back to the Golden Palace to get on with enjoying themselves until the world was saved. There was the annual ball to organise, and there all those violin lessons to have to be able to fiddle while the world crashed out of space.

The first thing that Fyrsil noticed was the wind. It howled as it blinded him with tears, which he thought was quite appropriate as he felt the Comfy Chair nosedive towards Alpoi. The second thing he noticed was the irate instructions shrieked by the Bobo to pull his joystick this way and that. He tried every variation, and then gave up, and lay back and closed his eyes. To his surprise the chair suddenly swooped out of the nosedive, and the booster kicked in. There was a flash of yellow light, and the chair surged up leaving a puff of white smoke to hover in the sky.

"Hip-hip – huzzah!" Fyrsil heard distantly as the chair shot passed Heaven. In the wing mirror he could see distant gods waving from the Golden Palace, and then they were gone.

"Right, let's try and get this thing working properly," the Bobo told him, as the booster wore off and their flight path flattened out. Using the heavily inlaid manual, the bird hit the control console – hard. After a couple of minutes of hesitation, the wings started to flap like a giant crow on mogodons.

"Always a technical stand-by," the Bobo told Fyrsil smugly. "Now how about you flying this chair properly before you get the same treatment.

Flicking from the manual to the DIY guide, the Bobo shouted instructions from its perch on Fyrsil's helmet. They stalled, banked, climbed, rolled, and dived as Fyrsil took more and more confident control of the joystick. It all became fairly fluid, and the chair was even flying in straight lines, and not keeling over at dizzy angles, and Fyrsil even began to start enjoying what he was doing – when he got it right.

"OK, so that's flying," he said eventually. "Now let's go and find Loot. Which way?"

It all seemed quite pleasant: the soothing whump-whump of the enormous feathered wings; the breeze caressing his cheeks; clear view of soporific clouds.

"Use the Autonav. How do you expect me to navigate from this height. I can't see a thing on the ground."

Fyrsil looked down, gulped, did something with the joystick, and the chair went into a dive again. There was still a lot he needed to learn about flying. When he got the chair onto a steady course again, he learned something new about the multifunction features of the Comfy Chair: use too many powerful programmes at the same time, and the machinery goes into overload. Unfortunately this happened when using the flight and navigation features simultaneously, so all Fyrsil got from the Autonav screen was a request to land to be able to pin-point to within 1.5 metres accuracy their exact position.

"Isn't technology marvellous," Fyrsil commented. "Try giving it a bang with the book."

"I don't think it would work with navigation. Too much software to take any hard knocks. But after that last dive I should be able to use the road map. I think I recognise these," the bird said, pointing ahead.

Craggy peaks dusted with snow rose majestically in front of the chair and its passengers. Below them verdant valleys meandered, as wandering rivers lazily criss-crossed their wide plains. The difficulty Fyrsil had with the Bobo's plan was, although he could make out several distinctive features of the countryside, roads were not one of them. There may have been sheep tracks on the hillsides, and even favourite paths for goats among the shale on the mountain tops, but good old rut and mud roads were not in evidence at all.

It was just a small point, and as long as the Bobo was happy squinting into the middle distance with the binoculars then Fyrsil was prepared to let it pass. Loud squawks of instructions in his ear at large numbers of decibels was not helping his learning experience with flight in general, and specifically the manoeuvring of a floral flying Comfy Chair around in that particular bit of sky.

He pondered on the Bobo's role in this operation. It seemed to Fyrsil that there was only one person who had a 'HERO' badge presented to him by Hap. There was also one person who was the security guard of the Golden Palace who had been entrusted by Heaven to save the world. That person did not have garish plumage, and was not wearing a flying hat and goggles. Yet the bird was doing all the talking. He might have left Alpoi as an almost apprentice Nutgatherer Mystic, but he was now an official hero – with a badge to prove it – and so Fyrsil considered that the bird ought to shut up and let him think.

The great synthetic wings protruding from the chair made a rhythmic whump-whump-whump as they propelled the party of two across the sky.

With nothing much happening, apart from being niggled by the Bobo, Fyrsil pressed at the buttons on the console in the chair's arm, hoping to get some action out of the Autonav. The screen remained stubbornly fixed on a street intersection of a deserted desert city. Apparently there were no reported traffic delays, but a lost camel train was expected in a month's time.

"Have you found out how this navigational system works yet?" he shouted to the Bobo behind him.

Perched on the back of the chair, the Bobo was flicking through the operator's manual with one set of pinion feathers, while holding open a copy of a road map for the upper continents of Glob in the other wing.

"Alright, alright, hold onto your hair piece, I can't do everything at once," squawked the Bobo petulantly. "Hoi, who turned the lights out?"

The bird had been very observant. Suddenly everything had gone dark in a yellow sort of way, and both boy and bird felt as if they had been enveloped by an enormous lemon scented courtesy wipe – the sort associated with restaurants which encourage messy eating.

"Urrgh! I hate lemons," sobbed the Bobo, who was unused to most sorts of personal hygiene.

"Urrg! I can't see," shouted Fyrsil, as he tried to wipe his misted shades with a corner of his toga.

"Arrrrgh!" they both screeched in unison, as Fyrsil had let go of the joystick, and the chair once again plummeted in a nosedive.

At about that time, a bored Crash Eagle was playing I-spy with itself as it notched up another aerial circumnavigation of Glob before summoning up the courage to crash land at its traditional breeding rock. As it soared undisturbed, it thought fatalistically of the impending courting ritual on crutches, the hospital romance, and hatching of offspring during recuperation. Such a pleasant interlude of excitement in comparison to years of loneliness on the wing.

Thinking slowly about the clue it had set itself in its solitary game, it had registered that it was flying under a lemon cloud. Then suddenly the cloud ejected a horrible apparition. A floral patterned comfy chair, and carrying a screaming man in armour, and ugly brightly coloured bird. On closer inspection, because it was much closer very quickly, it looked like the chair was going to drop on the eagle's head.

In a purely natural reaction the eagle closed its eyes. Born to be involved in accidents, the Crash Eagles knew that it was far better not to know exactly what is going to happen to you before you crash. Generations of this species had learned that the best way was to close the eyes and hope the result wasn't too painful.

"Where's the manual? What do I do?" shouted Fyrsil, with the joystick yanked between his legs.

"Mind the eagle!" the Bobo squawked, noticing that the other bird had its eyes squeezed shut.

The chair screamed past the bird's beak in a noisy rush of pandemonium and slipstream. (It was only a continent later that the eagle thought it safe enough to open its eyes, and that was only after crashing into a mountain peak.)

Half a mile below, the Bobo was trying to flick through the clattering pages of the manual appendices, as the chair's wings started to hum ominously.

The great expanse of wingspan projecting from each arm of the chair was quivering dangerously, as Fyrsil tried all the movements that bought the chair back on course before. His stomach was in his mouth, and his eyes could see far too much of what was on the ground hurtling up to him. With a desperate yank he pulled the joystick, and winded himself as it knocked into the pit of his stomach. As he wheezed with pain, he felt the Comfy Chair just nudge out of its vertically downward course. He pulled again (avoiding injuring himself for a second time.)

"Pull back energetically on the joystick – repeatedly," shouted the Bobo, as he found the appropriate madly flapping page, and pinioned it with its feather.

"What next?" shouted Fyrsil, as the chair skimmed along a climbing mountainside.

"Don't stall."

"Don't what?" Fyrsil asked.

"Too late," the bird told him as the chair toppled above an ice-topped mountain peak and went into another roller-coaster dive.

"Now what?" screeched Fyrsil, several shades whiter than his normal pallid complexion.

"Repeat first instruction."

"How about landing procedure?"

"Why?"

"We're…"

Actions often speak louder than words. This was one of those occasions.

The Bobo's question was answered as the chair, Fyrsil and the Bobo, in that order shot through the centre of a picturesque haystack, several white picket fences, a washing line, and embedded themselves in a thatched roof of an equally picturesque wayside inn.

"Any more of those stunts, and you can write the sequel to *DIY Flight In 30 Minutes*," the Bobo announced from beneath a personal thatch balancing on its head.

There was no response. Looking around the crater in the neat roof where it sat, together with the upturned Comfy Chair twitching its wings, the Bobo could see no sign of the recently appointed HERO from Heaven on whom it wanted to vent its spleen.

It had not been impressed by the landing technique, and it was piqued that Fyrsil should land the chair without doing so under instruction in the laid down sequence from the manual. To make matters worse it found that its whole body was constricted by something that smelled alarmingly of a relaxing hot bedtime drink.

Up to the impact of the crash, the Bobo had seen what was about to happen in crystal clear slow motion. After the impact, everything was a bit of a blur. This fuzzy part of its memory had in fact been filled by the bird being catapulted through the leg of a pair of chocolate brown leggings, which had been happily hanging out to dry in the soft warmth of the two pink suns.

Finding itself unable to wiggle its wing quills, the Bobo did what came naturally: it squawked loudly, and without mercy.

There was a rustling of thatch reeds, followed by a small eruption, as a dazed Fyrsil, helmet askew, surfaced with a breastplate full of eco-friendly roofing.

"Wha...what's that noise? Where am I?" said the confused apprentice hero.

"You are where you landed the Comfy Chair. Most improperly I might add. Now, get me out of this thing."

"Mmm, this smells nice. There's a sort of homely aroma to this place – whatever it is," Fyrsil said, as he fingered the Bobo's restrictive body stocking.

"Never mind what it smells like. Get me out of it!" the bird screeched in its best military imperative.

Fyrsil took a good grip of the Bobo and tugged.

"Carefoool. That's the only head I've got, and I'm quite attached to it," the Bobo squeaked through a clenched beak.

A sudden plopping sound, accompanied by a surprised squawk, announced that the Bobo was free. It didn't take long for it to orientate itself again.

"Right, let's get this mess sorted out. We want a full check and accident report of the vehicle, followed by a repair schedule prior to take off and resumption of flight. And get tidied up. You are an ambassador of Heaven, and don't you forget it," barked the Bobo as it re-asserted its military credentials.

"Um, do you know anything about repairing flying chairs?"

"Not my job."

"Not mine either. Edible nuts are my speciality. I can identify 237 different varieties and their hybrids at the last count. Multi-functional chairs just aren't nuts," Fyrsil told his military advisor and travelling companion as he pulled thatch from his toga in a truculent manner.

"Excuse me friends, can I be of any assistance to two weary travellers?" asked a strangely rich creamy voice.

VI

There was either something very strange about the inn, or it had been the subject of a complete make-over by a seriously pastoral theme-pub chain. It managed to incorporate every element of anybody's idea of a picturesque country inn, and should have had an army of chocolate box illustrators crowding round its portals in an admiring semi-circle of easels.

There was the thatched roof, the friendly smoking chimney, dark oak beams contrasting the sunny white plaster. The welcoming countenance was enhanced by the regular diamond beaded windows smiled at the outside world, as they dispensed dappled light onto the authentic flag stone floors, and an interior décor that seriously favoured horse brasses and highly polished agricultural implements of yesteryear. The rural charm exuding from the rafters and ruddy faces of the dun clothed occupants was so oppressive it made Fyrsil feel quite light headed.

The artificially aged sign swung spotlessly above the heavy studded main door announced the building went under the name of *The Rest Inn*. A monk was depicted ecstatically sniffing the vapours of a bowl of very brown soup. It reminded Fyrsil that he hadn't eaten since taking off from Heaven, and was famished.

Taking in his surroundings from the high table of the chocolate box inn, Fyrsil noted that everything seemed a little too clean for even a sparklingly presented theme-pub. Everything from floors and ceilings, to the long trestle tables and benches bore all the scars of being devoutly scrubbed.

Despite the over-riding aura of benevolence that wafted around *The Rest Inn*, there were one or two things that rang alarm bells in the back of Fyrsil's brain. The first was that he was at that moment sat in the seat of honour for what was apparently a hastily put together feast. The normal reaction of most small communities on Glob who had experienced a stranger dropping out of the sky in a mini maelstrom of destruction, would be to ritually burn the stranger in a specially constructed wicker basket, as an offering to a local minor god. The very least to be expected was a good lynching.

Instead, Fyrsil and the Bobo had been treated to an un-nerving display of good manners, and being feted as long lost friends. They had been helped down from the thatch, and given a thorough medical to check for whiplash, and any cranial injuries. During this process a tubby turbaned figure who called himself Shamir Smartie Bar-Button, who Fyrsil presumed to be the manager of the inn, rushed about clapping his hands ordering a feast to be prepared for this grand occasion. Fyrsil had found it very disconcerting to be the centre of such fulsome attention. He was used to being shouted at, and making honey and nut sandwiches and that was no preparation for being lauded as a welcome extra-terrestrial.

Sitting precariously on a pile of sumptuous cushions, a slightly dazed Fyrsil surveyed the table in front of him. Despite its stumpy-legged solid construction, it bowed under the weight of dishes wobbling in competition for mouth-watering awards. Each pile of faultlessly presented sugared delicacies had its own little card indicating in copperplate print the country of origin, ingredients, number of additives, and the amount of calories along with allergy warnings.

"So, where you go from, that you travel in such a hurry in your flying machine?" asked the Shamir in a voice that hinted of creamy soft centres.

"Heaven," Fyrsil replied distractedly.

The distraction was a delicious girl with a big white smile splashed across a creamy chocolate fine-featured face piling his plate with a selection of the choicest dishes from the groaning table.

At the mention of 'Heaven' small clouds of anxiety darkened the tranquil expressions printed onto the faces of Fyrsil's dining companions. Of course the Bobo never wore expression that could be described as amiable at all, and in contrast to the rest of the assembled company, was frowning in disgust at the piles of food in front of it. It glared with beady hooded eyes suspiciously at the serving maidens as they piled on delicacies on to the plates of favoured few on the top table.

"Heaven? So you are a god, yes? Let me guess…Claimform god of Chaos…"

Tearing his eyes away from the plentiful goodies in front of him, Fyrsil turned to his host and pointed to his hero badge.

"No, security guard to the Golden Palace. Spearholder and Cupbearer to top god, Hap-i-Glob, Keeper of the Golden Orbs." Fyrsil said. "Or at least he was. Which is why I'm here, really. They were stolen by the Stormtroopers of Murk, and we are on our way to find them and take them back to Heaven."

"I see," said the Shamir, shaking his turban so its studded jewels blinked in disbelief.

There was a silence.

To fill it, Fyrsil toyed with a round gooey nugget that called itself as a Cocoa Fluff Ball. The flying and landing experience had seemed to give him a more than healthy appetite, and he was about to dispense with all the manners that required him to be asked to dig in, when he noticed everyone staring at him in a funny way. Wondering whether there was some local custom that he hadn't observed, he bit back his hunger and embarked on a bit of small talk.

"Not really the sort of wayside inn I'm used to where I come from. It's a rather extraordinary pub you run here, if you don't mind me saying Mr Shamir."

This didn't seem to have the effect Fyrsil was hoping for at all.

"I mean, it's a very homely and pleasant establishment: extremely friendly, indeed." Heaven's representative found that diplomatic conversation was not one of his strengths if the expressions of Shamir and his companions was anything to go by. "I wish all inns could be like yours."

It was not a good conversational gambit. The Shamir's milky complexion turned a threatening midnight mint black.

"This is not an inn, or a hostelry, or whatever. This is a sacred community. We are persecuted by unbelievers and market traders, who do not understand our ways, so we have to disguise our houses of worship to deceive those who would do us wrong. Our laws call for peace, understanding, and full hospitality to visitors, even if it means sacrificing our last chocolate drop."

The Shamir leant forward and pulled his lips back in a smile that revealed two rows of blackened stumps where once there had been teeth.

"All over Glob we are persecuted. They say we have spots; they say that we have no teeth; they say we are fat; they say we are completely goo-goo in the head. It is all lies!"

Fyrsil stared drop-jawed at his host. The foul smell of the Shamir's breath left his lungs fighting for clean air.

"This is a shrine. A shrine to the sacred bean that feeds all desires. We have no Heaven but the heaven that is the taste of the fruit of the sacred bean. And we have no Murk, but the evil that is being starved of the bean and all its delicious, crunchy-munchy varieties. We are the Chocolate Communion, sometimes known as Brown Robes, whom some people sometimes shame us by calling us Brown Bottoms," the Shamir declared, shaking at the top of his pile of cushions in fervent anger.

"Oh," said Fyrsil. "Well, this probably would not interest you then."

Unzipping the bumbag which was dangling at his waist, he rummaged about and pulled out a golden scroll inlaid with platinum and decorated in intricate designs with most of the precious stones found on Glob. Hap had given Fyrsil the scroll as a diplomatic aid and possible conversation piece at school reunions. It seemed the perfect time for the budding hero to see if was of any use. It bore a sacred command from Hap to whosoever it may concern (in the 1,786,933 official languages recognised by most of Glob) to help the bearer in whatever capacity the bearer may command.

"The point is," said Fyrsil, as he unravelled the document, "I am on my way to save Glob before it is too late, and any help will be rewarded by…At least I am sure I could put a lot of cocoa beans - or whatever - your way if you, and your Chocolate Browns are suitably hospitable and helpful." He was not quite sure how to hand out a blessing from Heaven to people who believed in a bean instead of some sort of deity.

The Shamir turned the scroll over in his hands, muttering: "very nice, very nice indeed," as his eyes feasted on the inlay and the assorted gems. A dreamy look came over his eyes, which worried Fyrsil enough to ask if his host feeling alright, before the Shamir suddenly stiffened and clicked his fingers. Descending from the pile of cushions on Fyrsil's other side, the wafer thin Chamberlain to the Shamir flowed to his master's feet. Whispers were exchanged from behind the Shamir's plump hand. From up his sleeve, the Chamberlain pulled out a magnifying glass, and putting it to his eye examined the scroll with a professional air, getting very excited in a sniffy sort of way.

More whispering behind bejewelled fingers followed the inspection.

"You're meant to read the parchment. It's terribly good, and it's in all sorts of languages," Fyrsil told them helpfully.

"Yes, yes. Now eat; eat. You must be hungry after such a journey from so far."

Without any more prompting Fyrsil bit into the Cocoa Fluff Ball which had got stuck to his fingers.

"And your companion, the talking bird. Eat, eat, must be good."

The Bobo didn't think so, and declared that as a species they had an aversion to chocolate.

"I don't like this set up, there's something fishy here," it told its hosts diplomatically.

"No, no fish. We just take the goodness of the chocolate, and are friendly. Very friendly. See," the Shamir told the Bobo and tried to pat the bird.

"Very friendly," the Chamberlain emphasised in a not very assuring way to Fyrsil.

"Bobo's don't like chocolate," it repeated.

(Somewhere in the collective memory of the breed of war birds, there was an in-built dislike of confectionery. This may have been because of all the recipes employed by the Gastrognomes in cooking a Bobo included force feeding chocolate before they were given the chop and prepared for the spit. On the other hand it may have been because sweets gave Bobos the runs.)

"How can Chocolate Community be friendly if bird no eat yum-yums?" asked the Chamberlain petulantly.

"I'm allergic, and besides I don't want to be friends. Bobos are very picky," it squawked loudly. And with that it crossed its wings in front of its chest and wore a scowl that told anyone who was interested, that the only way this Bobo was going to eat the brown stuff was to prise open its beak and ram the food down the throat. And that was not without a fight.

The jovial atmosphere that had pervaded the hall, disappeared. The contented ranks of brown robed chocoholics who lined the trestle tables suddenly became excessively quiet. At the top table you could hear a pin drop, as well as the clattering spoon Fyrsil dropped.

Thinking as quickly as possible, Fyrsil did the only thing he could think of to improve the atmosphere before the situation got nasty. He had an important job to do, and had a badge to prove it, and did not want the mission to save Glob to flounder all because the Bobo wouldn't eat any chocolate pudding.

"If they want it eaten, well, let's show some enthusiasm," he told himself, and quickly stuffed the another Cocoa Fluff Ball into his mouth, followed by a handful of Midnight Crème Delights, a whole chocolate sponge, chased by rolly-polly pudding, and an assortment of dark and milk chocs with different fillings.

"Delish...yum...yum," he managed through a mouthful of mixed cocoa-based foods.

The Shamir stared agog, as plateful after plateful disappeared from the table top.

A silence turned to shocked intakes of breath that filled the dining hall. Was it sacrilege? The brown robed disciples were unsure how to react to this treatment of the fruits of the blessed bean.

The knitted black lines of the Shamir's eyebrows parted, as a benevolent smile licked at the sides of his face, and throwing back his head he laughed uproariously. His amusement was taken up by the Chocolate Communion as Fyrsil grabbed at bowls and dishes and slapped their contents into his gorging mouth.

"Quick, my children, eat! Before our honoured guest devours your portions," squealed the Shamir in delight as Fyrsil licked at the plates that had been piled high for the Bobo.

The Shamir's toppling turban shook as he clapped his hands energetically and shouted at the serving maidens: "More – more food for the hungry one. We must have an eager convert."

The hall was in uproar, as everyone laughed and giggled and made strange faces at each other as they gobbled mouthfuls of chocolate flavoured delicacies. Puddings, pies and cakes; Death By Chocolate, blancmange and chocolate ice chip cookies, disappeared from in front of Fyrsil as he munched his way maniacally through course after course, licking plates with an exhibitionist flourish for the giggling maidens who queued to serve him more.

"Feed the faith! Feed the faith!" the Shamir chanted happily, and the cry was taken up around the tables of the hall.

Frenziedly scooping up handfuls of this and that, and flinging them at his open mouth, Fyrsil played to the crowd.

Quite suddenly, the whooping ceased, and Fyrsil chewed sedately on a Flake Snowball Goo as the awed assembly fell silent. From the kitchens the Chamberlain marched forth bearing a silver salver, in the middle of which rested a tiny, shiny nugget of confectionery.

"May I present to such an appreciative guest, the ultimate in cocoa taste explosions: the Chocolate Truffle Bomba," he told Fyrsil, through a disconcerting smile.

Not wanting to be rude in the face of such an obvious honour, Fyrsil finished off the Snow Flake, and picked up this obvious treat. He balanced it in his hand. There didn't seem to be anything exciting to him about this gourmet gift.

"Most kind," he said. "Such a special treat demands a special delivery."

Using a trick he had perfected when gathering nuts on cliff ledges amongst the crags of Alpoi, he flung the bomba high into the air, knocked his head back, and waited for it to drop into his waiting mouth.

The Shamir fell backwards off his cushions, weeping with laughter as Fyrsil caught the confectionery projectile on the tip of his tongue, and rolled it into his mouth. Seeing their leader fall backwards, the disciples immediately laughingly fell off their trestle benches in a domino fashion.

Fyrsil didn't notice this. The truffle bomba had just produced a stunning taste explosion that made his eyes water and his tongue quiver with delight. He sat down heavily as different flavours and hints of palate tickling tangs reverberated between his teeth. Then suddenly his mouth went numb with a delight as the most exquisite oral sensation buffeted his taste buds, and left him in a bewildered state of satisfaction. He sat bolt upright, belched loudly and fell head-first into a bowl of chocolate banana yogurt.

With disgust written all its face, the Bobo lifted its beak in disdain, and walked out to try to repair the Comfy Chair.

VII

As far as he could make out, his eyelids were welded together. No matter how often Fyrsil blinked, he couldn't glimpse a peek of light.

Waking to find he was blind was bad enough, but he also didn't feel the same self as he had felt before whatever had happened to cause him to lose his memory. There was an awful aching in his stomach, his teeth hurt, and there was a pounding in his head worse than anything brought on by having an ear tied to a pneumatic drill. And it seemed incredibly stuffy.

On top of that he felt sick.

An overpowering aroma of chocolate seemed to permeate every pore of his skin, and in the back of his mind there was something saying that he positively hated chocolate. This was strange, as he had always liked a little nibble now and again.

He felt his midriff, and found he could pinch far more than an inch, but that was all he could do. His arms seemed to be stuck to his sides.

Bright light suddenly assaulted his eyes. Dazzled, it took more than a couple of blinking squints for his eyes to adjust. After a time he was able to make out the shape of the Bobo's head, which was strangely upside down.

"Who's been a naughty boy then?" tut-tutted the bird smugly.

"Where am I? What's happening? What am I?" stammered Fyrsil.

The world had obviously not ended yet, but it seemed to Fyrsil to be fairly close.

"The answer to the last question is: I am not quite sure apart from a disgrace to Heaven. As to the second: you are hanging upside down in the Shamir's treasure store. You are doing so because you have been a very naughty boy and have upset the whole community. As a result instead of confirming you as a convert and then taking all your worldly goods, the Shamir and his cronies are going to torture you until you deliver the cocoa beans you promised, or at least large amounts of treasure from the bumbag. As to the first question, it looks like a treasure vault."

"Oh no," groaned Fyrsil. He would have liked to have said something much stronger, but he was feeling a bit fragile, and so didn't feel up to it.

"As a personal favour, I removed the sack from your head. Hopefully this will enable you to prepare yourself, so you can then get us out of 'ere," the bird told him.

After some difficult orientating inside his head, Fyrsil could just make out the details of the dimly lit chamber in which he was suspended, manacled to the ceiling. The only light came from the discreet illumination of special works of art and special porcelain tea sets in their display cabinets. But all around piles of gold, silver and outrageous jewellery collections glinted in the dark.

"What happened?" Fyrsil asked weakly.

"You remember that spot of lunch we were invited to, where you made a great display as Hap's representative of Heaven on Glob – well it all started when you stuffed so much of that revolting chocolate into your mouth."

Fyrsil could feel a lecture coming on.

"That was only because you were creating a situation that could have turned nasty. Everyone seemed very put out that you wouldn't eat. It seemed the best tactic to keep them amused – a diversionary tactic, which…" Fyrsil protested with a tongue that tasted like pure mud.

"Which has ended with you hanging upside down, while the Shamir and chocoholics think up their worst torture to get you to hand over the treasures – real and imagined – contained in the bumbag. After you showed them the *'HELP-ME'* scroll from Hap, the Shamir decided that rather than help us in our mission to save the world; he would help himself to all the riches you carry.

"That last little treat, that you consumed with such aplomb, was a cunningly drugged delicacy to make you spill the beans – and all your goodies. In fact, I did discover from certain sources, that all our portions were slightly dosed. That's how they get all their converts. Fill strangers with nicely doped delicacies, wean them onto chocolate dependency, and then Wham!Bam! – a chocoholic willing to part with all their worldly goods in exchange for a regular fix of chocolate. It's disgusting." The Bobo almost spat at the thought.

"So, what's going to happen now? I take it I didn't behave as I should have done, or I would not be in here hanging upside down, and listening to you," Fyrsil said wearily.

"Well, as it happens, you are the cause of all ills in this Chocolate Community at the moment. You remember the Chamberlain? The slimy one who handed you the poisoned pill. Not a nice man. You wonder what he is doing in an organisation that proclaims peace, harmony and pacifism. He's walking around with a very large bandage on his hand in a mood that can only be described as 'dark midnight minty'. And do you who he blames?"

"The weather," suggested Fyrsil.

"No! It's you. He was trying to have a rummage in the bumbag, and nearly got in to it. Only the Snapper lock interrupted him, and he's blaming you for his misfortune. But don't worry, they have to get round one or two moral problems before they can do anything seriously nasty to you, because you see…"

With Fyrsil suspended upsidedown, and not feeling in a talkative mood, the Bobo had the perfect audience to bore with all he had discovered about the chocoholics and their community. This took them from the initial rites, the worship of chocolate in small drinking houses, to the Great Persecution when it was banned for public health reasons across the planet, to the establishment of the underground sects. The Bobo droned on, and on, and on…

"While you have been hanging around doing nothing, I at least have managed to do something constructive," the Bobo told the suspended Fyrsil.

"Oh yes," said the rather miserable security guard from Heaven, who was even more convinced than before that a hero's boots were too big for him.

"Yes," said the Bobo sharply. Fyrsil was contemplating the funny feeling of being able to sense every strand of hair on his scalp, and was not even attempting to concentrate on what the Bobo had to say to him. "For a start, I've mended the Comfy Chair's wings. All spruced up, with every joint well oiled. Then I managed to stitch together a set of new covers, which I think it would be safe to say, the chair is very pleased with."

Fyrsil could sense the bird's smugness, even if the dim light of the chamber prevented him from seeing it written all over its face. He revolved his eyeballs to be able to squint at the chair's new clothes. It was difficult peering up to look down at the Comfy Chair, but Fyrsil managed it, and wished that he hadn't, as he distinctly saw the chair wave its cushions in delight. If he hadn't been so concerned about his state of suspension Fyrsil would have agreed with the chair. The horrible floral whorls had been replaced by a covering of rich velvets, tasteful piping, and golden tassels in all the right places. It made him sick just thinking that the Bobo who would have hardly threaded a needle before this incarceration, had been able to produce such a professional example of upholstery.

"I got bored waiting for you to come round," said the Bobo after waiting overlong for a congratulatory comment. "Once the rest of the chair was fixed up proper, there seemed little else to do. Anyway, the Chair has been in a bit of a mood since you crashed it. It seems happy enough now, though."

To confirm this, the chair gave another happy wave of its cushion.

"How long have I been here?" Fyrsil asked, ignoring the new velvet attentions of the Comfy Chair.

"Hard to tell, really. Could be hours. Days. Or even months. I was too busy repairing the chair and seeing that it was alright to worry about the time. I would guess that we have been here a good long period though. The Shamir and his Chamberlain are getting impatient. They seem to think that you are hiding in your bumbag a sack of cocoa beans big enough to last the community at least a year. They also seem to think it contains a host of treasures that would outshine the Shamir's present collection."

"What a load of rubbish. Who told them that?" demanded Fyrsil, lowering his eyebrows in surprise.

The Bobo coughed, and in the dim light blushed a luminous orange. It admitted that under duress of mental torture he had told them anything they wanted to know, and anything else the bird could make up. The torture was very simple: the reading of recipes for the basting and stuffing of highly colourful birds with a variety of chocolates, and having a handful of chefs give their views on how best to serve the last Bobo on Glob. Live spit roast seemed to be a favourite to make the Bobo babble.

"My quill ends were as limp as glue, and the scales on my legs had all slipped around my claws. I just said anything to please them."

Fyrsil looked at the bird, which was still glowing dimly. "So now they are going to torture me to get beans and treasures from my bumbag that are not there. I thought Bobos were the ultimate war birds. I think there is more than a little chink in the species psyche armour here."

"Well I'm not the hero. That's your job. I'm only here as a military consultant on secondment from heavenly duties, with specific instructions to give you help and guidance."

"Well, you could at least help by untying me. My head is hurting."
The Bobo shook its head guiltily.

"Why not?" demanded Fyrsil.

"There is only me and the Chair here. Of the two likely accessories to aiding and abetting your escape, I have a feeling they would plump for the more edible one. Oh! Those recipes were horrible. And anyway, sometimes the bravest thing to do is nothing... and in my view, this is one of those times."

Fyrsil decided to follow suit, after a lot of huffing and puffing. But then again, he could not do much else, so he simply stared at the golden glow of riches that were piled in toppling towers around the vault.

Elsewhere in the *Rest Inn* there were others making tough decisions on what to do. The trinkets on the Shamir's turban shook with his indecision, and his hands splayed upwards and outwards in self-doubt as he wrestled with his conscience.

"I know your arguments, Chamberlain. It's just that it goes against the whole spirit of the Rule of the Wrappers. To be a chocoholic doesn't just mean total devotion to chocolate. Being a member of the Chocolate Community is more than just a loving addiction to the bean. It is a peaceful existence, where love can flower, and everyone can share, because sharing is love."

"Including sharing the contents of the vaults?" the Chamberlain asked. His beady eyes darting at the flaccid features of the Shamir.

"That's different. That's a perk of the job – reward for the heavy responsibility of looking after the well-being of the community," sniffed the Shamir, shifting his baggy pantalooned bottom on his cushion.

He looked around his private apartments. Dripping with silks, his impossibly soft bed stood like a vessel sailing with gossamer sails of valuable hangings in a sea of decorative finery, sumptuous scatter cushions, and valuable occasional furniture. It was a stark contrast to the drab browns and nicotine yellows which coloured and decorated the rest of the communal building.

"I suppose you are right Chamberlain. After considerable consideration, I must conclude that the application of medicines and remedies cannot *really* be thought of as a form of torture. He must be sick in some way, or he would not have been able to eat all that chocolate and still be alive."

A plump finger rested on plump red lips in deep thought.

"And it is all for a good cause," the Chamberlain told his spiritual superior, waving his bandaged hand. " With a supply of beans of the size the bird told us about - we would be free of those cursed bean traders, allowing the community to lead a more peaceful and prosperous existence."

"Oh well, in that case, bring your potions, and let's get on with it before my conscience gets the better of me."

Waving his bandaged hand in glee, the Chamberlain disappeared to his private quarters to select the most potent of the malevolent medicines he had concocted in his spare time.

VIII

"Urrrgh..." The sound of assaulted taste buds echoed rebounding off the glittering gloom of the treasury vault.

"That's revolting," screamed Fyrsil, trying to spit out the foul taste of a medicine that was now trickling out of his mouth towards his nose.

His tongue had shrivelled in terror at the first taste explosion. He spat again, trying to clear the residue of municipal refuse tip flavouring.

"What did you say that was for?"

The Chamberlain peered at a curling brown label.

"Frog bite, category two spider stings, and any nasty purple lumps that appear under the armpits. Oh dear, dear. It says here: *External Use Only*. It must be the light, but I don't seem to be able to read these labels that well."

The Chamberlain smiled with satisfaction, and peered over at the trolley of small bottles with disintegrating corks and corroding glass stoppers. The contents occasionally frothed in a continuous reaction of fumes and chemical fireworks.

"Now, open wide, and let's see if this spoonful of medicine persuades you to open the contents of your magic satchel."

"Do something Bobo!" Fyrsil cried in terror.

The Bobo squawked as he was sat on by the full weight of the Shamir.

"No heroics, please. It is a very peacefable request, which will earn you the eternal gratitude and felicitations from the whole of the commune, and probably help you to a better health than with the aid of the medicines," the Shamir requested in a voice that dripped honey balm to Fyrsil's afflictions.

"But I have been appointed the HERO from Heaven. It's on my badge. It's more than my job's worth to open the bumbag for unauthorised personnel. And anyway it only contains the essential travelling kit, and couple of little trinkets," Fyrsil pleaded.

"That's not what the bird said. And it will be telling the truth, or it will be auctioned off for a special feast for hungry Gastrognomes. Time for more medicine. If you would oblige, my Most Holy Chocolate Button."

Peering at his fuming chemical potions, the Chamberlain selected a steaming livid green bottle from the extensive collection – each one a colourful cockpit of brawling molecules. The Shamir stood next to the suspended figure of the prisoner, and with a flourish of sleeves firmly pinched Fyrsil's nose. The Chamberlain poured a big noxious spoonful of sizzling liquid, which bubbled and burped like sherbet dip on the tongue.

"Now, open wide…there's a good little pumpkin," said the Chamberlain as he shoved the large frothing spoon deep into Fyrsil's open mouth. Before there was time to spit out the taste of rotting mackerel and maggots, the Shamir clenched Fyrsil's mouth shut and gave him such a big push that his nose bounced off the ceiling.

"…And swallow," predicted the Chamberlain.

Fyrsil wished he hadn't as he swung like a clock's pendulum. If the foretaste was fishy, the aftertaste was something that had been dragged up from the depths of the most sulphurous marsh from the boggiest of swamps gurgling on Glob.

"Urrrrgh!" he yelled, not afraid of repeating himself.

"All we ask is for you to open your little baggy. A very reasonable request," the Shamir wheedled "Old ladies are asked it all the time in dark alleys of cities all over Glob."

Fyrsil was vibrating and jerking as the Shamir pleaded for co-operation to a face that had turned a dangerous colour of bilious purple.

"Al-lright, ar-right-t. I n-nev-ver wanted this h-hero job anyway. You can h-have the st-tupid bum-bumbag," he said through chattering teeth, twisting uncontrollably as he swung to and fro. "Just let-let me d-down, and no-no more m-medicine."

The Shamir and Chamberlain smiled at each other with satisfaction, eagerly anticipating the rewards of their labours.

"Your hands will be untied, but your feet touch the ground only after you have delivered the goods," the Chamberlain cautioned, suspicious of any representative of things they didn't believe in.

He was very wary of the bumbag and its many hidden secrets, having found out the hard way about the effectiveness of the Snapper lock. The Chamberlain had also found out after blunting several of his sharpest knives that a bumbag of the gods could only be opened and worn by its designated owner. The Bobo of course had told him after each failed attempt to prise the bumbag's zip open or cut it free from Fyrsil's waist, but he had not been convinced by the annoying bird. The lycra belt seemed so pliable and easy to cut, but the blade of a knife made no impression on the material. And what really made his blood boil was the Bobo smugly predicting exactly what would happen with every attempt to saw, rip or tear the bumbag free.

And besides, the Chamberlain hated know-alls. He was going to take no chances in getting the pile of cocoa beans and other treasures from the cornucopia of a bumbag. After all his efforts he considered the treasures his by right.

With his hands free, Fyrsil found where he had written on his tunic the combination code to de-activate Snapper lock. Punching in 1-2-3-O-P-E-N, he pulled back the zip, and dug his hand in the wide open spaces of the unknown dimension which had been sewn into the inside of the bumbag.

Below him the Shamir rubbed his hands and shuffled his feet in a little dance of gleeful anticipation. The Chamberlain was still peering closely at the Snapper lock, trying to convince himself that the combination was not so obvious.

"Well?" cried the Shamir excitedly. "Beans please, Mr Hero, lots of beans. Shower me with beans, and any treasures too." His eyes shone expectantly.

Cocoa beans, especially large piles of them, was not something that was stored in the unknown dimension Fyrsil was fumbling in. He was in a bit of quandary. If he did not produce the goods, his fate would be to be left hanging by his feet and fed diabolical medicines. On the other hand, as he did not have the requested beans, it was inevitable that he would be soon subjected to the medicinal torture again – and this time it was bound to be worse.

He felt a lot of junk in the internal pockets of the bumbag, including: thermal socks; a carton of scented easy-wipes; an odd collection of rare coins; and much, much more. But no cocoa beans.

While thinking hard what he should do, Fyrsil continued to riffle around the bumbag.

"Come on, come on," muttered the Chamberlain impatiently as Fyrsil pulled out a 24-piece dinner set, a rubber duck for bath time, and a multifunctional travel alarm clock.

All heads turned as the door to the vault groaned ajar, and the bashful head of a chocoholic sous chef from the kitchens poked into the gloom.

"Can't you read?" shouted the alarmed Chamberlain. "The notice on the door clearly says: *Pass Holders Only*. There are only two people with passes; our great leader His Holiness the Shamir Smartie Bar-Button, and me. Now get out of here."

The tentative figure in its brown apron shrank behind the massive weight of the steel door until only pale moon of his face remained in view.

"I...I..." he stuttered nervously.

"Spit it out, spit it out!" the Chamberlain barked.

The sous chef did – twice, and then looked up guiltily in the sure knowledge he shouldn't have been so literal.

The way the Chamberlain started to hit his palm with the big medicine spoon did not help settle the sous chef's nerves.

"Now, calm down Chamberlain. The brother here would not have interrupted our important work for the commune unless it was something very, *very* important. Would you brother?" assured the Shamir, in a tone of voice that warned that there would be trouble if the matter was not important."

Still hiding behind the door, the cook nodded his head vigorously while simultaneously saying "No, no, no."

"Well, what is it then?"

"I think we are being attacked...or at least that is what old brother Prothero says. He says there is only one sound like it on the whole of Glob – the drumming of empty bellies of a Gastrognome hungerparty. There has been a distant rumbling for a time, but it has been getting louder...and now it's deafening. . . and I saw them from the top window... coming down the mountain...it's horrible...they're horrible." The chef's stumbling rush of words faltered.

A stony silence filled the treasury vault. Even the tinkling of riches and treasures admiring each other in the dim light was quiet, as the Shamir and his Chamberlain stood rooted to the spot with mouths agape.

Fyrsil's mouth was already open because it seemed easier that way when hanging upside down. The Bobo gulped loudly. Into that heavy silence crept a steady ominous rhythmic beat of three hundred loudly grumbling stomachs. (The traditional number in a hungerparty is 100, multiplied by three, the number of stomachs possessed by the average Gastrognome.)

The face of the chef quickly disappeared after giving its message, and the interruption was only the pit-pat sound of running feet down the corridors of the extensive cellar stores, overlaid by the increasing volume of the rhythmic rumbling – one of the most feared sounds on Glob.

Whole landscapes had been left barren deserts after a Gastrognome hungerparty had carried out the compulsive eater's equivalent of wanton pillage and destruction. A hungry Gastrognome in a feeding frenzy knew no fear, and would eat anything in sight. Exceptions tended to be musical doorbells, old diesel engines and canine lavatories.

Realising his mouth had been open for what seemed a considerable time, the Shamir tried to say something.

"Wha…arrrgh," was all his vocal chords could manage. It was the last thing Fyrsil heard him say, as a trouser press, complete with tie mangle attachment, fell out of the bumbag and onto the Shamir's head. Not even the tiered padding of his turban saved him from the terrible impact of the plummeting trouser press.

The Chamberlain froze in shock, and gaped at the still form of his spiritual and bodily leader, flattened by a still quivering trouser press system – still in its shrink-wrap plastic and with a large notice advising customers that if they are not satisfied with the product, they should return the goods undamaged within 28 days for a full refund.

This, Fyrsil sensed, was one of those critical moments in a crisis when one ought to do something.

He started making frantic signs to the Bobo to peck through the rope suspending him from the ceiling while the Chamberlain's attention was diverted. In fact the Chamberlain, in an act of religious sympathy, had fainted and was prostrated across the fat folds of the Shamir's breathless frame. In his distress, the hood of his robe had slipped back to reveal a bald and blotchy scalp and large floppy ears.

The Bobo was oblivious to Fyrsil's frantic signals. It was flat on its back amongst a pile of tiaras and assorted crowns, laughing uncontrollably and pointing at the Chamberlain's ears. Even the Comfy Chair was shaking its tassels in merriment

Quickly, Fyrsil dug his hand into the bumbag to see if he could find something useful to cut the rope and escape.

It seemed that a worrying drawback of the bumbag was that although you could get an almost unlimited amount in it without it weighing more than a couple of rounds of egg and cress sandwiches, there was no way of finding what anyone wanted when they needed it. Only those things that were completely useless for the task at hand seemed to be grasped and pulled through the zipper.

Through the open vault door Fyrsil now heard a horrible loud burp at the top of the cellar steps, and the beat of three marching stomachs approaching. He glanced over to the Bobo, which had heard the belch, and quickly shut its beak. In contrast to the raucous laughter a moment earlier, it now wore a grim and worried expression. Taking up a defensive position in the Comfy Chair, it prepared its posterior to fire pong pellets at any Gastrognome that thought the last Bobo – ever - looked like a tasty morsel. After a quick flick through the chair's manual, the bird of war selected a couple of options. Out popped a myriad of hands, raised in ready *en guarde* position, and from under the skirt of the cover a dozen legs sprouted sporting big boots poised for kicking.

Fumbling desperately around the bumbag, Fyrsil's fingers wrapped round a large knobbly handle. It felt as if it might be some sort of knife. He tugged at it, but it seemed stuck. He grabbed at it with both hands and heaved. And heaved again. Rearranging his grip, a finger brushed against a switch. Almost imperceptibly a new force crept through his fingers, and up his forearms. New bodily hairs pinged as they sprouted up his arms, and continued at a pace of a roaring forest fire to cover his chest, back and legs. His body began to tingle with a strange electricity as his normally puny biceps began to bulge. His chest filled out until it moulded into the contours of the breastplate. His thighs bulged, transforming his normally baggy underpants into tight, revealing briefs.

The force moved down into his head, and Fyrsil gave an involuntary grunt. With a slow and measured movement of his arm, Fyrsil drew out of the bumbag the Sword of the Mighty MkIV(manual temporarily mislaid.)

The long blue blade ending in a glinting razor-sharp point, shimmered with a pure aggressive energy. The perfect symmetry and balance of the sword made it weightless in Fyrsil's hands, as his eyes ran down the decorative scrollwork which intertwined with magic symbols and runes. He felt the power of the weapon, as its energy seeped into the marrow of his bones. And in that moment he understood why Crusher had given it away – it was frightening!

By gripping its jewel encrusted handle, anyone felt they could do anything, conquer everywhere, and vanquish anyone. Fyrsil gave what he thought would be a practice flick of this blue gleaming monster as a bit of a dummy run. Before he knew it, the sword had executed a swipe that cut the rope, and propelled Fyrsil head over heels in a dramatic double backwards somersault with knee tuck and twist.

Amazingly, or at least Fyrsil thought so, he landed on his feet like a champion gymnast. While he wondered what to do next with the super-weapon in his hands, the Sword of the Mighty sniffed the air like a dog, and with a fluid motion of Fyrsil's wrist shredded the trouser press system into hundreds and thousands of flying splinters. They momentarily filled the air before landing in a pile which resembled a matchstick model of Bankrupt Tower (the tallest building on Glob – built by a property speculator who wanted to be remembered by all his creditors.)

"Wow! Did you see that?" Fyrsil grunted excitedly at the Bobo.

Unfortunately the war bird missed the display, as it had been lining up its bum at the doorway through cunning sights on its tail feathers. It squinted studiously down the sights, taking no notice of any distracting exhibitionism of the Sword of the Mighty. The heavy footsteps and grumbling stomach rumbling down the corridor had first claim to its attention.

Fyrsil adjusted his grip on the hilt of his sword with his newly enlarged fingers, and in doing so nudged a button.

"*Welcome. Your Sword of the Mighty MkIV is registered as GoreReaper a sword for all occasions to rid you of your enemies. Functions include showman swordsmanship; decapitation; disembowelling; maiming and much, much more. Personalised killing signatures can be programmed. Please refer to the manual for maintenance,*" a metallic voice told Fyrsil.

The Chamberlain, regaining consciousness just in time to hear *GoreReaper*'s specialities, tried to feign another fainting fit while his teeth chattered uncontrollably.

While *GoreReaper* was sniffing the air again for its next target to attack, Fyrsil was trying to work out how to switch off the sword's talking message loop (which was already in its third repetition) and to find out what the various function buttons did without the aid of the manual. Although the trick with the trouser press had been impressive – obviously something to do with the showman tricks, it was not really what he wanted *GoreReaper* to concentrate on. He remembered from his single disastrous lesson in military arts at school that the most important part of swordplay was to have full control of your weapon. It was an element which was obviously lacking in his relationship with *GoreReaper*. The energy emanating from the long cool blade was that of an independent operator, which happened to be a significant appendage to Fyrsil's sword arm. Worse than that, when Fyrsil tried to put the sword down to have a better look at the controls, it would not leave his hand.

By pressing a number of combinations of the inlaid ruby, emeralds and sapphires, a tiny mother of pearl screen displayed Fyrsil's horoscope, the date, and a list of recommended dealers for the Sword of Mighty to be serviced at. The message loop also stopped. But whatever else he pressed, he could not change the constantly flashing AUTO sign, which was inset in a corner of the screen.

Desperately Fyrsil pressed randomly at buttons, as the unmistakable sound of a frenzied Gastrognome chomping his way through carefully stacked crates of pickled onions and beetroot. The crunching din and crashes of this digestive process reverberated through the semi-darkness to the treasury vault with nerve tingling screeches that penetrated even the unconscious consciousness of the Shamir. He groaned and touched his turban where the trouser press had embedded itself before being transformed into a matchstick tower model. The trinkets decorating the turban tinkled, and then clattered to the floor as the carefully coiled headgear slid off.

The Chamberlain stared wide-eyed at the crushed remains of a sacred chocolate egg laid by the even more sacred Chocolate Chicken – the commune's most holy of relics – matted into the thick abundance of the Shamir's hair.

"What's…what happened…" mumbled the Shamir.

"The egg, the sacred egg," cried the Chamberlain, suddenly discovering mobility again.

"My head, my head," groaned the Shamir, and then looked at his Chamberlain and burst out laughing: "Your head, your head," smirking at his loyal lieutenant's embarrassment.

"Duck," said the Chamberlain firmly.

"Where?" asked the Shamir vaguely.

Before his question was answered and blinding flash of a furious blade swiping swift, deft cuts in a fine display of swordsplay around the Shamir's face. *GoreReaper* had got bored with Fyrsil's frantic button pushing, and was relieved when the figures on the floor stirred dizzily. As it was in auto mode it had been unable to decide whether the head of the commune and his chamberlain were a threat, or just plain offensive. Its lightning executive decision was, whatever they were, it was time for a little target practice.

With a speed that caused Fyrsil to be pulled head-long behind, *GoreReaper* dived on the bundle of discarded cloth that was the Shamir's turban. A flurry of whisking sword strokes put up a cloud of cloth and trinket butterflies floating through the air in a gosh-gasping display that would have brought the house down if it had been a conjurer's trick.

It was obviously too much for the chocoholics. With an agility that belied the Shamir's bulk and the Chamberlain's calculated dignity, they both made a headlong dash for the door. Fyrsil had just landed on his feet again, and was of two minds whether to be impressed by the pretty butterflies or concerned that he obviously had no control over *GoreReaper*. He didn't have time to decide between the two. After a quick pause, looking for some sort of appreciation of its artistry of the gleaming flourishes of its dextrous display, the Sword of the Mighty realised that its potential practice targets were making good an escape, and hurtled after them – Fyrsil pulled flying in its wake like the tail of a kite.

At that moment the inviting doorway that promised escape for the Shamir and his Chamberlain, transformed into a black hole. To be exact the mouth of Gastrognome preparing to belch. The indecision of the Shamir and his Chamberlain was only momentary: they both executed a two-footed equivalent of a handbrake turn, and dashed along the maze of pathways between the piles of gold and treasures.

GoreReaper braked in mid air, hovering undecided whether this new player on the scene was going to be a better target, while Fyrsil dangled limply from the hilt.

"Hoi, you're in the line of fire. Get out of it."

The Bobo, who had been listening grimly as the Gastrognome ate its way through 469 bottles of pickled vegetables, had tensed itself in preparation to fire its defensive pong pellets. As the double boom of the grumbling stomachs and heavy footsteps came ever closer, the Bobo never took its eye off the aiming sights amongst its tail feathers. Now when he had the Gastrognome in range and ready to release a bullseye barrage of pellets, Fyrsil appeared out of nowhere and hung helplessly from his headstrong sword in the line of fire.

The Gastrognome blocking the doorway, burped contentedly, licked its lips with a saliva drenched yellow tongue, and wondered what would be next to appease its demanding gastric juices. Standing at just over 1.5 metres high, with a similar width, Fyrsil looked at this foodie specimen from the inner recesses of Glob, and decided it was all mouth.

In its indecision *GoreReaper* dropped Fyrsil on the floor. This was too close to comfort to the dark green throatal abyss lined with double files of crunching molars and incisors, with bad breath to match. He also noticed that this small hairy creature with a large appetite was also armed with a vicious looking skillet and a large electric whisk, with a well-used rolling pin tucked into its belt.

"Eaaarrrch!" the Gastrognome belched loudly, and blinked its saucer eyes in appreciation of the latest addition to its digestive system. The propelled odour of mashed pickled beetroot and onions hit Fyrsil full in the nasal passages.

"Get out the way, nam-dam," the Bobo squawked as Fyrsil sat on the floor with streaming eyes.

He couldn't. The problem was he was still attached to *GoreReaper* who had very different ideas from Fyrsil as to the best action to take. His body might have taken on heroic proportions, but his natural reaction was to run in the opposite direction to the glaring Gastrognome who was making menaces with a nasty looking whisk in a stomach-churning manner.

"Yarrgh!" Fyrsil found himself shouting, and instead of running away from the belligerent eating machine, found he was whirling *GoreReaper* in a distressingly brave fashion.

"Yum-yum, yerrah!" the Gastrognome rumbled its feared war cry, and charged at Fyrsil.

Instead of his body turning to a quivering jelly, the muscles of his inflated body tautened ready for action. Adrenaline (a novel chemical for Fyrsil's system) pumped its excitement into every limb, as he found himself taking the bewildering action of leaping into the fray with an attempt at a blood-curdling yell.

The two combatants collided with a massive wallop, shaking the nearby piles of carefully counted coins. Fyrsil kicked himself away from the dangerously chattering teeth trying to bite at his ankles, and ducked a mutilating thrust from the madly whirring whisk. Giving himself space to wield the sword, he threw it into action (or maybe the other way round) with a couple of deft flicks of the wrist.

The whisk went flying across the vast expanse of the vault as Fyrsil waded in. After a flurry of short jabbing strokes with *GoreReaper* the skillet was no more than a heavily holed sieve and a series of slicing cuts left the remains of the rolling pin scattered like slices of cucumber on the floor.

The Gastrognome froze. Nothing like this ever happened on raiding hungerparties. It blinked a couple of times, as the little bit of face that wasn't taken up by mouth registered its surprise. Fyrsil was too busy yelling the cry of Alpoi goat herders – "Yarrrgh" – to notice this reaction. With hardly a pause to consider whether he was putting himself in unnecessary danger, he twisted and flicked the flashing blue steel until the coiffured arrangement of Gastrognome's previously straggling beard lay at its quaking feet.

Gingerly it felt its chin, as Fyrsil towered high in preparation for the final crashing blow, and the Gastrognome burst into tears with terrible howling sobs.

GoreReaper teetered above Fyrsil's head in surprise. A sudden crash from behind him, made Fyrsil pirouette to take on a new attacker. The creeping figures of the Shamir and the Chamberlain turned a sickly shade of pale, as they froze in mid-step and stared with imploring wide eyes. They had been trying to sneak through the vault door while the Fyrsil and the Gastrognome were locked in combat. Ready to make their dash for freedom they were crouched beside a pyramid of gold ingots. The thought of leaving behind all his collected treasures had proved too much for the Shamir, and he already had coronets and tiaras piled high on his head, and had filled the Chamberlain's hood with precious gems too valuable to leave behind. As they watched the fight, the lure of the gold had been too much for the leader of the chocoholics, and the Shamir had pulled a single ingot from the pile. The unbalanced pyramid teetered painfully slowly, and then crashed in an avalanche of noise around the Shamir.

A snorting barrel-chested Fyrsil and his dreadful flashy sword confronted them menacingly.

"Peace? Owwwh!" said the Shamir, raising his left hand in a three fingered salute of the Chocoholic Nut, and dropping the ingot on his foot.

I might not have been an intentional ruse to disarm Fyrsil's immediate intention of dicing them both into dog food, but it worked. The heroic sword arm of Heaven's security guard was stayed in mid stroke. He wondered momentarily what was the proper chivalrous behaviour in this situation.

The Shamir and the Chamberlain were probably just as unsure, but they did what came naturally, and dashed passed Fyrsil and out of the door, making for the cellar steps. The Gastrognome, who had been blinking with saucer eyes, stunned by its sudden nudity of having no facial hair, ran off howling in embarrassment after the two chocoholics. Not being slow on the uptake, Fyrsil in his new heroic persona took up the chase, yelling the most terrifying "Yoddle-ey-de-di" any goat had ever heard among the crags and ravines of the Alpoi mountain range.

When Fyrsil crashed through the cellar door in pursuit of the galloping clean shaven Gastrognome, he skidded to a halt as he burst into the dining hall, where he had been entertained so lavishly after his crash landing in the Comfy Chair. Where there had once been cleanliness and order, there was now chaos. The clean milky walls were splattered with chocolate smears; tables were overturned, half chewed benches were strewn around in disorder; and even the wood effect concrete roof pillars had large bites in their plinths.

With the marauding Gastrognomes storming around the room, slurping and gnawing at everything in their path Fyrsil hardly recognised the room.

His reverie didn't last for long. A Gastrognome began licking his leg with its yellow tongue, in preparation of an exploratory nibble. Flicking his – by now trusty – sword into action, he gave the little monster a quick shave and dust down, and played an old nut gathering tune on its teeth before knocking them into the back of its throat.

Quickly unzipping the bumbag, he groped for the Shield of Righteousness, and pulled out a garden fork. He shrugged, thinking it might come in handy anyway.

A crowd of cautious Gastrognomes surrounded Fyrsil. Usually the reputation of Gastrognomes on a hungerparty induced such fear that people either fled or just put up their arms in defeat and let the feeding frenzy pass as quickly as possible. Having witnessed the pasting dealt out to their comrade, they were universally annoyed. The time it took to deal with that sort of thing dug into valuable eating time. Slowly the slathering mass of Gastrognomes closed in, the ranks of small rotund warlike blobs of hunger swelling with every passing second.

Their stomachs began to pound in unison, eager to get back to the feeding frenzy. Fyrsil was an unwanted distraction from their feast, and they wanted to deal with the problem and get back to gorging their three stomachs again.

Thinking in a clear and precise way that had always escaped him in the past, Fyrsil acted with uncharacteristic decisiveness. Shouting

"Yoddle-oddle-doddle-doo" as aggressively as possible, he leapt into action. He leapt so far he nearly cleared the ring of smacking lips, and flailing out with the sword and garden fork, he bounced off the head of a Gastrognome and landed with a perfectly executed parachute roll on the flagstones beyond.

Shocked by his own athletic agility, Fyrsil was about to congratulate himself, when he saw there wasn't time. A herd of small gnashing people armed with deadly kitchen utensils was stampeding towards him. Nimbly leaping onto a solid wooden table, he shaved a Gastrognome here, pronged another there, and blatted others indiscriminately on the head, as *GoreReaper* displayed its prowess with dangerous flashing patterns of cold steel painted in the air.

Just as the table legs gave way after the tactical eating by a group of hungerparty braves, Fyrsil posed momentarily and then sprang into the air, using the fork to swing on a handy low-slung candelabra. A perfectly timed release landed him far from the pursuing posse, executing another perfectly executed parachute roll on the flagstones, before making an easy run out the doorway. After watching this athletic performance with goggle eyes, the munching marauders realised their prey was getting away and rushed after him with rumbling stomachs, and banging dinner gongs in pursuit.

As hordes of Gastrognomes poured from out of the *Rest Inn* to pitch in at Fyrsil, at the back of his mind memories of one of the Bobo's tactical military instruction sessions clamoured for attention. "Go for the advantage of the high ground," it kept on repeating as the Sword of the Mighty lived up to its name in cutting a swathe through the massed ranks of Gastrognomes. But no matter how many *GoreReaper* bopped on the heads, shaved, or cut the legs from under them, more of the rampaging hungerparty kept coming at him.

Jumping up on a cart Fyrsil made a stand there, but had to jump off hurriedly as the wheels, axles, and draw bar were eaten away by the howling mob of pursuers.

Leaping clear again, Fyrsil hacked a path of flying arms, legs and kitchen knives through to the steps leading to the barn's loft. Step by step he was forced higher and higher, as he slashed with *GoreReaper* and pronged and poked with the garden fork.

Slowly he became aware that his arms were getting tired. The Sword of the Mighty was becoming so mighty heavy that his parries and ripostes were becoming dangerously sluggish. It seemed ages since he was able to make the jabbing series of cuts to leave a shaven

Gastrognome with the message "Have a Nice Day" on its otherwise shaven pate.

Glancing down at the sword's function display, a warning light bleeped, telling Fyrsil that something was going to happen.

Then it did.

With the effect of an inflated party balloon being let go to career around a room with farting noises, Fyrsil suddenly found himself launched into midair, making remarkably similar sounds to a balloon as his pumped up body deflated. *GoreReaper* with Fyrsil still attached shot up, spinning round and round, and circling the barn before shooting over the *Rest Inn*'s half eaten thatch. Looping the loop several times, and spinning round the chimney as his biceps disappeared, chest shrunk back to its normal narrow ribcage, and his underwear got noticeably looser, Fyrsil hung onto the sword wondering what would happen next. His breastplate rattled and his tunic flapped as he was uncontrollably propelled across the ravaged mountainside, which only a couple of hours before had been the model of agricultural husbandry and rural tranquillity.

Rocketing over the roof of the inn, Fyrsil looked down through watering eyes and glimpsed the familiar sight of the Comfy Chair. With wings outstretched, the Bobo was manoeuvring it to face downhill.

"Aarrgh," shouted Fyrsil as his legs bicycled wildly in suspended animation in midair. The party balloon that had been his body had run out of puff, and he plummeted in ever decreasing circles, landing in a crumpled heap of limbs and armour into the Comfy Chair.

"Oi, watch it! You could have squashed me, falling out of the sky like that, and then where would we be?" squawked the Bobo, which had been knocked off its perch on the back of the Comfy Chair as Fyrsil made his fortuitous landing.

As falling from a great height in a giddy descent is not the best thing for good humour, Fyrsil would have expected something along the lines of: "are you alright" or even "that looked nasty". He gingerly felt bits of himself, to check that they were still there, and then hobbled over to his Sword of the Mighty, which had buried itself up to the hilt in the earth.

"Where have you been anyway? We loaded up and have been ready for take-off for ages, while you have been running around having fun with those Gastrognomes," the Bobo continued, oblivious to Fyrsil's black looks.

"I have been fighting off that horde of hairy monsters, and it has not been fun. Cut one down and there is always another in its place. And then all of a sudden I shot up the air. I could have been killed."

The Bobo looked knowingly at Fyrsil as he struggled with *GoreReaper* which was refusing to budge from the ground. The bird fitted its flying cap and adjusted its goggles.

"Batteries went dead, I presume?" the Bobo enquired. "Personally I never rated the MkIV – too many new fancy bits and pieces, and not enough good old fashioned cold steel. Things get a bit hairy when it all goes wrong."

"I found that out," said a puffing Fyrsil, still wrestling with the obstinate sword, which was refusing to even wiggle a little bit.

"Forget that…"

"But it's my sword…"

"Maybe, but it looks like we've got company, and unless your sword decides to join you soon, then me and the Comfy Chair are leaving."

Fyrsil looked behind him. A herd of hungry-looking Gastrognomes is not a pretty sight, especially when they are extremely angry and galloping downhill in your direction, stomachs booming, and waving a collection of kitchen utensils designed to do the maximum damage to any sort of flesh.

Regretfully, Fyrsil ran jangling over to the chair and arranged himself in the pilot's position. The flying controls were ready. Pressing the button sequence for take off, he hit the yellow button marked 'F' in his joystick. He was then reminded that nothing happened in Heaven when he used the manual-approved method of take off, when nothing happened again.

"Come on, come on, we haven't got all day. In fact more like about 60 seconds at a very round estimate," the Bobo squawked in his ear. "I will try and hold them off with a rearguard action, but it won't buy us much time."

"Don't fire until you see the yellow of their tongues," Fyrsil said, automatically quoting a famous phrase from the infamous Cooking Pot War as the Bobo manoeuvred itself in the pong pellet firing position.

Fyrsil hit the F button again. Nothing. He hit the control console with his fist. A painful hand and burp from the internal workings of the Comfy Chair. He hit it again. Another burp, more pain for the hand, and slowly the extended wings of the chair started to flap up and down.

"In the name of Hap, let off the HANDBRAKE!" yelled the Bobo.

Feeling foolish, Fyrsil eased the lever down, and pushed up on the flap rate lever for take off speed. The chair trundled bumpily down the slope on its casters. He glanced behind, and wish he hadn't. The gritted teeth of the enormous mouthed Gastrognomes were fixed in horrific smiles (complete with bits of food stuck in between the teeth) as they bounded towards the chair. The dribbles down their beards were becoming very clear to Fyrsil.

"Fire! Give it to them. Pong them off the face of Glob," he shouted at the Bobo.

"I can't see the colour of their tongues," it replied, as the chair lurched at sluggish speed over the bumps of the meadow.

"That's because their mouths are closed. Fire and that's an order."

"OK, keep your hair on," the Bobo told him, and taking aim through its tail feathers, fired a rapid volley of pong pellets at the front rank of racing Gastrognomes.

A couple of direct hits, and stunned Gastrognomes fell to the ground, knocked out by the excruciating smell from the plasma capsules. Those immediately behind crashed into the leaders, but some jumped over the instant pile up, and pressed on in pursuit.

The Comfy Chair, bumped off the ground, but refused to climb as Fyrsil pulled back desperately on the joy stick.

"What's wrong? It doesn't want to fly," he shouted as the Bobo fired at point blank range at the galloping Gastrognomes in almost arm's reach of the chair.

"I took the liberty of loading as much of the treasury vaults into the chair as would fit down the sides of the cushions. Bound to come in useful for bribes in Loot."

"But not for take off," yelled Fyrsil. He drew his sword he had used for ceremonial duties outside the Golden Palace and swiped at a Gastrognome brandishing a gleaming blender with some very nasty attachments. There was a crunching noise, and he yanked his sword free. Large teeth marks serrated the blade as the Gastrognome chomped gleefully.

With enormous effort the Comfy Chair started to rise, painfully slowly flapping higher, inching its way above the jumping Gastrognomes, as Fyrsil and the Bobo fought off the attempts to board the chair. Stabbing at the nose of a ravenous Gastrognome, who was hanging onto some of the chair's new golden tassels, Fyrsil banked hard, and picked up speed to soar away from the mountainside. Turning on its perch, the Bobo fired into the open mouth of the clinging Gastrognome as it was about to bite off Fyrsil's head. The saucer eyes expanded in shocked surprise as its yellow tongue turned blue and green, and it started to exhale dark fumes as its stomachs tried to deal with one chemical reaction too many. Fyrsil gave it a jab with what remained of his sword. It fell back off the arm, grabbing at the tassels on the skirt as it dropped into thin air and exploded like an egg in a microwave above the rest of the hungerparty as they stared up at the escaping chair.

"Now that's what I call *bad* indigestion," Fyrsil said and laughed heartily. He had read somewhere that that was the sort of things heroes should say after such tight scrapes.

He wiped away the sweat that had suddenly broken out on his brow.

The Bobo said nothing. It even ignored the corny remark. It was flaked out on the back of the chair, and was contemplating its very sore bum. It was the second time in a comparatively short time that it had found itself having to resort to these tactics, and it was very painful.

Steering the Comfy Chair between mountain peaks towards the two pink suns that hung over the middle of Glob, Fyrsil reached beneath his tunic and pulled out the Being Stone. He did not know how long they had been at the chocoholic commune, but the veins of blue were spreading through the gold of the stone. Its translucence was losing its lustre as the dark blue web ate into the warm glow of the stone's colouring.

Time was running out for Glob. He hoped that recruiting the pirate crew would be easy. The sojourn at the *Rest Inn* had cost Glob valuable time.

Maybe its future.

IX

In the eternal half-light that passed for night or day, the rain played its sinister tattoo on the grim castellated structures teetering out of the gloom. The black outline of Castle Gloom leered a crooked smile of turrets and barrack blocks, gatehouses, and a sprawling bailey on top of a huge sulking crag overlooking Murk's vast marshy wasteland. Lichen disfigured gargoyles poured pure filth, pestilence and plague down the high walls of massive granite blocks into the moat as figures of demons, troll, imps, ghouls and other servants and soldiers of Trachidambabble, the Lord of Murk, scurried about their business.

Down, deep down, the labyrinth of corridors that sank in layers beneath the castle's superstructure, a long steam-soaked room bustled with more activity and noise than was considered normal in the headquarters of the world's sloth.

A spaghetti of steaming pipes lined the walls, sometimes detouring to huge rusting hulks of cisterns. Large engines with long rotary arms hissed and spat clouds of ghastly vapours into a claustrophobic atmosphere. At the centre of the noise and confusion, in which half seen shapes flitted in and out of layers of purple vapours, stood 13 great vats, brimming with gurgling viscous fluids.

"What does it look like?" the Balck Warlock called up to his new apprentice swaying at the top of a ladder propped against a vat.

"A bit like slurry, only nicer."

"No, no. What colour?"

"Oh still yellow," the apprentice called down.

"Well add some more pigment and give it another stir," the warlock called up, swishing his tail in annoyance. He didn't like. He didn't like at all.

It was bad enough having to get used to his new legs, welded on after the last dip in the moat – the hooves did not fit comfortably with a reptilian torso – but the real insult was the job of mixing the new Murk manufactured Ness. It was an offence to his powers.

As the Balck Warlock he was high priest of all sorcerers and warlocks on Murk, most long surviving advisor to the Dark Lord himself, and Chief Executive of the Future Planning Department of Castle Gloom Enterprises. He had been in the job for so long, that he had forgotten his own name, and if anyone else knew they didn't dare use it. He felt horribly over qualified.

If being treated like a common alchemist wasn't bad enough, having to wear a boiler suit with *BALCK WARLOCK –Production Manager* was adding injury to insult. He felt naked without his dark robes of every hue of purple swishing at his feet. The mystical signs covering them gave him strength, and was a crib sheet for the various elements of spells and summoning incantations that were the core to his sorcery. And warlock power shoulder pads looked ridiculous in a boiler suit.

There was a cry from the top of the vat.

"Is it blue yet?" the Balck Warlock yelled up into the clouds of steam that swirled around the vat's open mouth.

As an answer close to "glub" filtered down, the Balck Warlock assumed his apprentice had fallen into the bubbling hopper.

He sighed. Apprentices weren't what they used to be. This one couldn't stand heights and got vertigo when he stood on tiptoe. Not very helpful when it came to surfing clouds on a chariot drawn by 12 ravens of the damned, as you chased the horned dog of chaos across the green moon at every equinox – an essential part of the sorcery field work practicals for the warlock diploma.

His fangs drooped as he remembered his auger reading of the night. The demise of the apprentice was only the first of his inauspicious waking hours. The fins down the Balck Warlock's back tingled with portent. He ruminated darkly as he sensed the impending surprise visit of Lord Trachidambabble to check on the progress of the Ness2Mess programme.

One of the distinct disadvantages of being a warlock of major powers, was being able to hear the voices of the Crones of Fate gossiping on the edge of reality as they wove the yarns of different lives into the tapestry of Time. The snatches of chatter overheard between the clicking of the needles were not encouraging.

Squeaking leather and the jangle of chains followed in the wake of the plodding footsteps of Trachidambabble's troll bodyguard, following them along the slime dripping corridors towards the lift. The ground hissed where the Lord of Murk's billowing Cloak of Darkness gave it a fluttering touch. Lurking spectres and malevolent spirits disturbed from their dozing nightmares fled deeper into the bowels of the castle.

The troll Blackguard detachment halted outside the onyx columns of the lift, and the Captain of the Guard pressed the call button. The lift doors opened, and Trachidambabble swept in, crackling with evil energy, and sat down on a miniature throne.

"The dungeons again, O Dark Master, for a little light relief?" asked the little black goblin, perched on his poisonous mushroom beside the communication mouthpiece.

"Lower Bowels, and make it snappy," the voice of a thousand iron filings grated.

"Wrong you are Dark Lord. We'll have you there in a jiffy," the goblin whined obsequiously, and picked up the mouthpiece. "Lower Bowels, and make it snappy, or you lot will be in the moat faster than I can say Gloop food."

From above their heads there was a muffled crack of a whip and a chorus of groans as the manacled ogres on elevator duty ran inside a large wheel housed on top of the lift.

The newly painted giant Orbs stood empty in blue rows at the end of the clanking machinery of Workshop One, waiting to be filled with a batch of the new Mess. Above them an octopus jumble of filling pipes hung from a hopper operated by rusty link chains and pulleys. The Balck Warlock fingered an Orb; its paint was still wet. He wiped his finger on his boiler suit and picked his way through the tangle of contorted machinery by the distilling cisterns, and back to the vats. Emerging from a sudden hiss of a vapour cloud from a pressure pipe, a chattering imp gripping a grease gun nearly knocked him off his newly grafted feet. All around the vats in the centre of Lower Bowels Workshop One the worker imps, devils and demons scurried here and there, and back to here again, babbling loudly, energetically achieving nothing much apart from noise.

The Balck Warlock picked up the imp by the ear and held it to his face.

"What's the commotion?"

"The trolls are jangling down the stairs...and the lift is squeaking closer...never...never been down to the Lower Bowels...the lift...what's to be done...there's lots to be done...got to make it all mucky...there's no muck, and no Mess..."

The Balck Warlock let the imp drop to the floor and made his way to the nearest of the vats, swatting imps and demons as they ran out in front of him. Agitatedly he turned the tap at the bottom of the vat his apprentice had been inspecting and poured a couple of dribbles of Mess into the bottom of the sample pot hanging from the tap. The warlock held up the pot and examined its contents. He grimaced happily through his forked tongue. The Ness had at last turned to Mess. A quivering purple had subdued any hint of golden hues that had obstinately remained in the early batches of Mess. Now all he needed to know was whether the power and weight of the original Ness had been maintained during the colour change.

He took the sample over to a cubicle where a steam driven pair of scales sat hissing. He poured some of the fluid into a measuring cup and pulled a lever. A small red hand on the scales wavered and then shot to the far end of the dial marked HEAVY. The warlock grinned horribly, and touched the unlucky black toad charm tattooed on his neck.

If Trachidambabble wanted Heaven's golden Ness to be turned purple and called Mess, while retaining all the same properties, no one - not even the Balck Warlock - argued. Through the many lives of the bodies he had inhabited, he had never been biodegraded, and didn't want to test whether there was a possibility of life after biodegradation.

He walked back to the vats, kicking at a demon who was rushing with a bucket of muck, splattering it at every surface in sight.

The voices of the gossiping Fates nagged him at the edge of his consciousness. He recognised his name in their chatter and shivered. His yellow eyes turned orange in trepidation. The thin red tongue darted around the scaled snout, and his tail frisked from side to side.

"Scab!" he called up to his apprentice. "Stop playing in that tub, and get down here. There's work to do."

An imp dragged a large can of foul smelling oil and tipped it on the floor, splashing the warlock's boiler suit as it slopped a slick in the middle of the main corridor of Workshop One. The warlock was starting to steam at the ears. He needed time to think. He tugged at his sleeve to release his favourite thigh bone wand, and tapped the ground with the old bone to activate its carved mystic symbols.

Waving the wand in proscribed loops and thrusts, the Balck Warlock muttered deeply into his beard. The mutter turned to rant, climaxing in a yell, as the wand twisted and kicked in his hand.

The air was still, even the steam froze in the atmosphere, and every little imp and demon that had been scurrying around the Balck Warlock's feet were turned to concrete. As the bad air of Workshop One settled back into relative normality, there were little movements on the edges of the spell forcefield. Little red imps skulked into the shadows, and stunted black demons scuttled into dark corners behind machinery parts.

When the Balck Warlock started lashing out with spells and curses, even the most cold blooded reptile on Murk shivered and made itself scarce.

A grimace of satisfaction of a spell well worked played on the specially filed teeth of the Balck Warlock. He returned the wand to his sleeve, and climbed the ladder leant against the vat where he had taken the Mess sample to see what was keeping his apprentice. Moving awkwardly on his hooves, he climbed through layers of poisonous gases to reach the lip of the vat with puffing breath. Scab was nowhere to be seen. He peered over into the Mess, which was bubbling the colour of squashed blackcurrants, and on its disturbed surface floated the wooden stirring spoon and clogs of his apprentice, drifting in an ominous circle.

The Balck Warlock huffed. Another apprentice gone. It looked like another journey to Glob on a recruiting tour – always a very tedious affair. And sorcery was not the flavour of the month at the moment amongst talented young fortune tellers and astronomers. They seemed to be content with becoming media stars, and living in thte lap of celebrity. Of course he had to admire their laziness, but despised the lack of dreadful ambition, which would stretch their minds and abilities with the practice of the balck arts. Of course longevity was not a guarantee as a warlock on Murk. But what was that, when for even a short time a bad warlock could be really nasty, vindictive and cruel with the most potent spells and curses on Glob?

He opened a descent umbrella and jumped off the ladder. At least he had found a way of turning the golden Ness into a purple mess. He would have to see if a few imps and demons would have the same effect.

As he landed lightly in the middle of the slick of oil, the atmosphere suddenly changed for the worse. Particles in the air jittered and molecules split themselves asunder. Plumes of vapours froze all across Workshop One and no machine dared splutter or let off steam.

Trachidambabble's Blackguards smashed their way through the scattered concrete figures as they stamped their way towards the Balck Warlock. Behind them the crackle and spitting of the Cloak of Darkness announced the arrival of His Most Disgusting Darkness.

The warlock furled his umbrella, made it concertina to the size of a matchbox, put it in his pocket, and waited to be ceremonially thrown to the ground by the Captain of the Guard.

Dripping with oil he raised his head as Trachidambabble spoke.

"Well Balck Warlock, how is my Mess progressing?"

"Badly, most Terrible One, very badly."

He took the raising of a long arching eyebrow as a sign of approval.

"We have at last discovered the secret ingredient to give Mess the correct colouration, as Your Disgusting Darkness decreed. All we have to do now is fill the Orbs and store them until the Mess is ready to be catapulted onto Glob."

"How horrendous," Trachidambabble whispered in a voice that rattled all the nearby pistons in their casings.

"And what is this secret ingredient?" the Lord of Murk enquired.

"Erm...my apprentice sorcerer. He fell into that vat," said the warlock pointing, "and the result is remarkable. Good colour, without detracting from the weight and viscosity. A disastrous blend indeed!"

He even allowed himself a small grimace of triumph.

"And how many apprentice sorcerers have you got?" rumbled Trachidambabble.

"That was my only...last one," said the warlock and gulped quickly. "But I will be going on a recruiting drive. Anyone can produce the Mess now, as long as they can read the recipe."

"Anyone?" grated the sinister tones.

"Well almost any..." backtracking desperately.

It was too late. Trachidambabble had extended his hand, and with a flick of his finger, the warlock, who was still lying at a respectable distance from the feet of his Dark Lord, was catapulted into one of the nearby vats.

The gurgling sound of the Balck Warlock as he was pulled down into the Mess produced a rare smile on the lips of the cloaked Lord of Darkness.

"Troll Captain, can you read?"

The captain of the Blackguards, who had been indulging in a huge smirk, wiped it off his face instantly. His clutch of brain cells were working as fast as they ponderously could. Everyone knew that trolls never learned to read. That was time away from hitting and terrorising anything in the vicinity.

"No Boss," the captain replied.

He had not risen to the rank of Captain of the Guard by disagreeing with his master.

"Ghastly. You are now promoted to Production Manager of Mess, for which you will need all the stupidity you have so far shown in your present position. This career change is effective as from now."

The troll, who had enjoyed abusing his position of power, was not so sure this was promotion. But, self-preservation prevented him from saying anything that might be construed as anything less than unenthusiastic.

"Most dishonoured Boss. I will do my worst to give you a horrible Mess."

"I am sure you will. Do your worst, and we will keep Murk on top, running Glob the way it always should have been," the voice grated.

With a swish of his crackling cloak, Trachidambabble swept back towards the lift with the remaining Blackguards, treading heavily on the scattered concrete remains of imps and demons.

The new Production Manager leant his spiked club against a bucket and scratched his head. He had never done anything that hadn't involved hitting things before. He wondered what to do. Workshop One in the Lower Bowels steamed back into life, pouring filthy vapours, hissing, hooting and clanking with machinery as the lift doors closed. From a dark crevice underneath a nearby piston engine a demon inquisitively poked his head out to test the air. The troll instinctively picked up its club and smashed it down on the demon.

He was getting into his new job already, and could see that he might like it.

He dragged the demon out, and held it up close to his gnarled, wart covered snout.

"Can you read?" snarled the troll.

The proximity of vicious fangs and withering bad breath was enough to persuade the demon that it could. It shook its head vigorously in agreement. The troll grinned menacingly.

"Bad. Go make a Mess."

The demon landed on the floor and scampered away into the darker recesses of the workshop among the more impenetrable steam vapours.

Somewhere at the bottom of the vat of Mess, the dissolved particles of the Balck Warlock were seeking each other out. The brain molecules had gathered together and were lurking with evil thoughts and devising nasty plans for when it came to a time suitable for rebirthing. Finding oneself at the bottom of a vat of Mess was proving to be a difficult mental exercise, but they were powered by terrible thoughts of revenge on an erstwhile appreciative master.

X

The great wings of the Comfy Chair kept up a steady whump-whump-whump as it flew high over territories of Glob, casting a strange giant shadow as it passed over the changing topography.

"I'm not so sure that this is the right way at all," Fyrsil told the Bobo as he dug his nose into the relevant encyclopaedia from the Golden Palace library.

From what he could decipher from the pages on Loot, the pirate citadel was surrounded by water. Miles and miles of it. At least that was the last reading before a massive burn out by the printed word made more recent updates indecipherable, with pile ups of frazzled carcasses of letters littering the margins.

With a lot of guess work and supposition Fyrsil was able to string along a theory that Loot was the only inhabited island of a strung out group of dollops of land – mainly weather beaten marsh mounds – known as the Fever Islands. These were situated in a hidden corner somewhere in the middle of the Blood Sea. Even when large and powerful civilisations bothered to send a fleet to stamp out piracy, they inevitably got lost, scattered by storms, eaten by mythical sea monsters, or any combination of these fates.

By the same token, it was only the roughest and toughest outcasts of every tribe and civilisation on Glob who survived the journey to Loot – often finding it by mistake after taking the wrong turning at the north star during astral navigation. And it was only the most brutal scumbags who were able to carry out their daring raids of wanton theft, destruction, pillage, murder and every other associated crime, and a lot of others not even thought of. The result of their recreational activities were then taken back to Loot – if they could find it again – where they would generally squabble over the division of the spoils, drink too much Knock Out Punch, and spend all their money on the traditional parasites of ill-gotten gains: wine, fast women, and faster catalogue shopping.

The city port of Loot itself was situated on the smallest of the Fever Islands, due to the prevailing hearsay that it was less prone to mad fevers from the marshy swamps. The town itself was described as a cross between a shanty town and a set for grand opera. The latter due to the intense rivalry of pirate chiefs in displaying their ostentatious wealth. The former was popular with everyone else because Loot was subject to every sort of natural disaster from earthquakes to hurricanes. With a life expectancy of a maximum of three years for any building, it didn't seem to make much sense in putting up any structure that couldn't be reassembled quickly after a flattening.

With a funny look in his eye, from trying to read too many pages that looked more like whole colonies of squashed ants than neat typescript, Fyrsil related this all to the Bobo.

"I know," the Bobo told him, "but the instruments say this is the right way, and I have more faith in them, than any blotched old book – no matter where it comes from. While you was messing around and gorging yourself on chocolates, I had the good sense to read the Chair's manual. Especially interesting were the chapters on the Autonav, astronavigator and autopilot controls, which I took the liberty of programming properly before take off."

Fyrsil couldn't think of an answer for that, and had no alternative ideas. Instead he consciously finished the last packet of crisps without offering the Bobo any at all. He was also tempted to stick his tongue out.

After a particularly sticky silence that seemed to last an eternity, Fyrsil ventured: "The astronavigator estimates that touch down is not far off, but for the last thousand miles I have not seen anything that looks like water, let alone a Blood Sea."

The long flight had given Fyrsil a few bored moments of his own with the Comfy Chair's manual, and had taught himself how to read the banks of flashing numbers and diagrams.

"Well, all I know is the astronavigator is guaranteed to be right. I know because I have seen the warranty."

"But what if it is wrong?" Fyrsil asked, worried at the reliance on technology that had not proved to be 100 per cent reliable on the first leg their journey.

"Then we are lost, and when we do land, we will have to ask the way," replied the bird with Bobo logic.

Fyrsil looked out onto the expanse of red contours that looked like a desert stretching below the chair. The tassels of its new claret coloured velvet covers hummed in the humid heat as they flew towards the twin pink suns that hovered above the middle of Glob.

Sighing heavily, Fyrsil put down the telescope with which he had been scanning the horizon for any sign of wet patches that could on an outside chance be a sea in disguise. Reluctantly he pulled out the game of Monarchy and Media he had been playing with the Bobo, and tried to think through a move of how to evade the paparazzi to be able to visit the royal mistress.

Being a hero was becoming worse than he imagined. Not only did it include an insufferable companion, but long and boring bits between the action. Even flying was not that exciting once you got used to it. Everything seemed so small from their cruising height, that there was nothing to write home about as far as exotic foreign lands they crossed day after day.

* * *

The wind rustled lightly through the reeds with a touch of a tender caress under a cloudless pink sky. There was no other sound to be heard except the occasional mournful cry of a wading bird calling for the sea. It had become exceptionally mournful lately, as the sea had suddenly left, without leaving a note where it had gone.

Behind a carefully camouflaged hide, hid two figures dressed in khaki disrupted pattern trousers and jackets, large sensible gumboots, and wearing green bobble hats with their names – Boac and Twa -knitted into them.

"Mister Boac, keep still, if you please," hissed the smaller of the two companions, as he painfully slowly swept the horizon with a heavily camouflaged pair of binoculars.

"But I thought we be twitchers," groaned his tank-like buddy, jiggering up and down on a flimsy collapsible stool.

"Me thinks there's a mite of misunderstanding in that supposition Mister Boac. I be the twitcher. You be the twitcher's mate. The reasoning is plain to see: *you* carry the thermos and sandwiches, and *I* do carry the binoculars," Twa told his companion, poking with his forefinger for emphasis.

For years Twa had been kicked around as the smallest member of any raiding party crew, and now he was making the best of his new found importance as chairman of the Loot Bird Watchers Association.

He cast his mind back to how he had been spurned by all but the most desperate pirate molls - the unfeathered variety of birds found on Loot. Even when he had booty clinking in his pocket. He had put it down to prejudice against people of small stature with unfortunate carbuncles on their noses. The molls and floosies put it down to horrendous personal hygiene (even by pirate standards) coupled with a warty nose, buck teeth, and bandy legs.

Forced to take up an alternative pastime to the traditional raging parties at the end of a raid, Twa resorted to expeditions into the outlying marshes to record sightings of different sorts of birds inhabiting or migrating to the Fever Islands.

He was disturbed from his reverie by Boac humming a little sea shanty and tapping his feet.

"Hisst," Twa told him irritably. "The wobble-bottom goose has a very acute hearing disposition. 'Tis quiet you must practice, if a real twitcher you want to be," Twa told his companion sternly.

"Arr," said Boac, because he was used to saying those sort of things. "And how is it that you be so sure that this wobble-bottom will fly this way?"

"Because, my intelligence does tell me so." Twa knocked a boney finger to the side of his nose, carefully avoiding the carbuncle. "You'll know full well when it does hove into sight. Faith Mister Boac, faith is all I ask."

By this stage Boac had lost all interest in being a twitcher. Admittedly things had to change since the Blood Sea disappeared, but it was not the sort of life he had expected after overcoming multiple dangers to enrol in the world's most notorious pirate brethren. A life of carousing and biffing had been the main attractions for the sort of life he had chosen for himself, and birdwatching did not come under either of those two headings.

Sighing heavily, Boac picked up his binoculars, not noticing that Twa still had his head through their strap, and glumly scanned the horizon through the hide's viewing slit.

"Bird ahoy! On the starboard bow, flying steady with the breeze," he whispered excitedly.

Pushing his burly companion aside in his eagerness, Twa adjusted the focus on the binoculars, and peered eagerly at a spot above the horizon. His forehead creased in doubt as he pulled out the Bird Identification: The Complete Guide from his rucksack.

"Well?" whispered Boac.

"Well, goose it be not, especially of the wobble-bottom variety," Twa said as he flicked through pages of silhouettes of the rare bird section of Glob bird life compendium, "and the outline of it does match nothing I have ever seen before. A rare bird, indeed, a very rare bird indeed."

Now Boac was starting to get a small dose of that tingle of excitement and the slight butterflies in the tummy that he used to experience
as the decks were cleared for action on sighting a hostile ship on the
Blood Sea. (All other ships were automatically hostile, as none of
them liked the idea of an invitation by Loot pirates to play special
games like *Walk the Plank* or *Give Us Yer Dosh*.)

Training the binoculars at the rapidly distinguishable spot in the
sky, Boac stared intently at the bird that was looking less and less like
a bird. Twa nudged his way beside his companion to see for himself,
glancing down at the illustrated pages to try and match the silhouette.

"Maybe a strange variety of Great Ork, from the snow-bound
wastes of Fro Stibite; or perchance the Hercule Condor, which according to all manner of reliable sources, has been known to be tamed by
the rock dwellers of Vertifalldon for the purpose of delivering winter
wheat to their caves."

Boac was not convinced.

"To my mind, it has the appearance of a flying armchair," he said
sceptically, now able to hear the steady whump-whump-whump of the
wing beat.

Twa cursed the stupidity of amateurs. Of course it couldn't be a
flying armchair. They have castors and are pushed around withdraw-
ing rooms in large residences, or filled up corners in the lounge. Silently he counted the interval between the wing beats. No, it couldn't be
the Hercule Condor he thought. He pulled out his handset. He needed
a witness for this sighting. It could be a first, or even a discovery
which could be named after him. It would mean fame, interviews, lecture tours, best selling books - and everything else he could wish for...

Twa's mind raced with the possibilities.

His fingers worked nervously at the pages as he flicked again
through the section on giant birds, cocking his ears as the rhythmic
sound of wings ceased, and he started to make out the strange call of
this mysterious bird.

WHAT'SITDOIN'. IT'SALRITE – IT'SONREMOTE.
WHAT'SITDOIN- NOW. IT'SALRITE – IT'S ONREMOTE.

He tried to make it out, as he tuned in to the Fever Islands Twitcher frequency.

"Busby One, Busby One. Twitch alert, I say again, twitch alert.
Mysterious and rare bird with no previous identity. Truly, a remarkable first arrival to these islands. Scramble, scramble with haste – Dead

Man's Marsh. Out." Twa enunciated in clear tones over his crackling handset. "Could be of the Hercule Condor spec…"

"Duck!" shouted Boac in his ear.

Twa was about to point out the basic dimensions of a duck, and the fact that this bird was far too big for that, when a powerful hand pushed his head facedown into the squelching mud. Seconds later he heard a loud ripping noise, as the hide was torn from where it had been embedded, and a noisy rush of air indicated that the body of the strange bird had just passed at great speed where his head would have been.

The reeds stirred windlessly. The sound of a long wet kiss indicated someone was trying to extract themselves from a clinging bed of mire and mud.

Picking up his helmet, Fyrsil strode through the springy morass, the dirty moisture of the saturated turf squeezing between his toes as it seeped over his thonged sandals. He made his way to where he could hear the Bobo squawking to free itself, as it dangled from its safety belt.

"Well if that's what happens on autopilot, it's no different from the last landing, which was on manual controls," said Fyrsil looking at the upended chair.

"There's a lot of difference. What happened just now was a technical error. What happened at the *Rest Inn* was pure stupidity reinforced by inexperience. Now get me out of this!" the Bobo screeched impatiently.

"But it's for your own safety, and I think you ought to stay here quietly while I scout around. There might be a need for heroics, and I'm not sure I can count on your nerves after the failure to untie me in the vault at the chocoholics."

He was enjoying the predicament of the Bobo, who squawked and rolled its eyes in a way that indicated Bobos did not like being suspended from tangled safety belts.

"And I think you ought to keep your squawks down. If the Autonav is anything to go by, we are in the allotment fields of Loot's suburbs. But if my eyesight is anything to go by, we have landed nowhere near. It could be bandit country," Fyrsil said, fiddling with switches and knobs on the navigation screen.

He picked up the remote from its pocket, and with the press of a couple of buttons the long expanses of wingspan neatly folded and disappeared under the velvet covers into their stowage compartment in the chair's arms.

"As we are meant to be penetrating the heart of pirate country, I don't think their reception for us would be any different from bandits," sniffed the Bobo.

"I would like to remind you that you need a military advisor to be able to make swift tactical appraisals of situations with potential hostiles. It was only the overwhelming fact of being threatened with a stuffing, basting and roasting, that I was unable to aid any escape you may have wanted to initiate at the *Rest Inn*. I was waiting for the optimum opportunity to be able to effect any escape and that only presented itself with the arrival of the Gastrognome hungerparty."

"Alright, let's stop bickering…"

"Who's bickering?"

"You are."

"No I'm not."

"Yes you are."

"You both be bickering."

"Who said that?" said Fyrsil and the Bobo in unison, simultaneously ending their misunderstanding.

XI

Thoughts of heroics quickly fled from Fyrsil's mind. Dangling strategically, the Bobo took up its defensive position of baring its red bottom from among the fronds of day-glo feathers.

Fyrsil looked at the two apparitions in front of him, gulped, and wished he was grading nuts for winter storage in one of the deeper caves of the Alpoian mountains. One large and one squat mud monster stood before him. He slowly shifted his sword to behind his back, hoping that they would not mistake someone armed as being dangerous.

"Aquavita sends her compliments," Fyrsil tried as a friendly opener, after the three of them and the Bobo's posterior had eyed each other for a couple of minutes.

"Who, pray, is Aquavita?" asked Boac wondering whether it was permissible under the new scheme of things in Loot to at least bash strange people on the head with a thermos flask.

Twa seemed to be saying something angrily as he jumped up and down, spitting out moss between incomprehensible gargling.

"We're emissaries from Heaven. And Aquavita is goddess of Gushing Water and Muddy places. Looks like a bedraggled weeping willow. I'm sure you should have a shrine. At leasr she should be your sort of deity," Fyrsil said, playing for time, and wondering whether any act of pure cowardice was worthy of someone who had been given a HERO badge by Heaven's top god.

"Well blow me down in a typhoon – strangers from Heaven! There was a temple for Crusher - once." Boac scratched his muddy locks on his head. " Me thinks it was converted into a veggie-burger restaurant. My companion, Mister Twa here, he may have had an inclination for religion."

"Gurrrgh," replied Twa spitting out the last of the mouthful of sludge he had swallowed when Boac pushed his face into the marsh.

"No," said Fyrsil thoughtfully, "I knew all the gods in Heaven, but that was not one I ever came across."

"Knaves! Scurvy vagrants! Barbarians! Do you know what you have just done?" shouted Twa very loudly for someone so small.

"Landed," said Fyrsil innocently, and immediately regretted it. The muddy figure in front of him was armed with nothing more dangerous than a large reference book, but it was being wielded in a very aggressive manner.

"Don't move or my bird will fire," Fyrsil warned, moving to give the Bobo a clear target.

The threat did not seem to penetrate the consciousness of the hopping figure of grey mud.

"Lilly-livered idiots! Cretinous worms! How can you perpetrate such an act of vandalism? This marsh has only just had an order of preservation put on it. The plans to recreate the traditional fever marsh, complete with a visitor centre and themed retail outlets, have only these past few weeks won approval from the Save Fever Islands Heritage Council. This is an outrage. The last colony of Yellow Wasting mosquitoes and the few remaining breeding pairs of Quikstiff flies were gathered together, and much attention was given for their daily good health," Twa ranted.

"Really?" said Fyrsil and Boac together.

"Vouch safe I speak the truth," Twa continued in an annoyingly shrill voice. He pointed a righteous finger to the long dirty groove in the crust of the marsh that ended in the mud hole where the chair sat in its splattered regal velvet. To emphasise the point he jumped into the muddy scar, and maniacally rummaged in the squelching slime until he emerged triumphant with a couple of battered examples of vicious looking insects and a sign now reading:

INFESTATION AREA
DO OT DIST RB

"Oh, I'm terribly sorry..." Fyrsil began.

"Good bloody riddance. I once ate a Quikstiff – it's still painful to remember the indigestion. The only thing they are good for is to be swatted," the Bobo interrupted.

Twa stood mouth agape, as he struggled for thought as an ardent conservationist.

"A curse on you for saying such a thing," he protested wondering who had made the offensive comment, "they are close to extinction. There is an order of protection on them as a species of historical value to these islands. Their rights to the freedom to be able to live and breathe on Glob are the same as any other citizen."

He paused, looking at the Bobo's rear end quizzically. "And who said that anyway?"

"They are disease-ridden pests, which should be squashed on sight. And don't talk to me of extinction; *me* the last of the Bobo war birds. I can tell you a thing or two about that state of affairs," the Bobo said, twisting its head through its tail feathers to give a more forceful argument for extinction.

Twa opened and closed his mouth several times as blinked in the glare of the Bobo's stare.

"Did you say bird? Bird watching is an activity that I have recently commenced as a pass-time. May I observe you, if I do so very quietly and according to the code of the club?" asked Boac, unsure whether you were meant to ask permission of the subject.

"Certainly," said the Bobo. "is there anything you want me to do while you are watching me, because it would be easier if you let me out of these straps."

Lumbering over, Boac untangled the Bobo, and placed it in the chair. But Twa was not happy. In fact he was excitedly unhappy.

"You blundering mule dung, that be not birdwatching," he shouted, as Boac cleaned off the lenses of the binoculars and studied at close range the ugly features of the Bobo. "The authorised manner and code of practice for birdwatchers of these islands is to hide from the bird, in order to take notes and observe them in their natural habitat."

Boac looked puzzled, shrugged, and pulled out his Birdwatching Notebook from a muddy pocket, licked his pencil, and started asking the Bobo questions to fill in the helpful headings of particulars such as: species; single/breeding pair; call; distinguishing plumage; and others on the parchment pages.

"...No, haven't had a mate since I was grabbed by Sorefoot and dragged farting up to Heaven...Call me Bobo – most people do..." the Bobo answered for the record book.

"This is a travesty. Birdwatchers do not *ask* their subjects the details when filling out a twitcher's notebook. It is fraudulent cheating, and will not be allowed as a proper way to undertake the calling of the twitcher," Twa ranted, interrupting the slow deliberate forming of Boac's entry into his notebook. "And besides, the Bobo is extinct. It is quite clearly stated here in solid print," he said pointing to the relevant page in his book *Bird Identification – The Complete Guide.*

"Prove it," said the Bobo.

Looking at the illustration of the extinct Bobos Twa was holding up to prove his point, the Bobo sniffed: "if that is meant to be cousin

Waldo, he definitely is extinct. I read the restaurant review where he was the main feature of the meal."

Twa did not take this challenge to his expert knowledge of his chosen hobby lying down. Throwing his bobble hat on the ground, he declared with all the dignity he could muster in his stunted frame:

"Ye may be a bird yourself, but I be the chairman and founder of the Loot Birdwatcher Society. As such I am the foremost authority on avian subjects in this vicinity, and it is for me to decided, as some-one of such importance, when a bird is, and is not, extinct."

Fyrsil, who had been leaning against the Comfy Chair wondering where they were if it wasn't Loot, pricked up his ears. Having dis-missed the idea that the birdwatchers were a) not muddy monsters from the mire; and b) not blood-thirsty pirates from Loot, he won-dered where on Glob they were.

"Loot, did you say?"

"The very same, and incorporating all the Fever Islands as well. They don't call me Birdman Twa with no light reason."

"Shouldn't you be pirates, buccaneers, or at least cut-throats? And where is the Blood Sea? We've been looking for it for ages."

Having lost interest in the Bobo and Boac's question and answer session, Twa sighed, and sat down in the marsh.

"It's a long yarn, but it be like this...," he began.

Before the day the Blood Sea ran away, and never came back again there were interesting things afoot in downtown Loot. In an unprecedented move, the warring pirate chieftains had gathered around the table and decided to co-operate. It was unheard of, but the constant gang warfare that raged within the citadel in between raids to foreign lands had become a bit tedious for everyone concerned. Apart from anything else it was a waste of energy and good murder-ous talent.

Despite the protests of the undertakers and crematoriums that the move would cause mass unemployment with the sharp downturn in trade, the chieftains declared a truce. They all signed an agreement in blood to only murder, maim and torture those peoples who were not part of the brethren of the Fever Islands.

To celebrate this historic accord amongst some of the world's most discordant characters, the biggest and boldest expedition was organised for all the pirate chiefs to sail in one great fleet to maxim-ise the amount of booty-taking ravaging of as many rich destinations in as short a time as possible. It proved to be such a successful combination, with the pooling of the wide range of skills in devastation and general pillaging, that the fleet went about its business for three years.

Eventually the fleet returned to its home port, with every galleon and captured craft laden with stolen treasures. But the town they left was not the Loot they came back to.

Those trades people who had found themselves out of work by the lack of dead bodies hanging around the streets, had gone into a communal huff. After a certain amount of hot air, they decided to set themselves up as priests of a new sect of Lifers, who preached the total sanctity of life, invoking inviolable rights for every living person, creature and insect. This move had been started by a rumour that there was a lot of money to had in religious cults, but it found favour with a section of pirate floosies who had become bored with no pirates to fleece of precious gems and pay for their essential shopping sprees. To relieve the tedium between hair salon appointments a few pioneering harridans had formed self-help groups to help find themselves – there was precious little else to do in Loot.

What they found was they didn't really need men anyway, as most had enough of a stash of goods from previous expeditions, and they were glad to have a bit of peace and quiet around the house. But they went even further, and decided that if they didn't need men, they could let their cellulite and crows feet march across their features and still feel good about themselves.

This did not matter to the returning pirates. In their typical macho way they presumed that what ever was wrong with their favourite girls, they would soon come round once the fineries and jewels from four continents started being dished out. In the meantime there was the traditional end of expedition party to organise. And this was going to be the biggest, most magnificent celebration Loot had ever seen.

Within hours of the fleet docking and disembarking, the fountains flowed with Knockout Punch, the streets resounded with music and dancing. Fashion shows of looted designer warehouses took place in the central square, bouncy castles, and any number of party games to choose from. As if from nowhere, bunting festooned public and private buildings, and trestle tables groaned with festive fare, and the best foods from the best delicatessens anywhere.

For two weeks the party rowdily raged in a constant sweeping tide up and down the citadel's cobbled streets. Finally exhausted, and the Knockout Punch drunk dry, the population of Loot lay snoring in crumpled heaps amongst the bones of the feasts, sleeping off the excesses of the Party to End All Parties.

And that was the end of the old Loot of a thousand legends in their own short lifetimes. When the first couple of figures started to stagger around holding their heads, there was a definite feeling in the air that something had changed, and life, as those who were still alive usually recognised it, would never be the same again.

Although it was universally agreed that there had been a seismic shift in something, no one could put a finger on what it was. Until, that is, the giant chief Grunt decided to clear his head with a swim in the sea. He staggered down to the quay and dived off the end of a jetty. He was later found up to his waist in mud with his feet waggling helplessly in the air.

The Blood Sea had gone. Overnight it had packed its bags and moved off to other climes.

In its place was endless miles of mud, cutting off Loot from any communication with the rest of Glob. This ultimately pleased kings and potentates within raiding range, but at that time they were too busy dealing with flood damage to think about other implications.

"So what has happened to the pirates who go anywhere and attack anything for a bit of a laugh, and a whacking great pile of treasure?" Fyrsil asked.

"Oh there be none of them in these parts no more. Them pirates and buccaneers have given over their old ways in favour of digging vegetable allotments and breeding edible insects. Life is one great big harmony in Loot. The pottery wheel has taken the place of the cutlass and the pike. The Lifers came out of hiding after the Party to End All Parties and declared it was because of all the wrong-doing that the sea left. So it's a life of peace and harmony in these days, and all told to us by the Lifers who guide us to The Good Life," Twa said as he finished his recent potted history of the fall of Loot from debauchery.

Standing up, Twa noticed a look of disappointment on Fyrsil's face.

As an emissary of Heaven, his short introduction to heroics with the Gastrognomes had left Fyrsil wanting to leave all the maniacal stuff to the pirates who enjoyed such antics when they raided Murk to find the Golden Orbs. Without their assistance he could not see another way of saving Glob. An expedition of just himself and the Bobo was not an option to be considered.

The light was fading as the twin pink suns above Loot dived into the muddy horizon. Fyrsil pulled out the Being Stone and watched the choking ivy of blue veins encircling the golden globe.

"What is your purpose in these parts in any case," Twa asked.

"Just a tourist," Fyrsil replied, not wanting to reveal his mission, as he tucked the Being Stone back into his tunic.

"What's a tourist?"

"Someone who goes visiting other places to see what they are like, buy useless mementoes there, complain about the food, get sick, and then tell their friends what a wonderful time they had when they get back."

This puzzled Twa.

"Well, baulk my timbers, I never heard of no one like that before. None in Loot at any rate. Only people that came here of their own volition before was those what wanted a life of a greedy pirate."

"You don't know any good hotels, then?"

Twa didn't. No one had ever thought of building a hotel in Loot, because no travel agent in their right mind would ever put it on a holiday itinerary.

"Being a peaceable old sea rover, you be welcome to string your hammock at my shack. Your bird be welcome too," Twa told Fyrsil. "Now this tourist thing, it do sound harmless as an occupation...Ye can tell me all about it over a bowl of porridge in front of a nice cosy fire."

Fyrsil nodded wearily. At least he would have a bed for the night. Longhaul flights in the Comfy Chair could get a bit uncomfortable after a while.

XII

A dispirited Fyrsil sat at the dining table studying scenes from the mother of pearl inlay depicting very odd myths, which appeared more interesting and appetising than the raw leek on his plate.

The opulence of the room, with its hanging silks, finest tapestries, intricate carvings, busts on classical columns, and glittering knick-knacks from countless raids on a wide variety of civilisations, was far too grand a backdrop for the mean meal in front of him.

"Right, explain again how this tourism business and its workings," Twa said, as he frowned at a scrap of parchment on which he had been scribbling notes.

"These 'attractions' and 'marketing concepts' do strike me as awful strange, and my head do hurt sore from thinking about how to make them work proper for Loot."

Fyrsil agreed. As far as could ascertain from the last couple of days in Loot, there were no attractions.

"The secret is not so much in attractions, but in an allure; pulling power," he said at last, after gulping down the last browning remains of his obnoxious vegetable.

"The real attraction will be that no one will have been to the city that once produced the most feared raiders on the whole of Glob. Make up some highly exotic stories about famous pirate chiefs, do little tours of their old haunts, produce cheap momento merchandise, and *Hey Presto!* You have a tourist industry. It's out of curiosity that people will visit the now tamed Loot, and it's out of gullibility that they will pay a high price for that privilege."

Twa eyed his tutor in tourism with grim suspicion.

"Sounds like robbery to me. That sort of thing ain't allowed no more under the New Way. No deception or nasty vices, etc, etc and etcetera," the ex-pirate said, tut-ting as he shook his head.

"It's nothing of the sort," Fyrsil retorted quickly. "It's a way of providing a service to visitors from strange civilisations, while taking into account the stresses and strains this influx puts on the local infrastructure. Alpoi has been practising this sort of thing for centuries, with the Golden Stairway to Heaven, and all the temples to every single one of the gods and goddesses. It's so easy that the guides didn't even have to fiddle the exchange rates for any of the strange currencies."

There was a sound of cascading dandruff as Twa scratched his head.

"But we ain't got no temples or rich staircases. Loot is a major marsh and mud city, with mucky higgledy-piggledy streets and a fall-down shanty town.. The only interesting bits were closed down by the Lifers – for being too regressively interesting. "

Fyrsil tried not to look too blankly at Twa. It had seemed a simple deal when they had first trudged in from the marshes. He would teach Twa the rudiments of tourism so that he could establish a trading monopoly, and in return the ex-pirate would help him get a ship together with a crew prepared to save Glob by enrolling to attack Murk. Simple really – rather like horse-trading.

As with horse-trading, where you rarely bought what you bargained for, it looked unlikely that Fyrsil's side of the deal would ever materialise. Excluding the high possibility of being unable to get across the rudimentary principle of tourism to Twa, the other main factor was that piratical ways were out of fashion in Loot. Permanently. There was no sign of their adventurous past on the faces of the citizens of the pirate citadel. Where shops once displayed wares of devices for maximum mutilation, they had now proudly presented their vegetarian wholemeal dispensary services. Ship chandlers now sold nothing resembling tar, cordage, or big brass fittings which no one knew the use for. Instead they stocked home-made baskets, pots that didn't stand up straight, and wobbly clay goblets.

"Now, souvenirs – explain them again laddie," Twa said as they got onto the last of the headings on his list of notes.

"Any tasteless, useless article with the name of Loot written across it in large bright letters. To be a proper souvenir, it has got to be something that tourists are embarrassed to admit buying when they get back home," Fyrsil replied quickly, wanting to wrap up his part of the bargain as quickly as possible.

He felt the Being Stone through his tunic, and could almost feel the inky blue fingers creeping through the stone, as its yellow glow of hope diminished.

"That it, then? Must say, seems awful simple to me," Twa said, caressing his carbuncle confidently.

"Good. Now how about finding a likely crew of swashbucklers to help save the planet. All that's needed is a bit of a sense of adventure, taste for the spice of life, and the advantage is that it's all in a good cause – self-preservation."

"What's that then?"

"Our agreement: Ship and crew and all the things that sail in her for a successful mission."

"Oh-ho-ho, you're still on about that. 'Fraid that people round here are all afeared at just the mention of weighing anchor, let alone the saving the planet mularky. All them hearty shipmates are nowheres to be found – unless it is tending lettuces on their allotments."

Fyrsil had been sure that it would not have taken much to rescue the former perpetrators of most crimes known to humanity (and several that were not) to forsake their drab existence, and have a last assignation with excitement. He had been wrong, and the Bobo took great delight in underlining the miscalculation.

He had canvassed the new beancurd bars, trying to solicit encouraging grunts from the fiercest looking customers sipping at their morning mossweed beverage. The big men backed off as if he had the plague.

In desperation, he had stood with the Bobo and the Comfy Chair by the fountains in the middle of one of Loot's octagonal squares and tried open bribery with the proceeds of the Chocoholic treasury vault. There were no takers. Material wealth was dirtier than the sewage system that kept on breaking down under the city streets.

Even the chair looked down cast as they had woven their way back to Twa's authentic pirate shack which was undergoing alterations in preparation for its grand opening as a luxury hostelry. The Bobo, accompanied by a loitering Boac, had stomped off muttering through its beak about doing something useful.

Fyrsil looked despondently at his plate and the truly inedible leaves of mulching vegetation that were wilting there.

He empathised with their wilting, and guilty for that empathy. So he went of for a sandal-dragging wander along Loot's myriad maze of crooked thoroughfares, and felt relieved that he was pounced upon by a group of weird looking men in beards and utility sackcloth robes.

Whatever they were going to do to him couldn't be any worse than sitting in despair while the planet plunged towards self-destruction.

XIII

The light of the two pink suns that rose everyday over Loot squeezed through the fortified tinted glass of the window and lay limply among the calming pastel shades of the Tranquillity Room at the Aggression Rehab Centre.

"Take the worm. All day he travels freely through the ground and the muckheaps as he digs his hole, not bothering anyone or anything. The worm doesn't hit or mutilate its fellow worms. It lives in harmony with its companions and its environment..."

"Until it becomes breakfast and gets chomped by a big bird with a hungry beak," a raucous voice interrupted through a rattle of chains.

The faintest ripple of a frown appeared on the smooth domed forehead of the stringy Lifer standing in the centre of the circle of foam chairs. The pastel shades of the chairs had been chosen to complement those on the padded coverings of the walls. They were not the colours for frowns. Neither were they the colours of loud and rude remarks. The different shades had been selected after extensive studies to encourage peace and meditative interaction.

"The worm is just an illustration of how to live a harmonious life, without aggression, without anger, and so we can all make a useful contribution to the ecological chain that makes up the complex - yet balanced - equation of life on this common sod of earth in our sea of mud," the Lifer continued undaunted.

"What do you want us to do next? Grow roots and live in a hole in the ground pretending to be a manglewurzel?" asked someone from the circle, who looked like a couple of large animated pumpkins with a face like a Halloween mask. His harsh orange skin clashed horribly with the bright red pantaloons tied with a mauve sash, and the very curly green slippers he wore on his feet.

"Umm, that would be preferable to your previous behaviour," said the Lifer, as he fiddled with straggling hairs of his spade beard which every Lifer grew to prove their commitment to vegetation.

Looking around the occupants of the chairs, the uncharitable thought sometimes crossed his mind that he was glad that they were all shackled by unbreakable chains to toughened steel rings set in the floor. He was also glad that the chains were short enough to ensure that he was always out of reach of this motley collection of desperadoes still clinging to attitudes of the old culture.

He was there to bring them into the fold of the New Way, but even an optimistic assessment of their progress could only class it as erratic. One session would see him exulting in the ability of miserable sinners seeing the light and taking to the teachings of the New Way. Then it would all go horribly wrong, and it would be back to barbaric square one. Like now.

"...So some idiot can come along with a spade, lop my head off, then chops me up in one of them vegetable regg-a-tagg-a-gooeys we keep on being fed," the pumpkin-faced pirate continued on his ranting line of reasoning.

"What a thought – ending my days with a veritable collection of lentils and cabbages in a stew pot. Bit like this collection of suet duffs I have to keep the company with in this prison cell."

A chorus of boos and rattling of chains rattled the Lifer, as he cowered in the centre of the circle.

"I'd rather have my gizzard nailed to a post," shouted the enraged pumpkin over the noise. Ugh! It makes a good pirate want to vomit with abandon."

The tranquillity of the Lifer's expression clouded over, and he tried to arrange his face to give it a stern expression. Being born with a countenance that reminded anyone who cared to be, of the soppiest of cuddly toys, made this a difficult task.

"Now, now Big-Gulop if you keep on failing to renounce your barbaric animalistic affinities and attitudes, you will have to have a reforming spell in the Solitary Meditation Unit."

"Is that a punishment? I am truly sorely afraid. If you are going to do something properly in the punishment department a little more vigour is needed. I could do with a good whipping whilst hung by the toenails. That would be a good diversion from these ghastly walls, and same ghastly company."

"That is a very regressionist thought, and you've been doing so well Cuffbert," the Lifer shot a worried look at the stunningly dapper figure in a well tailored blazer and cavalry twills, with a cravat secured by an elegant stick pin of a skull and cross bones.

"Captain Cuffbert to you! By gum and damnation I would have had you flayed for such presumption."

A natural arrogance sat easily on his finely chiselled features, which he drew attention to with a quick flick of his midnight curls that flounced in front of his eyes.

"Besides, to use your phraseology it is environmental conditioning. Papa said I must earn my way to lead the most exclusive buccaneer band on Loot. Joining the company at the bottom meant taking the whippings like any other social climbing member of the crew. One becomes accustomed to excess, and come to miss it when it's not there," Cuffbert explained happily, while carefully re-arranged his gilded chains so he could cross his legs more elegantly.

"So if you would be so kind Paxo, anytime you're feeling at a loose end just pop along and a deal out a good thrashing, there's a good chap," he said fixing the Lifer with a charming smile.

"I do wish you would behave," the Lifer huffed, tugging at his beard. "We have a new member of the discussion group here today, and I was hoping the occasion would make you rethink your positions and show some progress towards peaceable behaviour."

"Now Fyrsil, you are not to take any notice of all this. The group has made great leap forwards in past sessions, and this obviously a temporary relapse," Brother Pacis addressed the trussed Fyrsil to try and regain control of the proceedings.

Fyrsil nodded. He couldn't say anything because his mouth had been taped to prevent any dangerous vocal emissions. The Aggression Rehab Centre manager, in between meditation chants had decided that even a mention of language such as 'raid' could lead to behavioural difficulties amongst the New Way study group.

He remembered when he had first been forcibly admitted, and had been considered so dangerous that he had been put immediately in a Solitary Meditation Unit, tied into a straight jacket. A candelabra in the ceiling burned with the light of its 100 sweating candles. The only visitors were a succession of Lifers for intensive counselling sessions.

Occasionally novice Lifers peeked through the grille on the door, to witness the ultimate regressionist sinner who had tried to incite enthusiasm for a new raid.

A clipboard hung on a nail by the door monitored the progress of his counselling sessions, and resembled a ragged mountain range as he floundered in the downward drift of telling the truth, until he discovered that the only way up was flagrant fibbing.

At first it seemed ridiculous to admit murdering all the cattle on the Fever Islands, teaching mosquitoes to bite, and forcing dogs to chase cats in dark alleys. After a time, purely out of a sense of rhythm Fyrsil started agreeing to alternate accusations.

"Real progress at last," the interviewing Lifer told him at the end of one flagrant steam of lies.

It seemed the reward for his flights of fancy would be admittance to group therapy. For Fyrsil in a state of inverted suspension, anything was better than watching inky hues creeping into the sky as he peered through narrow bars at the occasional fluffy lemon cloud.

Finally by confessing to selling fraudulent shares in the Sea of Blood Water company on the stock exchange at Metroslix through a shell offshore company, did he make the breakthrough.

The Lifer was positively slavering as he made his notes on this heinous crime.

And so chained and gagged Fyrsil was allowed back into some sort of society, and was watching Brother Pacis trying to progress ex-pirates into useful social vegetables.

"Look, guys – oh of course gals as well - I'm here to help you help yourselves. Unless you co-operate you won't be able to relate to each other as rounded beings, and integrate back into the new society as a useful and positive member of the community."

In an attempt to regain control, Brother Pacis launched in to a confession session, but his group seemed in a funny mood. Every time he asked an ex-pirate to confess sins against Life and the New Way, within the first couple of sentences it was howled down by a chorus of "Heard it!" and "Boring!" until there was group stamping and clapping, demanding to give the new boy a chance.

Against his better judgement, he was heckled into un-taping Fyrsil's mouth, just to hear a fresh confession.

Regret was written over Brother Pacis' face as Fyrsil launched into a story he had been working on during extra dull moments of his detention. It was such a sophisticated web of fabricated fibs that any spider would have got lost without a proper map. A roar of applause and foot stamping from the study group greeted the traditional phrase signifying the end of a confessional. Pacis had gone a paler shade of pallid as he nearly retched in disgust before he heard the final words of "...I admit I am a criminal against Life."

Apart from the Lifer's reaction, the critical acclaim took Fyrsil aback, and he stood to take a bow, and promptly fell over, tangled in his chains.

XIV

The once gaudy paint on the topsides of the high-sided galleons was forlornly faded and peeling. Old sails flapped dirty and neglected at the yardarms, and figureheads drooped dejectedly on once proud prows of ships that were now stuck in the mud like a school of beached whales.

"Who owns these boats?" the Bobo asked Boac as they stood on the deserted quayside.

"Them be ships, but it be difficult to say who do own them now. Marooned and deserted, with no one wanting 'em no more. I've 'eard that the Port Authority still wanted their mooring fees, but it is difficult trying to find the old captains when everyone has turned to the New Way.

"Those not in the Aggression Rehab Centre changed their names and denied all past deeds anyway. Probably explains why the Port Authority is bankrupt now."

"So there would be no objections to taking vacant possession of one of these hulks."

"I bain't saying that. Someone always sees to mind anything 'ee do these days," Boac replied sourly.

The Bobo strutted up and down in thought, followed in its tracks with the Comfy Chair swinging its tassels at every turn.

"We can't sail away, because there's no water. There must be another way," the Bobo thought out loud.

"Well knock me down with a wet haddock if I can think of anything," Boac said helpfully, scratching his head in support. He looked wistfully across the bay at the wooden walls of the ships he had once sailed. He sat down on a bollard, and tried to look like an ancient mariner with tall stories to tell, but just looked like a bored ex-pirate without a pension.

The chair was flapping its cushion excitedly at something out in the harbour. The Bobo folowed the general direction it seemed to be indicating.

"Umm, yes, I think that could solve the problem nicely, thanks to a little help from this rather clever bit of furniture," the Bobo decided, stroking the bottom of his beak sagely.

"What be 'ee doin?" asked Boac, roused out of his pose.

"Climb aboard. We're going for a little hover over the mud to recce a particularly attractive looking craft."

"Well bump my bunyons," said Boac in a conspiratorial whisper, and jumped aboard the chair with the Bobo.

The war bird pressed a sequence of buttons on the Comfy Chair's remote. A whooshing of air lifted the chair's skirts, and with a hum from its innards they floated off the end of the provisioning pier to skim amongst the relics of what was once the most feared fleet on Glob.

XV

As the door closed behind the departing Lifer, the room was filled with a clatter of jangling chains dropping from wrists and ankles, as secreted hairpins and favourite bits of bent wire worked their trick in fractions of seconds.

Trying to chain down veterans of more jails, hangmen's nooses, and other sticky situations than most people change their underpants, was never going to be very realistic. But the inmate study group found it more amusing to let the Lifers think they were safely manacled – they anticipated that there would always be the possibility of going back out into the outside world when the rest of Loot had come to its senses again.

The only person who remained wrapped in his chains was Fyrsil, who was busily wondering what was going to happen next. He had presumed that he would have been escorted back to his lonely cell, and so wanted to make the most of being out of isolation.

He wriggled un-noticed on the floor, making grunting noises to try and solicit some help in getting out of his straight jacket. But the other members of the therapy class made no effort in recognising his existence at all. They were too busy re-arranging their chairs to face a blank wall, while Captain Cuffbert nonchalantly stepped over Fyrsil's writhing body to press an indiscernible spot on the wallpaper. A secret panel slid aside to reveal a large screen, which jumped to life with a fuzzy picture once Big-Gulop had fished a remote control device from his voluminous pantaloons.

After plenty of button pushes, the screen filled with the image of cartoon characters chasing, hitting, and generally bashing each other.

"One of my best raids in retrospect. Never into home entertainment myself, but a full warehouse was a full warehouse, and there's no denying the quality of the goods in store," said one of the ex-pirates who seemed to have an identity crisis. Outside his skin tight black lycra bodystocking he wore bright red underpants. His seaboots were polished to perfection, including the silver buckles, over his shoulders was draped a daffodil yellow cape, and over his head was clamped a funny wide-brimmed hat.

If Fyrsil could have seen his breast patch, he would have been able to read **The Masked Marauder** under a lightning logo. That little detail passed him by, as at that particular moment Fyrsil was wondering who had kicked him in the ribs.

A giant shadow had fallen over the trussed hapless hero on the floor. Squinting from behind his shades, Fyrsil looked up at a mountain of muscle lightly concealed in flesh.

"What are you doing down there? If you were so damn heroic on your supposed exploits, it would be no problem to get out of a simple straight jacket and chains," the giant demanded.

"Not really my *forte*. Escapology was not one of the subjects I majored in at buccaneering college," Fyrsil replied, hoping that there was an educational establishment on Glob that specialised in those sort of career courses. "You couldn't give me a hand to get these things off, could you?"

"You ever heard of Groggie, the most fearsome, teeth-rattlin', fantastic and spectacular of pirates ever to tread the timbers of a marauding pirate galleon?"

Fyrsil wondered whether it was a trick question. "No," he said at last, wondering whether he had made the right choice of his 50:50 option.

"Ah," said Groggie. "In that case you wouldn't know that no one ever asked favours of Groggie the Giant, except to plead for mercifully quick despatch before being skewered on my cutlass."

With his adam's apple bobbing from multiple gulps, Fyrsil admitted that he indeed was not aware of that sort of information.

The lumbering lips split into a lopsided grin from amongst an uncontrolled bush of beard.

"Well, just this once I will help 'ee. But don't you ask me of anything more."

Without the big man seeming to tweak a tendon, Fyrsil felt himself tossed up in the air in a series of back twisting arcs, and land on a pile of chains and his discarded straight jacket.

"Wow!" said Fyrsil fatuously, once he had regained some of the breath that had been knocked out of him.

"Just something everyone picks up from Mad Harry in the dungeons of Scummdumage. He didn't like jackets or chains or restrainers, and no one could keep him in them for longer than it takes to squash a slug." Groggie shrugged his shoulders and made a grunt that made Fyrsil aware that it was a simple thing to do.

The big face then leered dangerously close to Fyrsil's nose, and in a conspiratorial voice demanded: "You didn't sell the Blood Sea shares did you? So if you would like to take off those shades for a minute, you can tell me exactly what you are doing in Loot."

By this time Fyrsil had gathered that the giant Groggie was not one of the gentle variety.

"OK," said Fyrsil meekly, and told him everything. Well, of course, not everything, but starting sensibly from being a security guard at Heaven to his stay with the Chocoholics and the brush with the Gastrognomes.

"...And so I came to Loot to recruit a crew of pirates full of dash and daring-do, to help save the world and put a bit of plunder in their pocket and liquor in their bellies."

He looked at Groggie strangely. The big man had tears streaming down his face.

Unable to contain himself anymore, the giant let a loud hoot and fell over backwards in laughter.

A communal "sssh" came from the lips of those trying to concentrate on the cartoon.

"What's so funny?" asked a miffed Fyrsil.

Gulping for breath between the whooping guffaws, a tear-blinded Groggie managed to splutter a barely understandable sentence along the lines of: "you saving the world?...just look at you!"

Fyrsil did. He looked down at his body. It looked the same as it always had – nothing special, but none the worst for that. And suddenly he quite inexplicably flipped. Whether it was a manifestation of Solitary Cell Syndrome, or a momentary blip in his behavioural pattern, he was never able to establish properly. The result was Fyrsil found himself ranting uncontrollably.

"What's wrong with me saving the world? I've got all the equipment. Look!" he shouted as opened the bumbag, and dug deep. He pulled out the Shield of Righteousness with a very trendy bright protective covering, a complicated anti-bugging device, some X-Large thermal underwear, and the scroll from Hap commanding everyone on Glob to assist Fyrsil in his task in countless languages.

"And what's more, it is your sacred duty, as decreed by Hap-i-Glob, top god of Heaven, to help me," Fyrsil told the assembled gawpers who found his furious jumping up and down more entertaining than the cartoon.

To make sure Groggie got the message, Fyrsil bounced up and hit him on the head with the scroll.

In the stunned silence that followed, Fyrsil hopped about the centre of the Tranquillity Room, and pulled from the bumbag the Golden Spear of the Good (which got caught in the zip) the most ferocious spearhead and shaft that had ever come into existence. Imbued with so many magical powers that a touch of a particular hieroglyphic could send the spear to kebab a platoon of well armoured soldiery. The sharp pointy end wibbled up and down as it sniffed menacingly, working out the best impaling angles on the various bodies presenting themselves as targets.

"And that goes for you lot as well," said Fyrsil, pointing the Spear of the Good menacingly at the ex-pirates who were too busily trying to appear to be just watching TV.

"How are you going to save the world then, wonder boy?" asked Groggie, feeling the lump on his head caused by the weight of a thousand languages.

"We're um…we're going to start off by, going down to the harbour, taking a galleon, and sailing off to attack Murk."

"The ships won't be going nowhere. They be stuck in the mud, as fast as fast can be, 'cos the sea's all gorn, and without the sea we ain't going nowhere neither," a voice from the crowd argued.

"We'll cross that bridge when we come to it."

"There are no bridges in Loot. They were all symbolically burnt," the Masked Marauder remarked pedantically, gyrating his hips to make his point.

"Sounds more fun than baiting Lifers," Captain Cuffbert considered aloud. "Any fighting involved, and you can count me in."

"Lots of fighting, and when we get the golden Orbs back to Heaven, or anything else you want. One hundred and ten per cent guaranteed."

"Absolutely spiffing. Count me in old chap, sounds absolutely tip-top hole," the dapper pirate said with relish. "And me," "and me" echoed around the Tranquillity Room for anti-aggression therapy.

"If there's Knock Out punch with ice, I'm your man," Peg piped above the general din, stamping her wooden leg and making gestures with her power dressing shoulder pads.

"Right let's go," declared Captain Cuffbert. "It's domestic science lessons in half an hour, and I want to be down on the quay by then. Follow me!"

Pushing past the TV he disappeared into the wall with running feet following behind him.

"The palsy-brained fool has gone the wrong way. Follow me!" shouted the Masked Marauder, as he pushed a particular pastel flower on the wall paper and disappeared down another secret passage, with those slow off the mark stampeding behind the fluttering cape.

"Shouldn't they be following me? I'm the leader," Fyrsil asked no one in particular, as they had all left by secret passages that had immediately gone into hiding again. So Fyrsil used the door out of the Tranquillity Room, and wandered down the corridor until he found a lift. He pressed the down button and waited.

The doors opened, and a gaggle of excited looking Lifers scrambled out, pushing past Fyrsil, and dashed up the corridor opening and slamming doors, and shouting at each other as they looked for the escaped ex-pirates.

So Fyrsil walked quickly into the lift and pressed the button for the ground floor.

The lift made its little ting, telling Fyrsil that they were at ground level. He peered out of the doors, and started walking towards the doors marked EXIT. It seemed the only sensible thing to do, and he had no one else to ask.

"Oi!" called a semi-recumbent form of life from behind the reception desk.

"Where do you think you are going?" the receptionist bawled, and donned his official Lifer felt hat to emphasise his authority.

"Out," Fyrsil said, unconfidently, feeling like a startled rabbit in a spotlight.

"Oh," said the receptionist. "Alright. If you're allowed – I suppose. Going to set up a self-help group then, like everyone else," he sneered.

"The P-p-p-persecuted P-p-p-pirates P-p-p-p-pride and Discovery Co-operative Discussion and Self-advancement Group, to be exact," Fyrsil stuttered in disbelief, as he realised he was going to be allowed to just walk out.

This was the first time anyone who was not part of the staff had ever tried to leave the centre, and so the receptionist was not quite sure how to deal with it.

"Well in that case, fill out form L26b, regarding change of status and a forwarding address."

"Righty-ho," said Fyrsil, looking confused.

After a lot of slapping of piles of paper on the desk, the receptionist adjusted his hat and declared: "Err, I think that's it. Never done this before…"

At that moment, a wall, or at least part of it, with an explosion of noise and rubble, fell out into the foyer into a cunningly crafted stairway, down which fell a pile of pirates.

"What about that lot; anything to do with you?" the receptionist gesticulated at the bodies lying untidily all over the floor.

"Yes. Yes they are actually. Other members of the self-help group," said Fyrsil, a bit more confidently. "Do you want me to sign them out? Writing to discover the inner self is one of the main focuses of the group focus. A signature is more than most can manage at the moment, though."

Appearing from a silently removed slab in the floor, the Masked Marauder and his followers were crawling towards the double front doors.

"And that lot as well, I suppose," the receptionist sighed, resigned to it being one of those days.

Fyrsil glanced out of the corner of his eye and nodded. Finishing with a flourish of his quill, he slapped the paper in front of the receptionist.

"Right-ho, let's move out," said Fyrsil, trying to lead out the party of squabbling pirates, all elbowing to be at the front of the procession.

Once outside, the therapy group who had volunteered to save the planet were afforded the squalid panoramic view of Loot, which could only be seen from the vantage point of the Rehab Centre. It was the only building on top of a sheer face rock that leered over the rest of the citadel. No one was interested in that. Their concern was to rush to the cable car to get the best seats for the short trip down.

As the swaying, squabbling contents of the cable car rattled down to its station in the town, the specs of two climbers, linked by rope, stopped picking their way between tiny hand holds up the sheer face of the pillar of rock.

"Oh Murk and all its Messiness."

Instantly the words were whisked away from the Bobo's beak by tumbling groaning zephyrs criss-crossing the rock face. The climbers turned their heads towards the descending cable car.

"What?" called Boac.

"That crowd in the lift includes our glorious leader and saviour of Glob," said the Bobo. "Just typical. Couldn't wait to be rescued, has to break out on his own."

"So what do we do now?"

"Go down," said the Bobo testily, ruffling its feathers in ire.

There was a poignant silence.

"Can't do that," Boac told the bird.

"Why not?"

"Well, like I said, I took the rock climbing course, but gave up half way through, so I only know how climb up. Don't know about getting down."

The Bobo made a face that said a lot of things – none of them complimentary.

"Alright," it said, "let's get to the top, and then take the cable car down. But hurry! We better catch up with worthless nam-dam of a security guard before he does something really stupid."

XVI

The crowd of exotically dressed, unreconstructed pirates did not create a stir of interest in the old wharf area of Loot Bay. The reason for this was because it was deserted, and had been since the water had left the shores of Loot.

There had been frisson in the air as Fyrsil tried to lead the therapy group down to the docks to start on their venture of saving Glob. The noise, the excitement and the constant raspberries blown at the slammed doors and drawn curtains that proceeded their procession through the winding streets of the town. Followers of the New Way made the sign of the four fingered asparagus and scurried out of sight as the raucous bunch bustled its way down to the docks.

The reason for the majority of the noise was the barging, cursing, tripping and free use of the elbow to be at the front and lead the way with Fyrsil.

The route from the cable car to the bay of abandoned galleons was a wiggly one, mainly because the only one looking at where they were going was Fyrsil, and he didn't know the way. For the rest of them, those at the front spent all their time looking over their shoulders preventing those at the back from barging their way into pole position.

After the speedy meander though the by-ways and lesser-known alleys of the citadel, more by accident than design, the pedestrian cavalcade came to a halt on the quayside. Once there, they milled around in the way that crowds do when left to their own devices for too long.

The line of empty and decaying warehouses, dusty chandlers chock-a-block with equipment that nobody wanted, was a sobering sight to the collection of ex-pirate chiefs who had known it in its rumbustious heyday.

"Do you remember when...?" moped the Masked Marauder.

"Don't. I know. To think that it could all come to this," sniffed Big Gulop, wiping a crimson tear from his pumpkin face.

They looked out at skeletons of once proud vessels, which had been stripped of their timbers to build sturdy potting sheds for the growing allotments on the outskirts of the city.

"So what do we do now?" asked Groggie.

"Dunno," was the universal reply, and they all looked at Fyrsil, who tried to look like he knew what to do, but didn't.

He shrugged his shoulders.

"It's obvious. Find a galleon that's seaworthy, and prepare it to sail away. You're the experts, so I will leave this bit up to you."

There were a couple of blank expressions because of the odds of the Blood Sea returning to sail out on were very long. But as it was all part of the job description of a pirate to achieve the impossible and turn up where they were least expected, a few rusty cogs started turning, and thoughtful expressions covered the faces of most of the assembled band.

Doing the most sensible thing, Peg found an abandoned sedan chair and put her feet up. Others looked at their feet, some struck up poses reminiscent of mariners when spinning yarns, while a small group toyed with the puzzle of getting to the nearest mud-locked galleon using two barrels, a couple of planks, and a pulley.

"Lash the two planks, and tie them to the first barrel, and then using a tripod with the pulley..."

"You can't use a tripod, it's not in the rules," the Masked Marauder told Groggie, who was outlining his ideas to anyone who was interested.

"What do you mean rules?"

"We're playing that leadership initiative game that all management executives play in Monolith on their annual compulsory business survival courses."

"Blow me down with a wild west wind, this is no time for fripperies. I am making practical suggestions to get us onto a ship, and you stand on sidelines quibbling about rules. There's no time like the present, and no time for a committee if we are going to get seriously stuck in to having some fun," Groggie told anyone who would listen.

"Committees have always worked in the past. It's tradition, and they often throw up good ideas. For example, ideas like: a scavenging party should be organised to find planks and barrels to erect a permanent walkway," the Masked Marauder insisted.

The big giant of a pirate and the man with the corny comic-book outfit were squaring up for a heated discussion when an "Oi!" squawked very loudly announced the arrival of the Bobo, bursting into view in a flurry of perspiring feathers, with Boac loping easily behind.

Fyrsil, for once, was pleased to see his multi-coloured companion from Heaven.

"What do you mean by rescuing yourself. If someone takes the trouble of trying to rescue someone else, the least that someone else can do is hang about and so they can look pleased and appreciative when they are rescued."

Even Groggie stopped trying to work out how to swing the planks into place on the barrels, as the Bobo fluttered its feathers angrily.

"I thought that as Heaven's official HERO, I was the one who was meant to be doing heroic things, exactly like escaping from inescapable prisons and fortresses. Like the Aggression Rehab Centre, for one very large 'for instance'."

"You signed yourself out under the pretence of setting up a self-help group for ex-pirates," the Bobo said in a tone of voice that indicated that it was not impressed by Fyrsil's feat of escaping from the Rehab Centre with a crew of volunteers.

"Same sort of thing," said Fyrsil huffily. "It was a cunning ruse."

"I'm not going to argue. It's just not something a Bobo would have done. Now, what's going on here?"

Fyrsil explained that they were milling around while Groggie tried to make a couple of planks and a barrel stretch to the nearest galleon. He pointed in the direction of the galleon in question, which almost on purpose slipped over on its side with a tremendous slap, sending mud flying into the air.

The Bobo gave a withering look.

"While you have been lounging around, watching TV and chatting all day, me and Boac have been hard at work. We have found an appropriate ship, and with a few more adjustments, and some provisioning we will be ready to leave in a couple of days."

A cheer went up from the crew.

"So instead of tangling yourself in ropes, it would be a good idea if you followed me!" the Bobo said.

It then led the recent inmates of the Rehab Centre down to the end of the quay, where the down market suppliers of rotten provisions had once sold foodstuffs well beyond their sell-by date, onto a zig-zagging structure of walkways supported by stilts pushed into the mud.

XVII

The stench of a rotting fish market assaulted Fyrsil's nostrils in waves as it wafted in through the ship's stern windows. He sat in the main cabin of the galley that also doubled as the temporary official HQ of the Ex-Pirate Self Help Group (a measure to keep happy any inspecting officials from the Life Council of Loot, until the secret preparations to set sail were all ready).

The Bobo may have said that all the ship needed was provisioning and victualling before leaving, but there were also one or two technical hitches. While Fyrsil had been incarcerated in the Rehab Centre, the chair had been undergoing tests of the upward propulsion kit, devised and designed by the Bobo, which had been constructed between squawks by Boac.

Fyrsil had been assured that the few teething problems had been ironed out, and only a couple of glitches remained.

More of a problem was persuading the collection of pirate chiefs that a mere galley was a suitably classy mode of transport for such an important body of men. The general consensus was that galleys were for petty commanders, who lacked dash, grandeur, and large ornate cabins to be able to lounge around in. Big gaudy three-masted galleons were the only way to travel once you had got to the top of the buccaneering tree. Individually or in groups they now insisted on telling Fyrsil - backed up by clutches of medals they had awarded themselves, and personally written CVs highlighting their noteworthy raids – that essentially the vessel the Bobo had chosen was not in keeping with their rank and titles amongst the buccaneering fraternity.

"A galley? I'm not setting foot on a galley. I've got a reputation as the biggest high roller on the quayside. I can't be seen to be slumming it in this sort of craft!" Groggie foghorned to everyone loudly, as they had all wobbled down the precarious walkway.

"No self respecting pirate would be seen dead in a galley – mask or no mask. It's for those pipsqueak corsairs and sea scoundrel co-operatives," the Masked Marauder had declared as the Bobo had led them out beyond the grand galleons in the bay of mud.

If the leaders at the front were not going to set foot on the galley, then Boac with all the obstinacy of a barbarian, was not going to turn round along the plank walkway. For one, he was carrying Peg and her sedan chair on his back, and it would be a tricky manoeuvre on the rickety structure of planks and poles.

Surrounded by murky plooping mud, and with a walkway straining to support such a large number of hulking - if expensively dressed – bodies, there was no alternative. To very vocal protests, the band of reprobates made their way reluctantly onto the deck of the galley.

Immediately a pirate council was called to discuss the matter. They sat in a circle on the deck, and to start with decided councils weren't as much fun as they used to be, and decisions were not as easy to make without constant flagons of Knockout punch.

Being called to speak to the council, the Bobo spoke at length about the advantage of a galley over a galleon for the purposes of a raid against Murk.

a)   Because the oars had been stitched together with a canvass covering to make rudimentary wings – because sailing there was out of the question, and so flying was going to be the only option.

b)   All the work had been done to convert the galley into a flying ship, and the Bobo was definitely not going to start again just because it ruffled a few social feathers of passed-it pirating big wigs.

This did not impress the mutinous crew.

What did was the economic argument.

To get back to the quay they would have to use the plank walkway. Boac, as builder and nominal owner, demanded a toll for anyone using it. However loyal members of the crew for the expedition to Murk were offered a free season ticket. As no one had thought of bringing any money with them when they had fled from the rehab centre, and the laundry bills would be extortionate if they reached the quayside, it was decided unanimously to stay on board – for the time being, anyway.

With the ship's company all gathered together, it seemed a good point for Fyrsil to establish a few ground rules – like who was the leader of the gang. He could admit to himself that he did not have the physical bulk of Groggie, or the frightening bright orange demeanour of Big Gulop, but he had other qualities that meant he should occupy the top job with no squabbling. Fyrsil thought about these – but not for too long. They amounted to: having a badge denoting a 'HERO'; being told by Hap to save Glob; being the official security guard for Heaven; and …er, being the only one with a bumbag full of the best weapons that Heaven could provide.

"Ahem," he announced to the assembled crew. "About this leader business…" and outlined his compelling reasons for commanding respect and some semblance of obedience.

Fyrsil paused. The ship's company were all looking attentive, but not at him.

"Who is in charge here?" asked a dry voice from behind him.

On the gangplank stood a Lifer, holding a briefcase and clipboard. On his yellow bowler hat was pinned a badge with the feared word of 'Inspector' printed on it.

Fyrsil found all fingers pointing at him.

This he recognised was another problem. Of all the words that always struck the most fear into the hearts of dastardly reprobate pirates, it was always 'INSPECTOR' that left them quivering. A pirate was always up to no good, and inspectors, by their nature were there to make sure no good was not being got up to. With the coming of the New Way they had become feared, as armed with forms and different coloured pens, they slapped banning orders on any activity that was not in the spirit of the peace and harmony of the New Way and the Life Community.

Although Fyrsil had wanted to establish himself as leader, it was primarily to ensure that he got the best bunk in the ship. Signing forms in triplicate was not one of the attractions, nor was taking responsibility for knowing the duties and requirements of running a voluntary sector group.

The spade beard of the Lifer seemed pedantically aggressive, as it waggled up and down on the chin as staccato questions were fired off about the Ex-Pirate Self Help Group.

"Has the self-help group a Constitution or Articles of Association?"

Fyrsil shook his head sheepishly, and a black mark was noted on the inspector's form.

"Before entering into an association, had the LZw1590 been filled in and completed for submission, and notices posted in Loot, for the requisite period of time on recognised billing sites?"

"Hem," Fyrsil answered, and felt it was not really enough. He was under pressure, which grew as the list of crosses against requirements grew.

"…And how will the group contribute to the well being of the community as a whole?"

"Ermm…by encouraging otherwise potentially aggressive citizens to work through their violent urges by constructive projects and activities," answered Fyrsil, getting the hang of the vocabulary required for this sort of conversation.

The Lifer wasn't impressed.

"And what would those be?" he hissed almost maliciously.

Fyrsil looked at the crew on deck.

"Investigation and identification of edible mud for the production and sale of Fever Island mud pies as a useful contribution to the society of Loot, and as a therapeutic dispersion of aggressive tendencies through the positive process of creation."

"Ah! Have you a licence to sell to the public digestible foodstuffs?"

Wondering whether a licence was needed to sell indigestible foodstuffs, Fyrsil answered the Lifer inspector. "No, but we are only at the initial stage of testing and putting together a marketing plan to survey the consumer tastes and needs. Market testing will commence after several pilot products have been fully developed."

The inspector's face fell. He was not used to credible responses to his inquisitions, and so could only grudgingly inform Fyrsil to apply for a licence and make the premises available to inspection by the Department of Public Hygiene For Comestible Vendors.

The beard wagged up and down.

A soft splatt of something soft and unpleasant landing on the bowler hat interrupted the scratching of the Lifer's notes.

"Well, hang, flog and keelhaul me rotten! The jumbo gronk seagull," cried Boac excitedly as a teeth-rattling shrill cry filled the air. "Very rare for these parts it be; wingspan five foot; usually found only in colonies on abandoned liferafts in the Blood Sea. They have never been seen in Loot before – except once as part of a casserole." Excitedly he reeled off the breeding and feeding habits of the big sea bird that was strutting around the crow's-nest at the top of the mast.

The inspector's expression softened as he looked up, and watched the big bird scuff and peck at the platform high up in the rigging.

"Isn't life wonderful," the inspector declared, as he wiped tears of joy from his cheek. "The first jumbo gronk, and it personally tells me that it has found sanctuary here in Loot. It's all very touching. It has touched me with its essence of life."

He put away his clipboard and told Fyrsil to make the appropriate applications, and to collect a ream of forms that should only be filled out after carefully reading the accompanying leaflets. Lost in wonder he tottered off down the walkway in search of other transgressors of regulations.

"Strikes me, the sooner we weigh anchor and are off to Murk the better. I've no liking for this kind of poxy insanity," Big Gulop told anyone who would listen.

"The longer we remain here, the more pestilent meddlers will put their big noses where they shouldn't be. They'll be asking for a flying licence next," the Masked Marauder joined in, and struck a pose to show that he was putting his oar in.

"Or what's in the stew," said Groggie, looking at the gronk and smacking his lips.

In a rare moment of solidarity to a very distant avian cousin, the Bobo squashed the idea of jumbo gronk for supper.

"If there's a bird in the stew, then this bird doesn't fly. And if this bird doesn't fly, then you're stuck in the mud," it said emphatically.

There was a miserable nod of heads around the deck.

"Um, we will probably need a plan if we are going to fly off to Murk," suggested Fyrsil tentatively.

There were cries of amazement as the ex-pirates slapped their foreheads in wonder.

"Cor, he's a deep one, a thinker more like," said a scrofulous shape who had forgotten his name after being marooned on a deserted island for 15 years, but generally answered to Capt'n Crud.

Pirate plans were generally rather loose affairs: beyond the horizon there were thousands of cities and countries just begging to be stripped of all their treasures. Sail in any direction for long enough and a ship was bound to bump into at least one, so best be getting on with it, rather than waste time talking about it.

Spontaneity was the key to most of these ventures, and that usually did not involve much planning. In fact the most common spur for a raid was a couple too many drinks in the tavern with some cronies, and the next thing a pirate knew, they were in the middle of the Blood Sea under full sail, heading for who knows where with a stonking headache.

So when Fyrsil mentioned the need for a PLAN the pirate chiefs were taken aback. It was almost a forgotten word in Loot, and one that was used as often as beef dripping in cooking since the New Way.

In a hap-hazard way Fyrsil detailed various bodies to different tasks while he drew up a draft plan, which would be put to a Raid Council for approval. He conceded to this part of Loot's piratical tradition. But as traditionally that never took place until they were well at sea (to allow for hangover recovery) any worries about the council could wait.

Without Fyrsil making any attempt at task allocation, his crew busily set about organising themselves into search parties to requisition the necessities for a raid. That was fine with Fyrsil, who went below to his library he had retrieved from the Comfy Chair so he could put his nose into his books for some solid research. Hunting out facts about Murk, and obscure maps of its topography, would make a pleasant diversion from trying to work out a plan that no one in his crew would take any notice of.

XVIII

A gentle wind blew across the stern of the galley, ruffling the papers spread over the table in the master cabin. Ten neat piles of parchment lay on the table, with the top leaf of each marked with various titles in neat copperplate script. There was the *Plan for Flying To Murk*; *The Plan For The Attack Of Castle Gloom*; *The Plan In Case The First Plan Did Not Work*; and more than a few others in note form on the back of old bits of parchment.

At that moment Fyrsil was sat at the table, fingers in pages of books spread out in a fan in front of him, sorting additional reference piled at his feet with his toes. He was working on the *Plan To Effect Lift Off From The Mud*. Picking through a tome taken from the library of the Golden Palace, his fingers stopped running along the line of script, and he scratched his quill quickly over the fine parchment. Hurriedly scattering sand over the drying ink, he rushed with flapping toga out onto the quarter deck.

"I have a plan!" he announced to the slumped figures around the deck of the recently renamed *Rover Woof-Woof*. (The collective pride of buccaneering big wigs, however ex- they might be in active terms, had insisted on a change from *The Jolly Rowlock*. Unfortunately as imagination was not a pirate strong point, they opted for a name much in vogue at the time of the Party to End All Parties. *Rover Woof-Woof* it was.)

A rasping noise from Big Gulop's funereal rendition of a hornpipe tune on his harmonica led the chorus of groans from the lolloping crew scattered about the deck.

"Not another one!" they moaned.

"No, no, listen. This is a *very* good plan."

"That's what you said about the last one," groaned Groggie as he carved an intricate whistle from a block of recyclable horn substitute.

An air of stale inactivity squatted along the length and breadth of the galley. The first buzz of activity in converting the sea-going vessel for flight had been quickly and efficiently carried out under the directions of the Bobo. After the polishing of all brass knobbly bits, splicing halyards, and lashing various items in the right place, there was little else to do. The oars had been lengthened, strengthened and strutted according to the Bobo's aeronautic stress ratios, and heavily cured tarpaulin sewn onto these outriggers to create stiffly flappable wings. The mechanics of this operation had been linked to the internal workings of the chair for powered uplift and forward power in flight. A new mizzen mast had been stepped, with its sail linked to the wheel so the ship could be steered while in flight, and the big lateen sail was repaired and patched up to let the Comfy Chair have a rest if it started wheezing under the strain.

At intervals among all this activity, Fyrsil had been running out of the master cabin with various 'plans'. While not adverse to a bit of forward thinking to avoid foolhardiness, the pirates of Loot were not used to this 'planning in detail' malarkey. The main reason was to avoid any blame if things went wrong, as being hung off the yard arm by erstwhile shipmates was not a good career move for an ambitious pirate.

As far as they could see, the major problem was that the *Rover Woof-Woof* was stuck in the mud. No amount of slopping around in the reddish-black sticky morass seemed to be able to pop the galley from its gooey berth. Ropes and pulleys failed to budge it. The first experimental flaps of the chair-driven wings on the *Rover Woof-Woof* didn't even produce a tremble towards lift off. And the explosive option of small charges of gunpowder buried in the mud to break the suction grip only achieved an extra busy wash day for both pirates and clothes.

As the catalogue of attempts to get airborne rose, so the moral of the crew sunk. Even Fyrsil could sense this, and he spent most of his time with his head buried in books – an activity viewed with extreme suspicion by the pirates, whose only use for books in the past had been to stoke up the fire during the celebration feast at the end of yet another good sacking of a bastion of civilization.

"Looking at the problem of flight delays, I have broken it down into elements," Fyrsil announced to his troops tentatively. "First the ship is stuck in the mud. Secondly the Comfy Chair cannot flap its wings fast enough for the vertical lift needed. Thirdly, which results from the first two, we need to create that necessary whumph to be break free of the mud berth."

"How, pray, is that to be achieved?" asked a laconic Captain Cuffbert, his slumped disinterested body sunk in bilious pantaloons of sheer velvet.

"Air. Very light air, captured in sacks, and strapped to the hull. Then once the ship is hovering, the chair starts flapping the wings, and its up-up-and-away!"

Howls of laughter danced across the deck, colliding into bulwarks, coiled warps, and anything else hanging around as nautical clutter.

"And where are we going to get this floating air?" Big-Gulop demanded through his hoarse guffaws.

There was more than a short dramatic pause, as Fyrsil shuffled his sandals and managed not to look anyone in the eye.

"You! A collective you... I've read all about how to do it."

It seemed a considerable time before every pirate worth his salt had stopped rolling around the deck, and wiped his tears of laughter from his face.

Striking a dramatic pose with one foot on the aft hold hatch, Fyrsil continued when he thought he had his crew's attention again.

"Methane bean flatulence," he announced bravely.

A sea of puzzled faces looked at the gangly squirt who was about to lead them on the most ambitious raid in Loot's far from glorious history. They looked at each other, as the toga-wearing bean pole went red as a beetroot and squirmed in trying to give a proper explanation of his plan.

"From here," Fyrsil said, pointing to his posterior. "We're going to have to fart our way into the sky."

He waited for the resumed hilarity to die down, which took an inordinate amount of time as it seemed that the whole idea had hit the pirates' collective funny bone.

"Trust me," Fyrsil told them. "It's all very scientific."

Unfortunately the two things that any apprentice privateer would tell you distrust when starting out on a career as a seawolf were: the phrase 'trust me', and science. Both usually required a good kick to get any sense out of them. But given the option of terminal boredom, or a return to the Rehab Centre, they were prepared to give anything a try. Once.

In his poring over reference books and encyclopaedias that had been transported from Heaven in the Comfy Chair, Fyrsil had come across the interesting practice of a tribe of nomadic marsh fishers. Known as the Levitaguff people, they began the pre-fishing trip ceremony with a huge feast of methane producing flatulence beans.

The purpose of the ceremony was functional in its most basic form. The fishing technique developed by the tribe was to float over the water on reed platforms suspended in the air by inflated giant toad bladders. By lucky coincidence, the other staple of the Levitaguff tribe was the bean with the extraordinary methane flatulence properties.

How or why anyone should have wanted to discover these properties, was a mystery even to the encyclopaedia containing this nugget of information.

When the prevailing wind was in the right direction, the Levitaguffs used the huge bean feast to perform the communal task of filling the toad bladders. Fyrsil's plan required a slight variation on the purpose, but the technique of placing an inflatable bag over the buttocks to catch the man-made wind seemed tailored for his particular sticky problem. It all seemed to depend on the number of balloons needed for lift off. Not being terribly good at mathematics, Fyrsil did a rough figure, and doubled it – hoping that it would be enough to get *Rover Woof-Woof* unstuck and flying.

"There may just be one problem to this very fine plan, my fine young toga togs. Where are we going to get these beans? I presume you are talking about the Levitaguffs from the delta region of Grungol River, two continents and a few thousand leagues from our jolly party here in the Fever Islands."

Captain Cuffbert glinted his perfect set of teeth in a self-satisfied smile, twisting the ends of his moustache smugly at his pertinent question.

"Ah," said Fyrsil waving his index finger wildly, and waving a piece of parchment. "According to *The Complete Guide To Vegetables And Their Uses on Glob* I have found out there is a very similar bean which grows wild in the marshes around here. My research shows that they were until recently essential eating for top performers of the pyrotechnic dance craze called 'The flaming Bum-bums'."

Big-Gulop's face creased in happy memories of the dance, and the wild parties at which they had originally featured.

Without much prompting from Fyrsil the grinning crew mobilised itself into various activities needed in preparation of lift off. Despite the feeling that he ought to be standing in the middle of the throng waving his hands and shouting orders, everyone seemed to be happy organising themselves. With a shrug of his shoulders he left them to it and went back to the cabin to check his calculations for the number of balloons needed to get airborne.

A search party organised itself and left to sniff out large quantities of beans. Meanwhile the Masked Marauder and Peg headed up the balloon section, stitching sail cloth remnants into airtight receptacles for bottie gases.

The Bobo, who had been ashore scavenging for leather strops to strengthen the wings, was amazed by the sudden hive of activity, when it returned on board. It found the whole idea of important developments going on while it was not there very worrying.

"What's the sewing circle on deck in aid for?" it demanded as it strode into the divan scattered master cabin, which acted as Fyrsil's office, library and sleeping quarters.

Peering at a model of the *Rover Woof-Woof* in that particular goggle-eyed way everyone peers at miniatures, Fyrsil was scratching his head with a quill as he tried to work out from the scale model the ratios of weight and lift.

"Come on, come on, what is it? Either you told a very funny joke, or there is something very fishy in the air – and both are unlikely."

"Lift off!" Fyrsil told the Bobo and excitedly outline his plan.

If the Bobo had an eyebrow to raise, it would have done so at that point. Instead it had be content with rapid blinking with its violent violet eyelids.

"It looks like my plan will work. And what's best is that it is my plan, thought of by me, with a lot of research and brains, and no brawn at all," Fyrsil told the bird smugly.

For every day the Bobo had been trying to fly the galley out of its mud berth, pretending that it was just another practice when the short beating of the wings produced nothing more than a squelchy sucking sound from the wooden hull, along with ominous whirring and clanking from the internal workings of the Comfy Chair.

At every failed attempt, Fyrsil had pulled out the Being Stone, and examined the blue fingers strengthen its grip like a sickening cancer on the bright yellow glory of the crystal. Every rolling dawn that washed in from the horizons surrounding Loot seemed to have a deepening dark tint to the sky. And Fyrsil's thoughts had grown correspondingly despondent. The threat was not only from the creeping colours of Murk, but more immediately from the Council of Lif in Loot.

To conform with the requirements of establishing the pirate self-help group, there had been concerted efforts in the production of edible mud pies. They were not only useful for trading in exchange for foodstuffs for the journey, but it was an effective front while a contraband collection of weapons of gruesome potential was secreted away from the eyes of prying inspectors. Unfortunately in 99 per cent of cases the mud pies had been found to be inedible, despite the sales team's protestations, and they came up as fast as they went down.

As the number of complaints was roughly equal to the number of sales, and the life enhancing properties claimed couldn't be further from the truth, it was obvious that the venture was running on borrowed time. Only bickering between the Health and Safety Directive, the Department of Trade, and the Re-Education Ministry over whose responsibility it was to prosecute on what promised to be a headline case was saving the *Rover Woof-Woof* from being closed down in all its trading capacities. The forced re-admission to the Rehab Centre for the crew seemed only a matter of time.

"When do we go?" the Bobo asked.

Fyrsil looked up from holding the model galley upside down to make the miniature paper balloons look as if they were working. (Somehow it didn't look quite right.)

"By my calculations," he said flourishing a series of squiggles which looked vaguely like mathematical calculus, "at three bowls of beans per balloon, and 10 balloons per farter, it looks like an all night feast, followed by lift off at first light, after the balloons have all been secured in place from the rigging and to the hull."

The Bobo nodded, almost confidently.

Out on the deck a squatting circle of ruthless cut-throats eyed the bubbling cauldron of beans with mixed emotions, along with the personalised cards with the quota for the number of bowls that needed to be consumed. As these were excessive, and unreformed pirates of every kind of denomination loved excess, a jovial mood wafted among the buccaneers readying themselves for the bean feast.

Quickly Fyrsil outlined the rules for the ceremony and took up his position in front of a full bowl of the most unappetising looking beans he had ever seen.

"Drop trouser!" squawked the Bobo in its most military manner to the circle of competitors.

"Fix balloon bags. And in your own time, eat and fill the said bags. Come on, come on don't be shy. Hands up when you're empty, so as I can fill them bowls with beans, and you can fill yourselves," it barked as it ladled out beans left, right and centre, and back again.

From the benches huddled around the cauldron there was only the sound of concentrated chomping, accompanied by waving of the air in front of the mouth.

"I'th hot," Groggie gulped, as he poured a bowlful down his throat, determined to fill the most balloons.

"Maybe needs a bit of celery salt, and a sniff of turmeric," announced Captain Cuffbert between mouthfuls, as he masticated elegantly. He peered with a practised eye at the assortment of glimmering red pebble beans, long lozenge yellow beans, and little vicious orange beans that made up the recipe of beans in bean sauce.

"As a gourmet taster of long standing, me thinks my taste buds do detect the influences of tobasco, rosemary, and if I'm not mistaken crushed dill dried in the sun."

He did. Fyrsil had found a spice rack in his bumbag, and thought it might make the recipe a bit more digestible.

A cheer went up as Big-Gulop managed to squeeze the first *parp* into the posterior-attached bag soon after shovelling two high speed bowlfuls down his gullet. Groggie racing for pole position soon came up with his own offering. The Bobo strutted around with a clothes peg firmly secured over its beak as the deck became a broadside of flatulence, steadily filling the balloon bags. As a surprise outsider Captain Cuffbert galloped along with the first inflated balloon. He waved his broad brimmed hat with its cocky feather, and bowed deeply as Peg secured the first balloon on the taffrail.

"How did he do that?" Groggie asked suspiciously through a mouthful of bean mulch.

"Simple finesse and style, my dear chap. It's not the quantity but the quality that counts – along with devilish good looks that could lure a mermaid off her rock. You either have it, or not, and I've got a treasury of it all," he told Groggie haughtily, and nibbled delicately on a spoonful of beans.

More and more balloons were tied to the rails around the galley, jostling with each other in the rigging. The air of amusement grew stale on the benches. Indulging in tricks, like playing bum-burping tunes into the balloons, lost its appeal as they failed to receive even a grunt of approval. As the Bobo heaped more bags of beans into the cauldron, the molars started to tire, and the buttocks started to feel raw with the highly charged gases escaping from the bodily pipework.

At this point two figures to emerged out of the gloom, and into the light of the lanterns suspended above the cauldron guffing area.

"Well feed my gizzard to the sharks, and my spleen to seagulls – if it isn't Juicy Lucy and Lizzy Spanker. Haven't seen you two lovelies since that wrestling in caviar during the Party To End All Parties – at least you were lovely then," exclaimed Groggie.

"My *new* name is Buttercup, but I will accept Buttie if you are respectfully friendly," declared the ex-Juicy Lucy, the ex-celebrity beauty and best dressed show off of the quayside.

"And my *new* name is Daisy. And I will not accept anything but the full thing. Especially from any uppity chauvinist who still clings to the old ways. It's only 'cos we want to help save the world, from what MEN has made a mess of. Typical MEN – just fiddle-fiddle-fiddle, and can't leave nothing alone. Then they get surprised when they bust it – whatever they've been fiddling with," said the ex-queen of the IT girls as she sauntered by.

Dressed in uniform baggy brown utility clothing, their voluptuous figures had seemed to have gone to seed and borne fruit.

"Yeah, it's typical. A manifestation of a domination complex which is a result of a natural inferiority complex and jealousy of women's superior intelligence and better nature – subjugating the mother Glob karma that should be naturally bubbling up to the top of everybody's awareness," Daisy pouted.

Several loud bubbling noises saw a scowling Peg rushing to tie off several hastily filled balloons.

"You obviously need a good female touch," Buttie loudly declared. "Look at you all. You've been sitting in the bay for days without getting nowhere. Luckily we got wind of this little adventure, otherwise you lot would not be able to benefit from us as true caring *female* beings wanting to dispense happiness on the planet."

"Now, now ladies. We are charmed I'm sure by your generous offer," Captain Cuffbert told them, "but the task at hand is hardly that for the feminine physique. I may be wrong, but I believe that women just don't."

"Huh! Men!" snorted Buttie. "Just proves you know nothing, and never have known nothing. Come on Daisy, drop your drawers, and let's give it one or two blasts for womankind," she said, forcing her way onto the bench.

"You can't do that," said an aghast Masked Marauder.

Fyrsil was inclined to think the more the merrier, as he did his mental arithmetic with the quantity of beans in the pot, and the number of balloons dancing in the rigging on their straining tethers.

"Why can't we?" demanded Daisy in a very unfeminine tone.

"Because it's a man's job.""Why?"

"Because it's nasty, smelly and dirty."

"Sounds like a husband I once had," scoffed Buttie, and dug into a bowl of beans proffered by the Bobo, who appeared to for once agree with Fyrsil's thinking.

"Fwwooarr, these are hot," she cried, before realising that was not fighting feminist talk. "Let's have some more."

The silence of the night descended over the *Rover Woof-Woof*, as jaws crunched their way through bowl after bowl, and blow after blow into balloons. Only the clatter of spoons, the cheeky trouser chuckles, and woofs of spent air interrupted the tranquil that settled over the sea of mud.

On the deck bodies rolled in agony as they tried to lead the race for filled balloons.

"Only twenty more to go, so let's have a big push," Peg announced as she pirouetted energetically in front of the crew.

Groaning and holding their large protruding stomachs, the pirates murmured their agreement to give a final big push, to launch them on their mission.

"Come on, push!" Peg encouraged, sauntering around the deck swinging her hips and strutting her wooden leg.

The light of the two pink suns started to get a finger hold on the horizon in preparation for the quick heave to bathe Loot in light.

"Put your backsides into it, and heave. We ain't got all night," barked the Bobo at slowly munching bodies strewn around the cauldron.

"There can't be more, there can't be," groaned Groggie through a mouthful of mushed husks as he rolled around the deck in agonies of an over-packed belly.

"Huh, call yourself a man," snapped Buttie, as she chewed and delicately pouted into her bag in a business-like manner. "Pull yourself together. There's a job to be done, and we've all got to play our part. So stop whinging and get farting."

Groggie screwed up his face and winced in supreme effort as he inflated another canvas balloon with a great gust from his rear end. The effort left him motionless in the scuppers, until the Bobo placed another bowl in front of his nose. A thin whimper escaped his lips as flakes of dried beans dropped pathetically from his lips.

"Typical! No staying power: that's men all over for you," Buttie declared as she dug with business-like gusto into her bowl. "Just proves my theory of the underlying superiority of the female. Men, they're all full of wind about what they can do, but at the end of the day they just don't do a job properly. "

A dozen balloons from wilting ex-pirate chiefs suddenly filled, to keep the rear-ends up in the pecking order that Buttie was laying in to.

The first of the pink suns leapt into the sky and declared the day open for business, revealing to the world the deck of the *Rover Woof-Woof* littered with groaning bodies. Expressions, limbs and even their attire, all seemed to have wilted during the great bean feast, as the collection of hairy buttocks pointed at the sky like a strange new fad in garden furniture.

XIV

With eyelids drooping from exhaustion, Fyrsil noted that there were only five more of the balloons left to fill, and hoped his calculations were correct. He had no doubts that the collection of rag dolls on the deck, pooped from giving every puff their digestive systems could squeeze out, would soon rouse themselves with an appropriate punishment if he was wrong.

Having come so close, he could not bear to fail now. He heard Peg and the Bobo securing some of the inflated canvass sausages to the underside of the hull in preparation for lift off. It might have been his imagination, but he could almost sense the lightness of the galley as it gently slurped from side to side, still held in the gooey clasp of the red mud. He slowly eased his bum bag to a more comfortable position, taking pressure off his bloated belly, which seemed as taut as skin over a drum. His jaw was numb from bean crunching, his teeth ached and he tasted the blood from his bleeding gums. He almost wished his bloated pot belly would pop and end it all, there and then.

"Ahoy there you lot! Wake up, I want to buy my tickets," an irritable voice called out.

A communal inquisitive groan escaped the mouths of the collective of bean-bloated bodies.

"Tickets! What tickets?" squawked the Bobo, who popped up from the engine room where it had been carrying out last minute tinkering. A wrinkled and craggy old man, supporting himself on a walking frame, stood at the gangway.

"The tickets for the ride around the bay. I presume that is what the notice on the quayside says. It would be a pretty stupid sign if it said anything else. And I want a discount. There's got to be at least one advantage of growing old."

A more concerted groan of recognition rose from the felled figures pinned to the deck by the weight of their stomachs. Quiet desperation hung like a dark cloud over the company of men, women and a bird as everyone apart from Fyrsil and the Bob realised they could not escape the pestering belligerent demands of the notorious Crock.

Having had a reputation as a fearless sea captain and leader of lunatics, Crock now polished a fearsome reputation in Loot as an awkward campaigner for pensioner rights, and general contrary demands on anything and everything. Before the disappearance of the Blood Sea, the sight of his withered body entering a room was quickest way of ending a party. Now with the coming of the New Way, citizens and Lifers alike fled in terror at the possibility of having to actually sympathise with any of his ranting complaints.

"There are no joy rides. If you could read, you would know that. Now bog off. We haven't got any time to waste on senile illiterates," the Bobo told him.

There was a collective holding on breath. And then the storm struck.

"I know my rights! Luring old men on unsafe gangways on the pretext of a trip around the bay. Where's the respect for yer elders? The least yer could do is offer a poor OAP a bit of breakfast. Manners! Huh, them all left with the bloody Blood Sea. I may be old, but I deserve better treatment than being told the big 'E' by a bird that looks like an accident in a paint factory."

Crock drew breath, and prepared himself for the next blast as his indignation boiled, and he unexpectedly let rip an enormous fart that would have normally had everyone running for a gas mask. He was rather bewildered to see Peg running towards him with a large canvass bag, and even more surprised when she started pulling his trousers down. His stomach continued to rumble like a dormant volcano about to have another go at throwing rocks and lava into the world.

"Quick give him a bowl of beans," Fyrsil yelled at the Bobo, who was too busy running for the cauldron to answer back.

Crock muttered something from beneath his dirty walrus moustache as he searched amongst the fluff and dirty handkerchiefs in his pockets for his eating dentures. He might not like the look of the fluorescent bird, but it seemed to be making up for its rudeness with a big bowl brimming with tasty looking beans, and he rather liked the ministrations of pretty Peg, as she fixed the canvass bag to his nether regions. He hadn't had so much attention for ages.

Taking out his special spoon that he kept behind his ear, the old man dug into his breakfast with noisy concentration. Then he noticed everyone was watching him with strangely intense stares.

"This isn't a trick to get me into one of those homes?" he asked suspiciously as he filled two balloons with ease as he masticated his way carefully through the contents of the bowl. "I've already made my views on them plain enough. I'm not going to stand for it. Being sat in there with all those miserable old gits, just waiting to die. And all them busybodies being so nice and understanding. It's just not natural, that's what I say."

The chemical reaction of the beans and Crock's vinegared gastric juices had the desired effect, and another balloon was whisked away and tied to the forestay.

Like a collection of bean bags scattered on the floor, Fyrsil and the crew shifted their bulks and watched in fascination at one of the finest displays of flatulence seen on the planet.

Expectation hung in the air. It might have been wishful thinking, but Fyrsil seemed to feel the ship swaying tantalisingly in its mud berth. Only a couple more balloons and they would be airborne.

"What're you all gawping at? Ain't you never seen no one eat a bowl of beans before? And you can stop fiddling around with me nethers," he told Peg as she tied off another bag full of guff to loud applause.

Despite himself, Crock started to grin. Sensing he was the centre of attention, but still not able to work out quite why, he wiped his lips with the back of his hand, blew his nose loudly into his sleeve, and let rip again.

He was about to slap the woman who kept on fiddling with his backside with his spoon, but was distracted by the ragged cheer, and she slipped off out of range clinging to the latest inflated balloon.

"What's going on here? Come on. There's something yer not telling me, and I likes to know what I don't know," Crock shouted.

With just two balloons to go before lift off, Fyrsil staggered to his feet and sat next to Crock to explain the situation, and make sure the momentum of the old man's intestinal system kept popping.

Suddenly realising that he was the centre of attention, Crock farted uncomfortably to rapturous applause. Peg took the inflated offering, almost losing her grip as she tied it to the prow.

The galley deck seemed almost light-heartedly tippy. Feeling that the time was nearly nigh, the Bobo slipped below to prepare the Comfy Chair for take off.

There was a scraping over the scrubbed boards, as the rolly-polly figures of the crew crawled forward to get ringside seats for the giant guff that would take them off on their mission.

The expectant stares turned to concerned chatter mumbled around the cauldron. Crock had gone beetroot red. His constant chewing jaws were clammed shut.

"What's the matter?" asked a worried Fyrsil.

"Stage fright," whispered Crock. "I've come over all shy. Nothing is happening down there, and I prides meself on farting at will, at any occasion. It guarantees to get you noticed, yer know."

Fyrsil nodded with forced sympathy. The muffled sound of clanking and creaking came from the rowing decks as the mechanics of the wings started to flap in slow sweeping strokes.

"Come on! Every one is waiting for you," Fyrsil blurted impatiently.

Crock sat miserably considering his shrivelled navel. The first time in years he had been paid any proper attention, and he was failing his rapt audience.

Strutting towards him across the deck was a grotesque gaudy coloured bird with a massive camera.

"Smile for the camera," the Bobo told him, and an extended portrait lens poked towards Crock's grizzled features. "Just something for the album."

The dazzling brightness of the flash unit caught Crock like a frightened rabbit, and with an almighty roar that had been bubbling up inside him, he let rip and fell off the bench.

Only with the deftest of movements was Peg able to nip and tie the neck of the balloon as it threatened to shoot off over the side with the force of the blast. Steadying herself, she climbed the companionway and secured it in pride of place at the back of the poop deck as the ship erupted in a roar. "Lift off" she declared as she marked off the final balloon on the scoreboard..

"Hip-hip hurrah!" "huzzah!" and even "hip-hip-hippit-hop!" resounded from the mouths of the tired crew who not so long ago had found it difficult to groan with conviction. Groggie and Big-Gulop, danced a little gig, banging the boards of the deck with the flop of their feet, and even Buttie and Daisy gave Crock a congratulatory slap on the back and a motherly hug each.

When the shower of tricorn hats had landed with a patter back on deck, and the joyous leaping about had died down, silence carpeted the crew, and all eyes turned accusingly to Fyrsil.

What happened was nothing.

All the balloons had been filled only after a gastronomic hell, but the galley still remained stuck in the mud. The wings were flapping, but there was no upward lift, and Fyrsil looked deflated. He had just found out why the pirates of Loot did not make plans – just in case they went wrong. The consequences could be dire, and he felt he was about to experience more than just a delicate taste of those consequences.

"Just a minor miscalculation," Fyrsil announced, and staggered over to the wheel to ring down for some faster flapping.

"If the Comfy Chair flaps any faster all its springs will go. Why don't you talk to the mud and ask it let go – it might be more useful," was the answer he received up the communication tube from the Bobo.

Fyrsil momentarily wondered why the bird that was meant to be his aid and companion on this mission from Heaven, when it so obviously failed on both counts.

"Just a technical hitch," Fyrsil told the glowering crew, who were eyeing him in a most unfriendly manner.

"Inspectors ahoy!"

Boac's cry diverted the attention from Fyrsil's sheepish expression by the wheel.

From the quayside a party of inspectors, followed by muscled attendants from the Aggression Rehab Centre in bulging white coats, were making their way across the bay of mud along the suspended plank walkway.

On the other side of the deck Crock didn't hear any of this, as he had turned his ear trumpet off during all the shouting and applause. He was too busy showing Peg his party trick. Bending over, he lit a match, and with a little grimace sent a roaring sheet from his backside into the rigging.

"Ooh, my word," he said, almost apologetically, as burning bits of tarred rope dropped from the ratlines. Quickly he pulled his trousers up, and grabbed for his walking frame, to try and melt into the crowd looking out from the gangway.

He only got halfway across the deck, before a big bang rocked the galley as a couple of balloons exploded simultaneously, and burning bits of canvas balloon covered the deck sending everyone diving for cover. By chance, one of these swirling pieces of burning material landed (as these things tend to do in these sort of situations) directly on the balloons the Bobo and Peg had strapped to the underside of the galley.

As the first Lifer inspector strode purposefully onto the gangplank with an impounding order form the Community Administration Director, busily wording in his mind a noise abatement compounding order, he was suddenly hurled into the sticky morass that had been below him.

A big whoosh, followed by the sound of the biggest and wettest, sloppiest kiss heard on the face of Glob, reverberated across the muddy bay. With a blue methane tail, the good ship *Rover Woof-Woof* launched into the air like a suddenly released party balloon as it broke free of the grip of its mud bed.

Completing a loop-the-loop, the ship buzzed the rooftops of an awakening Loot, before shooting off at great speed in the direction of the two pink suns sitting at the top of the sky.

XX

The outriders of imps rein-whipped their giant vampire bat mounts as they swooped through the portcullis and over the moat of Castle Gloom. Hard on their heels the two frothing wyverns pulling Lord Trachidambabble's rusty iron chariot buzzed the drawbridge, closely followed by the rest of the cortege of the imperial bodyguard of trolls in studded leather uniforms standing on raven driven sleds. Almost absent mindedly Trachidambabble thrashed his driver, as the driver in turn whipped the wyverns into the dark blanket of rain and hail that was travelling across Murk on its scheduled sluggish weather front.

After a more than respectable interval, an old heavy framed tandem rattled across the slippery boards of the drawbridge. A sign hanging from the crossbar announced: Balck Warlock – master of the nastier black arts by appointment to his Nastiness Lord Trachidambabble.

"Peddle faster. We're losing them," shouted the black cloaked figure as the bicycle was steered into the storm.

He muttered deeply to himself.

As the newly appointed Balck Warlock of Murk, he had expected a more dignified form of official transport than a tandem. No one took any notice of a rusty bicycle, and there didn't seem much point of cheating, lying and surviving long enough to land the top job in the profession, if this was all you got as a perk.

Being the most senior warlock in Murk must have some advantages, but he had not discovered them yet.

For a start off he had to deal with name confusion. For most of his career as a warlock he had gone under the name of Darren. It was not the best name on Glob, but he had got used to it. He had been informed that he ought to change it to something more sinister. Hoodoo was accepted, so Hoodoo he now was, and was getting used to his new name along with his new duties.

The first job had been the recruiting drive in Loot, which had proved far from satisfactory. It was all very well Lord Trachidambabble want to run the world, but Hoodoo had a feeling that the consequences of stealing the Golden Orbs from Heaven and the Ness recipe had somehow upset life on the rest of the planet. The famed repository of all the most evil and malicious people on Glob was unrecognisable, and the quality of the goods he was able to come back with begged an enormous question. But beggars can't be choosers and Hoodoo was definitely not going on another recruiting drive. He was having trouble reading his fortune stews – big dark messy things with all sorts of nasty surprises in them – which happened to be his speciality having majored in it at warlock college. And that did not bode well for the Balck Warlock, the most powerful magician on the planet.

Having had to resort to taking a stall at the Loot Annual Horticultural Show, Hoodoo did not have much success in getting the quality of candidate for an apprentice. In fact he could interest no one in this once in a lifetime opportunity to become a key functionary in the Murk hierarchy, with plenty of opportunity to create havoc on Glob. It was only through promising that there was a large bag of sweets at the bottom of his sack was Hoodoo able to bundle his new apprentice away from Loot. It was a pity that horrible little retard said nothing more than "beep-beep", but that might be a blessing in disguise. And looking on the bright side if you are going to have an apprentice its just as well to have an utterly disgusting and revolting specimen that looked like he had just emerged from festering in the sewer. And he seemed quite good at peddling, which was a good thing considering the official mode of transport.

The Balck Warlock hit the disfigured humpback while he wondered whether the apprentice he called Beep-Beep had been attracted to the potential of power that he had included in the job resume, or whether the creature had been practising his reading.

Not wanting to admit that his long journey to Loot had been a waste of time, Hoodoo had decided to stick with what he had. But that did not mean he was happy with what he had. Just to demonstrate this point he gave the stupid back of his clumsy apprentice another big whallop.

"Faster you moron!"

"Beep-beep," panted Beep-Beep, as he steered the tandem through the open gutters of the suburbs that had grown up around Castle Gloom. They scattered all in their wake: retired trolls, deformed imps and other lesser fiends that had settled in the shanty town that mouldered close to the castle walls. The warlock and his apprentice sped down the garbage strewn streets, hoping that it was the right direction for the site of the important ceremony they were going to conduct. It was an important point, because Hoodoo knew that despite the obvious disadvantages in the mode of travel, if they were not in position by the time the Dark Lord landed, he would be very much an ex-Balck Warlock.

"And use the bloody gears," Hoodoo shouted as Beep-Beep's feet whirled in dizzying circles.

The Balck Warlock pulled his potato clock from beneath his official cloak of office. It was a nifty timepiece, and his only souvenir from the horticultural show. The problem was it told too good time for Murk, and had not stopped once when Time had its nightly power cuts and failures in Castle Gloom. He reset it again and frowned, worried a bit, and then gave a reluctant sigh. "There's nothing for it," he thought, and with a quick intonation and the flick of a wrist and Hoodoo's hapless apprentice was transformed into a manic winged poltergeist.

"I'll change you back when we arrive at the factory," he shouted at the new form on the front seat, gripping the handlebars tightly as he experienced something close to Mach 5.

(There was an un-written rule in the code of conduct for warlocks, and that was that a warlock never transmogrified his apprentice. The reason for this was very simple: REVENGE. Contorting the body and mind into another form was an agonising business, which could leave lasting psychological scars. When freed from apprenticeship, it had been observed through studies by people who bothered about the subject, that the former master was often turned into small squashable little creatures by their big boot wearing former pupils. Hoodoo hoped that Beep-Beep was too stupid to register concepts like retribution. (All the signs had pointed to this, but you could never be sure.)

*   *   *

On a site of bland post-industrial non-productive factory units, the Castle Gloom cavalcade ripped down through the storm to land on a pitted tarmac road leading to the new Mess factory building.

It wasn't really new, but newly occupied. However, the Castle Gloom marketing department had got its teeth into the task of truth warping for the ceremony.

After capturing the Orbs and ordering that the Ness recipe should be changed to purple Mess, Trachidambabble had brooded deeply in his damp inner sanctum. He did not like the thought of so much potential goldenness within the castle walls. True, it was deep down in the Bowels, but he reasoned that the dark unmentionable quarters were always where dissent and potentially hazardous ideas emerged from. And Trachidambabble felt he ought to know, because that is where he tended to experiment with most of his nastiest ideas.

A directive was sent to the Production Manager, telling him to move all the Orbs, manufacturing cisterns, and mixing vats to the empty brown field site beyond the shanty town of Deeper Gloom. The official reason was to be able to launch the Mess into Glob's atmosphere more easily through shortening the supply chain logistics of transporting it from the Bowels of Castle Gloom to the newly laid out catapult launching pad. This was an ambitious project to infuse an unhealthy hue to Glob's stratospheres, working on the smaller scale operations of the manufacture and launching of rain clouds formed out of the muck collected from Castle Gloom's dreaded dungeons.

Because the sight of the once golden orbs might upset his brooding, Trachidambabble also ordered that everything should be taken from Castle Gloom without the possibility of him glimpsing any part of the process.

The Production Manager, as former captain of the Dark Lord's Blackguards, knew all about obeying impossible orders to the letter. He quickly set about installing himself in an office that was convenient for organising the indiscriminate flaying of workers. As a separate issue he told a fiend with administrative flair to oversee the digging of a tunnel under the moat, which was to emerge at the factory site beyond Deeper Gloom. It did eventually.

*   *   *

The cavalcade landed and performed fussy taxi-ing procedures on the runway. As everything came to a halt a loudly clanking missile cut across the line of landed bats at bone-shaking speed and crashed loudly into the side of the factory.

Hoodoo picked himself up shakily from the mangled wreck of the tandem, leaving the groaning Beep-Beep on the freshly painted blue grass. The warlock gave him a cursory glance, to make sure he had returned to his normal disfigured form. Hoodoo wasn't quite sure if the groaning from his apprentice was from being transformed back to his old self, or whether it was because Beep-Beep had taken the brunt of the collision into the factory wall. Quickly adjusting his official hat, the Balck Warlock decided he didn't care.

By the time Hoodoo had picked himself up, Trachidambabble was already on the specially erected podium for the official opening of the Mess factory.

Resplendent in his finery, wearing rows of medals, with the black star of the Order of Darkness on the onyx black sash tied with a purple blood knot across his chest, the Dark Lord hissed visibly as he waited for his Balck Warlock. He needed to know what augured for the public opening of the new enterprise, and it better be bad.

(By public, it did not mean anyone with nothing better to do. It meant carefully press ganged imps, demons, and other assorted spooks of the domain swept from the dark corners of the factory building to practice booing loudly at the proper intervals. To ensure this was achieved properly the spindoctors from Castle Gloom had prepared different coloured cards for each response required from the crowd. Important ghouls from Trachidambabble's private office were positioned to wave paddles with the cards stuck to them, for proper orchestration of crowd reactions.)

On the podium in a heavy metal cauldron bubbled the Stew of Mistery Hoodoo had prepared earlier in his kitchens at home and stored in his larder until getting the special banshee couriers to deliver it on site in readiness for the ceremony. He shakily took his place, alongside the new Captain of the Blackguards, giving his cloak an impressive flourish to conceal the patches of chain oil splattered on the mystic symbols.

"'Ope you got insurance. The cost of replacement of that particular Castle Gloom International transportation you've just trashed will come out of your salary," the captain said grimly out of the corner of his mouth.

"Sod off. I'm a director," Hoodoo told him bravely. This might have been a silly move, because trolls usually reacted to such remarks by tearing the voicebox out of flippant little pipsqueak.

Despite being the most feared and respected of all warlocks by dint of his office, Hoodoo knew that the captain of the Blackguards was not a troll to tussle with. The Blackguards were chosen for being the biggest, meanest and hairiest trolls on Glob. They were also tested for an astonishing lack of IQ before they made it into the hallowed ranks of Trachidambabble's personal bodyguard. The Dark

Lord reasoned that you had to be really stupid to obey most of his commands, so he set stringent standards on strength and stupidity, which fortunately more often than not coincided. Being of this disposition the Blackguards never trusted anything that was 'clever', and this included magic – mainly because they couldn't understand how it was done, and usually involved warlocks doing a lot of reading, which was the basis of being clever.

"Thank you warlock for your company. So good of you to join us," Trachidambabble hissed in a voice that had all the attraction of a sewage sluice opening.

Grabbing the microphone, the Dark Lord threw back his head and boomed his address to his disloyal subjects and workers.

"Worthless scum, villains, and miserable lowly proles of Murk."

(A loud hissing erupted from the crowd as an oily figure in a suit raised a coloured paddle in the air.)

"...Welcome to this historic moment in the task of reasserting Murk as the driving force of Glob," Trachidambabble continued in a voice as warm as a glacier.

The different coloured paddles went up and down with a speed and variety that confused the crowd into a cacophony of simultaneous booing, hissing and jeering at their leader. The oily oik in the suit had lost his place in Trachidambabble's scripted speech – not surprising as the Dark Lord had started *ad libbing* after the first sentence - and was panicking at the thought of incarceration in the dungeons.

"...But to prove the totally inappropriateness of this venture, I call upon the Balck Warlock to read the signs of the unseen dimensions. The directorship of Glob is mine. Now, let us hear how the Stew of Mistery maps out my purpose."

The Mess factory workers recognised the part of the Balck Warlock holding up his ladle, and gave him a great jeer. Hoodoo dipped his magic ladle into the unwholesome broth and stirred so that its carved runes played their secret tunes from the hidden rhythms of the universe. The crowd grew silent in anticipation. Not as silent as Trachidambabble, whose predatory black thoughts sucked into oblivion any possible sounds on the podium.

Using a complicated routine of ceremonial steps around the cauldron, as laid down in *Warlocks Cookbook: Spells, Stews and How To Read Them*, the Balck Warlock worked his craft. He kicked his apprentice, who gave a satisfying painful "beep". Standing over the bubbling morass of the worst cuts of offal and severed limbs mixed in a vile gravy, the warlock gave an imperceptible twitch of the hands and disappeared behind a cloud of smoke.

Hoodoo winced and scrunched his eyes. He didn't like doing these simple tricks of smoke and garbled mumbo-gumbo, but on an occasion like this you had to give the audience a bit of theatre – it's what is expected after all.

He stirred the Stew of Mistery with his ladle again, and heard it hum a tune. A rat's tail covered in mucus bubbled to the surface. He stirred again. A decapitated toad stuck to a kitten's paw bobbed up and down as the runes on the ladle sang their dirge.

The warlock knew these were not portents, just ingredients, but they impressed the peeping trolls and ghouls on the podium. Even the rune spoon's tune was an amusing dirty ditty, popular with a small race of gnomic miners. That didn't matter either, because the spoon was singing it in the language of large poisonous plague aphids, and as mumbo-gumbo it sounded impressively authentic.

"Get on with it warlock!" a voice that could have stripped a carcass to the bone whispered loudly in his ear.

Quickly Hoodoo mumbled an incomprehensible jumble of words, and tapping the cauldron three and a half times with the ladle (mainly to stop it singing the stupid song) disappeared into another cloud of smoke. Coughing as the vapours cloyed at his throat, the warlock waved his hands to clear a visibility hole over the surface of the stew.

A ripple stirred, and out of the muck a claw clutching a crumpled piece of parchment thrust through the surface skin of offal fat. Hoodoo grabbed it eagerly, and in a glance committed the scribbled message to memory. He pushed it back into the talons and waited for the claw to submerge again. From the sediment at the bottom of the stew a sound very much like "Hem!" boomed. Quickly the warlock slipped a quartz coin from his sleeve to the claw, and it sank back into the vile concoction.

"Well warlock, what is the word of the Stew of Mistery?" Trachidambabble rumbled in a voice that threatened an avalanche of retribution if the answer was not to his liking.

Clearing his throat, Hoodoo spread his arms wide and declared to the crowd: "The stew has spoken, and so spake it with these words:

When up is down and down is up
Who can tell on what they sup?
When gold is blue, and blue is Ness

Is there an end to this terrible mess?
When down is up and up is down
And castle rules are all around
Who can tell if mess is Ness
When Glob does spin in backwardness?"

There was a silence on the rostrum, and not a murmur from the crowd as Hoodoo's words trailed off. If there is a universally puzzled look, it was at that moment being worn by the crowd of Murk's henchmen outside the new Mess factory.

"If that makes sense then if I'm a dung rat's left testicle," a troll pondered out loud.

A dark blue presence rattled his brain, and before Trachidambabble could speak the words, his Balck Warlock simply announced: "The interpretation of the Balck Warlock, Master of the Black Arts of Murk, is that Glob will be blue and the whole enterprise will be a disaster."

A great jeer erupted from the crowd, and smirks were exchanged on the stage platform between the dignitaries.

The dark holes of Trachidambabble's eye sockets glinted with delight.

"I do like my projects to be terrible disasters," he hissed.

"Absolutely not," agreed Hoodoo, shaking his head vigorously. "Nothing but absolute disaster."

He didn't dare mention the other half of the message, and its abundantly clear meaning. But as repeating that would have meant instant biodegradation, he held his own council and his tongue until the cavalcade had soared back into the storm clouds towards Castle Gloom. He calculated whether it would be in his interest to drop heavy hints to the dragon patrols to look out for a flying ship looking for Murk's gold. As this sounded rather ridiculous, even as he thought about it, because gold had never glinted in Murk a) because it was the colour of Heaven, and b) because it was worthless in a society that used crusty cowpats as the largest denomination of coinage. Anyway the dragon patrol commanders were never known for their intelligence, and so subtle hints would be beyond their comprehension.

He looked at Beep-Beep, and kicked him into the front seat of the buckled tandem, and they clanked their back towards Castle Gloom.

XXI

Fyrsil wondered vaguely whether the condition he was suffering could be called seasick when his ship was flying rather than sailing. Whatever it was, he wasn't feeling well at all.

From his bunk amongst his books in the master cabin he could hear the rhythmic groan of the stays as the big lanteen sail strained at its spar. If he had been feeling better he would have felt in sympathy.

Restlessly Fyrsil tossed and turned on the crunchy straw mattress, known bewilderingly to seafaring folk as a donkey – maybe because of its stubborn refusal to give a comfortable ride. Not being able to sleep, he dressed and went out on to the heaving deck as the *Rover Woof-Woof* lurched into an air pocket. He found sailing in a ship hundreds of feet above the surface of Glob an eerie experience.

He waved at Groggie, who was peering sternly towards the prow as *Rover Woof-Woof* flew over the shaded banks of fluffy clouds. A gust clapped at the canvas of the main sail, and the rigging groaned under the sudden surge of pressure. The decks slipped violently, and Fyrsil followed it downhill on his bum, and crashed into the rail. Grabbing at a conveniently secure rope, he steadied himself, and prevented his first experiment into sky-diving without a parachute.

"Brace yerself when you come on deck. Haven't you got your sea legs yet?" Groggie bellowed, and broke into a raucous laugh as Fyrsil was violently sick over the side.

It was a sight that Groggie regarded as Fyrsil's natural state: pale, helpless and sickly. It struck the pirate chief that this was a very strange choice of emissary of Heaven. And it bugged him that this sorry collection of limbs was nominally in charge and had been telling him what to do. Even if it was only from time to time. Taking any orders from anyone – no matter who – stuck in his gullet.

In the dark corners of his mind (which took up the majority of his thought process) there were already nasty ideas lurking with gruesomely appropriate ends to Fyrsil during the raid on Murk. An unfortunate bop on the head, a dangle by the neck with a long rope, or stuffed into a flaming hot oven, perhaps. The problem was the bumbag. Groggie recognised the bumbag as a great prize, which anyone on Glob would be envious of. He decided it was just the sort of travel accessory he needed, and would be a good trophy from the raid.

Secretly he had spied on Fyrsil dipping into the bumbag and pulling out all sorts of treasures as he searched for a bottle of seasick pills. Groggie's eyes had grown as large as saucers at seeing how so much came out of such a compact bit of kit. He had watched as Fyrsil had gone through some sort of special ceremony involving pushing buttons, with lots of waving of hands and occasional muttering of magic words that sounded like: "Damn! Wozza-number?"

Groggie needed to know more about the bag that was dangled around Fyrsil's waist, before he could decide whether Heaven's security guard had passed its use-by date. His thoughts darkened as the *Rover Woof-Woof* surged plunging into an acrid smelling cloud.

"Murk ahoy!"

The cry from the crow's nest brought the crew scuttling up on deck. Straining eyes scanned the horizon through the skittering crow-black clouds briefly obscuring the outline of the ink black Stairway of Damnation, which sprouted like an un-natural weed from the purple range of spikey mountains thrusting up from Glob's surface.

"Clear the decks for action!" Fyrsil called weakly through his loudhailer, suddenly feeling even more sick at the sight of their destination.

"Why?" asked the Bobo, who had come up from the engine room to see what all the stamping feet was about.

"Just in case. That is Murk you know, and it is the source of all evil, and generally horrible things."

"But it's all automatic. I had to do something with my time while you were lounging around in the Rehab Centre. Games of Imperial Scandal with the Comfy Chair lost their appeal after the 100th time in one day. So we decided to have a bit of a tinker. The AutoNav was relatively easy to adapt into an armaments directional firing system, actually."

With a flick of its pennant feathers the Bobo pressed a button on the side of the compass binnacle to reveal a display console that unfortunately reminded Fyrsil that the AutoNav system had not been very successful in working in its proper operational mode.

"Ah," he said in hopeful encouragement.

"The great thing about it," continued the Bobo enthusiastically, "is that as well as the 32 and 24 pounder cannons independently and automatically tracking any incoming target, there are also settings for 'broadside' and 'fire at will'. It's called the Automatic Rapid Fire Defence and Attack System - or ARFDAS. There is also the 'repel boarder' option, but I had difficulty programming the friend/foe identification, so that should only be used as a last resort."

The delicate state of Fyrsil's stomach took a sudden dive at the thought of having to rely on some of the Comfy Chair's operational extras.

"If you hear a high pitched whine, that is the 10 second warning to dive for cover," the Bobo added cautiously. "After that the decks will be raked with grapeshot for five minutes of continuous fire by the canister swivel guns on the poop and at the fo'csle."

"Sounds quite effective," Fyrsil gulped.

"Terminally."

"What do the crew think. Rather makes them redundant, doesn't it?" Fyrsil asked, worried whether having their function replaced by technology would have an adverse affect on a difficult morale.

"Oh they love it. Groggie bought up a consignment of deck chairs to be able to watch the fun in comfort. Crock grumbled a bit, but he's not happy if he can't be grumpy about the present not being like the past. It has taken all the hard work out of battle stations, and with no more powder monkeys and humping and heaving of munitions after a cannon is fired, I think you have a very contented crew. Captain Cuffbert even intimated that it would be a pleasant change being a spectator."

Fyrsil looked down on the quarter deck, and sure enough, the pirate band was sat in viewing positions, tooled up with their favourite swords and pistols stuffed in belts and dangling from broad sashes just in case some of the action got a bit to close for comfort. Captain Cuffbert waved as he knotted a natty handkerchief at each corner for a hat, rolled up his trouser legs, and took a bite of a toffee apple.

"Ready for action in two minutes. Not bad considering these chairs are damn tricky to set up," he called jauntily.

"Well in that case, let's make for sail for Murk: for fame, fortune, and a place in Heaven for giving that damnable Trachidamnbabble such a good hiding, that if he lives he will never forget the brave adventurers from Loot," declared Fyrsil in as strident tones as he could manage.

The "hip-hip hurrah!" that followed was lost amongst the gathering storm clouds, as the good ship *Rover Woof-Woof* sailed on to its demonic destination.

XXII

"Well what is it?"

The gangling demon drew himself up stiffly and punched out the best grisly salute he could perform, and quivered a bit on his hooves. As an ambitious Generalissimo of the Murk Border Defence Force it was not often that Scabbatch had the displeasure of having to entertain the company of his supreme commander. And for the Dark Lord to come to Scabbatch's Command bunker was a great dishonour – as long as it did not result in the terminal ending of the Generalissimo's ambitions by being biodegraded.

"We've picked up something on the scanner near the Stairway of Damnation. Not the usual adventure tourists or shark salesmen. Too big for that. I would say some sort of ship, if there was any water near these mountains."

"Really," grimaced Trachidambabble, in what could possibly have been taken for a smile on any other being.

With a hiss of pure malice he turned and headed for the dimly flickering banks of screens blinking on the wall.

"Show me."

Scabbatch cowered as cravenly as he could, slipping on the ordure as he led Trachidambabble to the screens. A manacled imp who was fiddling with a daunting array of dials, switches and big colourful buttons with Danger! stamped on them, was knocked appreciatively to the floor with a backhand slap. The Generalissimo stood back proudly so the Dark Lord had a clear view at the blob that bleeped weakly as a radial arm swept over the dial decorated with the local topography around the Stairway of Damnation.

"Not what I expected, but if Intelligence is as stupid as it claims to be, I think our visitors have arrived."

"Visitors?" blurted Scabbatch before he had time to cut his tongue off for questioning the Dark Lord. He followed it with a grimace of such putrefying obsequiousness that even Trachidambabble was distracted from his usual jerk reaction of reducing a questioner to a heap of instant ashes. Scabbatch thought this rather odd, when he had recovered his dirty colouring.

Entertaining guests was not part of the make up of Murk. There were resident devils, demons, imps, werewolves, ghouls and the usual misfits and crossbreeds of vicious disposition. But visitors were unheard of. "Whatever it is, there may be a chance for promotion," the demon thought to himself.

"Now what sort of reception party shall we organise for them?" grated Scabbatch's lord and master.

The Generalissimo in all his long years as a totally ruthless career backbiter, had never attended, let alone organised a party. They were meant to be jolly affairs, and Murk was never a place for that sort of thing.

"A bad party?" he enquired – this time prepared with his ceremonial dirk to cut out his tongue if it was the wrong answer.

"The question was purely rhetorical, dunderhead," came the icy reply, intimating that any further uncalled for contributions to the conversation would fatally damage career prospects – literal interpretation only.

The Generalissimo stiffened happily at the insult. That's what he understood. A good beating or two as well, but generally insults were within his comprehension.

"What I want you to do, you useless dolt, is personally see to it that the lovely little blip on the screen is extinguished. My friend Hap has finally made his move to get his Balls back. You will ensure that this cretinous little expedition gets nowhere near my stairs, and doesn't brighten surface of Murk with their ghastly clean countenance. Understand?"

The Generalissimo didn't, but he did shake his head in the affirmative very positively.

"I want you to exterminate that blip!"

The Generalissimo beamed, smashed the screen, and executed a smart salute with his bleeding fist.

The dark pits that were presumed to house Trachidambabble's eyes bored into the commander of the border guard.

"Now go and destroy the real thing by launching your lovely little squadron of dragons which you have been training for a time such as this. And with large cannons and lots of blood and noise, obliterate that alien ship. And I want pictures to prove it, or I will have to devise a pleasant way for you to wish that biodegradation came to you the moment you were born. Get a film crew, I want the results for many hateful evenings of entertainment during the long summer days!"

The words hit Scabbatch's eardrums like a storm of giant hailstones.

"Well!! Don't just stand there gawping – do it!"

With an angry of hiss of a swirling anthracite cloak, the Dark Lord turned on his heel and left the Command Bunker. The telltale squeaks and clanks of the troll BlackGuards faded into the distance, leaving only the steaming gobbets of pure evil burning pockmarks in the granite floor to mark Trachidambabble's visit. The Generalissimo watched them in a trance for a couple of seconds, as if foreseeing his future if he failed, Pulling himself together, he quickly sucked his bleeding fist, punched the imp to the floor and listened to it howl in satisfaction.

He was back in control. He nearly lost it, but who didn't in the presence of the Dark Lord.

"Right you delicious bunch of fairies, like the Dark Lord says, I want that blip blatted – now! Emergency briefing for all top brass in my office in 10 minutes. Jump to it Stooge, or I shall personally see to it you will never jump again – mainly because you will have no legs."

"Already done," said an oily demon wearing the insignia of a General Disaster, as it scampered off on its cloven hooves to bash an inferior into action.

Long years in Murk's military service had taught the Scabbatch one thing above all else: delegate, so if it all goes horribly wrong, there is always someone else to blame.

XXIII

The deck of the good ship *Rover Woof-Woof* was awash with good spirits as it bobbed at anchor amongst the clouds. Knockout punch was the particular spirit in question. And the couple of beakers of brew that Fyrsil had been persuaded to drink in toasts to open the traditional Loot pirates Raid Committee was not helping his concentration.

Tradition has a lot to answer for, and in the case of the pirate raids around the shores of Glob, it was a surprisingly democratic tradition. Every member of the crew had the democratic right to vote for any plan of attack, what was to be attacked, and when to attack. As this had always been written into any piratical contract, it was taken as read that these practices applied, even when none of the pirates entering into a contract could read.

The nuisance of democratic processes had traditionally been overcome by the more ambitious captains through the age-old universal political device of bribery. A couple of barrels of Knockout punch was usually all it took to incapacitate any independent reasoning by any difficult member of a crew. Usually the thought process of putting one foot in front of the other was severely damaged, let alone anything more complicated. By the time the sea bandits had emptied the barrels of punch and had woken up with a fully orchestrated headache, the captain would inform them of what they had voted to do in great detail. That was another tradition.

Fyrsil had not quite grasped the essence of this decision making process.

"Right," he said, and cleared his throat through a megaphone. "Now let's have a show of hands for Plan 22A: The Plan for Attack of Castle Gloom If All Other Plans Fail. No abstentions, and no voting partners on this one, if you please."

A ragged chorus of loud guffaws and heckling drifted from the sprawled figures in their deck chairs.

"Run through that one again," shouted Groggie between belches.

"Hear, hear!" cackled Crock, excitedly thumping his walking frame on the deck for emphasis.

With a growl of approval from the rest of the crew, except for Peg who managed a loud purr, Fyrsil sighed and picked up the pile of parchment sheaves marked 'Plan 22A' in big writing.

"What's the score so far?" he asked the Bobo, who was acting as the official votes recorder.

"We've got a tie for plans one to 15, all scoring maximum points, with a recount on 19, and a review of the situation on Plan 21 after spoiled ballot papers."

Fyrsil exhaled loudly, and steadying his feet on the gently rocking deck of the galley as it bobbed on hot bean-air balloons, he lifted the megaphone to his lips again.

"The Plan for Attack of Castle Gloom If All Other Plans Fail..." he shouted.

"Louder. Can't hear at the back," Daisy bawled as she sipped delicately from the bucket of punch which had been passed incorrectly from her right hand side, but no one cared by that stage about the niceties of traditions of serving drinks.

*   *   *

As the day dragged itself into existence up to the Gates of Murk, it seemed to be much like its predecessors. As with most days for those unlucky enough to be posted to the entrance of the Murk, boredom reigned supreme. Goblins picked their noses as they shuffled paperwork, imps on duty could be lucky if they got anyone passing through customs during an active month, and the dragons made unpleasant smells in their stables between snores, as the demon Dragon Squadron slept in unison at their post.

If a demon had any sense of aesthetics, those serving out a posting at the Immigration Control, would not be terribly impressed by their lot. A grumpy collection of huffy hills piled up into the decidedly unattractive Vom mountain range. On the plateau of the tallest and ugliest mound of dandruff scree, a series of squat and featureless buildings huddled under a large gargoyle infested concrete gateway bearing the legend:

PREPARE FOR YOUR FALL FROM GRACE
YOU ARE NOW IN MURK

('Up to your necks in it' was scrawled on the bottom of the sign, but as all the guards were illiterate they took no notice of it.).

Behind the onyx and anthracite gates stretched a tar-dressed monumental stairway, helpfully labelled The Stairway of Damnation. In front of the gates stood sentinel booths and turnstiles. Here bored imps lurked to check the passports of any creature of Murk returning from a bit of mischief making, havoc recreation, or just breaking out to have a bit of fun in the happening cities of Glob.

The arid trickle of traffic probably did not need to be checked out and checked back in again, but they were. And it was the job of slothful imps to be pernickety about dubious visas and return passes of the travellers. Contradictory signs pointed to different booths making it a multiple choice decision as to whether a busking poltergeist would classify itself as a Heinous and Horrible Murk Resident, or General Trouble or even Antisocial Detritus Inhabitant of Murk. Whatever channel they chose, there was no automatic wave through to the outside world and a view of Vom peaks. There was always the compulsory detention, strip search, interrogation, and a bit of ritual torment. That was just to get out. To get back into to Murk there was the compulsory confiscation of any souvenirs that might give pleasant thoughts, followed by a period of festering in the quarantine pound until considered vile enough to fit in on Murk again.

A short muck slinging distance from the quarantine cages lay a small landing strip where a Dragon Squadron flew the occasional routine patrol in the Exclusion ZapZone over the Vom mountain peaks. Their task was to ensure that nothing that ought not to, approached the Gates of Doom. As not many beings in their right minds, apart from the occasional over-adventurous package tour, thought that a visit to Murk was anything more that an unattractive proposition, the demon pilots blatted whatever was silly enough to move. It also relieved the boredom – and they were well and truly bored.

Boredom reigned supreme, with apathy, sloth and tedium installed as chief ministers in mean jerry-built shacks of the Dragon Squadron camp.

In an unlit corner of an office marked *Squadron Chief Basher* a telephone jangled into life. A string of oaths erupted from another corner, where the burly figure of Bruiser the Chief Basher had been so bored that he had been ironing his cap badge. The telephone's shrill bell took the demon so much by surprise that he had ironed most of his fingers before he registered to yell in pain.

On any other occasion he would have kicked his obsequious goblin gofer to answer the infernal ringing, but he remembered that he had suspended his kickable assistant from the toenails above the ever-boiling kitchen cauldron for a bit of a lark. Throwing the iron out of the window, Bruiser grabbed the receiver.

"What do you want?" he roared.

The voice at the other end told him, and Bruiser's face immediately turned sickly grey. The dashing bushy moustache favoured by the pilots of the Dragon Squadron drooped and quivered as he held the receiver away from his burning ear.

"No...yes, Sir, General Disaster...absolutely General...no, of course...always prepared...the worst condition possible...combat readiness? The XXII Dragon Squadron is always prepared for a... General Disaster...understood...and will ensure that my dragon aces leave no traces of any...General Disaster?...Film it!

Bruiser, the Chief Basher of XXII Dragon Squadron sucked at his throbbing recently ironed hand.

"A crew is on its way. Well I'm not sure I can spare a dragon for a bunch of wimpy ...In that case one of my worst fiery beasts will be available so the Dark Lord can enjoy the worst day's entertainment ever recorded."

The receiver went dead. Bruiser cradled it in his good hand for a moment, and then threw it against the wall with all the force he could muster. Instead of disintegrating into a thousand broken pieces, the demon-proof phone – standard military issue to withstand the tantrums of service personnel – bounced back onto the desk with a quick *tring*, and settled back to sleep again.

"Soap, pumice stones and ultra white detergents," the Chief Basher swore, as he kicked down the office door and stormed along the corridor, kicking holes in the plasterwork as he went.

"Sergeant! Scramble alert. Briefing five minutes in the stables," he bellowed, lashing out at recumbent bodies as he waded through the offices. "Where's that too good to be damned Little Basher. Saddle up all dragons," he screeched as he knocked two sleepy-headed demons together and booted them through a window. "Five armed with Muckraker missiles, the rest Splattguns and Vombombs," they heard as they landed in the grey ash parade ground, and scampered off to the dragon bays in the stables.

"This is going to be fun," Bruiser thought to himself as he burst into the Ops Room and set about slapping all the snoring operators awake, and then bopped them on the head again for good measure.

On the radar screen a static blot bleeped patiently. The blood red eyes of the dashing Dragon Squadron commander glazed over as Bruiser snarled in anticipation.

* * *

Strains of a jolly ditty sailed upwards into the billowing clouds, as all aboard the *Rover Woof-Woof* they bawled out the refrain of a traditional Loot raiding song, conducted theatrically under the frilly handkerchief of Captain Cuffbert. All apart a boy, a giant, and a brightly plumed bird of war.

These three were huddled over a pile of parchment slips, sorting them into piles, which were then counted individually.

"Right, that should be the lot," said Boac, licking his pencil stub with an air of finality. "As temporary counting officer in this election, I can declare that, including soiled voting slips – and some people have been very dirty – we have a dead heat between plans 7 and 15."

Fyrsil groaned. The Bobo ruffled its feathers in sympathy.

"Not again. Look at them. You won't be able to get a sensible vote out of them in the state they are in. That is the third time they have sung that verse, and it has been to a different tune every time. Big-Gulop is wearing his deckchair as a hat, and the Masked Marauder has been flat on his back and out for the count for the last three recounts," Fyrsil moaned miserably.

"Seems a complete waste of time. No good asking troops what they would like to do. Got to tell 'em. Specially if it's a dirty job. This democracy thing will never catch on," the Bobo said wagging its horrible head in exasperation.

"But it's tradition. They won't attack Murk without a proper democratic vote," Fyrsil said.

"In their state they won't know if they have voted at all by the time they have some sense in them," sniffed the Bobo.

Boac was about to say something about democracy, when something else struck him.

"Bandits," said Boac, pointing to a line of little black dots in the sky.

"Bandits – 11 o'clock," he said for emphasis.

The Bobo had got the gist of the situation, and had hopped down the main hatch to start up the Comfy Chair into emergency flight mode, and get some speed on.

"Prepare to repel boarders," Boac shouted.

"Prepare to repel boarders?" Fyrsil questioned incredulously.

"Repel boarders?" shouted Groggie, snapping out of his Knockout punch induced doze in his deckchair. And to prove that he had been wide awake all the time, he shot off two pistols into the air at nothing in particular.

Unfortunately the nothing in particular where the shots passed through, happened to be in particular two balloons that had been so carefully inflated by Crock's chronic digestive system, and had until that moment been keeping the galley floating among the clouds.

Diving for cover, Boac was just about to shout out the warning "There be dragons!" as three of the fiery beasts screamed down in bomb runs, with spear-wielding demons yodelling ferociously on their backs. Before the words could get out of his mouth two large explosions rent the air, and the galley suddenly lurched into a plummet and disappeared into a cloud as three deadly Vombombs whistled harmlessly overhead.

Flapping at idle in his tactical position of '*as high above the target zone as possible without losing sight of the enemy*' the squadron chief Basher swore by the Great Dung Beetle and all its unsanitary works. Not only had the target disappeared in a miraculous evasion manoeuvre, but he had just watched three of his fighters being frazzled as they flew into two balls of fire. Bruiser cursed again as they dropped out of the sky and crashed into the Vom mountainsides.

"This is not fair!" he screamed into the wind, desperately wanting to hit something.

His headphones crackled with the repeated reports of the flying galley's magical disappearance and the terminal fate of Blue Wing.

"All wings, repeat all wings. Stop this holy babble and find the target. I want that flying pleasure palace blown to smithereens. I want it in pieces. I want nothing to remain. And if there is any pilot who fails to do his duty, they will be strung up by their horns, disembowelled, and fed morsel by morsel to a colony of carnivore ants. No questions – just do it, and do it now!"

Wrenching at the reigns of his mount, he put the dragon into a steep dive, heading for he cloud where the galley had disappeared. The two demons keeping station on his wings kicked their dragons into maximum revs, and forming a 'V' formation, plummeted into a screaming dive, and hoped they would find whatever they were looking for.

XXIV

Crashing out of the purple mists of the cloud they had dropped into, the galley edged its nose out the death drop stall and pulled up into a face distorting loop packed with enough G-force to flatten a cannonball into a lead pancake. The canvas wings clattered on its oar struts, threatening to rip into tattered bunting, as Fyrsil pushed the wheel forward in a white knuckle grip and steadied the ship into a glide. He whistled down the speaking tube to the engine room.
"What do you want?" barked the Bobo.

"Ask the Comfy Chair for some power. We had better cloud hop from here on in. That was not a very friendly reception," Fyrsil shouted down the tube.

It was something about the communication tube – everybody shouted down it, despite the ultra sensitive earpiece that could pick up a mouse burping at 30 paces.

"What do you think I have been doing while you have been playing games up there? The Comfy Chair is in a sulk. That unprogrammed dive nearly pulled out most of its stuffing, and it is counting how many stitches have been stretched," the Bobo squawked so loudly that Fyrsil hd to hold the earpiece under the folds of his toga to save his lugs from the decibel onslaught.

"Promise the chair new upholstery – and new covers in a pattern of its choice – and get those wings working. I want you here to operate the defence system," Fyrsil shouted. And for good measure he added: "and that's an order," and instantly regretted it, hoping the Bobo wouldn't go into an insubordinate sulk.

After disentangling themselves from the ratlines and other bits of rigging that they had grabbed hold of as they fell through the sky, Daisy and Buttie led a quick spruce up of the deck. They busily stacked the deckchairs, told Groggie and Captain Cuffbert to pick up the cannonballs and put them in neat piles in the cannon loaders, and berated anyone who got their feet in the way of the vacuum cleaner. They found it exasperating trying to sweep up around the Masked Marauder and his gang struggling to take control of the mainsail, which was throwing a tantrum at being so rudely thrown out of shape.

Big-Gulop was peering at the control binnacle for ARFDAS in a frightening way. There was visible doubt written all over his face as to which were the right buttons to press to activate the system, combined with the determination to get it to work if it was the last thing he would do. This prospect sent the rest of the crew diving for cover again. It was the only sensible thing to do with Big-Gulop's reputation for putting his over-sized foot into situations to transform them into minor disaster areas.

"Um!" Fyrsil addressed the puzzled pirate in a hopefully authoritative tone.

"Er," he continued to Big-Gulop, "are you qualified?"

The pumpkin head of the giant orange buccaneer stopped in mid-finger pointing concentration. It always annoyed him when he was interrupted. Doing two things at once just wasn't his style – or more accurately within his mental capabilities.

"What?"

"It says in the instructions that only trained technicians with at least 50 hours of simulated tactical electronic defence training are authorised to operate the system."

Trying to glide the *Rover Woof-Woof* into the nearest available dense purple cloud while persuading Big-Gulop that his place was as far away from the control panel of the shipboard defence system was not going to be easy.

"Oh," said Big-Gulop in a manner that made it clear to everyone in earshot that he never read instruction manuals.

"It says it in big red writing, so I think it's rather important," Fyrsil continued, hoping to restrain the big man's twitching fingers.

"Is it a rule then?"

"No," replied Fyrsil quickly, knowing the pirate penchant for breaking any rule, and stamping on it very hard. "Just something that is very highly recommended if you want to keep your skin and gooey bits together."

The galley was losing height as it ran out puff on its angled glide. It was a toss up between continuing to wean Big-Gulop away from the temptation to start pressing buttons, and shouting down the tube to the Bobo to kick start the chair if necessary. The clouds seemed to be bustling out the way of the galley, so Fyrsil was having to turn the wheel this way and that to chase the purple fluff balls as they tried to hide from the sight of the dragon squadron.

A wave of relief flowed over Fyrsil as with a whump the oars rose and fell, giving the galley a big push forwards. The negotiations had obviously ended in an agreement. The Bobo climbed up the companionway from the hold, and went puce green with fright.

"But what I want to know, is what this button does..." Big-Gulop said pointing a ponderous digit closer to a red and yellow bulbous knob with DANGER written all over it.

The Bobo squawked nervously.

"I could tell you better if you moved away – NOW!" the bird shrieked, only just in control of its voicebox.

"Why's that ?" Big-Gulop asked, plainly puzzled.

"Because , if you were a trained technician with only five minutes simulated training, you would know that the particular button you want to press is called the *Deathwish* programme," the Bobo explained as it hustled the bulky pirate out of arms reach of the console. "In short, once activated there is no going back on a 'take no prisoners' self-destruction course of action. Simply put, it will blow up the ship and all who sail in her along with everything around it for a radius of two miles."

Big-Gulop scowled a bit, and then said: " Oh. Well why didn't someone tell me that before."

"Why don't you help Peg tie those pink ribbons in the anti-boarding nets," suggested Fyrsil, wanting to get the lumbering lump off the poop deck. "If you do that, you can have the first bash at any demon who comes close enough."

"You're on," Big-Gulop said, grinning at the thought of his most favourite thing: bashing things.

Fyrsil wiped his brow, as he swung the wheel and pushed the prow of the *Rover Woof-Woof* into a purple haze of cloud.

"That was close," he said.

"Probably as close as those dragons are going to be when we emerge at the other end of this cloud," the Bobo said, pointing to three circling specks flying in formation. "And it looks like their friends are joining them for the party."

Fyrsil thought "damn it!" and tried to think of a way out. "I have a plan," he announced to the ship's company.

The Bobo sighed heavily, and then disappeared into a purple silhouette as the galley sailed through the dense inner core of the cloud.

* * *

Small puffs of flame spurted rhythmically from the nostrils of the panting dragon as it soared amongst the scudding towers of cirrostratus decorating the mauve tinged sky. Sweat and blood dripped from its flanks where Bruiser's spurs had savagely driven it through a helter skelter ride in the gathering gloom. His flying goggles were misting up as he fumed at the voices crackling in his headset.

"What do you mean lost the visual, you bungling bunch of moat bait. I want blood, and if its not the blood of these aliens from Heaven, it's going to be yours!" the Chief Basher ranted.

The crackle stopped.

"Hello Black Leader this is Chief Basher. Do you read me? I know you are out there. Report your position, or I'll have you skinned and used as a bath mat. You had better read me. Hello?..."

Bruiser gnashed angrily, and chomped at his reins in frustration, sick to death of this cloud-hopping game of hide and seek. Not only had he lost sight of the rest of the squadron, but he had not had a peep of the ballooning galley. From time to time there were sightings, that made his fingers itch to use his Muckraker missiles, but then the ship would disappear into another cloud bank. To make matters worse he did not know where his other Wings of the Dragon Squadron were, and his only company was his personal wingmen and a dragon with the constantly recording film publicity unit.

Although the dragons were fitted with the latest direction finders, not one pilot seemed to have mastered how to use them. Not that Bruiser could either, but he swore into the wind and vowed there would be changes when they got back to base.

A hot shiver ran up and down his spine as he thought of the footage of the sortie so far recorded by the film crew. Lord Trachidambabble would not find it very entertaining so far. The performance had been a comedy of errors, and that was not the sort of film the Dark Lord had booked. The future would have a precarious feel about it, unless the right goods were delivered, and there was nothing so far that indicated his personal survival.

Yanking at his reins, the Chief Basher chucked his mount into a dive, getting speed up for a power climb, the two wingmen doggedly keeping close station, while the film unit veered off in a different direction.

* * *

"I don't like this plan. Can we have another one?" drawled Captain Cuffbert, as he leaned nonchalantly on the taffrail whisking his lace handkerchief in front of his long elegant nose.

"What's wrong with it?" asked Fyrsil as he negotiated their emergence from the cloud.

With his birdwatching skills, Boac was on station to spot for dragons as the *Rover Woof-Woof* made the aerial leaps between cloud cover.

"Well, to be honest old chap, it's a touch boring. You know lacking interest, excitement, zip, or anything like that."

"But it's safe," said Fyrsil.

"My point exactly. Odds bodkin, what we need is a bit of pep, vim, spunk or whatever. Something to spice up the trip before we get to Castle Gloom. Now a nice little *aperitif* would be thrashing a few demons, letting them feel a gutful of cold steel, and perchance collecting a few dragon head trophies to hang from the yardarm."

"Yer," agreed Groggie, who was standing pugnaciously in support of his dandy colleague. "Anyways, we've got to test out all this new kit the painted bird set up for blasting the enemy out of the skies. Best to give it a try out before we really use it proper like."

There were grumbles of agreement from the crew that had gathered around Fyrsil at the wheel.

"What are we that we do creep among the clouds like some wee mousie? Give a dragon a good poke in the eye, and any other place where it reveals itself!" the Masked Marauder declared, in his red satin Y-fronts.

Fyrsil gulped, hard.

"But," began Fyrsil, and then decided to change tack. "I like a bit of a skirmish as much as the next man..."

"And woman," interjected Daisy, swigging the last of the Knockout punch from a bucket.

"Quite so – and woman. But the most important part of the raid, as well as performing the most daring raid in the history of piratical plundering on Glob, is to save the planet."

"That's as maybe, but a smidgen of entertaining diversion is always required to keep a crew happy," Buttercup said, in sisterly support for Daisy, and to help promote the cause of equality in a fighting free-for-all.

"Buttie is quite right. It's not fair you men going off and having all the fun. Female intuition makes for a far more intelligent and effective blatting and bashing," Peg said, driving the point home with her wooden leg with wallops of emphasis on Groggie's head.

Fyrsil sensed that the discussion was not only losing the point, but was losing direction.

Saving the world had not been his idea of fun in the first place. Trying to do so with a bunch of suicidal maniacs who thought that it would be an amusing diversion to stop and have a tussle with demons on dragons, was complete madness. Fyrsil's plan had been quite simple: scuttle along from cloud to cloud, climbing high into the sky towards the pink suns and Murk. The strategy was based on evasion rather than confrontation of demons, mainly due to their reputation for enjoying all manner of senseless slaughter, maiming and disfigurement.

Besides, the important thing was to get to Murk as soon as possible, pick up the Golden Orbs and Ness recipe, and get back to Heaven as quickly as possible - hopefully in one piece. Glob depended on it. Hap depended on him to do it. And his own existence depended on it.

These were all rational arguments. Fyrsil tried his powers of persuasion (not very powerful); pulled the Being Stone from his tunic and showed how it was turning dangerously purple; and even whined a bit. In the end he resigned himself to the fact that the *Rover Woof-Woof* was crewed by a bunch of dyed-in-the-wool hooligans, who were determined to make their last ever raiding party ever a memorable punch-up. This could endanger the whole mission, and Fyrsil decided to dedicate a lot of thinking time to try and circumvent his crew's desires while keeping them relatively happy.

Time to think suddenly went overboard.

ARFDAS bleeped into action sounding like a frantic metronome, and the Bobo jumped to its station to try and work out what was happening.

"Action stations," shouted Fyrsil, more to be able to see what he was doing without a bunch of hefty pirates blocking the view.

A great cheer went up, and the eclectic crew of the biggest ruffians on Glob stampeded to take up the best positions in the deck chairs. Eagerly they fingered swords and pistols as they waited for the show to unfold in front of them.

"It's almost as good as the good old days," Groggie kept telling anyone every couple of minutes, until the communal "hist", followed by the chorused "shuddap", and emphasised by a belt round the ear with a wooden slops bucket told him that no one was interested in what he thought.

"What's happening?" Fyrsil asked the Bobo.

"Dunno. Can't work it out. There's something out there, but none of the cannons can lock onto it. The bow or stern chasers should be the first to engage an unidentified enemy craft. They're the ones with the range. But there's nothing on the screen." The Bobo scratched its plumed head and pushed a number of keys, to activate different projectile applications of the defence configuration.

Fyrsil didn't say anything. "Typical" is what he thought, but presumed it would not help the situation.

The bleeping emitted by ARFDAS was now just one long, piercing, high pitched tone.

From the deckchairs the crowd jeered, stamped their feet and chorused "why are we waiting?" as the purple mist of the cloud swirled around them.

Then it happened.

XXV

A sudden explosion of timbers upset the seating plan, and knocked the expectant spectators off their deckchairs and into a jumbled heap on the deck, as the hull of the *Rover Woof-Woof* shook with the impact of a projectile hitting its target. As the words "What the …?" formed on tongues, as low flying black shadows shot up either side of the galley in a gale of slipstream. ARFDAS, late but better than never, stopped its whining, and activated broadsides from both sides of the ship as the dragons shot by, heaving the *Rover Woof-Woof* into another hiccup in the air.

"Got one. Dusted!" cried Boac from his lookout position on the prow, and carved a nick in the stem with his shark gutting knife.

A ragged cheer rose from the lips of the crew as they rushed around reloading the cannons and cursing happily to each other. With the guns primed, and ARFDAS set on 'Fire At Will', Fyrsil had time to notice that there seemed no evidence of any damage to the ship. Perplexed, he went back to the wheel, and found that the steering didn't work.

"I've got no steerage. Can you check the hold Captain Cuffbert? We must have been hit below the waterline," he shouted to the nearest member of the crew, who happened to be adjusting his silk bandoliers. Peering into the hold, Captain Cuffbert twirled his moustache and grinned unpleasantly.

"My, my, I do believe we have a visitor: a rather irascible demon to be exact who seems to have come in through the back door. Me thinks we should extend a proper greeting to our honoured guest."

Drawing his delicately decorated rapier, with an elegant hop the dandy pirate disappeared down the main hatch.

Fyrsil groaned.

"Goodee. Leave him to me."

"He's mine. I need to test this special cudgel I made."

"No one finish him off until I've had a go…"

Like a lemming migration the crew jumped through the main hatch, scrummaging to have a bash at the demon who had flown into the bottom of the *Rover Woof-Woof.*

"Well that explains why ARFDAS initially failed to activate," the Bobo told Fyrsil above the howl of a demon that was receiving the full attention of a fun-loving bunch of pirates eager to get some bashing practice in before the fight got underway properly. With its head stuck in the hole in the bilge timbers it had created, it was not enjoying the undivided attention of the Loot veterans getting into their stride with good old fashioned pirate hospitality.

The Bobo gave a quick check to the Comfy Chair, to make sure it wasn't too shaken, nodded at the demon bashing session, and joined Fyrsil again at the wheel.

"I have a feeling that the enemy have accidentally found the ARFDAS blind spot in their first sortie. I would suggest the hanging of anti-demon mines under the ship as an early warning system," the bird squawked over the din of pirates at play with a victim.

After another quick inspection, it confirmed what Fyrsil had suspected. The dragon had broken the steering mechanism as it ploughed into the bowels of the galley. There was absolutely no response from the wheel, which gave Fyrsil a quiet panicky feeling, as they were starting to drift out of the cloud and into clear mauve skies.

Two equally pink suns, dangling like decorative baubles without a tree, appeared on the starboard bow as the *Rover Woof-Woof* sailed out of the safety of their cloud cover. Nervously Fyrsil scanned the skies for other members of the Dragon Squadron.

"You had better get tooled up," the Bobo told Fyrsil.

Non-comprehension was written large all over Fyrsil's face.

"Don your armour and buckle your sword. In short, find some weapon with which to defend yourself if the demons attempt to board the galley. It might come in handy."

Fyrsil thanked the Bobo for its advice, and with what was meant to be a nonchalant expression indicating that he was not the sort of security guard to the Golden Palace and Cupbearer of Hap who really needed weapons, rummaged around in his bumbag to see if there was anything useful stored there for self defence in the cramped spaces of a flying ship.

A succession of crashes and bangs resounded from the hold, while Fyrsil sorted through the odd oddments deemed useful by Hap and other gods.

He scratched his itching nose, and then remembered what it meant. It always itched in that peculiar way when Fyrsil was in particular danger. Out of the corner of his eye he saw that his senses had not lost their instinctive panic button.

"Bandits," he shouted.

"Oooh, goodie – where?" asked a grinning Big-Gulop. With as much as effort as it takes a practiced chef to flip a pancake, he scooped up the trussed and hissing demon and chucked it up on deck.

"This one is a bit tied up, for the moment," Big-Gulop laughed in a manner that only merciless buccaneers do when something very unamusing is about to happen to their victims.

As far as the demon had been led believe, this sort of thing was not meant to happen. People from the surface of Glob were meant to be afraid of demons. It stood to reason.

A distinctive whine filled air, similar to the amplified noise of child when it is told to eat up its greens.

Distracted from the pile of thermal socks, aqualung, novelty pumpkins, and trouser press that had been pulled from his bumbag, Fyrsil looked up to see the skies thick with the flaming Dragon Squadron. One formation in particular looked particularly unwelcome as it made a bee-line nose-dive for the *Rover Woof-Woof*. This was not going to be a friendly house call.

"Take cover," Fyrsil shouted, more to try and exert a bit of authority than as a warning to the crew, who were climbing out onto the deck again.

Happily chatting amongst themselves after the pleasant diversion of demon bashing, they re-arranged the deckchairs to watch ARFDAS display its true potential. After bagging his place in a prime spot, the Masked Marauder nailed the demon to the mast by the ears, so it didn't start any silly distractions during the impending action.

Having donned a special anti-flash cap, the Bobo tweaked the controls of ARFDAS as it bleeped reassuringly, waiting for the diving dragons to enter range.

"Bank to the right," the Bobo called to Fyrsil.

"Why?"

"To increase elevation trajectories."

"Alright, alright," Fyrsil called back, all fingers and thumbs as he tried to get to grips with the personal armaments he had found in the bumbag.

(After pulling out the Shield of Righteousness, Fyrsil had had to rummage hard to find anything else suitable for a fight. All that came to hand was a high powered water gun, and a cupid's bow and quiver of arrows.)

He cranked at a lever to stop the port bank of oars. ARFDAS latched onto target and emitted a solid beep, and the bow chaser sounded its booming report.

Loud cheers erupted from the deck as the pirate crew sat back and enjoyed the spectacle as the first dragon of the formation pirouetted in the sky, its demon pilot was catapulted from its saddle.

"Good shot sir! Slap bang on the bonce. Good shot I say!" applauded Captain Cuffbert as he raised his opera glasses again, eager not to miss the excitement of the unfolding drama.

ARFDAS sounded a long beep homing in on another target as the two remaining dragons continued their dive towards the galley. Two more guns blew blue smoke from their muzzles, and danced back on their trolleys, and two more dragons fell like ninepins from the sky.

The initial roar of applause stopped in mid voice, as what appeared to be two particularly nasty and stale Christmas puddings hurtled through the air towards the *Rover Woof-Woof*. The demons had released their Vombombs before being knocked out of the sky.

Grabbing at the levers, Fyrsil started to manoeuvre the ship into a bank to starboard, and held his breath as the bows yawed slowly round to clear one of the chemical cocktail bombs. Time did a bit of running on the spot as the crew stared in open mouthed apprehension. The Comfy Chair, sensing danger was flapping the port wing with great gusto. Time might have been running on the spot, but for Fyrsil it stood still, as he realised that there was only one place that the remaining Vombomb was heading for, and that was the spot he was standing on. Faced with the two options of : a) run for cover and hope to survive the explosion; and b) do something stupidly brave; Fyrsil naturally took the irrational course and started fumbling with the cover to the Shield of the Righteous to put it into action. Crouching behind the shield, Fyrsil carefully read the guarantee on the back of the shield and noted that explosive projectiles were not covered in the long list.

Deciding it was a bit late to worry about returning it to the manufacturer, he had a quick peep at what was happening to the Vombomb, and decided that it was too late to read the instructions for the shield. Disasters always have a slow-motion clarity about them for their victims just before they strike. This particular impending disaster seemed to be slowing down to display its sprig of holly doing dizzy revolutions as it pelted towards Fyrsil.

The next sensation was of his arm being hit by the biggest hammer made on Glob, as he skidded across the deck and crunched into one of the many painful solid obstacles that litter any ship. After that he lost touch with Time for a bit, and the next thing he realised was that he was baring his teeth for one of those extremely silly grins people wear when they have done something stupid, but got away with the consequences.

He looked around at the motley collection of oddities he liked to think of as his crew, who were all sitting stupefied in their chairs.

A big explosion rocked the galley, breaking the spell of incredulity and sending Loot's finest collection of buccaneers scurrying for cover. Only after the *Rover Woof-Woof* had sailed through a brief shower of scales, fins, a tail and lots of bloody bits, did anyone realise that Fyrsil had deflected the Vombomb and downed the other dragon with a direct hit.

Big-Gulop's mouth hung open unattractively in his creased pumpkin face, while the Masked Marauder's mask was contorted into a dumbstruck expression.

"Well, a hip, hip, and a jolly good hurrah for our fine young captain. Well done sirrah! A fine shot, and a fine first blooding if I'm not mistaken," declared a shell-shocked Captain Cuffbert, who advanced on Fyrsil raising his hat as the ship's company broke out into a chorus of spontaneous congratulatory yelling.

*　　*　　*

The Chief Basher fumed commands and spittle down his intercom at Green Wing, Grey Wing, and Mucky Wing. Suddenly remembering his priorities, he grinned at the cameras for the Castle Gloom Promotions Team who had pulled alongside on their supercharged griffin.

An enemy that fired back was one thing. An enemy that not only fired back, but downed members of his elite Dragon Squadron was not something that could be tolerated. It had never happened before. A couple of Vombombs lobbed was all it usually took to disperse any mistaken travellers lurking around the borders of Murk.

"Right, I want Muckrakers pasting that flying wreck, and I don't care whether it's in range or not. Undercover of the missile fire, all available dragons will attack at once. Form circle formation, and down that damn ship, or I will have all your gizzards ripped out and boiled for glue. Blat, blast and board that flying monstrosity. No surrender, no prisoners – everything must go! Go! Go! GO!"

He switched off the intercom and smiled horribly at the camera.

"Good training for the troops, this sort of exercise," Bruiser shouted at the camera crew. "A few losses means a chance of promotion for any really bad dragoneer, and gets some new blood into the squadron. What I want now is the blood of those clowns in that dinky floating fairground ride that might have once called itself a ship."

The microphone boom arm swung closer to his face as the cameraman came in for a close up shot.

"Survival of the filthiest – that's my motto. Come on let's go and have some fun."

Performing a perfect loop the loop, Bruiser the Chief Basher dived down to join his depleted squadron, and take up his traditional position at the rear of the attack.

✳ ✳ ✳

"Yikes!" is not an expression normally used in common parlance outside cartoon strips, but this, or something remarkably similar is what escaped Fyrsil's lips.

From the elation of making the Vombomb score an own goal, he looked up to a sky black with dragons assembling for an aerial charge.

"Hur, hur," said Boac, and gulped guiltily.

The ARFDAS bleeped as three dragons broke away from the encircling squadron, and in a swooping manoeuvre where the Wing spread out like the prongs of a trident, they fired their Muckraker missiles. The first whistled towards the *Rover Woof-Woof* with alarming accuracy, bursting through the lateen sail with an enormous roar and leaving a gaping hole that left Daisy tutting about the mess. Before the second dragon had time to fire its projectile, the Bobo put in a covering broadside, as Fyrsl tried to steer a weaving coarse by banking the galley with levers this way and that.

The bleep of ARFDAS filled the expectant silence, but was unable to lock onto its targets as the dragons jinked in different directions before firing their weapons. Another missile sailed past the bows, close enough for Boac to tap its tail fin.

177

The wings of the galley pumped up and down in their rowlocks, as the Comfy Chair motored on through the skies. The Bobo taking mannual control of the ARFDAS locked onto the last dragon as it dived down in a daring run. The bow chaser barked out its report as the dragon launched its Muckraker and skittered back up to the heights, where the rest of the squadron were jockeying for position in the planned charge.

With the knowledge of all mariners looking at the trace of a torpedo on target, the pirate crew watched from the rail as the missile sped towards the ship.

After the recent adulation of Fyrsil's last act of brave folly, he had been shaking his arm to try and revive some sort of feeling in the numbed limb. As he was doing so his noticed some buttons on the grip of the Shield of the Righteous. With a warning sign or two, and no proper instructions, he deduced that out of *Glow, Glare, Burn* and *Rebound*, one of these might a saving function for his expeditionary force.

One of them did, but afterwards Fyrsil had no idea which one, he pushed his way to the front of the ranks of spectators, who were busily taking bets on the fate of the ship. Resting his shield on the handrail, Fyrsil pointed it in the direction of the big black dart homing in on the galley. With a flurry of fingers he pushed all the buttons in every sequence he could think of in the hope that one might do the trick.

Something must have worked. From their stations on the deck most of the pirates said afterwards they saw a blinding flash, heard a midair explosion, and then went blind – for a good couple of minutes.

It was slightly different for Fyrsil, who had dropped his dark glasses, and was scrabbling around the deck to find them.

But to the Dragon Squadron charging to the ballooned galley while the defence mechanism was distracted by the Vombomb, it was an experience similar to flying into the flaming core of the pink suns.

As the Muckraker exploded, sending up a fizzing chemical curtain of shrapnel and all the nasty ingredients that made it the pride of Murk Armaments Laboratories, the Dragon Squadron had just bottomed out of their dive. Bruiser had given the order to the draw the five-bladed sabres in preparation for the final sprint and boarding. Then everything went light. Yellow light. Dragons reared and fell out of the sky in panic. Others flew through the chemical fallout, and crashed blindly into the timbers of the *Rover Woof-Woof.* Bruiser, taking up the rear had been grinning at the camera team behind him when he felt a heat wave strike the back of his head. Dumbstruck, he saw the cameraman's eye frazzle in flames as he caught the devastating flash down the viewfinder.

Wheeling his cavorting mount into a steep climb, it was a long time before the Chief Basher could pull up his blinded dragon and look down at the wreckage of his disgustingly venal squadron of demon pilots.

Those dragons which had not crashed into the galley were stampeding across the sky, belching gouts of flame in the pain of being disintegrated by the Muckraker chemical fallout. Far below there were small pockmarks of unseated pilots who had imprinted their fallen outlines in the barren mountain topography.

✳ ✳ ✳

With his shades firmly on his nose again, Fyrsil was just wondering if anything had happened when the retort of the explosion told him it had.

What followed that was a pandemonium of noise and action. The Bobo operating ARFDAS was doing a manic dance at the controls as it popped off canons left, right and centre, putting grapeshot, round-shot, chainshot and even buckshot into the sky, at the dragons and their demon pilots. The half blinded dragons tore through the rigging, knocked over the crow's-nest and got entangled in the boarding nets. Their hapless pilots who were not bucked off with the explosion, fell onto the deck and into the clutches of a slap-happy mob of old pirates who were busily dishing out hearty thwackings, a bit of cutlass slashing, and a general bashing.

Using the Shield of Righteousness to protect himself from demons falling out of the rigging, Fyrsil made his way back to the wheel, to see if he could steer the *Rover Woof-Woof* in any direction, let alone the one he wanted to go in. Jostling back towards the wheel, Fyrsil tried out the water pistol on an entangled demon, and was a bit surprised when it burst out laughing. Taking a closer look at his weapon, Fyrsil noted that the label described it as a Giggle-gun for pacifists, loaded with liquid laughter. He tried it again, and stopped a demented demon dead in its tracks as it charged at Fyrsil swishing its five-bladed sabre. With a look of pure non-comprehension on its face, it smiled beatifically, curled up its talons, and lay on the deck in a huddled ball giggling in hysterics.

It still couldn't stop laughing when Captain Cuffbert bopped it over the head and nailed it to the mast with his other trophies.

"This is more like it," yelled Big-Gulop as he chased a petrified dragoneer demon through the ratlines.

That seemed to be the common consensus among the buccaneers from Loot as they oiled their rusty skills they had enjoyed so much as pirate chiefs. They whooped and hollered as they chased the demons around the ship. Faced with the alternative of a fearsomely sharpened handbag wielded by Daisy, or the dangerous posing antics of the Masked Marauder, demons were quivering on the decks, whimpering and pleading for a quick dispatch to NeverNever. Boac and Big-Gulop were happily chasing the bewildered boarders up and down any existing rigging, dropping them on the deck for the Bobo to set about with vicious kicks with its shining war spurs. Those that thought they might have an easier time at the hands of the fairer sex, got a big surprise with Peg's lethal wooden leg and killer kisses. Groggie was just generally beastly to any demon that came in his cutlass chopping range, while Crock had found new youthful vigour with his specially customised walking frame, which proved very effective for puncturing and clubbing.

"Having fun?" enquired Fyrsil, as Groggie strode back to the stern with another limp body over his shoulder to toss into the clouds below.

"Yer, too right! Haven't had such a good time since…since the Blood Sea ran away. Oh it do bring back memories…"

Groggie stopped. Fyrsil wasn't listening. He was looking over he rail trying to figure out why the galley was listing to port and still not responding to the helm.

The old pirate's eyes narrowed. He heft the demon over the end of the stern.

Up on his toes he crept behind Fyrsil, carefully lifted the still askew helmet with its Bobo perch, and with a simple tap on the head, the saviour of Glob and security guard of Heaven lay concussed on the deck. Quickly hands fumbled around the bumbag and a knife tried to cut its strap. The lock could wait for later.

"A thousand curses – it's blunt!" Groggie quietly exclaimed, and then cut himself on the razor sharp blade of the Official Robber's Handiblade.

Cursing again, he sheathed the knife, and working faster than he had ever done as master pick-pocket in his youth, he flexed his fingers into every permutation to learn the secret of the bumbag's clasp.

Changing his grip, he felt a damp patch on his arm. The next thing he knew he had an inexplicable attack of the giggles. Nothing was funny, and despite mentally fighting against the desire to burst into a belly laugh, so his fingers could work on relieving Fyrsil of the Heavenly bumbag, he gave in to the overwhelming desire to act as if he was being tickled by hundreds of feathers while being told the world's funniest jokes. His stomach was in convulsions, and drawing great gulps of breath, he laughed raucously and painfully at nothing – again, and again, and again.

Somewhere through the rolling agony he heard a searing ripping of canvas and the popping of fart-filled balloons, followed by what he thought was an ominous crack of splintering timber. The *Rover Woof-Woof* seemed to be sliding downhill fast, instead of just listing to port, as on the outer boundaries of consciousness beyond his laughter he heard cries of alarm. He rolled into a scupper, and despite his hysterical humorous convulsions, managed to wedge himself between a couple of lashed barrel, and waited for his world to end.

Soon – hopefully.

Defying gravity the galley *Rover Woof-Woof* floated, suspended momentarily in thin air, and then slipped sideways into a gut-wrenching plummet through the dark ruffled clouds surrounding Murk.

XXVI

A cloud of pure evil hissed around the glinting jet throne. Trachidambabble was in one of those moods. Like a nagging headache, the fouler than normal mood had started as a slight irritation which had built up into a crescendo of white whining noise in Trachidambabble's head.

Multiple torturing of goblins, demon stamping sessions, and other normally relaxing pastimes just didn't seem to relieve the mood at all.

Even the slow decomposition in the slug pit of the Dragon Squadron's Chief Basher after the sinking of the mystery flying ship had not given much light relief. The scanner at Murk border Defence Control Bunker had noted the eradication of the obnoxious bleep as it disappeared into oblivion near Stairway of Damnation. The Lord of Murk had watched grimly as the manacled imps gleefully charted the whole bungled search and destroy operation of the ship, and the wiping out in a single action of the whole Dragon Squadron. Their gabbling excitement had only increased the intensity of the brooding mood. Even mass downsizing of the entire office workforce to nasty piles of foul-smelling dung to stop their gibbering, did not relieve the tension.

Hoodoo, the latest Balck Warlock, had given Trachidambabble measured portions of his delicious Cure-All Medicine Stew, which the Dark Lord found so nutritious he had to ratchet his adam's apple to be able to swallow it. Tension, the warlock had said, was probably the cause, especially with the Big Day coming up. Hoodoo was lucky Trachidambabble's eyes were streaming so much that he couldn't see to demonstrate instant biodegrading to relieve the warlock of the nightly grind of living.

"How would the warlock know what tension was?" Trachidambabble asked himself, as he tried to scrub his tongue with a scourer to eradicate the healthy taste of the stew.

Plans, plans, plans, for centuries, with only incompetents to execute them. Plans, plans, plans, to overturn Heaven and make Murk the force that moves Glob. Plans becoming reality. He should be feeling miserable, but he wasn't. he was feeling happily worried, and that worried him even more.

"Well, no matter," Trachidambabble hissed to himself, "at least it's not long to go now". The launch plans were well in place. The catapults had been tested, the Ness was a Mess, and the date of when Murk turned Glob dark blue had been announced to all incarcerated creatures of his domain.

With a swish of his meanest cloak, Trachidambabble left the regenerative discomfort of his throne and splashed through the puddles of accumulated damp on the flagstones, out of the Hate Hall throne room and into the anteroom of the Control Centre.

"How's it going?" he demanded of the hideous ghoul wearing a filthy lopsided turban, who had the misfortune of heading up the Disinformation and Disorganisation Department.

"Disastrous. Negatively disastrous with a capital N and a capital D. This is going to be the worst event Glob has ever seen, let alone Murk," Compost the department head slobbered enthusiastically.

The ghoul grinned hideously, displaying a row of purple rotting teeth with a large proportion of the last rotting cadaver it had feasted on still wedged in the dental crevices.

Rattling off the gruesome programme to raise the profile of the main event, including the publicity campaign and timetabling of the event itself, Compost failed to notice Trachidambabble's disinterest.

With a "huh!" full of invective, the Lord of Murk and All Darkness scattered the untidily stacked papers on the ghoul's desk with a sweep of the crushed velvet cloak, and made a full angry exit, complete with lingering ill-will.

The mood had taken over again. It was not something medicinal stews could cure. It was a doubt that had lodged itself in the black ghettos of Trachidambabble's mind as it wondered whether being top supernatural force Glob would be as attractive as it sounded. After all with nothing else to do except glory in that role, it might become tedious.

For the first time since Glob's creation, Trachidambabble considered the implications of reversing the driving force of the planet, and was a smidgen unsure of how he was going to put interest in his waking hours after it had been achieved. You might as well be a glorified mechanic if all you ever worried about was keeping the planet going. Causing trouble, pestilence and plague – now those were the interesting bits, the Dark Lord thought sullenly.

XXVII

If anyone had been watching the muddy skies over the Neverend of Murk, they would have spied a strange projectile whistling through the night sky on a kamikaze course to the ground. If they had been bothered to get out their telescope, they would have been able to see a collection of figures looking like gargoyles lining one surface of the spinning object. They may have wondered what these were. They might have wondered why the unidentified flying object was leaving a trail of splintered timbers and nautical knick-knacks as it rolled across the night sky.

More likely, they would have thought "that's odd" and gone back to examining the fluff in their belly button.

With a far from satisfying *plop* the object, better known to its crew as the *Rover Woof-Woof* nose-dived into a mountain of newly washed and fluffy conditioned laundry, smelling faintly of lavender.

With his head in a white linen pillowcase, Big-Gulop opened his eyes, blinked, and wondered if he was dead. He felt himself all over, and seemed to be all there, but found breathing a bit difficult. The eternal white horizon, and the inability to see other bits of himself was a bit worrying, but he decided it was something he could get used to.

A muffled laugh, sounding distinctly like Groggie in one of his rare moments of good humour, was a bit disconcerting. He wondered whether there would be any other sounds from his past, and thought of half a dozen he would definitely not want repeated.

"Take that pillowcase off your head, you addled haddock," was not one of the ones on his black list. And besides, it sounded like the Masked Marauder in a bad mood.

"What pillowcase? We're dead aren't we?"

"I'll just check," said a familiar voice.

"Oww! That hurt," Big-Gulop protested, and wrestled to pull his head covering off, now that the kick in the ribs had confirmed that he was very much alive.

Blinking a couple of times just to make sure of his whereabouts and bodily state, he looked up at the figure who resembled his old shipmate in every way apart from one. Big-Gulop puzzled over what it was.

"Welcome back to the land of the living, you pumpkin-brained son of a pestilent cur. Make yourself useful and help me look for my mask."

That was it, thought Big-Gulop, and cheerfully got up to wade through the neatly piled articles of laundry. Everything was normal again.

The horrific experience preceding the soft landing was now only a distant memory for Big-Gulop, and one that wouldn't bother him again as it got squashed by the over-riding simplicity of the giant's mind.

Fyrsil was someone else who would not be bothered by the frightening plummet of the galley, as it fell through the sky. Mainly because he was still out cold until they made their fortunate landing.

If the Splattgun burst had been more than a wild parting shot before the Chief Basher made good his escape, it would have been an award winning display of aerial gunnery. The brief blaze of fire from the bucking petrified dragon had torn one of the wings of the galley and burst too many of its supporting balloons.

With the good wing flapping in overdrive, the *Rover Woof-Woof* had spun out of control through the sooty clouds, while the crew held on to anything that was not detaching itself from the deck in the helter-skelter fall from the flight path. The combined din of an un-aerodynamic form crashing through the atmosphere, filled with yelling freebooters clinging on for dear life, plus additional howls of demons still nailed to the mast, would have reduced the president of any noise abatement society to tears. With the G-force playing disfiguring tricks on their faces, and the wind deafening them as it rushed past their ears, no one noticed the additional detonation of sound that indicated that they had crashed into the Stairway of Damnation.

It wasn't the write-off collision the manacled imps in the Control Bunker assumed, merely a glancing blow that took away the mast and flung all the nailed demons to a grisly doom below. The galley then barrel-rolled into the anti-gravity vortex at the back of the stairs, was yo-yoed by rogue currents, buffeted by anti-social air pockets, hit a hidden parapet, and was spat out of the vortex again and rocketed to the Neverend of Murk.

Which is where Fyrsil came to, and asked: "What happened?"

Captain Cuffbert, who was standing nearby when Fyrsil rejoined his ship's company, felt sick at the thought of what they had miraculously escaped from, and so just grunted a reply. Besides he was looking for his favourite wig, and he was damned if he was going to do anything else before he found it.

Although the crew had miraculously survived their fall to Murk, that couldn't be said to describe the state of the *Rover Woof-Woof*. Bits had survived. Most other features had simply disappeared.

Fyrsil lifted his shades and considered the galley. He felt enough to let go of the bulwark he had been holding, and lift his nose to try and work out what the funny smell was.

"Hoi!"

He turned his head and took in the disgustingly flamboyant plumage of the ruffled looking Bobo. It looked like the bird was trying to speak very hard but nothing was coming out except a groaning rasping noise. Saying "hoi!" had obviously exhausted its reserves of speech for the moment.

Fyrsil looked at the rest of the pirates, who, he observed, were disentangling themselves from where they were wedged, and tentatively trying out their voice boxes after yelling their way through the death-defying roller coaster ride no one would want to pay to go on.

Trying to get up, Fyrsil fell down again, which somehow hurt his head. The strap of his bumbag was caught in something. Disentangling the strap from a large nautical hook fastened to the deck, which had probably been something to do with the mizzen mast, he stood up successfully on the second attempt.

The scene that greeted his eyes was distinctly strange. The galley had landed in the middle of what was obviously a camp of some sort. Fyrsil also deduced from the high barbed wire fences, nasty spikey entanglements and brooding watchtowers that it was a camp for keeping people in. The odd thing about the camp was that whoever was being kept in, had obviously departed.

The big bright white steel gates had been pulled from their hinges, and there were telltale signs of some sort of struggle around some of the watchtowers, including a figure that looked like a white troll hanging upside down, and sounded like it was whimpering loudly.

In the middle of the camp there were huge bubbling vats, gurgling with soapy bubbles, surrounded on all sides by large spotlessly white barrack blocks. The rest of the space was taken up with the mountainous pile of linen, towels, knickers, and odd socks that had softened the *Rover Woof-Woof*'s landing. Elsewhere there were flower beds of white carnations bordered with freshly painted white rocks, an orderly display of dustpans, brushes, carpet beaters, a file of orderly vacuum cleaners, and other implements of domestic cleanliness.

The camp appeared as a dome of brightness under the dark sky.

"Very strange," thought Fyrsil, and wondered aloud where the inmates, whoever they were, had gone.

He took a couple of steps, and stopped as something clanged against his lopsided breastplate. He picked up the dangling Being Stone and taking it from its protective pouch looked at the little veins of gold tracing through the stone like delicate strands of a spider's web. His mouth went dry, and his adam's apple bobbed up and down as on the boundaries of his senses his inner ear picked up the faint clacking of giant knitting needles, as the three Fates of the universe knitted the enormous woolly pullover of Time.

On the ethereal coffee table in front of the Fates, steaming cups stood on piles of knitting patterns.

"Anyone got anymore of this Glob colour," the young Cloe asked her companions, breaking the silence of eons.

"Now look what you made me do," the flabby wrinkled figure of Lacha in her tweed and twinset tutted. "I've dropped a stitch."

Somewhere in the universe a black hole appeared and swallowed a couple of unsuspecting suns and a clutch of meteorites.

"There's always one, isn't there? I can't find this, I've lost that, can I borrow the other? I don't know this pattern, can you do it? Huh, the younger generation. Lose everything they ever had and then want to have some more. Well not this time young lady. If you can't find it, the universe will have to do without it."

The ancient sack of Attie, the last of the trio, clacked her sharp features and boney elbows at the youngest member of the knitting circle.

"Just asking, that's all," Cloe told them huffily, and began purling furiously.

"I don't know – the future generation," Lacha sighed a dumpy sigh and shook her head as Attie cackled in agreement.

Fyrsil's inner ear didn't quite pick up all this conversation, but it got the general gist, and it filled his consciousness with foreboding.

Straightening his breastplate, he strode forward along what was left of the poop to address the moaning pirates, who had assembled in a vague sort way on the remains of the main deck. After falling over Crock's walking frame which was tangled in stray tackle, Fyrsil picked himself up and stood in what he imagined was an authoritative stance, and then wondered what to say.

Ignoring the most recent events, as the last thing he could remember was the sound of Groggie laughing in a worrying way, Fyrsil spoke about the need for speed, urgency, and knowing where they were. This speech left a bemused crew collecting their thoughts while Fyrsil went below to deal with this last task personally.

The Comfy Chair was looking more than a little disgruntled when Fyrsil visited to consult the AutoNav. It was trying to unbolt itself from mechanism that the Bobo had created to flap the galley's wings. A free-roving spanner hit Fyrsil on the shins, just to show how upset the chair was at the rough treatment it had received during the end of the flight.

Another indication of the chair's disgruntled mood was the remote refusing to work until all the debris had cleared from its seat, and the covers were nicely dusted down. In the end the AutoNav didn't know where the surviving bits of the galley had landed. A message on the screen blinked 'OFF LIMITS' at two second intervals.

Giving the Comfy Chair a friendly tap on its arm as it shook out its tassles, Fyrsil wandered back through the wreckage to the master cabins and his books from Heaven's library.

He stepped carefully along the timbers of the lower deck to avoid gaping holes that revealed the muck that always collected in the bilges. The door to the cabin was clinging hopefully to its hinges, but gave up the battle and crashed to the floor as Fyrsil approached.

When the dust settled, Fyrsil could make out little of what had been his library. Books were scattered everywhere and in the middle of a mound of scattered pages still scratching out the changing history of Glob, sat Groggie nursing a big bump on his head.

"What are you doing?" asked Fyrsil in a tone generally reserved for children playing with matches.

"Um," said Groggie, in a tone generally used by children caught doing something they ought not to do be doing.

Surveying the scene, Fyrsil could see that Groggie had ransacked through his personal effects, leaving them all severely rummaged. What Fyrsil couldn't fathom was what Groggie was searching for. All valuables were kept in his bumbag. In fact most of the Shamir

Smartie Bar-Button's treasury was in there if he bothered to fish around for it.

"Um," said Groggie unconvincingly again, as he tried to get up, but banged his head on the bulwark, forcing him down on the floor again very quickly.

"What are you looking for?"

Groggie sat nursing his bump, and wishing he had the daggers he was trying to stare.

"Right, in that case I have no option," Fyrsil said, and opened his bumbag.

Groggie went white, and despite having very little voice left after the prolonged bout of laughter he had suffered, managed to blurt out: "Alright, alright, I'll tell yer. It's the map."

He had worked out that there were a lot of things stored in the bumbag, with more than one or two being potentially dangerous to his health and rugged bad looks.

"What map?" asked Fyrsil, more than slightly puzzled.

"*The* map," said Groggie with all the emphasis in the right place.

Fyrsil was still puzzled. "Map of Glob? Map of Murk? Map of Loot?"

"*The* map," Groggie repeated, still emphasising correctly. "Listen, in any of these sorts of adventures, there's always a map. Usually with an island, always with a big 'X', and it's always secret."

"What's the 'X' for?" asked Fyrsil, shaking his head sadly as he took out his notebook and quill from the bumbag.

Groggie gulped, not knowing what kind of lethal weapons the feather pen and little black book were. "Treasure of course. Gold, diamonds, jewels, valuable goods, and anything else that can be sold on the black market. You know, the things pirates normally go for."

Fyrsil re-assured him that he did know.

"But this is Murk, where all the nasty, cheap and worthless things on Glob originate from. All that is up here is Hap's Golden Orbs which we have to find…"

"I told you. Golden Orbs – there must be a map for where they be buried."

"No. I don't know where they are, and haven't made a map, and haven't hid it," Fyrsil said in an understanding and concerned way. "There is a rumour that Trachidambabble keeps a store room full of the most fantastic treasures used to tempt rulers and potentates into evil ways, but its only a rumour, and it certainly wasn't believed in Heaven."

In his notebook Fyrsil scribbled illegibly: <u>Groggie</u> - suffering from post-crash trauma. Ask Peg if she has any medical training ref. Maybe adapt some psychology.

Groggie afforded himself a sigh of relief, as the potentially dangerous quill and notebook were returned to the bumbag.

"Now if you want to do something useful, you can help look for the *Encyclopaedia of Everything - Yes Everything*. Hopefully it should have a …" Fyrsil stopped himself from saying 'map' just in time. He did not want Groggie to start getting excited again.

"…A …er…diagram, or chart even, of Murk. We've got to find out where we are, and where we want to get to."

"You nearly said 'map'. I know you did. I knew there was a 'map' in this operation somewhere," he said.

"No I didn't," Fyrsil told the burly pirate, lying badly. "And anyway, if I did, it has nothing to do with any treasure – buried or otherwise."

"What about the Golden Orbs? Sounds like treasure to me. Gold normally fits into that category."

"They are not treasure, they are the Ness dispensers which happen to be gold, because almost everything in Heaven is gold," Fyrsil told an increasingly confused Groggie.

"Well why don't we attack Heaven, if that's where the gold is?"

"Because if we don't raid Murk to get back the Golden Orbs and the recipe for Ness, there will be no Heaven, and no Glob, and so no nothing. When we get back to Heaven, I promise you that I will personally escort you round the storeroom and give you four times your weight in gold. It's just quite important to sort out the fundamentals first – like the continued existence of the planet."

Fyrsil was getting irritable with the constant explanations. Time was short, and the Being Stone was nearly blue. Precious moments were slipping by in a conversation that never got off the subjects of maps and buried treasure.

"Well if that's the case, try a few of these I found in my searches," Groggie said, pulling from his jerkin a fistful of maps, which had been busily redefining themselves with updates on landslides, floods, and other upheavals on the face of Glob.

The only map in existence of Murk was not easy to miss. On paper it appeared as a dark anvil-shaped splodge with a tail. The distinguishing features were very simple as there were very few of them. The tail was the Stairway of Damnation, and there was a large erratic fortified structure with broken curtain walls and a moat which was marked as Castle Gloom. Beside this was an area that looked like a soup stain on a shirt, which was the castle's suburbs of Deeper Gloom, there were a couple of brimstone mines and their associated works, a large fire pit, a few diabolic factories, along with occasional sweat shops and oppressive mills located in inaccessible spots and craters around Murk.

Fyrsil and Groggie pored over the map, wondering where the *Rover Woof-Woof* had landed on the splodge, and how long it would take them to get to where ever they needed to go.

"We're here, and that's where the Golden Orbs will be," said an authoritative voice as a fluorescent orange pinion feather pointed decisively at the map.

"How do you know?" demanded Fyrsil and Groggie in unison.

The Bobo sniffed and tapped the side of its beak knowingly.

"All it needed was a bit of initiative. I interviewed the troll who was dangling from the watch tower."

"So, where are we?"

"Here in the middle of the worst punishment camp devised on the face of Trachidambabble's domain – the Cleaning and Laundry Camp at the NeverEnd of Murk," the Bobo said, a little too smugly to win friends and influence people.

The Bobo continued to arrogantly relate all he had learned from the inverted troll. Although trolls are not usually the subject of sympathy, especially those who are the Camp Commandants of Murk's nightmare punishment centre, Fyrsil began to feel sorry for the hapless beast who had to suffer the Bobo's abrasive questioning.

The results, however, were useful.

Not only did the Bobo learn the exact location of where the *Rover Woof-Woof* had come to rest, but in its desire to give up as much information as possible, the troll burbled on about a camp revolt started by a White Wizard who had emerged out of the bubbling laundry cauldrons and spoiled that particular wash. This wizard had declared holy war to overthrow Trachidambabble, and as the inmates had nothing better to do, and anything was better than enforced domestic cleaning practices, the White Wizard had a 100 per cent conversion rate among the inmates. Knowing what was good for them, and also bored with their lot, the troll guard also succumbed with a 99 per cent conversion rate. The missing one per cent - called the Camp Commandant - was then strung up from the watch tower.

"And how did you extract this information?" Fyrsil asked, just to break the monotony of the Bobo's litany of information extraction.

"Easy. All I had to do was play the classic Mr Nicey-Nicey/Mr Nasty-Nasty routine. Tell me something interesting and he got a pong pellet in the face. Clam up, and ...," the Bobo exhibited a vile green tickling feather from amongst its armoury of covert plumage.

"It seems that trolls will do almost anything not to be tickled. Laughing, apparently is as funny to them as a prostrate hernia."

Fyrsil tried not to show his true feelings regarding modesty and Bobos as he stared hard at the map.

"It will take us days to get from NeverEnd to Castle Gloom. We can't fly off in this wreck. The Comfy Chair has decided that already, and has unstrapped itself from the ship's wings," he said despondently as he studied the contours in front of him in the vain hope of finding a way out.

"Not necessarily, and we don't actually want to go to Castle Gloom."

Fyrsil groaned inwardly. The problem was, he had never known the Bobo not to be right.

With an air of inevitability, Fyrsil and Groggie listened to the braying of the Bobo as it took them through a blow-by-blow account of everything else the troll commandant had revealed, and how it would affect the plans for retrieving the Golden Orbs.

As he listened, a plan started formulating in Fyrsil's mind, and wondered how and when would be the best way to present it to the crew.

XXVIII

For a troll with no real *forte* in thinking, the Production Manager at the Unholy Mess plant thought he was doing very well in his new role.

Mess was not so easy to produce as he first thought. Despite not being able to read, and relying on the most unreliable demon that he had pulled from under the steaming machinery, it seemed alright to him.

With blue being the important distinction of Mess from its Ness, and Mess converting back to golden Ness if there were not the added ingredient of live bodies, he had come up with a solution: the creation of the Dishonourable Suicide Club.

This was a purely voluntary group of workers who wanted to donate their bodies for the greater bad of Murk so it could become the driving force of Glob. A very unworthy cause Grump (the Production Manager) had thought, but it did not help him to get any volunteers. To get round this slight problem he declared that every factory worker was automatically made a lifetime member of the club – subscription payment by survivors only – and so he felt obliged to throw into the bubbling vats any shirkers or anyone not at that time actively engaged in production.

As the demons and imps who worked in the Unholy Mess plant were intrinsically shirkers and skivers, Grump felt morally bound to throw as many as possible into the Mess as he did his rounds as a manager.

It was an even better job than being Captain of the Blackguard, with even more bashing involved.

If there was one thing Grump hated, it was meetings. And at that moment he was sat in his office in the comfy chair, while a green ghoul from the Disinformation and Disorgansiation Department sat in his favourite back-breaker seat while it blah-blahed about the preparations for The Event.

The Event, of course, involving the lobbing of the contents of the Blue Balls of Mess into the atmosphere to make Glob blue, and turn on its axis in a Murk-type way, would be the official occasion to signify Murk's victory over Heaven and its dominating role in the running of the planet.

"Now, for the seating arrangements on the podium…" droned Baba Yaga.

The stage for his Lowness the Dark Lord was being constructed outside the factory car park. The giant catapults were all built and in position, crouching on the tarmac like a family of malevolent prehistoric creatures. The Blue Balls were stored for ease of filling at the back of the factory, ready to be brought round and bolted into position to throw the mucky Mess at the sky.

"…The procession will pass through Deeper Gloom on the highways indicated," wheezed the ghoul through its respiratory complaint, as it indicated on a flip chart the official route.

"Where," Baba Yaga continued, waving its mouldy green hand airily, "the crowds will boo and hiss unenthusiastically by order of the Dark Lord. Members of the Blackguard – your old mob I believe – will cudgel any deviation from the proclamations regarding the celebration of The Event…"

The steel door to the office slammed open, as an imp in a high state of excitement burst in unannounced.

Instincts came before inquisitiveness, and troll whacked the imp on the head.

"What's the meaning of this interruption? We're in a meeting, and meetings are always very important, which means no one can disturb them," huffed Baba Yaga. He would have taken a bite out of the imp's leg if Grump had not dragged the snivelling little creature by the scruff of its neck and dangled it in front of his ugly steaming snout.

"What's the story? It better be good or you're next in the Suicide Club cooking pot.."

The imp's red face waggled precariously in front of the bared fangs.

"Boss…boss, it's Castle Gloom. The place is being attacked. It's…"

There wasn't time for the little forked tongue to manage anymore before its body was flattened against the wall.

"IMPOSSIBLE!" Grump roared, and then thought about it. No imp would ever tell him such an outrageous story unless it was true. The consequences would be too dire to contemplate for the victim. And if it was true, it did mean a marvellous opportunity for bashing, and that was not the sort of opportunity to be missed. Besides the ex-

Captain of the Blackguard had his duty. That was an unquestioning knee-jerk reaction as well.

"Well, that has messed up the timetable, big time. Some people are so inconsiderate..." Baba Yaga complained to no one, because no one was listening, while he tidied his papers into a briefcase.

In one fluid movement Grump picked his favourite cudgel from its hook on the wall, and without even a practice swipe, brought it down full on the ghoul's seeping turban.

"Never mind the timetable – let's have some fun," the troll roared, and swaggered out to rustle up a posse of like-minded demons.

XXIV

REVENGE!

A sweet word, which figured highly in the White Wizard's top ten. A word that he had put to great effect when he had preached his messianic message to the inmates of the Cleaning and Laundry Camp. A word that had fed his new army of disciples on the long march to their position in the Garbage Hills that crowded close to Castle Gloom.

Undetected in the secret canyons among the mounds of rubbish that had been dumped for centuries by the Civic & Amenity Authority outside the castle walls, the White Wizard, or Double W as his followers fondly referred to him, had made his final plans for the assault.

"Everything ready O White Wizard. In addition there has been an interesting little development at the drawbridge which looks extremely disastrous…sorry, advantageous." The neat and clean devil in its well ironed white uniform stumbled over the new terminology as it stood bright eyed in front of its new leader.

"Good. It won't be long now. Revenge is sweet, but the waiting allows me to savour the taste," the wizard said, lifting his field glasses to scan the grim battlements of Castle Gloom's curtain wall and keep. A smile played on Double W's lips as he thought of Trachidambabble's reaction to this unthinkable act.

The plan had gone like clockwork. There was nothing to indicate that anyone in Gloom had any notion of what was in store for them. His shoulders shook in amusement. Like stealing sweets from a baby, he told himself.

So far, so good. And that was 'good' in the new interpretation he would impose on Murk when he sat on the Jet throne.

Under the cover of daylight special volunteers had crept out and poured powerful supplies of detergent into the Gloop infested moat. The effect had even surprised Double W. Overnight the stagnant waters had cleared, and reports came back to camp of a dramatic transformation of the Gloops. They had started performing ritual ablutions and were even observed preening themselves. Feeding frenzies over anything dropped in the moat was out. The new attitude was for any edible morsels donated to their living and feeding environment were divided equally and fairly by an appointed adjudicator. The Gloops had also organised themselves into action groups in between visits to the beautician and cosmetic dentist, and a list of demands for preferred menus had been sent to the castle kitchens and latrines.

The Poisoner Chef, head of the kitchen devils, nearly ate his tail as he frothed in a histrionic tantrum on receiving the list from a florid Gloop with waxed tentacles. It smiled sweetly with newly whitened razor teeth as it read out the petition demanding filo pastry delicacies instead of offal and floor sweepings from the kitchens.

It had taken a whole detachment of trolls to take the Chef into indefinite detention to await injustice, after throwing pots, pans, carcasses, cauldrons and their rancid contents, along with a week's supply of rotting cadavers over the battlements. Unfortunately the hail of equipment and foodstuffs from the kitchens rained down onto the inaugural meeting of the moat environmental awareness action group.

Within minutes the drawbridge of Castle Gloom was crammed with slippery globular Gloops with terrible makeup waving placards protesting at the ecological vandalism, and calling for a moratorium on all waste and chemical dumping in the moat. The result was Murk's first traffic jam causing a gridlock with enormous tailbacks into Deeper Gloom. Irritable giant skunks used to pull carts of festering flux in and out of the castle let off clouds of pungent stench in protest. The odour sat sourly over the scene, getting thicker and stronger, obscuring the placard waving monsters involved in road rage scuffles on the drawbridge, and choking the central freezing systems in the more run down residential developments in Deeper Gloom.

✻　✻　✻

"What is going on?"

The icy chill that scampered into the office of the Minister of Disinformation and Disorganisation told the drooling green ghoul that he was about to experience an unofficial visit from his lord and master. Scurbage, the long-surviving minister, quickly dropped the freshly microwaved snack-sized corpse into the waste bin, and adjusted his worst turban which was untidily unwrapping itself.

"Mobilisation of the populous of Gloom for The Event, Master of Darkness," he said, wiping back the saliva dripping from his rotting mouth, and kowtowed his slimy bulk on the damp flagstones.

The minister peered at the clock on the wall, trying to avoid the sensation of being stabbed by a thousand daggers as Trachidambabble aimed his glare at the prostrate figure.

"A couple more hours and we should be nicely late to ceremonially catapult the first batch of Mess into the atmosphere of Glob to herald the dusk of a new age for Glob," Scurbage monotoned unenthusiastically.

The only sound was the hissing of Trachidambabble's field of evil spitting small plumes of malediction along the edge of the pure black flexi-onyx cloak. The minister chanced a glance in the direction of the Dark Lord, and instantly regretted it. With a small gesture bony fingers snapped, and it felt like a giant yeti lifted Scurbage and swatted him against the stone wall. As he dropped slowly from the great height where his body had hit the blackened masonry, the minister's mind raced as it tried to think of what detail he failed to cover in organising the ceremony.

In the split second he had seen Trachidambabble, he had been awed by the pure dark majesty of the full regalia of his ruler. With meeting after time-wasting meeting with his subordinates and department tails, everything had been planned to the last grubby ogre waving its special souvenir flag along the official route. Even at the moment that he was momentarily suspended against the wall before crashing painfully to the floor, the Ministry Police would have finished herding all unwilling imps, devils, demons, sirens and furies to their appointed places. The temporary grandstand would be full of an impatient crowd being entertained by flaming hellhounds jumping through hoops of ice and other boring tricks.

Nothing could go wrong. Scurbage hoped.

"Urrgh," the ghoul managed to comment on his predicament.

The minister's turban fell off as gravity took full effect, and dropped him head first onto the floor, he revised his previous thought, and deduced that something had gone wrong. Badly. And Lord Trachidambabble was not being just playfully malicious.

"The moat is green – with lillypads – and there is not a Gloop in sight," Trachidambabble hissed ominously. "As Minister of Disinformation and Disorganisation you will tell me why. In five minutes. I will be recharging on my throne."

To kill time while he waited to lead the cavalcade out to the Unholy Mess factory for The Event, Trachidambabble had decided to feed the Gloops in the moat. A selection of squirming hobgoblins suitably lacerated were selected as titbits for his favourite monsters and assembled in the dark cavern of the royal bedchamber. The Lord of Castle Gloom took delight in dragging the first unfortunate hobgoblin out onto the battlements and throwing it gleefully over the balustrade. The screams of the hobgoblin as it fell towards the moat produced the familiar feeling of recreational ambience in Trachidambabble. There was the usual satisfying plop as one of Murk's smallest creatures hit the castle's liquid surrounds. Then nothing. No delightful scuffle and painful yells of a feeding frenzy as the ugly little body was torn asunder. Instead there was just a flopping noise of the supposed Gloop food doing a doggy paddle through the lilypads before scrambling up the moat bank and to unexpected freedom.

Lord Trachidambabble was not amused. Even less so, when before he could biodegrade the rest of the selected Gloop food, they all jumped over the battlements and into the monster-free moat. An unlucky troll, mouth still agape with the words of a question went up in smoke, and the Dark Lord went in search for anyone who might be remotely responsible.

✳   ✳   ✳

The aura of evil crackled noisily as Trachidambabble turned on his heel to leave the minister's office.

Scurbage shivered involuntarily. Forgetting the cold corpse in the waste bin, he pushed through a secret door behind an ornamental sarcophagus and fell down the unlit steps. As he crashed through the hidden door marked 'Prying Control Room' and looked up at he banks of surveillance monitors, he had more than an inkling that his future as Minister of Disinformation and Disorganisation did not have a long timeline.

All the operatives had been dispatched to the Unholy Mess factory for The Event – not that they ever watched the screens for the castle surveillance system. The constant hands of Black Knave and Shiver Poker were far more interesting than identifying miscreants, especially as everyone on Murk was meant to be up to no good anyway. Even if there had been a ghoul on duty watching the screens filled with protesting Gloops, none would have been so foolish to break the news to their boss.

Looking at the monitors, a particular scene was unfolding before his eyes that he did not care for at all. A camera was panoramically recording the view towards the Garbage Hills, where an orderly group of white garbed demons were taking off the camouflage from a line of siege catapults. Scurbage rubbed his eyes a couple of times, and then put them back in their sockets. The scene was still there, but getting worse. Who had ever heard of such a notion of white devils?

Pushing buttons for maximum zoom and magnification, he quivered as the evidence reflected on his face. It looked like an army of reprobate creatures from Murk about to do the unthinkable.

The minister looked down at his chains of office, his sash of the Order of the Gutter, and his medals of achievement, and made a career move. Now was not the time for an audience with the Dark Lord, especially when the moat was a temporary danger-free zone.

*   *   *

"All siege engines loaded with detergent and soap clusters, O White One," shouted an enthusiastic albino demon, almost cutting itself on the creases on its trousers as it threw a salute at the wizard.

From his vantage point on a hump of discarded reptile skin moults, the White Wizard looked down in triumph at his spotless little army; the catapults and giant slings; his regiment of imps on flying hogs waiting patiently in the wings; all just waiting for his signal. With a sense of history in the making, he adjusted his white peaked cap on his head, and after only a momentary dramatic pause, he gave the signal: two fingers thrust tauntingly at the dark outline of Castle Gloom.

"Fire!" he roared, and a cheer broke out from the assembled ex-convicts from the Laundry and Cleaning Camp.

Cleaning agent bombs of the most virulent concoctions known to Glob, let alone Murk rained down on the slime encrusted walls of the headquarters of all things nasty on the planet, and burst in great white stains which dribbled down towards the moat.

"Reload!" roared the Captain of Projectiles.

Busy hands heaped more bombs into the catapult cradles.

The White Wizard gave the two-fingered signal again, and the bombs exploded in tides of white cleaner against the dark walls of the castle, giving it the appearance of being dumped on by a giant seagull.

"Time for the sling shot," the Double W told his Aide de Camp, who was mincing around in the prescribed teapot posture demanded of all camp aides.

"Sling your shot big boys," the Aide de Camp yollered genteelly at the Captain of Projectiles, who immediately gave the two-fingered salute.

Carefully selected boulders of the hardest and heaviest rocks on Murk filled the air as the giant siege machine slings swung into action. The castle walls shuddered as the rocks crashed into them. The number of holes peppering the dark walls made the castle look like a chunk of Swiss cheese that had been lost in the fridge.

The ranks of white demons crouching behind their barricades howled delightedly as the sling shot toppled a watch turret.

Like a statue the Double W stood at his vantage position, and stared at Castle Gloom. Marshalling all his magic powers, he channelled his hate and directed them at the big blocks of stone that made up the ugly castellated structure housing the Administrative Offices and Court of Trachidambabble, Lord of Darkness - and lots of other things.

Whether it was the power of the Double W's wizardry, or the work of the extra powerful detergent bombs eating through the centuries of filth that held the castle's masonry together, was an academic debate that could wait. (It might have in fact been down to the fact that the construction of Castle Gloom had been carried out by a master builder who had bought his qualification through a correspondence course and hadn't properly understood the concept of mortar for stonework). Whatever the reason, Castle Gloom's walls began to crumble in large chunks and splash into the moat.

Drawing his white wand from his belt, Double W looked at his expectant forces arrayed before him, and waited for the wand to transform into a giant silver knobkerrie. He raised it above his head and shouted:

"In the name of clean underwear and freedom – charge!"

The barricades came down, and like crests of waves on an angry sea, the white army of demons and devils rose to breach the crumbling walls.

The White Wizard mounted his giant albino hellhound, and with a kick of his heels bounded to the front of his troops. His white robes flowed confidently behind him. All preparations had been made. He had laid down the magical signs and summoned friendly spirits of the Ether World for advice on his future's direction. The unequivocal answer had been: Gloom, Gloom and Deeper Gloom.

There could be no clearer message.

"This blinking thing is blinking rather a lot. We must be quite close now," said Fyrsil with acute technical observation on the workings of the Comfy Chair's AutoNav.

The flying seat whumped its great wings through the dark structures of cumulo-nimbus clouds.

"How observant," the Bobo noted.

"I think it's rather pretty," said Peg, as she adjusted her wooden leg to dig more uncomfortably into Fyrsil's back. "What are those blue lights?"

"Something very technical," Fyrsil told her, as he hadn't got that far in the manual.

He glanced in the wing mirror, checking that the floating raft crowded with other crew members was towing tolerably well. A lumpy spec in the mirror told him that the dragon that had been christened Cuddles and another raft loaded with provisions and pirates was still following.

Buttie and Daisy had found Cuddles cowering in the forward hold of the *Rover Woof-Woof* and Fyrsil had been pestered into allowing it to become a pet-cum-mascot. It had been hiding in a particularly dark corner which it had made its temporary lair, and was only coaxed out with lumps of charcoal and the sort of love and affection that is normally reserved for mangy cats. After that the dragon had become their permanent shadow and was given the name of Cuddles despite his uncuddly appearance.

"Poor Cuddles," Buttie would declare as she draped herself around the scaled neck. "When this is over, I'm going to set up a home for abused dragons. Oh, my heart went out to the poor frightened thing when I saw those pleading bloodshot eyes peering out from the dark. Reminded me of my first husband."

The rest of the crew, for the most part, were engaged in stripping the wrecked ship of anything that might be considered useful. They seemed to know which these bits were automatically. Captain Cuffbert deemed this all below him, and so was using the opportunity to clean his satin shirts, and hoses.

The problem Fyrsil faced was that the plan he had been developing involving towing floating glider rafts made from the ship's salvaged timbers and the remaining balloons behind the Comfy Chair had a major hiccup. The chair refused to tow more than one raft, and not all of the ship's company and the baggage could fit on this. It created a dilemma. As Heaven's official Hero and captain of the pirate crew, he automatically reserved his place in the pilot seat of the Comfy Chair. The Bobo's perch was only suitable for that bird, which meant everyone else was condemned to a very cramped journey.

As Fyrsil had never quite grasped the complexity of the pirate's voting procedures, there was no guarantee of the outcome of a council meeting. Even if he was captain, Fyrsil could not condemn the rest of his buccaneer band being marooned at the Neverend of Murk with only a moaning inverted troll for company.

As Cuddles gave another pathetic gronk of dismay to its emotional rescuers, the solution hit Fyrsil full in the face.

After that it was plain sailing, discounting the hours of anxious pleading with Buttie and Daisy to allow their pet traumatised dragon to pull a flying raft, and tedious hours of negotiations with the Comfy Chair.

The preparations for take off started with a brew up for a bean feast. Showing he was still not passed it, Crock led the party with a masterful display of rapidly filling balloons to lift the floating rafts into the dark skies of Murk.

Leaving the punching in of the co-ordinates on the Autonav to the Bobo, so it could be blamed if they got lost, Fyrsil had given instructions to Buttie and Daisy as they coaxed Cuddles into take off. The Comfy Chair lurched into the air again, dragging the bobbing raft of pirates who were behaving like a bus full of children on a field trip.

Even now, as he checked his wing mirror again, they were poking each other in the back of the neck, knocking off hats, and making secretive rude gestures to Buttie and Daisy who were riding the dragon together.

The Autonav beeped confidently as they came out of an ink black bank of nimbus cloud that had lost its cumulus, and there below the dirty sky spread like an overflowing dog lavatory in an urban park, was Deeper Gloom. Glancing over his shoulder, the Fyrsil could see the outline of Castle Gloom leering like a crumbling compost heap.

To Fyrsil's unprofessional eye, there seemed to be rather a lot of activity around the castle, with a mass of little white dots splashing about the moat, clambering over the castle walls, and rolling around with black dots. Up above the battlements buzzed what looked like white flying pigs locked in aerial combat with giant vampire bats, lobbing bleach balls and stink bombs at each other.

"I wonder what's going on there?" mused Fyrsil.

"No point in finding out. Let's find them Golden Orbs, and get out of here," the Bobo told him. "Looks like the Mess factory down there. Just beside the airstrip. Perfect."

"What's the airstrip for?" Fyrsil wondered out loud, and wished he hadn't.

The Bobo gave him one of its most scathing looks, which would whither a bed of roses at 60 paces.

"To land on, in an officially proscribed manner, on a runway built for the purpose of landing a variety of aerial transport. Something you have been incapable of doing up to now, so try and get it right this time."

"Oh well, tally-ho then," Fyrsil said more nonchalantly than he felt, trying to give the Bobo a prepossessed look.

"Now if you need a hand dear, I can read to you from the manual," Peg volunteered, unsettled by Fyrsil's cavalier attitude to getting down from the sky. "I have never been one for a rough ride. Never have done, and am not going to start now."

That settled it for the Bobo. Adjusting its flying cap, it started painting its goggles black. There was one thing it was not going to do: go wide-eyed into another one of Fyrsil's landings.

Fyrsil sighed and puckered his lips in concentration. He would be glad when all these histrionics were out of the way and he could get back to looking forward to studying for his nut gathering apprentice exams in Alpoi.

XXX

Only the least discernible outline of a face was visible to those who looked very hard against the deep intensity of black of the high backed sable collar of Trachidambabble's cape for State Occasions. Looking hard into the face of the Lord of Murk was not something, anyone or anything did for any length of time if they wanted to respire for much longer.

The present occupants of the throne room were uneasy. There was an aura of impatient dark anger sparking from the tall depressing pillars as everybody waited for the Balck Warlock's Fortune Stew to boil.

Steel false fingernails drummed on the ebony arms of the Jet Throne.

"What exactly are we waiting for Warlock?" grated a voice empty of any empathy for any living thing.

"Err, er, the Stew of Fortune to boil," quavered Hoodoo, the Balck Warlock. He would have thought it obvious, with his apprentice gently puffing at the fire under the cauldron

"It can't be hurried if a clear reading is required."

The warlock was not taking any more chances after the reading of the augurs for The Event had hand-delivered that ominous little ditty from the Stew of Mistery. Stews were Hoodoo's speciality. So much so, that he was not happy with any form of prediction process or sorcery. His recipe book had recommended the Fortune Stew for bad, dishonest, no nonsense seering. So he had bought bulk from the trade warehouse, and kept three portions in the larder and 16 in the cold store so as not to be caught out.

In a rumble of granite words thumping into place in Trachidambabble's address, the warlock's eardrums were assaulted by a terrifying collection of syllables.

"My dear Balck Warlock," the Dark Lord began, "while my disloyal and black hearted, cretinous garrison is being ripped, clubbed and cudgeled on the battlements; and while my monstrously stupid Blackguards are being massacred at the gates of this keep – because I burnt the stairway to cut off any retreat; and while I am impatient to know in this bright hour of my existence what the future possibly holds for such an undeserving wretch such as my bad self...WE WAIT FOR YOUR STEW TO BOIL!"

"But...but oh great Lord of Darkness, the stew must not be rush..."

Before Hoodoo could finish his sentence a ball of flame shot from a single black pointing finger, engulfing the cauldron in an instant inferno.

The Balck Warlock peered with singed eyebrows at the bubbling mass of unhealthy entrails and the more revolting bodies of 748 carefully counted insects, assorted reptiles and animals. He stirred it with his charred wooden spoon of carved magic symbols.

"WELL? If you cannot make any sense of your stew, I am sure your apprentice can."

"Beep-beep," said Beep-Beep noncommittally.

The stew had gone into a sulk. It was not forming any recognisable patterns to read the signs from. The warlock needed something – anything – and it better be bad, or his end would be sooner than predicted.

With relief he saw amongst the bubbling globules and scum on the surface a more specific stirring. He peered closer. The stew erupted splattering its putrid ingredients on Hoodoo's face. As he wiped his eyes a semi-detached blue baboon's tongue blew a long, loud raspberry at the Balck Warlock and disappeared back into the nether regions of the stew.

That was the last Hoodoo remembered of the reading session.

For no apparent reason, the cauldron suddenly rose up and swallowed his head. The Fortune Stew scalded his face, while various indelicate ingredients attacked his nose, ears, and any other bit they could get hold of in the dark.

Howling with his mouth closed, Hoodoo ran blindly around the throne room, clanging against pillars and slipping on the damp flagstones coated in bat droppings.

While everything went black for the Balck Warlock, the rest of the hall had a brilliantly illuminating experience that was so bright that it penetrated the farthest recesses of the rafters. A dark cloud of Splatt bats who had been undisturbed for centuries to soil the ceremonial rooms of Castle Gloom, rose up in a swarm and flittered about in a panicking cloud.

Trachidambabble automatically pulled his cloak in front of his eyes, to guard against the debilitating effects of too much illumination.

"Your future, especially the immediate future is very bright. Very bright indeed O pathetic Dibbledabble – or whatever you go by these days. So bright you are about to shrivel up and expire."

Hate Hall resounded with a gale of gleefully manic laughter.

"The time has come for you to meet your end at the hands of the new ruler of Murk. Prepare yourself."

The White Wizard thought that the demise of Trachidambabble deserved a bit of good theatre, whether in Murk-speak or not.

While his army of scrubbed devils poured through the castle walls to dispose of the garrison, he had made for the secret passage that only he knew of – only he had survived. Everything he had planned hinged on this confrontation; and he was the only one who could win or lose the ultimate fight.

It had been difficult climbing up the shute designed to deposit undesirables from in front of the throne into the moat, but Double W had had a long time to prepare himself. It was an added bonus, when he eventually hauled himself up on special suckered grips and a small spell, that he was able to hear that Trachidambabble was demanding a last peep at his future. Connecting up his electrolight 10,000 watt suit, Double W had gripped his knobkerrie, aimed it at the slab above his head and fired, quickly jumping out as Hoodoo clattered around Hate Hall with cauldron stuck on his head.

"Who are you, you blessed angel?"

There was a note of uncertainty in Trachidambabble's voice as it boomed not quite so loudly across the illuminated hall.

"Someone you have known, but do not know now," roared Double W. The jet throne sparked with a laser blast from the knobkerrie, but was deflected by Trachidambabble's protective cloak.

A flicker of shadows was the only sign that the Dark Lord of Murk had vacated his seat, and was hiding behind the throne.

Moving slightly uneasily within the constraints of the shining electrolight suit, Double W manoeuvred himself to bring the full beam on Trachidambabble's hiding place. There was a split second window to get off another blast as the shadow presence of the Dark Lord flitted behind a pillar. The shot hit the back of the high collar, ricocheting harmlessly into the ceiling - not that harmlessly for the frazzled bats that rained down among the falling masonry and dust.

Double W addressed the shadows where he thought Trachidambabble had retreated to. The White Wizard knew he had to target the vulnerable area that hid the face to get past the Dark Lord's defensive shield. It would be easier if it had not been recharged recently on the throne, but even then there was a weak spot that only Double W knew about.

"For centuries I served you disloyally as your Balck Warlock. And my reward? Biodegradation and demotion. Now is payback time," Double W bellowed.

Out of the corner of his eye he saw a movement, and just in time jumped to sidestep a fireball curling in for the kill.

"Not so fast, no so easy petty conjurer," grated the gravel voice of Doom as it dodged into another dark corner.

"Petty conjuror? Would a petty conjuror survive the Gloops of the moat?" screamed the Double W, lashing out with a laser shot to emphasise his point.

"Would a petty conjuror re-materialise himself after being dissolved in a vat of Mess?" A particularly cute surrealist sculpture disintegrated into coal dust. "Would a petty conjuror rise triumphant out of the wash tubs of the Laundry and Cleaning Camp at the Neverend of Murk to lead a white crusade to rid Murk of its pretty boy little prince?"

A fireball whizzed overhead and exploded into a maelstrom of shattered gargoyles and stone as Double W instinctively ducked.

"Pretty boy? I'll show you pretty boy," the voice of 100,000 iron filings scratched over glass reverberated around the decimated Hate Hall as red with fury Trachidambabble stepped out into the half light, and was immediately blinded by the White Wizard's searchlight beam.

This was the moment the former Balck Warlock had been waiting for. He took a step to steady his aim, and tripped.

The lights went out.

"Damn! Damn! And Double Damn!" he said as he hit his battery pack.

"Beep," said the obstacle he had fallen over.

Shaking his knobkerrie to try and get it to work, Double W bopped the cause of his downfall on the head and dived for the hole through which he had made his dramatic entrance only minutes before. The last sound he heard as he bounced down the shute towards the moat with a giant fireball at his heels was a peel of gloating triumphant laughter.

"Looks like it could turn out to be an unpleasant day after all," Trachidambabble grimaced grimly at the smoking hole in the floor.

He gave Beep-Beep an almost affectionate kick in the ribs, and said: "Come on, we've got work to do Balck Warlock. And don't turn out like the last two – that's your first warning, and you only get one."

A disastrously unpleasant day, the Dark Lord of Murk thought as he swept aside the fallen pillars. He looked around him and decided he had rather hated this new style of décor for the throne room, and decided to keep it as it an utter mess. Whistling an unhappy tune he climbed the stairs to the top of the keep, with Beep-Beep scampering in his shadow.

XXXI

Clipboard in wing, the Bobo stood in the loading bay of the requisitioned cloud glider and counted the number of Golden Orbs (scrubbed clean to their original colour) stored neatly in the hold. The irony of using one of the gliders used in the attack on Heaven that started the Armageddon crisis was not lost on a bird whose bum still twinged uncontrollably at the memory of the fateful day. But as the glider was lying around in its catapult on the airstrip, and there was no one around to tell them not to, Fyrsil and the Bobo felt that it was the easiest and quickest solution to getting the Golden Orbs back to Heaven.

It had not taken much deduction to identify Hap's big balls filled with festering Mess in the warehouse at the back of the Unholy Mess plant. A bit of scratching at the surface revealed their true colours.

Fyrsil was busy supervising the transport of the orbs and fending off the pestering of Buttie and Daisy to include their dragon amongst the passenger list back to Heaven. Fyrsil was trying to argue that it would be cruel to take Cuddles out of its natural environment, but his real worry was Hap's reaction to a creature from Murk, however friendly, stomping around the Golden Palace. As far as Fyrsil knew the only other creature allowed on Heaven was the Bobo, and that was one too many.

His arguments didn't stop the two ex-pirate molls pleading for their pet until Fyrsil gave in.

The Bobo looked at his list again as the last of the orbs were rolled into the cargo bay and secured in position. The bird ticked it off with a final flourish and thought: "Heaven here we come – at last!"

It had all been a bit of an anti-climax really, the Bobo reflected. The pirates were not happy at all, and it could see their point. They had come to Murk to do a lot of bashing, because it had been outlawed on Loot, and it was their last real chance to have a bit of fun. If they had paid good money for a holiday package that had promised bags of bashing, a bit of pillage, and some booty thrown in, the whole party would have chosen this moment to compose their letter of complaint to the tour operator. So far, Groggie had observed, apart from the attack by the Dragon Squadron (which was admittedly an amusing interlude) there had been decidedly little bashing.

They had landed at the airstrip, with very little incident, collected what they had come for with no hint of opposition, and were now about to fly out again. All the action was going on at the castle, and to the hardened buccaneering adventurer, it looked like *that* was where all the fun was.

Instead they were mooching around a light industrial site on the outskirts of the grey suburbs of Outer Gloom, with no light relief at all.

Groggie was humpfing around airing his views on breech of promise of a scrap and bags of fighting.

A lot of heads nodded in agreement.

"What 'bout 'em demons at the factory? We could rough up a few of 'em," Boac suggested as the buccaneering band of brothers and sisters hung around kicking dust balls while the Bobo made final adjustments to the glider catapult in preparation for take off.
The grandstand and deserted expanse of tarmac by the Unholy Mess factory seemed eerie in their empty state of preparation for some sort of grand ceremony.

"Hardly worth the effort. No competition at all. I gave a couple of those devilish creatures a few whallops about the head, and flung them in the vats, and it hardly raised a sweat. I was looking forward to something where I would really have to mop my brow after I had dealt with the vile vermin," Captain Cuffbert told the company, displaying his well laundered handkerchief as evidence.

They stood in a disgruntled group, airing occasional gripes against the management of the expedition, verging on the edge of half-hearted mutiny.

"Right 'o, that's the lot. Let's get your bodies in the glider and we'll launch off to Heaven," the Bobo said as he strutted up to the grumbling ship mates.

"What about the recipe, anyone find that?" asked Fyrsil, who was dispirited by letting into Buttie and Daisy's request to smuggle Cuddles into Heaven on the excuse that it would be handy as a firelighter once it got its confidence back.

"What recipe?" demanded the Bobo.

"The recipe for Ness. We can't go back without it. To save Glob Hap has got to be able to make Ness again, and for that he needs the recipe," Fyrsil told the Bobo in a tone that was rather too pleased that the bird had slipped up.

"Well it wasn't on the list."

"Yes it is. It's over the page."

"Huh, now he tells me." The Bobo looked as if it was going to sulk.

"Any volunteers? After that we're off," said Fyrsil.

There were grumbled sounds of acquiescence, and the mob of pirates led by a sprightly Fyrsil headed off towards the factory offices.

"What we want now is to have a nice big punch-up with a couple of devils and demons and things. Just to show who's boss," Big-Gulop told anyone who cared to listen.

"A hearty here-here! To that," Captain Cuffbert agreed.

* * *

The Minister for Disinformation and Disorganisation felt like a green splat as he hung flattened on the back of the door to his office. It was not the most pleasant experience in Scurbage's existence, being impaled by the coat hook, but that was a minor discomfort compared to the look of Trachidambabble who had slammed into the Ministry Rooms just as the minister was looking for a good hiding place. He had been dithering about jumping into the moat, and then had rushed back to his offices to hide from the clean white crusaders' bombardment of the ramparts.

It was a mixture of emotions that flooded the ghoul's luminescent body when he learned that it was the Dark Lord, and not the invading horde of white devils, who had squashed him against the wall.

"The Event? Oh that event: *The Event*. You want it to happen immediately. But, but what about…" Scurbage was gibbering for time.

He could still remember the decades when nothing of any importance happened. The job requirement had generally been to make sure Murk got a bad press on Glob, and as that was not particularly difficult.

Life and inactivity at the ministry had jogged on quite nicely for centuries without much real change to pace. The recent run of rapidly changing situations had unsettled him. There was no time to form committees, draw up the necessary documents, to be completed by all parties in triplicate and filed incorrectly on a pain of a long stint of dusting and polishing brass buttons. As minister he had been deeply dubious about the plans to attack Heaven, but a hint to

Trachidambabble and Scurbage would have been a vapourised ex-ghoul. Like every other fawning courtier, the minister had showed unhealthy scepticism and hoped it would all turn out badly.

Somewhere in the active thinking bits of his brain, Scurbage wondered if there was a link between what was happening on Murk, and the series of new developments in the Dark Lord's ambitions to be the propelling force of the planet. The minister's world seemed to have gone mad. White demons – a *non sequitur* if he ever thought about it – attacking Castle Gloom! Then there were the Gloops demanding a clean up of pollutants dumped in the moat - the monsters had evolved as a direct result of mutations born into the toxic cocktail of filth that floated around the castle.

"Absolutely Dark Lord, immediately," the minister managed the correct response after a small pause. "My department will maladminister The Event as badly and as quickly as possible. But what about the white…"

"Dealt with," Trachidambabble told Scurbage decisively, looking out of the slit window with satisfaction at the carnage of the white crusader army.

"The Gloops are back in the moat, their ringleaders disintegrating in the dungeon cesspits; the white army is torn apart – literally – and in total rout, and I am back IN CONTROL.

"It was an interesting, and most unenjoyable little diversion. But now we have had all our entertainment, there is no reason not to press ahead with the main business of the night. Domination of Glob by Murk, and therefore my most disgusting self cannot wait any longer. Organise it! NOW!"

"Beep beep!" said Beep-Beep, the new Balck Warlock, for emphasis, emerging from behind his master's cloak.

"Exactly," said Trachidambabble. "This new Balck Warlock speaks the best sense I have heard from a wizard."

With that, master and warlock swept out.

Scurbage tore himself off the coat hook and grasped a telephone on his desk. It was malfunctioning as usual, so he ritually threw it against the wall, and stormed through an adjoining door.

"We have situation Green Plus Plus on The Event," he shouted at the five messily turbaned Under Ministers who had all tried to hide in the waste bin.

"I want the crowds in place at the Unholy Mess plant like yesterday; cortege and outriders saddled up like an hour ago; and we have ETD – that's Estimated Time of Departure for those more intelligent operatives – of minus 10 minutes. ANY QUESTIONS?" the big ghoul roared.

There was a squeak as the Personal Private Secretary fell out of the filing cabinet.

"In triplicate?" asked the PPS.

"NO FORMS. NO FILING. JUST DO IT. NOW!"

The minister stormed backed to his office, thanking his lucky entrails that he had other creatures to yell at. Opening the bottom draw of his personal desk he extracted from behind the regulation directories a nice bit of elbow joint that had been festering tastily for a week.

Still having a job was a relief. Still having a life was better. Still having an appetite was incredible.

*   *   *

"Come on. Put some effort into it. The sooner we find it, the sooner we get to Heaven."

Fyrsil was searching the Production manager's office for the Ness recipe, which was like looking for a funny joke in a Christmas cracker factory. Disorganised piles of papers teetered everywhere, decorated by discarded tins from the vending machine and odd bits of broken mechanisms that must have had some use once. The only contents of the filing cabinet were an old furniture assembly manual, and a fungus forest that had once been a raw tongue sandwich.

Big-Gulop was holding up an imp by its wings and slapping its face in a nonchalent way.

"Maybe this one knows. It is only a bit concussed after I stepped on it," the orange flesh mountain said as he leant idly in the door frame.

The imp slowly opened a red eye, and quickly closed it again.

"Aha! No you don't, you little worm. I have some questions for you. Question one: do you understand what I am saying? Nod for *yes*, shake your head for *no*."

The imp nodded at first, and then shook its head violently.

"That's good enough for me," said Big-Gulop, and gave it a nasty clout on the ear.

"Now where is the recipe for this Ness stuff kept?"

The imp shrugged.

Big-Gulop gave it a thwack against the wall.

"WHERE'S THE RECIPE OR I WILL PULL YOUR TALONS OUT ONE BY ONE, AND THEN USE THEM TO NAIL YOU TO A STICK SO I CAN SOAK YOU IN BLEACH AND USE YOU AS A TOILET BRUSH. YOU DO KNOW AND YOU ARE GOING TO TELL ME, AREN'T YOU?"

Shouting at natives who did not seem to understand your own language was something that all tourists did at Alpoi, and it never seemed to work there. (This could be due to Alpoians adopting earplugs as part of everyday wear because they were always being shouted at.)

Fyrsil was about to mention this to Big-Gulop, when it became evident that it was the sort of language the imp understood very well. It shook its head a couple of times, before turning the shake into a nod on overdrive.

"WHERE?" continued Big-Gulop at maximum decibels.

The imp pointed to the notice board.

"It can't be," said Fyrsil, "I've been through every scrap of paper at least twice."

But the imp continued to point at the lopsided cork board, which was a forest of yellowed ministry regulations, cards for the educational services of mutant molluscs, and failed tickets for the rigged lottery. Even after an enthusiastic pistol whipping from Groggie, who wanted to get in on the act, the imp was insistent that the recipe for Ness was on the notice board.

"Aha!" declared Fyrsil in triumph, as he waved a scruffy piece of best quality parchment which the Production Manager had been using for a rota of volunteers for the Dishonourable Suicide Club.

The reverse side was a mass of gilt calligraphy with the title altered with a blue marker pen, but the original quite clearly reading: *Recipe for Ness*.

"Smile. One for the album. And another for good luck," shouted Boac, who had finally found a use for this part of his bird watching kit. The camera flashed at the mob of pirates making desultory noises of congratulations.

"Hold up the recipe. It do look pretty," Boac called to Fyrsil as he put a congratulatory arm around Big-Gulop's shoulders. Fyrsil willingly obliged.

"OK, let's get back to the glider," a relieved Fyrsil called in general announcement.

There was a shuffling of feet, as the pirate band realised that this was the end of the raid, which despite all the expected excitement, had turned out to be relatively humdrum. Their future from now on was going to be in Heaven, or a return to incarcerated boredom in Loot.

"What's that noise?" Boac asked over the disinterested grumbling.

Everyone was suddenly aware of a low rumble like a herd of stampeding big hairy animals that liked running in no particular direction and kicking up a lot of dust. What's more, the noise was definitely getting closer.

Looking out of the grimy window of the Production Manager's office, the tarmac in front of the Unholy Mess plant was being transformed, filled with every sort of devil and evil creature that called Murk its home. Whip-cracking trolls were corralling crowds of demons, imps, werewolfs, ghouls, and various odd dark creature that slithered or trotted around the down side of Glob into some semblance of disorder. Moaning and protesting, they covered the open spaces outside the factory like a an extremely nasty, thick hairy carpet. The skies swarmed with the traffic of dragons transporting strange mutant monsters from distant areas of Outer Murk.

"I think we're trapped," Fyrsil said, thinking of the large expanse of unhealthy weeds between the factory buildings and the glider on the airstrip.

"A slight understatement, me thinks," Captain Cuffbert agreed, twisting the ends of his carefully waxed moustache. "It could prove an amusing, if a trifle lively, venture getting out of this scrape."

With the Bobo back at the glider working out the controls, Fyrsil was at least spared a more caustic remark. But he thought it would be a good idea to be prepared to defend himself if the mass of Murk's population should discover them in the Unholy Mess plant.

Opening his bumbag, he found with surprising ease the Shield of Righteousness, which he had forgotten he had put back there. He couldn't find the cupid bow and arrow, but did find an implement that called itself an Angel Axe, so he slipped the strap over his wrist. There was also some colourful grenade type munitions which were labelled as Pavalov Dogs, so he hung their bandoleer across his breast plate for decoration. For some reason he thought a phial of Raw Love from Ffffworrrr goddess of Lust might come in handy, and so slipped it into the secret pocket in his under-tunic.

"I be wondering what 'em beasties be doin' here," Boac mused no one in particular..

"Some sort of ceremony. All the big nobs assembled on the podium, just waiting for the biggest nobbie of all, by the looks of things," said The Masked Marauder, peering out the window. "And by the looks of things, there is something to do with those catapults where we found those missing golden Orbs. Could be something of a holiday for Murk…"

He was interrupted in his guessing by a howl coming from the passage leading to the loading bay of the factory. A ruffled, but extravagantly swaggering Groggie was dragging a troll by its hair. Owing to the fact that the troll's limbs were tied in a series of complicated seafaring knots, it bounced along the ground at Groggie's heels.

"I can tell you exactly what's happening out there," smirked the big pirate chief. "This thing kindly imparted the information after a little gentle persuasion, if you get my drift. You've got to know how to treat your squealers right, eh Boac?"

To demonstrate, Groggie gave a practised tweak to the troll's little toe, and it howled in pain.

"Quiet! Scurvy weavel. It don't hurt that much. This one 'ere tells me he's the Production Manager of Unholy Mess, and so he should know, 'cos this is where they have been making it. Ain't that right, my little lovely?"

Grump howled in agreement.

"Well it seems like we are in the middle of the biggest event to hit Murk. In fact it's so big, that it's just called The Event. What it is, like, is launching Mess into the stratosphere to turn the sky blue, and make sure Murk rules Glob good and proper."

"Galloping hobnuts! We were just in time. That would have been the end of Glob as we know it, and probably for ever," Fyrsil exclaimed, but it sounded a bit weak, even to him.

"That also means, we are in the middle of the biggest congregation of all creatures on Murk, and have to fight or way back to the glider," said Groggie loudly, not liking being interrupted when he was the centre of attention.

"Oh goodie! Sounds like fun," said Big-Gulop enthusiastically.

"Sounds more like 'no escape'. We're doomed, and so is Glob," Fyrsil wailed, pulling out the Being Stone. Only a single gossamer thread of gold wound round the core of inky blueness.

"Oh you can still have lots of fun when you are doomed," Big-Gulop told him.

"You mean you've been in this sort of situation before?"

"Oh lots of times. Usually transpires that you are not so doomed as you first thought, and you come away with enough booty to have made it all worth while," he explained.

"Funnily enough, that's what I've always found," Boac confirmed.

"So what happens now?" Fyrsil asked. He seemed to be the only one of the crew who was worried about the prospect of being ripped apart by an angry mob of vicious demons and after dark beasts from the dark part of the planet.

"Well we have a Council of War and decide on what we are going to do next. Then something else happens, so you can't put the plan into action, but you have to slash and maim like your life depended on it – which it does. And then you have a lucky break, and it's all alright in the end. Otherwise it's not," Big-Gulop told him, beaming broadly.

"Sounds fail-safe to me then," remarked Fyrsil.

XXXIII

The rolling thunder of thousands upon thousands of slavering creatures opening up their throats to boo at the approaching Dark Lord reached a crescendo as his cortege circled below the gathering clouds. The giant vampire bats peeled off and landed along the designated strip near the podium, followed by Trachidambabble and his Balck Warlock in the state chariot pulled by two fiery wyverns. The convoy of raven powered sleds carrying the battered remains of the elite Blackguards landed behind to a cacophony of heckling and hisses.

On the podium the Minister for Disinformation and Disorganisation relaxed. It was all done. The crowds had been whipped into place and were showing all the lack of enthusiasm to give Trachidambabble a dismal welcome. The collapse of the grandstand after overcrowding had given The Event just the right disastrous start to get the crowd into the right mood. The sight of mangled bodies and severed limbs was just the sort of welcome the Dark Lord would appreciate, Scurbage mused.

But the minister had a happy feeling that something was missing. Something important, but he just couldn't put his finger on it.

It then hit him. It was so glaringly obvious he hadn't noticed it before. There were no Blue Balls of Mess. None of the giant catapults had spherical objects in their slings to turn the stratosphere blue. Around the base of the nearest catapult was a telltale puddle of dark blue liquid busily killing off the surrounding weeds.

"Where are the Blue Balls?" he demanded of his nearest under-minister.

"Dunno. Baba Yaba was co-ordinating the Unholy Mess end of operations. I thought it was a change in plan, and they were going to be brought on when the Dark Lord arrived. Build up of tension or something – that was the agreed excuse. Not my department."

Scurbage felt himself go yellow with rage. Striding down the line of dignitaries, he pulled Baba Yaba from his position of balancing on the edge of the podium.

"Where are the Blue Balls? The Dark Lord is expecting to launch the Mess, and not one catapult is loaded," the minister hissed, making sure no one else could hear the detail of the ministry's successful organisational cock-up.

Baba Yaga shrugged his shoulders.

"Dunno, I'm not the Psychic Warlock. When I had the last meeting with the Production Manager they were all ready and loaded in place. It must be something to do with that clever troll Grump. He must have done something since coming back from bashing the white army," the ghoul told his boss, quivering in the face of pure anger thrust into his nose.

Jets of vaporised ire hissed out to Scurbage's ears, as hiss head changed from yellow to muddy brown in pure rage. All those plans running as badly as the worst thing that that had ever been run on Murk before, and the whole point of the exercise was not there. The Event would be a non-event.

"If you want to know what happened to the Blue Balls, there's a bunch of pirates in the factory who know," the Psychic Warlock called from his seat on the podium.

"Well, why hasn't anyone done anything about it?" fumed Scurbage, his jaw snapping open and shut on his tongue in a spat of deranged departmental fug.

"It wasn't on the schedule," came the reply.

The minister shot a smouldering glare at Baba Yaga as this statement sunk in. Then with a sweep of his enormous arm, he knocked his underling's head off, and left the body to jump down and look for it in the milling crows. Storming through a pack of baying werewolves Scurbage headed for the door of the factory offices, just as the Dark Lord dismounted from his chariot.

Kicking indiscriminately at the booing and jeering crowd, Trachidambabble, Lord of Murk and All Black Rainclouds, Diviner of Destruction and Head Demon of Doom, was going to make sure that this was a time to savour. He had worked, planned and schemed for centuries to bring about his domination of Glob, and now in his moment of complete and unmitigated disaster, the lowest depth of his existence, he was going to really hate it. Really hate it.

The din of boos and catcalls was almost unbearable as he lashed out at the unenthusiastic crowd. Swaggering so that his pitch black cape flowed most demonically behind him, Trachidambabble mounted the podium. He stood feasting his eyes on his creatures of malice, stupidity and cruelty, and drank in the atmosphere. He stepped up to the microphone and taking a deep breath launched into the speech he had been practising in private for decades:

"Horrible demons, devils, and all nasty creatures of my domain. This night is an historic night. This night is the night when Murk with its iron fist moulds Glob, and forges a new direction for the planet. With these Blue Balls launching Mess…"

Trachidambabble stopped and stared at where the balls should have been.

There were no balls.

"Where is the Minister for Disorganisation and Disinformation? Get me that gooey ghoul so I can liquidise him painfully," the Dark Lord hissed at the Captain of the Blackguards.

"Beep beep."

The new Balck Warlock pointed to a green figure steaming through the sea of ugly dark monstrosities towards the Unholy Mess plant.

"I want that idiot torn limb from limb and deposited in an unpleasant pile at my feet, so that ghoul can tell me the meaning of this…"

The Blackguards captain already had a nasty grimace on his face, and was leading his troops squeaking and jangling on the chase.

*　*　*

"I think we have a visitor," Peg on lookout told the assembled Council of War.

"Oh good," declared Big-Gulop, "that means we can abandon all these plans, and just get on with it."

This was a relief to Fyrsil, who had been getting very worried about both the sanity and intelligence of his pirate brethren – not forgetting the sisters – in their plans to escape.

"What sort of visitor?" asked Fyrsil.

"Oh, only a big green ghoul with a turban that looks like a bandage for a bad headache."

There were groans of disappointment from the crew sitting as a council.

"But the ghoul is being followed by a large number of trolls," Peg told them.

This news was greeted enthusiastically with shouts of "ooh goodie", and "that's more like it". The pirate chiefs were starting to bristle with excitement; giving their pistols and extra clean, practising the slash and debowel techniques with their cutlasses, and generally getting twitchy. Fyrsil was feeling queasy and had butterflies in his stomach.

"Got an idea of how this will all end?" Peg asked Fyrsil quietly.

Fyrsil's imagination was working overtime, and it was not very pleasant.

"Very messily," Fyrsil replied, "especially if no one knows what they are going to do."

"My thoughts exactly. How about doing something in that department? It can't do any harm."

"Like what?" Fyrsil asked desperately.

"I've got an idea or two, dearie, you just use them as you see fit," she told him.

In the couple of minutes it took for Scurbage to get to the factory door and tear it open, Fyrsil had got his crew into position, with a plan for a first and second line of defence, and even an emergency exit for the hurried retreat.

Fear can do a lot to people. Supreme fear of the sorts that was bubbling in Fyrsil's innards revealed qualities that he could never have discovered in a lifetime dedicated to the philosophies of the Nutgatherers of Alpoi. He actually barked orders that were obeyed by a mob that in other circumstances would have endlessly disputed whether such actions would be included in the constitution of the Council of War. He found, to his surprise, he quite liked the sound of his own voice. It was even better when fearsome pirate chiefs like Big-Gulop asked if he was standing in the right place.

"First customer coming up," hissed Peg.

"Give the ghoul a good Loot welcome to the party: make it a night it has no wish to remember," Fyrsil called out almost inevitably, in the manner of military leaders who want to recorded for brave words in history books.

There was no time for anything else. Scurbage rushed at the factory door. Groggie obligingly opened it for the fuming green minister, lifted the turban, and bopped Murk's second most important uncivil servant on the head. An industrial sized hook was pulled down from the overhead pulley system, and the big noise in the Ministry of Disinformation and Disorganisation was hauled up, guided across, and dumped unceremoniously into a bubbling vat of Mess. The concoction paused briefly, burped loudly, and turned an excitable indigo.

The trolls of the Blackguard rushed after Scurbage at the open factory door, and then clattered into each other like a derailing locomotive as Groggie and Big-Gulop allowed the first two in before slamming the door. A couple of perfunctory blows to the bonce stunned the troll advance guard, who were quickly trussed up like the minister, hauled away on pulleys and dropped into bubbling Mess vats.

With the door being battered by the elite but not too intelligent Blackguards, Groggie assessed the situation.

"We wont' be able to hold them if we open the door again," he shouted above the hissing mechanism of the engines that were scattered along the length of the factory floor.

"Back to the first defensive line. Vat teams ready, on my word," Fyrsil squeaked, unable to contain his adrenaline rush.

In the tense moments as the door was bombarded by ramming trolls, Fyrsil decided to arm the Angel Axe which dangled by its thong from his wrist. He guessed it was not a manual axe, the sort which normal marauders would use. He pressed a button above a small LCD screen displaying the legend *Audio Instruct.*

"WARNING:" announced the pre-recorded message. "THE *ANGEL AXE* MK2 IS A DANGEROUS WEAPON AND COULD SERIOUSLY MAIM OR INFLICT TERMINAL INJURY ON SINNERS. ALTHOUGH THE *ANGEL AXE* IS GENERALLY USER FRIENDLY, IT'S PRECISION BLADE MADE OF THE TOUGHEST PATENTED MATERIALS, HONED AND SHARPENED BY THE FINEST CRAFTSMEN SUB-CONTRACTED TO HEAVEN. IT BLOODY WELL HURTS IF YOU CUT OFF A LIMB, SO DON'T SHOW OFF IN FRONT OF FRIENDS."

"OH, TO ACTIVATE, POINT *ANGEL AXE* AT SINNER AND GIVE COMMANDS OF: *REPENT* FOR WOUNDING, *TOO LATE* FOR SLAYING, OR *BYE-BYE* FOR CRUSADE."

With a satisfying crash the trolls came streaming through the flattened door, and piled up in a mountain of squeaking leather and entangled chains. A chorus of laughter echoed around the chamber of the factory. The trip wire rigged by Groggie and Big-Gulop had over exceeded its expectations.

"Wot's all this? Get going, get killing. I want whoever is in here in pieces before I can count the fingers on my left hand," shouted the Captain of the Blackguards, kicking his select force to their feet.

As an esteemed leader of Murk, the captain had naturally brought up the rear in this potentially dangerous engagement. Officially this was to be able to know who to award medals to. Other reasons included self-preservation and cautionary cowardice.

The empty silence of expectation descended like a nasty wet dog blanket over the Unholy Mess plant. The roar of the crowds outside seemed to be suddenly distant, as the gently jingling trolls picked themselves up and peered into the gloom. The rows of vast vats brimming with bubbling Mess, the occasional spats of escaping steam, and the central avenue between all the paraphernalia of production disappearing into a dark cavern.

The problem with the troll's simple thought pattern is they need to know, at least vaguely, where their intended victims are. If this isn't he case, the automatic rush of desire to beat up and rip to shreds just isn't there, and they are inclined to sit down and almost amiably smoke a foul smelling pipe. As a result Trachidambabble's bodyguards were gathered in a cluster looking rather lost and patting pockets for their pipes and tobacco pouches, despite the kicks and yells of their captain.

If they had been listening to other things, they would have heard from the darkness a careful clank-clanking. It wasn't heard by the trolls, because they were concentrating on avoiding being kicked. They were also being pushed forward into the unknown by a growing mass of ogres, demons, imps etc, who were pouring through the flattened door in hope of a gruesome spectacle.

An object whistled out of the darkness, and landed with a small bang on the captain's head. He scratched at the irritant sticking to his hairy scalp like a leech with super suction power. The red pear shape object steamed away happily on the top of his head and then disappeared in a cloud of gas as it made a sound very much like '*plop*'.

It was not the effect Fyrsil had hoped for, especially as it was such an accurate lob. Something dramatic like a loud *BANG* was what he wanted. He had assumed that as Pavlov Dogs were grenade shape, they would make loud explosions in the same sort of way. And in picking the red one, he had hoped that it would make a bigger bang than the rest of them – especially as it was his signal to the rest of the crew to put the next part of the plan into action.

The Blackguards Captain, if he had registered that he had been hit by a piece of military hardware, would have probably preferred being blown up. The trolls of his elite force suddenly started giving him funny looks. Not odd ones, but unless he was mistaken, adoring ones. It halted him in mid yell, as a spectating ogre started to ogle him with a long lingering look. Being extremely ugly, as well as brutal, the Blackguard Captain had never had this sort of attention before. Now he was the subject of cat-calls, and puckered lips, and he didn't like it.

"Now," shouted Fyrsil, quickly assessing the situation. He ascertained correctly that Operation Washout had got off to a bad start because no one had seen the start signal.

"Get those wagons rolling," he called to the pirate band, as he ran to join them at the back of the factory.

The Blackguard captain didn't hear Fyrsil's brave words. The troll was still stunned by the smacking kiss his sergeant-at-arms had just planted on his lips

The mechanics of the Pavlov Dogs would probably not have interested the commander of Murk's elite troops as he tried to fight off the bottom pinches and unwelcome kisses of the crowd around him. Although the Dogs were packaged to look like a grenade, they were mainly used by minor gods in the event of sticky life-threatening situations when touring their shrines on the surface of Glob. Essentially the Dogs were colour coded for the craving that they induced. Green was for a double cheese burger with onions and relish; yellow produced an overwhelming desire to run around imitating sheep; anyone who sniffed the gases emitted from the white Dog fell on the spot into peaceful sleep; and the black Dog induced immediate violent projectile vomiting. The red Dog was the most powerful, and caused everything to fall in love with whoever it landed on.

Fyrsil was passed caring what effect the Dogs had. His concern was to get back to the relative safety of his shipmates, who should have swung the plan for Operation Washout into action. Skidding to a halt at the end of the long line of Mess vats, Fyrsil nearly knocked Crock over, who was meant to be on lookout for approaching trolls, but was watching avidly as a huge concrete block swung on chains from a gantry in the roof. Two teams of pirates hung on the guiding ropes, rushing forward to give the swinging block momentum, and then letting out slack to allow for back-swings.

"Let's have one big heave, and then we can all sit down and enjoy the entertainment," called Captain Cuffbert through cupped hands to the two line of sweating figures.

As the concrete block swung back, the two teams took up the slack and raced forward. With a loud clang, the block hit the lip of the nearest vat of Mess. The vat teetered on its carefully weakened front legs.

"One more time and it's a gonner," Fyrsil encouraged the sweating teams.

"Absolutely. Give it the good old heave-ho me hearties and we are as good as home and dry. Good effort chaps," Cuffbert told his shipmates, waving his plumed hat in an encouraging sort of way.

The concrete block swung back again, the guide ropes were pulled tight and with a great roar the teams cantered forward. There was a deafening crunch as concrete pebbles showered in all directions, and the vat lurched into its neighbour and spilt a great wave of the highly volatile Mess on to the factory floor. The next vat in line toppled forward, knocking its neighbour down, which then pitched forward into the next in line. Within seconds there were vats hurling their contents forward at increasing speed to the accompaniment of the thunderous clanging of large metal containers going down like ninepins.

"Well, that's the domino theory kicked into action," Crock told Fyrsil, as the undefeated master of dominoes along the quayside taverns of Loot.

It was uncertainty at the other end of the factory whether the extra noise was noticed above the raucous chaos that gripped the seething mass of creatures. The demons and imps outside the Unholy Mess plant had got wind of the fact that there might be some juicy mutilating of victims going on in the building, and didn't want to miss out on a good gawp. As they scratched and kicked to fight their way into the Mess works, they were caught up by the growing band of onlookers wanting to kiss the Captain of the Blackguards. Competition was becoming so great that fights were breaking out amongst the most fervent suitors, and fur started flying as tails whisked jealously from side to side. Those that weren't caught up, formed a vulture's ring around the action to be able to get on with some serious gloating in preparation for something really violent.

It did, but it was not what the crowd expected. With a roar the massive wave of activated Mess hit the milling crowd and flung it against the factory wall.

Fuming on his podium while the assembled dignitaries of Murk chittered at the delayed proceedings, Trachidambabble turned to see a geyser spurt of blue Mess explode from the factory door. As he juddered with anger, the end wall of the building collapsed, and crumpled to resemble a stricken ship going down at sea.

"What is going on? Who is responsible for this?" he roared at the collection of warlocks who were looking very exposed in their special seats.

They shrugged and waggled their tails (if they had them).

"Looks like the work of the Department of Disinformation and Disorganisation," said a junior warlock hopefully.

Trachidambabble hissed pure wrath, and turned to his faithless uncivil servants. Too late. Their section of the podium was already deserted, and the only evidence that they had been there at all was the knocked over chairs, and the green baggy bottom of the late Minister for Disinformation and Disorganisation's PPS crawling into a crowd of unexcited devils flapping their wings and gibbering at the back of the podium.

A sharp gesture of his arm, and the disappearing backside, along with the immediate crowd of devils, was nothing more than a charred and smouldering crater.

The warlocks fidgeted on the podium muttering unlucky charms and protective spells as the cloak of Trachidabmbabble sliced through the air. He faced them again. For a few cold moments they collectively looked into the face of instant extinction as the Dark Lord considered their fate.

The noise of the rest of the factory buckling and crashing to the ground momentarily distracted Trachidambabble from his intention to biodegrade the surviving senior advisors to his court. After slight consideration, he decided to spare them – for the time being. Having lost his entire personal bodyguard and the upper echelons of the uncivil service, he decided to take time and enjoy decimating the magic department. So he ranted about who would pay for this 'success', stamped his feet and fizzed alarmingly until the podium collapsed under the pressure of his fury.

Enough was enough. It was the final straw for the Lord of Darkness. Centuries of planning in tatters. And so with a final kick of the podium, he stomped off to his state chariot, and kicked his Balck Warlock into the driver's seat to take him back to the ruins of Castle Gloom.

The fight against the forces of Double W had drained his energies more than he had thought, and he needed to get back to the jet throne to boost his powers. The King of Evil never sleeps, but the whole apparatus needed regular recharging, and internal warning showed that he was hitting emergency reserves of the dark energies.

"Find out who is responsible for this spectacular achievement, and bring them to my chambers for well-considered and drawn out injustice. I don't care who it is – anyone who will scream a lot," he shouted at the warlocks scrabbling to find their lost wands and magic circles amongst the debris of the podium.

The state chariot of Trachidambabble whisked up into the night sky to the sound of whipped wyverns bellowing over a scene of confusion so complete that it would have taken three decades of planning from the Ministry of Disinformation and Disorganisation.

* * *

Another group which had been considering their fate was Fyrsil and his raiding party from Loot.

They had whooped as the tidal wave of Mess had carried kissing trolls, demons and all before it. But their shouts of joy had been suddenly cut short when Crock, using his infra-red spy glass had cried out as he spotted a back wash of Mess coursing down the factory floor to where they all stood.

Piling through a door in the factory wall, they ran through the Blue Ball filling station and into the empty warehouse where they had discovered the disguised Golden Orbs. Puffing and wheezing they collapsed in a heap by the doors to the warehouse, as the sound of the factory caving in reverberated in their ears.

Outside there seemed to be a change in the sound of the crowd. The concerted booing and hissing had turned to anxious howls. Sounds of stampeding weirdbeasts mixed amongst indecisive yells and squeaks.

"What's going on?" Fyrsil asked Boac, who was peeping through a crack in the door, trying to ignore Crock's grumbles.

In the spirit of saving a shipmate from drowning in Mess, Boac had grabbed Crock and heaved him over his shoulder as they escaped from the collapsing factory. Only when they were through the filling station did Crock remember that he had forgotten his walking frame, and yelled at Boac to go back for it. The big barbarian told him plainly to stop whining. Heaven was bound to have a nice golden one knocking about.

"Complete chaos," Boac told Fyrsil after swatting a still whingeing Crock.

Fyrsil considered Boac's answer with more than a little concern, and took a look himself.

"Great – just what we needed. Nothing like a bit of chaos for sneaking away with bags of booty. I've done it loads of times," said Big-Gulop happily.

"That's right, shipmate," agreed Groggie. "I remember the time I was in this place called Dome. The plan was to …"

Half listening to the tale of daring-do Groggie was reciting to the still panting collection of buccaneers, Fyrsil looked across the mass of milling Murk creatures, to the outline of the cloud glider. It looked a short trip to the airstrip, but through an angry and confused crowd meant that journey would seem forever. The prospect of walking nonchalantly – whistling a jaunty tune if possible – into that throng seemed to Fyrsil like an appointment with an end called Suicide.

"Let's have a look," Big-Gulop said, bored of Groggie's tall tales.

Expertly casting his eye over the scene, the pirate chief decided that a little more confusion was needed.

"Bung one of your grenades out the door, and let's see what happens," he suggested.

"You can't tell with these. They might do anything."

"Let's try another colour. It could be interesting," Big-Gulop told him.

So, selecting a yellow Pavlov Dog, Fyrsil pulled out the pin, counted to four, and hurled it into the crowd outside. It landed on a passing ogre, who paused momentarily to wonder what the new itch in his tousled thatch of hair was. Something when 'plop' amongst the matted mane, and the ogre sniffed the air, and then had an uncontrollable desire to get down on all fours and bleet.

"Baa-baa," bleeted the ogre, and scampered willy-nilly amongst the crowd, knocking as many off their feet as possible. Buffeting its way to a clear patch of weeds, it settled down to graze. It was only distantly aware that a pack of werewolves that had been looking at the ogre with hungry eyes, were now also on all fours, baa-ing and buffeting, and giving occasional frisky skips as they milled around looking for someone to follow.

"Well, it's not what I expected, but it has definitely created a lot more confusion," Big-Gulop declared, scratching his head as he watched the scared sheep/werewolves creating mayhem.

Without any prompting, Fyrsil suddenly knew what to do.

"Right, gather round you lot. This is what we are going to do," he told the pirate band.

"No more running I hope. I worked up quite a sweat from the last little gallop, and it always stains a good shirt. We want to arrive in Heaven looking our best, ain't that so Groggie?" Captain Cuffbert said, twisting his moustache with concern.

Groggie looked at himself and scowled.

"No more running. As Groggie and Big-Gulop have suggested, it will be a pleasant walk through the crowd to the glider, with just a little help from the *Shield of Righteousness*, and the Pavlov Dogs. Keep your weapons handy, just in case of a worse scenario scrap. But otherwise play it ice cool."

Captain Cuffbert adjusted the feather in his hat, while Buttie and Daisy gave each other a sisterly hug, and Crock stopped grumbling about his walking frame, as they waited for a suitable gap in the crowd.

Closing his eyes and making a blind selection from his dangling Pavlov Dogs (a green one this time) Fyrsil lobbed it at a vicious looking devil who had been sniffing around the warehouse doors suspiciously. It didn't notice the Dog land on one of its horns and go *plop*. At least if it did, it was more worried about the strange desire look for a burger van to satiate the strange desire for a double cheese burger and all the trimmings. As it lurched through the crowd in its desperate search, one horn steaming evocative vapours, more and more creatures became caught up the search for the elusive special burger.

Neatly, but not too closely, Fyrsil stepped out into the gap in the crowds created by the burger-hungry devil and its following. Holding before him the *Shield of Righteousness* (still covered and in its small round easi-portable mode) and axe dangling from his wrist, Heaven's representative and official hero tried to look as un-selfconscious as possible.

With the general unattractive demeanour of the pirate crew being pretty close to the more attractive ogre, all it took were a few growls from Groggie and Boac for the mass of evil creatures to let them pass as unusual residents of Murk.

Pushing confidently towards the glider, they were making good progress, with the occasional Pavlov Dog thrown ahead to clear any congestion in the crowd.

The swirling mass of confused Murk populous behaving like a collective headless chicken took little notice of the unusual band. They seemed to escape any inquisitive attention from any of Lord Trachidambabble's disloyal subjects.

All apart from a giant ogre who took a fancy to Buttie.

Captain Cuffbert alerted Fyrsil to this romantic problem as the ogre shadowed the pirate party and leering in Buttie's direction in an almost affectionate way.

An ogre getting hot under the collar in the love department is not easy to miss – their big dish eyes turn purple and revolve in a giddy fashion.

Disconcertingly for Fyrsil, this is what it was doing as it tried to catch Buttie's attention.

He threw a white Dog at the amorous monster, but in an unusual display of intelligence the ogre picked up an imp and tried to bat the grenade away. When the Dog stuck to the imp, the ogre simply threw the imp away as well, and then disappeared into the crowd.

Taking precautions against any more direct displays of affection, Buttie was hidden behind Groggie in a tight phalanx, who not even an ogre was likely to have a soft spot for, while Boac and big Gulop and Boac hemmed her in at the sides.

As they neared the edge of the disordered collection of milling bodies that now constituted The Event, the crew relaxed as safety seemed within their reach.

Suddenly all Fyrsil could see over his shield was a pair of huge revolving eyes as the ogre jumped out in front of him.

"I want!" demanded the ugly creature, pointing threateningly at the cowering Buttie.

Groggie's infamous scowl was no more than a friendly smile to the beast, but Daisy's handbag had more effect.

"You leave your great hairy mitts off my friend. You've got a cheek making nasty eyes at her like that," Daisy screamed, as she fetched the ogre a clout about the ears. "Now clear off, and go and pester someone else."

The clout about the ears was something that the ogre understood only too well. It was the opening exchanges of its species mating ritual, and the biggest come-on for any hairy lump on Murk.

"Shoo!" tried Fyrsil defensively, as he tried to protect Daisy from her new-found admirer. Unfortunately "shoo" – even with an exclamation mark – was not going to deter a giant ogre in luv. It took an irritated swipe at Fyrsil, who automatically raised his shield in defence.

Fortunately for Fyrsil, but unfortunately for the ogre, its swipe caught the quick release toggle on the Shield of Righteousness cover. With the shield pre-set on BURN in case of unforeseen trouble, after a searing flash all that remained of the ogre was a smouldering pile of something that resembled an old fur coat that had been rescued from a bonfire.

A vulture circle of demons formed around the pirates. What had been a confused crowd moments before, now had a focus – the interloping party of buccaneers who had just made toast of the biggest ogre on Murk.

"Everyone behind me. We'll push through with the shield, but any nonsense and defend yourselves as best you can," Fyrsil told his band that was looking increasingly more desperate by the minute.

There was a sound of cold steel rasping on scabbards, and the ominous clicking of pistol hammers being primed for action as Loot's finest clenched their teeth and inched a painfully slow path towards the glider through an increasingly menacing crowd of drooling monsters of the Dark Domain.

Switching the shield's mode from BURN to GLARE to conserve the batteries, Fyrsil was able to keep the surrounding creatures at bay. Swinging the shield's ray in all directions, he was acutely aware that if the power suddenly failed, his buccaneering bunch would be reduced to what butchers often advertised as 'oddments and off-cuts'. The baying of the encroaching wall of howling imps, demons and other fearsome creatures battered at his ears, and he switched the Angel Axe setting to CRUSADE and kept his finger on the safety catch.

They were making careful progress towards the tantalisingly close structure of the cloud glider when a black shadow flew across Fyrsil's path.

XXXIV

Having the Shield of Righteousness on your left arm, and an Angel Axe in your right hand, is little compensation for the feeling of pure fear that broiled in Fyrsil's stomach. That was F-E-A-R in capital letters.

A couple of seconds before there had been a wall of gargoyle gawping faces. Now there was a thrall of black smoke lifting above the lip of a crater, where assorted nasty creatures had once been.

Fyrsil looked behind him. The formation of shipmates which had been following him had disappeared.

"Ah," thought Fyrsil, and knew he was on his own.

Lying uncomfortably on the ground, Fyrsil fleetingly wondered what would have happened if he hadn't tripped up.

A misplaced foot placed amongst a vicious tangle of brambles pole-axed him as he looked up to see what was the cause of the icy shadow that had passed over him. As he fell, his thumb unintentionally flicked the switch on his shield from GLARE to BURN. A midair explosion brought the rest of whatever was flying up there very quickly down to the ground, to create a big smoking crater.

Now, if he wasn't mistaken, he had been deserted in the face of something that even Groggie would not take on. As he got to his feet, as a precaution, he keyed the code on the shield for full body height protection, and peered through the viewing visor. Fyrsil wiped the screen where it fogged up from his heavy breathing. He wished he hadn't, when he saw what confronted him.

The sight of Trachidambabble was an occupational hazard to courtiers at Castle Gloom. They, at least, knew what to expect. Fyrsil didn't. It made him wobble on his feet to see the Dark Lord pushing through the smoke that wafted from the charred remains of the state chariot and its fiery wyverns.

His knees played a clacking tattoo as the flapping black cloak paced towards Fyrsil hiding behind the Shield of Righteousness. The sinister emissions from the daunting black figure could be felt through the shield's safety fields (a special feature only found on the model for gods and semi-divine heroes). Fyrsil made a note to check the manufacturer's guarantee to see if he could sue for undue fear and trepidation, contrary to claims made of the product.

It was only the thought of why the GLARE or BURN settings of the shield was having no effect, that Fyrsil was able to pull his mesmerised eyes away from the apparition in front of him. The reason why they were not working was the thumb that had frazzled Trachidambabble's chariot had also switched off the other settings when he was rolling around in the brambles trying to get back onto his feet.

Sinister decibels reverberated in Fyrsil's ears.

"So, we meet at last."

Fyrsil blinked, bewildered.

"Pardon?" he said.

"WE MEET AT LAST."

The words played bongos on Fyrsil's eardrums. "I presume I have the displeasure of meeting Hap, my nemesis from the Other Place, whose interfering has turned The Event, which should have been Glob's darkest hour, into a glorious fiasco."

"Oh, I'm not Hap, just his Spearholder ..oh, and Cup Bearer," said Fyrsil, reassured by the mistaken identity.

He was also more than a little preoccupied by trying unsuccessfully to keep the Angel Axe from jerking excitedly in the direction of Trachidambabble. It seemed to have self-activated the CRUSADE mode, and no pressing of buttons could persuade it otherwise. As a result, Fyrsil was engaged in an unwieldy sort of dance, as he tried to prevent the Angel Axe, with himself attached, dashing off in the direction of the faceless dark figure in the high collared cloak.

"WHAT?" boomed Trachidambabble, steam spurting out of where it would be presumed his ears were. "A mere security guard has foiled my plans and made fools of the mighty forces of Murk?"

There was a sound of a thousand hissing vipers, as the ground around Trachidambabble's feet boiled in pure vindictive anger.

"Um, if you say so," replied Fyrsil, who appeared to be bobbing up and down behind his shield in a strange ritual dance, as he tried to restrain his axe.

He made a mental note to mention the general uncontrollability of the armaments when he got back to Heaven. It could lead to dangerous accidents, he thought. Then another thought struck him: "If I get back to Heaven…"

"You shall pay for your meddling, you delightfully cretinous spawn of a skunk dung weavel. You piffling little…you…imbecile…you…"

"Beep, beep," said a scorched Beep Beep, as he crawled out of the crater.

"SHUDDUP," roared Trachidambabble, and kicked his Balck Warlock back to when he had crawled from.

The momentary distraction was what he Angel Axe had been waiting for. With an almost imperceptible hiss it sliced through the air and propelled itself at the Lord of Murk. Being attached by the wrist, Fyrsil and his shield followed.

The extra drag caused by the axe's supposed wielder saved Trachidambabble. Having booted his sidekick, he turned to zap Fyrsil, and ducked instinctively as he spotted the strange procession of projectiles hurtling towards him.

"Bye-bye," yelled Fyrsil trying to retain the pretence of control over the axe, as he remembered the command for CRUSADE.

It might have been the speed at which he was flying through the air, but as Fyrsil whipped past the Dark Lord, he was sure that he could see that

Trachidambabble had no face. The high collar of the cloak kept in the shadows the image of a thin mean nose and slightly pointed ears. There also appeared to be an odd little moustache floating about. But they were fleeting images rather than solid features, and it was like looking at a reflection in a muddy pool.

The one thing that Fyrsil was quite sure about, as he landed in a heap under the Shield of Righteousness, was the face, if it was really a face, had stuck its tongue out at him.

The spectating crowd took a collective sharp intake of breath and held it.

Peering through the shield's viewing visor, Fyrsil watched petrified as Trachidambabble turned the pointing finger of his right hand, while his left hand and a swathe of his cloak dropped with a dull thud on the ground.

The crowd of onlookers quickly exhaled and gasped in unison.

For a moment is seemed as if Trachidambabble had not noticed his loss. With a deft movement the Dark Lord picked up the missing part of his body, wrapped around it, and using the index finger of his right hand as an acetylene torch, dexterously soldered the hand back onto his wrist.

"If you want to play rough, that's the way I like it," the Lord of Murk growled.

The words reverberated through Fyrsil's skull, with a finality that drained almost all the strength from his body, as he struggled with the Angel Axe which was embedded in the ground.

"Nice little toy you have there, but hardly enough to defy the Lord of Darkness. But the next act in this play will give me extreme displeasure, I assure you."

Looking at the sharp point of Trachidambabble's steel fingernail, Fyrsil felt his insides turn to jelly. There was only one thing to do: let the first natural reaction have its head, and...run.

Grappling with the axe, he tried to get up, and was immediately knocked down. And then blasted up. And then while still airborne, blatted down.

Tethered to the embedded Angel Axe, Fyrsil was being played with as he hid behind the Shield of the Righteous. Biodegrading blasts from the Dark Lord's fingers bounced him between land and sky, as he clung desperately to the underside of the shield. Like a powerful laser show, the jets glanced off the shield and shot off at wild angles, wiping out great swathes of assorted creatures as they ricocheted into the crowd.

Cackling with sinister enjoyment, Trachidambabble demonstrated his supreme power by zapping Heaven's champion in midair. Fyrsil gripped the shield with his left hand, leaving the technology of his coal black shades to hide the worst effects that dazzled from the viewing visor.

"Oooooaaargh!" he cried out loudly, when what he meant to say was: "Help! I can't take any more."

Even thoughts of him having to survive to save Glob had difficulty forcing themselves to the forefront of his mind as his limbs screamed blue murder from being torn in different directions.

The shield, with Fyrsil clinging underneath it, lurched again in midair as it soaked up another direct hit, which scudded off at an oblique angle to waste a pack of milling werewolves. With an almost inaudible hiss, the last jolt pulled the Angel Axe from the turf and Fyrsil's arm felt a momentary release from the agony of being stretched by its tether.

The relief was only momentary. Before he could utter: "Bye-bye" the axe shot up in the air, and pulled Fyrsil in the direction he least wanted to go – towards Trachidambabble.

"Bye-eeeeeee!" Fyrsil shouted, as he flew towards what he presumed to be his doom.

"Yep," grated the Dark Lord in confirmation, and shot from the hip.

The axe that had been pulling Fyrsil in a screaming flight towards the black caped figure of the Dark Lord, was suddenly transformed into a catapulting ball of flame heading up towards the stratosphere. Left with an outstretched arm and a scorched hand, Fyrsil suddenly discovered the meaning of the word 'plummet'. After an instant's hover, Fyrsil and the shield took the fast way down to earth, and landed in a crumpled heap.

He closed his eyes as he lay waiting for his aching body to get its final farewell from Trachidambabble's potent fingers. He waited, and waited, and opened his eyes. The black caped figure of pure, unadulterated evil appeared to be bathed in a halo of some sort of illumination. After a shake of his sore head, Fyrsil could see that his adversary was transfixed by the blinding light of the Shield of Righteousness.

Somehow in the crash land, he must have switched the GLARE mode on. Fyrsil was too relieved to remember that he had thought that the GLARE setting had been incapacitated.

"This is alright for the moment, but what happens when I try to move?" Fyrsil asked himself. He might have stopped Trachidambabble in his tracks, but he couldn't stay there for ever. For a start off, the shield's batteries would eventually run down. Secondly, to save Glob, and himself, he needed to escape with the Golden Orbs back to Heaven, and this was definitely a stalemate, with neither combatant going anywhere. And thirdly, a being as evil as Trachidambabble was certain to have a trick up his sleeve to escape the shield's GLARE function. Then it would be back to square one of being one breath away from a pile of burnt ashes.

Feeling with his raw hand, Fyrsil fumbled with the zip on his bumbag, and felt with faint hope for something useful in its cavernous storage space. It was a tricky operation, keeping the shield aimed at Trachidambabble to keep him a dazzled state, while a growing pile of inappropriate articles was thrown on the ground.

An inflatable bed, portable vending machine for clean underwear, a couple of recipe books, a shoe-shine kit, and several golden ornaments from the chocoholics treasury soon sat beside Fyrsil's prostrate figure.

"Aha," thought Fyrsil, and looked at a vial he pulled out of a cranny of the bumbag.

His brain started to whir with activity other than severe pain reports from almost every part of his anatomy. Handling the phial marked *RAW LOVE* gingerly, he read the label carefully. When he had packed this contribution to the bumbag from FairCorker the goddess of lust, Fyrsil had assumed that it would be pretty, but useless baggage. But on closer examination of the instructions and warnings on the label, Fyrsil registered that it could come in very handy.

Most of the label was taken up with small red copperplate script warning of the dreadful properties of *RAW LOVE*. In big bold purple type was the cautionary note that unless diluted the contents could cause mass riots. Recommended dosages for everyday applications included one drop per barrel of water being sufficient for permanent infatuation.

Quickly delving further into the bumbag, Fyrsil pulled out an inflatable tree, a guide to common plagues on Glob, and a valuable collection of marbles, all of which he impatiently threw aside. His fingers gripped on a promising shape, and he pulled out a multi-loading recoil-less automatic crossbow. Taking an elastic plaster from the first aid kit which was sitting conveniently close at the base of the pile of bumbag contents next to him, Fyrsil stuck the phial of *RAW LOVE* to the first dart in the crossbow's breech.

A quick glance towards Trachidambabble did not look promising. The back of the long cape and its high collar was all that was visible. As he watched, a small periscope rose above the top of the collar. It swivelled and peered with its single darkened eye through the glare of the Shield of Righteousness at Fyrsil. It gave him an uncomfortable feeling similar to being tied to a chair while a manic dentist warmed up his drills. There is an inevitability of something very nasty limbering up to happen.

Manoeuvring himself so the shield was propped up against his legs, Fyrsil pinned a Heavenly clothes peg on his nose, brought the crossbow up to his shoulder, and looked down the telescopic sights. As he did so, a hand appeared at the side of Trachidambabble's cloak, and Fyrsil found himself staring at a magnified steel fingernail pointing at himself. Finding the trigger, he squeezed.

At that moment there was a blinding flash as the pile of useless articles from the bumbag received a direct hit and was instantly transformed into an even more useless pile of ashes.

The sound of grim mirthless laughter stamped its decibels on Fyrsil's eardrums.

The back of the cloak became a pincushion of erratically aimed darts as the crossbow automatically fired off its magazine from where Fyrsil had dropped it.

"Nothing and no one, gets the better of the Lord of Murk, Custodian of Gloom, and Glob's most efficient Agent of Biodegradation," the voice boomed.

"Prepare for your end, and the beginning of the rule of Murk for all of Glob." The grim syllables had an aural undertow of pleasure as the dark figure turned to face its foe.

Totally exposed, with his shield blown out of reach by Trachidambabble's backward shot, Fyrsil sat transfixed as he watched the contents of the smashed phial of *RAW LOVE* trickle down through the smashed glass of the periscope. It seemed like the dart was transfixed above a flickering screen that projected an image of the Dark Lord's facial features.

Savouring the moment, a malicious grin was discernible, as slowly a black hand was raised and pointed at the forlorn figure with a peg on his nose.

The crowd of baying creatures closed in for the final demise of Heaven's hero. Clamouring devils, trolls and imps pushed forward, slobbering and slavering to surround their master in his moment of supreme victory over the forces of golden light and liberal practices. Amongst the rising din of voices, Fyrsil was suddenly aware of incongruous utterances of "darling", "sexy socks", and "gorgeous, pout this way".

Trachidambabble heard it as well. He swivelled his head, dispersing a small plume of ultra sweet vapour.

"Beep, beep," said a charred form lovingly, as it scampered up and kissed the hem of the Dark Lord's cloak.

"Cor, give us a kiss darlin'," roared a troll from the Blackguard as it fondled the behind of his lord and master.

It took a moment for Trachidambabble to realise what was happening, as a couple of imps jumped up onto his back and lovingly licked the flickering image of his earlobes. With a wild shot at Fyrsil that created a small crater in the ground at the Heaven's hero's feet, the Dark Lord wrestled with his over-affectionate subjects, zapping at them with all fingers blazing as they struggled to embrace him.

"Back, back. Get off you cretins. The fate of Glob is about to be decided, and...stop doing that – it tickles...and the future of Murk depends on this historic moment...stop slobbering over me like that..."

Fighting like a fury, Trachidambabble swirled and zapped until his hands glowed,. Standing back in a cowed circle making extremely big eyes, the massed creatures of Murk stood staring lovingly at their master. The circle pressed forward as those at the back who had got a whiff of *RAW LOVE* pushed eagerly forward.

"This isn't meant to happen. How can you do this to me? How dare you kiss me. It's girlie and cissy, and yuk!"

The grating voice was sounding more than a bit petulant.

"Bye-bye," said Fyrsil and blew Trachidambabble a kiss.

From the sky, a high pitched whine buzzed increasingly louder. A burning torch of what might have been a hi-tech Heavenly axe dived with unerring accuracy at the head of Trachidambabble as he looked up. With the screeching of a fanatic, the remains of the Angel Axe in its dying moments sliced through the head and body of the Lord of Murk, cutting as accurately as a sushi chef in a hurry, before burning out in a gooey puddle of metal on the ground.

A collective gasp escaped the mouths of thousands of potential huggers, as the body of Trachidambabble fell apart in two neatly cut halves. Inside sat a small boy with blonde curling hair and a angelic face gripping the joy stick of a playstation console.

The look of shocked surprise disappeared from his face, and an expression of pure thundercloud descended on his delicate little features.

"It's not fair, it's just not fair. It's my turn to rule the world!" the boy screeched and stamped his feet.

He jumped down from his teetering platform that was Trachidambabble, and kicked the fizzing remains of his electronic powered persona with which he had ruled Murk.

A werewolf howled hungrily from the crowd.

"Yummy," declared an ugly troll, licking its lips at the sight of the pretty little boy.

"Oh no," the boy squeaked, looking for somewhere to hide.

A collective baying rose from the throats of the creatures massing around the unexpected shape of what had once been their lord and master.

With a lightning movement, the blonde bob of curls shot between the legs of a slobbering troll, and dodged into the midst of the tumult of the ugliest and most vicious lifeforms of Glob noisily hugging each other.

Standing behind the Shield of Righteousness, trying to fend off the unwanted advances of a giant cyclops with a fading GLARE setting and a golden ornamental lamp found in the depths of the bumbag, Fyrsil felt a tap on his shoulder.

"Come on. If you have stopped messing around, I thought we still have a planet to save," Captain Cuffbert told him as he dangled from a rope with big wads of cotton wool stuffed up his nostrils.

Fyrsil looked up to see the Chair hovering above him, and the Bobo gesticulating impatiently, as the rest of the pirate crew clung to each other, piled untidily on the Chair's covers.

"It's only you and Groggie to come, but he seems to have disappeared. That bird of yours has been doing a great job. You did quite well yourself, mind you. Jolly good show!"

"Thanks," said Fyrsil, and smashed the ornamental lamp on the cyclop's toes before allowing himself to be hauled up off the ground by Captain Cuffbert as they rose above the heads of the cavorting beasts and headed for the cloud glider.

XXXV

"It's deserted. The Golden palace is empty, and there's not a god in sight," Fyrsil told the Bobo, because there was no one else in the vicinity.

The Bobo squawked noncommittally by way of an answer.

They were standing in front of the grand automatic doors entrance of the palace, where Fyrsil had tripped repeatedly when on his sentry duties. He fingered the Being Stone uneasily. It was only after intense inspection with one eye closed that he could find a mote of gold on the smooth dark blue surface.

Looking up to the roof of the Golden Palace he watched the pirate crew lower the Golden Orbs by pulley and tackle from the cloud glider's cargo doors. "I hope your flying days are over. Why couldn't you just land the thing on a flat surface like any normal pilot, instead of putting the glider into the roof of the biggest obstacle you could find?"

The Bobo was not in a good mood. It matched Fyrsil's.

"Why can't you shut your stupid beak and do something useful for a change?"

"Useful? Useful! Who saved your worthless hide from the fiends of Murk, and the Gastrognomes of Hotchili, and sprung you from the Rehab Centre?"

Fyrsil pursed his lips, not answering the question.

"If you're so clever, where have all the gods gone?"

"Dunno, they didn't leave a note."

The Bobo glared at Fyrsil through slits of opaque florescent eyelids.

"Er, excuse me: ZEE END IS NIGH."

Fyrsil and the Bobo spun round at the sound of the strange voice.

Standing behind them was a craggy old man in a soiled homespun robe, preening a permanently windswept beard. He was leaning against a homemade placard on a long pole which read:

'THE END IS HIGH'

"Who are you?" demanded Fyrsil.

"I am ze Mission Man. I was given zis mission by the gods to warn all of Glob of ze impending dooming. Ze boom vich vill spell doom, ven all dis stuff around us goes blue."

"Why did they choose you?" the Bobo demanded as rudely as possible.

"I vos chosen because I had ze honour to be trodden on by all ze gods ven they stampeded down ze Golden Stairway to Heaven. I vos having my picnic. One of zem says: 'Zis one vill do," and I get ze job, by order of ze pantheon of all gods. Ze mission is to tell all people zat ze vorld is ending, so everyone have a good time, yes! So I tell zem all so."

"All of the gods?" Fyrsil and the Bobo asked in unison.

"Apart from ze big one – Hap-i-Glob, he stay, I sink. But anyvay, I say to ze gods rushing for ze good time: 'What do I do when mission is over'. Ze scratch zere heads and say: 'Go to Heaven' and so – I am here now. No one listen. So up here I help in ze garden and discuss ze goot old days. Vee vait for kaput."

"Haven't I seen you somewhere before?" asked Fyrsil, scratching his head to encourage his memory.

"Wiv possibilities. I haf bin every-over-the-Glob. No place missed out. Loot also. I see you ven you fly from zere."

The Bobo squawked with impatience.

"No doubt you were at the chocoholics community when the Gastrognome Hunger Party was on the warpath."

"Correct. But for zem it wos too late. The end had nighed already. Now I come over to see what goes boom in ze roof of ze palais."

"Ah, I hoped that would attract some attention," Fyrsil said sheepishly, pushing his dark glasses up the bridge of his nose. "Did you say you were helping Hap in the garden."

"Zat is also so. This season will be vere goot for ze goosebumps, and also some redcurrents – zat is, if ze planet lasts zat long."

Patience with incomprehensible prophets of doom was not one of the Bobo's strong points.

"Well go and tell Hap-I-Glob that we can start saving the world," it squawked.

Fyrsil nodded in agreement, and added: "Tell him the Golden-ish orbs and the recipe for Ness have been retrieved from Murk, and so it is time to start production again."

Not even a flicker of excitement registered on the wizened old face at this news. The prophet of doom wheezed slightly and ran a grubby hand through his straggling beard.

"Jump to it!" shouted the Bobo.

"Do zis, do zat – where will it all end for an old man like myself. First eversing is ending, now it is no longer ending. What am I to know?"

The by now ex-prophet slowly turned on his heel and dragging his placard behind him wandered off in the direction of a border of bushes suffering from extravagant topiary.

"We will be in the laboratory," Fyrsil called after the bent, plodding back.

❊ ❊ ❊

A hurley-burley hum of activity resounded around the laboratory, punctuated by hisses of steam and noxious chemical reactions.

Hap tapped the glass of a vast glass vat, took a reading with a special instrument that bleeped contently.

When he had first appeared in the doorway of the laboratory of the Golden Palace, Fyrsil hardly recognised him at first as the top god of Heaven. The figure that congratulated Fyrsil on his successful mission was a more streamline model of the larger than life figure that had waddled around the golden corridors of his palace in globular glory. Along with a lot of excess weigh, Hap had lost his yellow leisure suit. The style for an old god about to lose his world was an off-white utility dungaree with grass stains on the knees and accompanied with a floppy straw hat.

Although Hap still referred to Fyrsil as 'Fuzzy' and puddled around in a larger than life sort of way, there was something missing in Hap's whole attitude towards, life, Glob and being top a god.

The missing element seemed to be enthusiasm, which was completely absent for anything except showing Fyrsil the secrets of how to read the recipe for Ness and the development of a large compost heaps.

It must have been a long wait, Fyrsil thought, especially with all the other gods deserting heaven. It looked as if Hap had given up hope, and had taken up gardening in preference to twiddling his thumbs while waiting for the end to come.

"Right, everything about ready. Just pull that lever there, young Fuzzy, and we'll be in business to put Glob back on the right tracks again."

Fyrsil was hesitant, but looking around at the eager faces of Captain Cuffbert, Big-Gulop and the rest of the pirate band, he gave a heave on the lever, and a raucous cheer leapt into the rafters. The geyser hissed, burped, and spurted hot golden Ness into the first of the Orbs.

"Calm down, calm down, it's only the start."

Hap, complaining of a bad back from too much weeding, left Fyrsil to roll out the first of the Orbs to the tipping point on the edge of Heaven. With a gentle final push, the Ness slopped from the Orb and poured gently into the atmosphere. The golden fluid formed a livid waterfall, splashing and dispersing into glittering filaments, glinting clouds as it dispersed and floated into the sky above Glob.

The party from Loot, being in a party mood, cheered, threw their hats into the air, and slapped each other loudly on the back, while throwing hats, wigs and wooden legs into the air.

"Does this mean that the Blood Sea will return to Loot, and we can get back to some real piracy again?" Big-Gulop asked Hap blowing the top off a large tankard of Heavenly mead.

"Maybe, and maybe not," replied Hap. "It all depends on what happens when Glob reverses its orbital spin."

"Well that puts a return to Loot out of the question. I'm not going back there unless I can have a bit of fun," Peg declared, hopping by as she went to find her spare leg.

A debate immediately started among the Loot exiles on what they should do now, having saved the world. The party dissolved into a melting pot of loudly shouted opinions, as everyone of the crew shouted at their shipmates that they didn't know what they were going to do. The only successful raid on Murk in history is a hard act to follow.

"I think this is probably a good time to make an announcement," Hap announced.

"I've been in this job for long enough, and it's time for someone younger to fill my sandals. To be honest, my heart has gone out of since my Orbs were nabbed by you know who."

"Fuzzy here has shown a certain sort of aptitude for saving the world, and so I am going to hand it all over to him. During this period since sending him on his mission, I have got rather keen on gardening, and would far prefer to do that."

It took more than a few seconds for Fyrsil to grasp what this would mean for him.

"Wh-what, me? Top god, and all that palaver!"

"Correct."

"What?"

"Do stop saying 'what'. There will be a little bit of work to do, re-dedicating shrines and temples, approving of new ones, and the like. And as it is my last Heavenly decree – you have no choice."

Fyrsil pushed his dark glasses up his nose to hide his reaction.

"I might need some time to think it over," he muttered.

"Does that mean we can keep our dragon?" Buttie shouted, and Daisy whooped in celebration before anyone could give an answer.

"Anything you want, as long as Fuzzy approves. I tended to let most of the gods get on with their own thing, and keep official meetings to minimum."

Rocking on his sandaled feet, Fyrsil was still coming to terms with what this would mean to his ambitions of nutgathering in Alpoi. He had to think about any possible trauma that he might suffer from this sudden status change, and how it would affect his lifestyle.

"What we want is a big drinking hall, with all the grog we can drink, and big fug up to give it a friendly atmosphere," declared Big Gulop.

"You can pull it all down and start all over again. It's all up to you now," Hap told them. "Now if you will all excuse me, I have my snap dragons to feed before their fires go out." And he slipped out towards the hedge bordering the formal gardens he had recently created, leaving the new gods to sort out the spiritual future of the planet.

"This calls for a council meeting," called out Big Gulop. "I want to be the god of ...I'll think about it..."

"That's what I want," said the Masked Marauder, and struck a pose that might have led to some immediate bashing.

"Do you think that we could start a cult to supply Heaven with a good wine cellar?" enquired Captain Cuffbert of no one in particular.

The Bobo put its wings over its ears and looked disparagingly at the newly appointed collection of gods and goddesses.

Fyrsil turned to appeal to Hap for help, but at that point the lumbering figure of the ex-top god gave a little skip and disappeared into the bushes and anonymity.

"Heavens...." he muttered to himself.

"Well come on don't just stand there," the Bobo told him. "If you're going to be the big boss of Glob, you might try and make at least a passing good job of it. Let's get some more of that Ness into the sky, and then we can sort out this god pantheon debate."

Somehow Fyrsil had the feeling that Heaven and being the top god was not going to be the totally celestial experience mortals on Glob might like to believe.

THE END

ABOUT THE AUTHOR:

WgWl (commonly pronounced Ooogol) is not of this planet. He is a demi-god from Heaven on a planet called Glob.

On Glob he was a scribbiner, a demi-god of Heaven who recorded all important events and salient details of the planet's geo-political structures for Heaven's Central Library. It was on a routine fact-finding mission that he fell asleep at the controls of his transporter pod and only woke up when he was in the next universe, and couldn't find the turning to get back to Glob.

Being semi-divine he was not able to die by just falling to sleep, so it came as a shock when he crashed landed on Earth at a music festival somewhere in Britain. While staggering around trying to get his bearings, his transporter pod was stolen by an investment banker who was desperate for the loo. As the transporter pod looked like a golden portaloo with a sign that resembled 'VIP' (but was merely a company logo for a standard vertical implosion propulsion creator) proudly on the door, this was not such a stupid mistake as it may first appear.

The end result was a WgWl was stranded without means of getting back to Glob as the golden portaloo transporter pod launched into the sky before he was able to buy a lucky dip roadkill burger or find out where he was.

He is now actively still looking for his transporter pod, and has penned this account of one of the famous legends of Glob to be able to finance his search.

Luckily he has been given a camper van which runs on chicken muck by a generous donor., and is trying to track down people who may ave seen him at a festival, or may be able to help to identify the banker in question.

If you have seen a golden portaloo with VIP on its side, please let him know.

Follow WgWl in his search for his stolen transporter pod at
www.armchairhero.com
He will appreciate the company. It is a lonely business being an alien on a strange planet.

Enjoyed the legend
Make a legend of the party!

Organise a party on one of the themes in Armchair Hero, and then tell everyone about it. By posting your pics and telling everyone about the highlights on :

www.armchairhero.co.uk

Choose from

- ## HEAVEN
- ## MURK
- ## MURK INVADES HEAVEN
- ## CHOCOHOLICS CHOCO FONDU PARTY
- ## LOOT PARTY TO END ALL PARTIES

Continue the fun, and share it with your friends

* * *

Ever wanted to shape a planet?
Fancy being a demi-god?
Here's your chance:
WgWI is looking for people like you to help him carry on his work of shaping and recording all activities on his home planet of Glob

He hopes that by recruiting people to help him carry on the work of recording what is happening and what has happened across the surface of Glob, he will not be in quite as much trouble when he finally finds his transport pod and returns to face the music in
Heaven on Glob.

www.planetglob.com - make it your world